RULE OF TWELVE

BOOK 1

DOUBLE TAKE

BRADLEY ALLEN

First published in Ireland 2022.

This second edition published in Ireland in 2024.

Published by TPAssist LIMITED.

ISBN 978-1-0686295-1-8

TPAssist LIMITED
14 Penrose Wharf
Cork, T23 W440, Ireland

www.tpassist.com

This book is dedicated to my loved ones, who put up with my

ramblings as I developed the story.

Prologue

While he could check everything from the controls around him, old habits die hard. To the annoyance of some of the newer members of his crew, he still insisted on someone visually double checking everything.

Those habits were formed over fifteen years of hauling. He knew it was less about safety now days and more about strengthening the discipline, the team needed when the shit hit the fan, which it often did.

He sensed Marr returning to the cockpit.

"Reactors two and three are running hot and fast," she announced triumphantly as if she personally turned the massive crank needed to spin them up.

Another one of Dukk's potential unnecessary precautions was to run all three reactors for the descent, even when one alone had sufficient power to guide them successfully into port.

He had been through too many situations when evasive action meant the difference between life and death. Which he also knew, wasn't relevant.

It was true that he, Marr, and the rest of his crew were high on this place's most wanted list. However, the rig he currently captained had more than it needed. They would easily slip in unnoticed by the EOs and their devoted followers.

Having a rig with these capabilities or being so highly sort after, hadn't always been the case.

As the autopilot announced it was about to break orbit, Dukk reflected to his first descent at the helm into his home planet. A time when he knew little of the truth about the world, he called home. While it felt like a lifetime ago, it was less than two months since.

Chapter 1 – A routine descent

1

The outgoing captain, Rachelle, had given him the conn shortly after leaving Drafuse. She wanted to start her retirement early, which suited Dukk fine. He had been first mate for over five years and had helped manage this old rig through many far more challenging situations. The run had been uneventful and the conditions for descent looked perfect.

Dukk was really looking forward to making a start on securing his own retirement. Which he knew meant clearing the many favours and debts accrued to get him to the position he was now in. And that being, about to become captain of the Dinatha. Two things had come together to enable that. Firstly, Rachelle had finally cleared her debts. Secondly, Dukk had finally secured the line of credit he needed to buy Rachelle out of her share. With the largest share, he would naturally assume the role of captain.

Dukk was average height. Wide shoulders and a big chest gave him a stocky look. Fair complexion. His petrol hazel eyes looked brown against his dark brown hair. He was attractive in an ordinary sort of way, with a warm smile but a seriousness about him. He was fit and worked hard at staying that way. Not an easy task when spending so much time in near zero-g.

The life of a haulier suited Dukk fine. He knew the risks but kept coming back. It was the only life, he knew. He had made that choice as a teenager and hadn't looked back. It wasn't an easy choice. He recalled the moment he first grappled with the hard truth of his choice. He was about to board a rig for the first time. He was at a port waiting for the arrival of the rig that would be his new home. A port worker noticed Dukk there looking anxiously out at the approaching rig. He came over and looked out too.

"I wouldn't ever see myself in one of those contraptions," he said.

And, then added, "it looks like a gigantic twentieth-century space shuttle. One of these days it will share the fate of Challenger."

Dukk still had no idea what the port worker was talking about and put it down to madness.

2

The decision to apply for an apprenticeship as a haulier was made after the results of the test, at the age of ten. The test marked him as very unlikely to get above level eleven. The observer said he would never reach level one to become one of the twelve EOs whom ruled each citadel.

The test results said he lacked the necessary identity characteristics to excel in the Rule of Twelve training. So, there, and then he chose the status of deprivileged. He accepted the life of someone who would never be assigned any level of privilege.

Besides, he found those that embraced the Rule of Twelve training cold and repulsive. He assumed EOs would be the same. He much preferred mingling with fellow deprivileged, who worked hard, were authentic and treated each other with respect.

Annee was one such fellow deprivileged. She was short, but strong. Her muscular and fit body was only second to her sharp tongue and cheeky grin. Her dark brown and cool toned complexion added to her poise and style.

At this moment, she stood in the hatch that separated the cockpit from the passenger seating area. Dukk had given her the task of seeing that the passengers were ready for the descent.

As she complained to him now, Dukk was reminded that there was a time when he had fantasised there could be something between them. But that idea was extinguished long ago when she and Rachelle stopped hiding their companionship. It wasn't clear to Dukk, what would happen when they reached port. Annee was a talented haulier, and she would be hard to replace.

He was hardly listening as she shared her concerns about getting the six passengers and the observer strapped in before they pointed the nose. Dukk wasn't paying attention to those worries, as he knew Annee was well able. He smiled as he realised, she was simply lightening the mood, as if she could read his thoughts.

As the door closed behind Annee, Dukk parked the thought of her leaving the rig. There were far more important things to do right now. One problem at a time.

The hatch indicators on the panel before him, showed him that Annee was already through the passenger seating area, and onto the landing. The landing was the top of the stairs to the lower levels. Beyond the landing was the transport pods and airlock that made up the rest of the upper deck.

Soon she would be on the accommodation level yelling commands at the guests. The twelve-hour delay in orbit would have increased their anxiety, but also increased their complacency. They'd need a good barking at now to snap them into line so that their effects could be stowed securely, and seats taken in the upper level.

3

Dukk now returned to the pre-descent checklist. He had already accepted the approach offer from the port authority and shared the access codes he got from the observer.

Having the observer on board was a necessary evil. No-one he knew, liked either their presence or what they represented, but it was the only way he knew of getting into and out of the citadels. And that was where hauliers picked up their contracts. Putting up with the observer was far better than the alternatives, which included working in the labour camps at the citadels or playing lackey to one of the odd creatures in any of the other systems.

At least here on the Dinatha there were boundaries. Some concessions. The observer had to stay within the passenger areas and wasn't allowed into the cockpit, storage areas or engine room. "Operational safety always comes first" is what Dukk and the crew would say if the observer tried to push their privilege.

It was true that the observer held the power to make changes on a whim, but the crew had to be free to run the rig.

Dukk checked the allocated pad number and entered the coordinates into the Nav. He knew this pad well. It wasn't too far from the bars that would give him both access to downtime and his first contract as captain.

His mind wandered to the moment they cleared control. The moment his identity chip was read, vitals scanned for and cleared of contagions, he would be off to secure a new contract. The others would be well able to unload the passengers and cargo.

His thoughts were interrupted by a squawk in the comms, the multi-channel communications implants located just behind his ears.

"Heat shield locks, four and five are not going green."

It was Bazzer, the Dinatha's main engineer. He was a stout and fit man in his late forties. Fair complexion, dark green eyes and unkept long red hair that was often secured in a low ponytail.

Whilst older than Dukk, Bazzer had no desire for his own command. Interested instead in the technical workings of these grand old birds.

Dukk had known Bazzer since his first job and there wasn't anyone else in the galaxy he trusted more.

Bazzer was at his usual pre-descent station deep in the rig's inners. He was at the engine controls overseeing both the starting of the second reactor and the positioning of the heat shields for re-entry into the atmosphere. Monitoring the starting of the reactor was his priority.

Dukk could see from the dial before him that it wasn't fully spun up yet. Bazzer would be stuck at the console for at least another couple of minutes.

The heat shields had been acting as counterbalances to the solar panels, while they ran the gravity emulator. They deployed the solar panels on emerging from deep space. Using solar energy to power the rig's essential systems was cumbersome but saved precious hard fuel. It made sense to use them in the dead time, like orbiting a planet waiting for a docking slot. As the solar panels were retracted back into the body of the rig, the heat shields needed to be moved back into position and locked into place. Unfortunately, space debris could get lodged into the tracks and stop the shields from locking neatly. That would result in a sudden and fiery end to the descent. An eventuality everyone was keen to avoid.

Dukk responded, "Larinette, how is it going?"

Larinette was also in the engine room, monitoring the retraction of the solar panels. She was using the inspection cameras, scouring for any damage to the flimsy surfaces.

A lifted panel might clip the compartment doors as the panels slid down the inside of the rig. If the compartment doors didn't seal properly, a fate similar to malfunctioning heat shields would await them as they raced through the outer atmosphere.

"Two more minutes," Larinette replied.

Whilst momentarily distracted by her silky voice and the thought of time together when they were planet side, Dukk had to focus on the problem at hand. Two minutes was too long. He had already committed the Dinatha to the descent. Altering the plan now would prevent him from making the docking window.

Dukk was already unbelted, up and moving. Before leaving the cockpit, he grabbed his cuffs from their docks. He cringed as the standard announcement echoed through his head, "Remember to keep your Rule of Twelve sanctioned wrist wrap devices always charged to above twenty percent. Your devices are currently near sixty percent."

Instead of making his way back through the passenger seating area, Dukk headed for the hatch in the floor at the back of the cockpit. Whilst not the fastest route, using the floor hatch meant his absence from the cockpit wouldn't be noticed by the already anxious passengers.

Having no one at the helm as they commenced descent wasn't ideal. However, with Rachelle taking it handy in her cabin, Chuk's no-show before leaving Drafuse and the rest of the crew occupied, Dukk felt he had little option. The window was too tight. He was well aware of the scarcity of descent slots. He knew there were at least a dozen other rigs eagerly waiting and willing to take his slot if there were any delays.

The hatch gave him access to the forward airlock compartment, which served as the main airlock for bringing cargo on and off the rig. This compartment also served as the storage for miscellaneous tools and spares.

Solving this problem fast would need plenty of strength to propel himself through the guts of the rig. The g-suit wasn't helping either. While fitted, it was bulky and could catch latches and handles. However, wearing the g-suit was essential for survival if there was a sudden depressurizing. Besides, it also kept his muscles strong which he needed if he wanted to walk the moment, he was planet side.

To complicate it further, he was sensing his own odour. He tried to change his inner layers daily, however he hadn't factored in the extra hours waiting in orbit for port clearance. Sweat had accumulated and the exertion was amplifying it. The image of a powerful long shower on the planet he was born, came to mind as he opened the hatch to the hold.

The main hold gave him access to the starboard storage hold. This hold mirrored the one on the port side. It housed the various fuels, oxygen, water, and other supplies. The superstructure that housed the storage spaces also functioned as crude wings that made flight possible within atmospheres.

Along the forward wall of the space were the massive pump handles needed to manually lock the heat shield panels in place. The age of the rig meant these handles were used more than they should be, but what could you do with margins so tight and competition for loads so high. Comprehensive maintenance wasn't a viable option at the moment.

The warning lights on locks four and five were blinking an angry red. Dukk first pumped the handle on lock four. A faint pop and the light blinked green. Next, he pumped the handle on lock five. Nothing. He waited a moment before pumping it again. A pause, then a faint pop.

Just as the second light went green there was a massive shutter. The rig groaned. It was a sound that would bring more anxiety to the folks strapping themselves into their seats. However, Dukk smiled. He knew this rig well and knew the message he would hear in his comms a moment later.

"Solar panels secure," Larinette announced from her position at the engine room console.

She had just shut the doors which closed off the solar panel bays. Dukk could hear Bazzer next to her confirming the heat shield locks were all in place and reactor two was stable.

It was time to return to the cockpit.

As Dukk stepped through the starboard storage hold hatch he saw Bazzer and Larinette accessing the stairs to the mezzanine and then accommodation level. Dukk retraced his path swiftly, closing hatches as he went.

He was just closing the clasp on his harness as Annee, Larinette and Bazzer entered the cockpit from the passenger cabin. As he winked back at them, he caught a glimpse of the passengers harnessed in and peering around, trying to get a glimpse of the cockpit, and looking anxious. And rightly so, they now faced the riskiest stage of their descent.

5

For the descent, Larinette took the seat next to Dukk. She had her sandy blond hair tied back; thus he could take in fully her fine features and light blue eyes. It felt odd, but nice to have his companion at the controls with him for this maiden descent. It was odd because usually he or Rachelle sat there as the other was at the helm.

As second, Larinette's role was to monitor the thrust and pitch controls. Annee sat at the console behind her and was tasked with monitoring other traffic and handling communications. Bazzer sat in the back of the cockpit monitoring the reactors and other rig systems. Dukk would keep an eye on the Nav, autopilot and oversee everything else, ready to step in if something didn't feel or sound right.

Whilst all automated, systems weren't infallible, and this rig was old. Knowing what was happening just before something breaks, helped reduce the chances of overreacting and making it worse.

"Dukk, make it a good one," it was Rachelle on the comms.

"Will do, Captain," Dukk replied.

"I don't want anything getting in the way of my celebration this evening," Rachelle added.

"Where are we going, Shell?" said Bazzer joining in the comms.

"Not the Auld Dubliner again, I hope," piped Annee.

"Cheek of you! You suggested it for old time's sake!" Rachelle retorted.

Annee chuckled to herself at her console.

"Well at least no-one will get lost again, hey Bazzer," Larinette joked.

"So, who's buying the drinks, you or Dukk," Annee added.

"Don't look at me, every EU I have is committed to putting the captain happily into retirement," Dukk replied.

"You buy the first round, and the rest is on me, how's that Dukk?" Rachelle said.

"Deal! Now time to focus or no-one will be doing any celebrating later," Dukk concluded.

The comms went quiet.

With everything in place, Dukk engaged the descent sequence on the autopilot. This started with the port bow thruster pivoting the rig one hundred and eighty degrees.

The rig shook and groaned. Even Dukk felt his stomach turn. The necessary maneuver and the resulting g-force push the g-suits to their limits. Being familiar with the feeling didn't make it any less unpleasant. He was glad as always that he wasn't sitting in the back with the passengers.

Next the main engines gave a quick burst. This slowed the rig so it would drop out of orbit. Another burst of the bow thrusters brought the rig back one hundred and eighty degrees again.

Now a final burst of both tail and bow thrusters pointed the nose into the forty-degree angle needed for re-entry.

The re-entry alerts sounded just before the colour of their view changed to bright red. Then a thunderous noise engulfed them as they entered the atmosphere. They were now committed and at the mercy of their preparation.

It was a moment Dukk loved and hated equally. It was terrifying but also comforting. For a brief time, there was nothing further he could do but wait. Things were just as they were and will be as they will be.

Soon the view and the sounds changed. They were in the atmosphere.

Chapter 2 – Perspective

1

Marr was in her favourite place. Binoculars at hand and hidden in the bushes near the crest of a hill overlooking the approach to the port.

From there she could see both the approaching rigs and the port. She could see the nature of the activity in the dock.

Reporting on this activity was why she would typically be found in this hidden lookout. Her role was to report when there was increased security well ahead of the arrival of a rig. For typical cargo, the observers, sentinels, and ground crew would only show up after the rig breached the horizon on its final approach. However, for valuable cargo the dock was inspected and locked down sixty minutes before the rig arrived. This information was valuable for the raiders who would hit the rigs before they got near the citadel.

However, right now was different. At this moment, she was there by choice. In her free time, she often came to the lookout simply to watch the rigs come and go and reflect on the path before her.

This was one of those times. But with a difference. She knew things were in motion now. The waiting was nearly over. Soon she would embark on the path set out for her.

Marr was of average height and medium build. She had fair complexion, with a tint of olive. She had dark brown hair, and light blue eyes. She was attractive in a sense, but not obviously so. Her attractiveness was in the way her eyes smiled before her mouth. With the years of hardship and training, and because of the seriousness of the path she was on, that smile was rarely seen. This was useful, as it enabled her to pass by others barely noticed.

From her position on the hill, she not only had a view of the port, but the citadel as a whole.

She could see the seventy-foot-high wall and parts of the residential buildings which lined the inside of the wall.

The port was built into the wall. Huge doors would open to give access to the dock. Rigs could be parked inside the wall and the doors closed when the citadel came under threat.

So, since the doors were rarely closed during the day, she could see exactly what was going on.

Further in from the wall, she could see the vast green houses, incubation dorms, warehouses and factories that made up the middle ring.

And, beyond she could get a glimpse of the inner circle of the citadel with its fine buildings, huge stretches of greenery and towers.

Of course, she had never been to the inner circle. Her mentor was the only person she knew who had even seen anything of that part of the citadel.

She had lived in the middle ring until she turned eighteen, when she moved into the adult residential districts, embedded in the wall.

Marr had led a typical childhood.

She was born in an incubation centre and lived there until she was eighteen. She went to formal school until her tenth Birthday, which she shared with the eleven others in her dorm. On that day they all took the test. Her results meant she wouldn't be furthering her formal education.

Instead, the day after the test, she woke to a half full dorm room. Those like her that were left behind, had now finished their formal schooling, and were cycled through the various labour jobs.

She worked with the industrial cleaning teams. Spent time in the greenhouses and the factories. She also spent time in the kitchens and with housekeeping. The latter being her least favourite.

During the eight years in labour training, Marr showed particular interest and prowess with all technically challenging aspects across the various areas. This enabled her to apply for an apprenticeship role with the keepers, the maintenance teams who ventured beyond the walls. They maintained fences, tended to the larger livestock, and managed the vineyards and orchards.

So, on her eighteenth Birthday she moved out of the dorm and into a h-pod in the residential district. She then spent five years as an apprentice, learning the ways of the keepers in the wild. She still had to return to the citadel at night, to check in, upload her logs, eat, and sleep. And being outside was extremely dangerous, but the freedom of movement made it all worthwhile.

2

An alarm sounded in Marr's comms. She looked around. It was all quiet. Not good.

She crawled out of the hide and crept slowly down the path that led back to the orchards.

She soon came across a young woman lying flat on a small outcrop. She was overlooking Marr's colleagues sweating and toiling below. The woman was snuggled up to a sniper rifle with her eye in the sight.

Marr unsheathed her 6-inch blade as she crawled up behind the young woman.

As Marr brought the knife up. The woman whispered, "Cut it out Marr, you are spoiling a perfect view."

Marr put the knife away and stood up.

"Shit Marr! Get down. They will see us."

"What? You afraid of getting caught drooling again?" Marr replied.

"You are just jealous of the action I get. Speaking of action, what is the story with your primary companion? We haven't seen him for a good while?" Luna replied doing her best to change the subject.

"Firstly, Mentor is not my companion, primary or otherwise, you know that. You also know better than to ask questions of his whereabouts. Besides, we have nearly missed our check-in time."

"You worry too much, Marr," Luna retorted.

Marr's demeanour changed. Time for play was over. It was time to step back into teacher and apprentice roles again.

"You don't worry enough, and you know very well that if we don't put some seemingly legit chatter on the comms soon, the fake logs may raise an alarm. We really can't afford at this point in time to draw any scrutiny from the overlords."

"I know," Luna replied as she sat up and started packing up the rifle.

She then continued, "I just wish I knew more of what exactly was going on and what the plans for us are."

"Luna, you know that it is for the best that we only know as much as we need to at any given time. The stakes are just too high. All will be revealed to those that follow the path. Speaking of which, it's time for some revision."

Luna groaned.

Marr continued, "Recite the creed."

Luna replied, "Focus on that which is real in the heart. Create the space so that the process can emerge. Honour that which serves you well. Engage in the journey as it unfolds."

"And, again with meaning," Marr demanded.

Luna smiled but ignored her.

Marr had to admit, her smile was a killer. It could break the coldest of hearts.

Luna was twenty-one, ten years younger than Marr. And like Marr, Luna had been recruited by the resistance during the labour rotation. And red pilled at the age of eighteen. She had been under Marr's wing ever since. She was of average height, with dark brown hair and eyes that matched her complexion. Some would say her complexion was warm with orange-red undertones. She was slim but strong and incredibly agile. And she was one of the best snipers Marr had known.

Marr nodded.

They both then disabled their bracelets.

Marr then said, "that all looks in order, let's get ready for the pick-up."

Luna added, "excellent, I am tired and ready for some food and rest."

Then, they both waved a hand over the bracelet again and a slight green glow reappeared.

Luna looked up from packing away her stuff, "I still find it hard to believe the observers think we only talk once or twice every thirty minutes and that we only say that crap."

Marr shrugged, "it works. Why question it. For as long as I've known, they don't come looking, if we don't give them any reason to. If we keep them thinking it takes eight hours to run those checks and not one hour, then we've got the space we need to train, learn, and prepare!"

Luna stood up and they both then made their way back down the hill, using the bushes for cover.

"Now recite the Story," Marr requested.

Luna slowed and looked back. "What if it isn't true? And don't go reminding me about poor Billy and his mentor getting picked up for reciting the story without their bracelets being active. I know the overlords crack down hard on any mention of this story. But what if they just want to protect us from lies?"

Marr stopped dead. She grabbed Luna's shoulders and spun her around to look at her.

"What is real in your heart?" Marr demanded.

Luna looked embarrassed. Her expression saddened. She then stood up properly. Pulled her shoulders back. Allowed her focus to drift and was quiet. Within a few moments, her smile returned. Her whole face lit up with an expression of both love and knowing.

Then she shared, "The story is the truth."

"Right, now recite it," Marr replied with warmth and forgiveness.

3

Luna turned, picked up her pace and started to speak. She spoke with confidence and grace. She gave the story love and in that she gave it life.

"There was a time when vast cities covered the planet. Life wasn't perfect but it was far easier than today. There were wars and famine, and lots of work to do, but for most it was a safe time. A time when people could make a life for themselves. They could choose how they spent their time. They could work or not work. They could own things. They were properly rewarded for their work. Yes, there was imbalance and hardship, but there was equal access to opportunity.

"Then came the Reset. Utopian dreamers had installed sufficient numbers of their brainwashed followers into political, governmental, educational, and commercial systems. They made their move. They changed the laws and used influence within large corporations to twist and corrupt the minds of the overly trusting majority. They forced the societal systems to align with their utopian ideals. They used various trojan horses, including equality of outcome, reparations for past inequities and sustainability. They used tools like ESG, programmable centralised digital currency and military-grade psychological operations. They broke the balance. They moved society away from competency hierarchies. They broke the systems that had enabled tens of thousands of years of growth. They moved the emphasis to power and identity hierarchies. They insisted that everyone should own nothing and be happy about it. This left societies incapable of functioning properly as increasing numbers of their citizens had to devote their time to the dysfunctional bureaucracies needed to enforce the utopians' ideology.

"The impact on the poor was immediate. Services stumbled and became incapable of serving all but the well off. Pandemics and other health crises became common place. Overreach, blind incompetence, and adeptness at covering up the truth took over as the prominent skillsets. The systems no longer served to provide refuge for the less fortunate. The systems simply provided support for the madness.

"The impact on the middle-income earners came too. Mass unemployment and the burden of the hugely inflated bureaucracies left whole countries laden with debt. The burden was too great, and societies crumbled. Fighting became common place. Neighbour fought against neighbour. Whole suburbs fell into disarray as the fighting escalated.

"More and more cities fell into anarchy as those with means left and then regrouped. They congregated in an ever-decreasing number of cities. But the worst was still to come."

Luna continued,

"In the fifty first year after the Reset the rich elite achieved the seemingly impossible. Shielded by their wealth, from the chaos and mayhem that confronted the majority, they had blazed ahead with their space programs.

"The fruits of these programs had been largely mute until that year. In that year they successfully breached the galactic horizon. A manned craft from the Musk corporation had successfully used dark matter technology to jump from our solar system into another and back again.

"The opportunity presented by reaching new systems took all their attention. The priority became forging ties with other solar systems and accessing their tech. Up until this point the elites had protected sufficient elements of the societal systems to serve their needs. However, when they put all their attention into the riches beyond the skies, nothing stood in the way of the utopians from taking complete control.

"This was the final straw for those that opposed the utopian madness. They fought back hard. This was despite billions of their number being lost through negligence, war, and genocide. The latter being achieved through pandemic counter measures. The resistance regained control of most places. They re-grouped and concentrated their efforts on the six remaining utopian controlled cities. The resistance nicknamed these cities Tangoalfa, Indiasierra, Alfadelta, Mikelima, Alfaecho and Tangoecho.

"However, this massive push was all in vain. Unknown to most, the utopians had been planning their escape. Under the banner of saving the planet they had established five eco-friendly urbanised regions. This was common knowledge. However, it wasn't understood that at the heart of each region was a self-contained and heavily fortified citadel. The resistance named these citadels Kuedia, Inquis, Norline, Genda and Utopiam. Those names have stuck and were even adopted by the overlords.

"When it was clear the final six cities would slip from their control, the utopians retreated to the citadels. From there they released weapons of all manner on the rest of the world. Chemical, biological and traditional. Whole regions became unliveable. Billions perished. Some directly, but most from famine as the systems outside the walls of the citadels were destroyed, polluted, or rendered useless.

"With the world in chaos, the utopians played their final trick. Already in control of all sources of communications and masters at delivering false narratives, they laid blame for the destruction at the feet of their opposition. Then they offered conditional sanctuary to anyone who came to the citadel gates. They housed them in the walls to discourage attack and they put them to work in the various factories and green houses. Using the growing knowledge of alien tech, they fortified their positions. Within a few years, the citadels were the only place where people could exist in relative safety."

Luna took a pause at this point as her, and Marr had reached the edge of the hills.

Before them was a nine-foot-high chain link fence. The fence disappeared away towards the citadel to their right and into the distance on the left. Beyond the fence were the vast tracks of grazing lands, vineyards, and orchards. Just on the other side of the fence was a stretch of bushes and shrubs. This buffer also disappeared into the distance in both directions.

As they slid through a gap in the fence, they checked their comms and looked around.

"The transport is still a few minutes away, tell me what we know about what happened next," Marr asked.

Luna continued, "The years of conflict and turmoil had been put to good use by those behind the utopian dream. They saw first-hand how their strategies hadn't worked. It had simply created stronger division. That division awakened and strengthened the resolve of those they saw as oppressing them. Instead, the utopians used their newly acquired authority afforded to them by the citadels to shift gear. From this they conceived the Rule of Twelve.

"The Rule of Twelve said that all were equal, but only when at the same level of assigned privilege. They conceived the model with twelve levels. Each level would be granted certain privilege, and with it, power, and entitlement. Level one having the most, and level twelve having the least. They appointed sixty of themselves as the first EOs for this new world order. Twelve for each citadel. They decided that EOs would remain in these positions until their death.

"Appointment of EO replacement is from the level below. This in turn opens opportunity for promotion for the level below and so on. Each can have up to twelve devoted followers, or observers, who occupy the level below. This propagates down to level twelve. In reality each really only has one to two subordinates.

"Most, start and remain at level twelve. Known as the deprivileged, they are destined to work their entire lives. They live in the walls of the city without not much more than subsistence-based rewards for their toil."

With that, Luna stopped talking. They both listened. Without speaking and at the exact same moment they both launched into a sprint. Dashing through the stretch of bushes and shrubs and running as fast as they could in the direction of the citadel. Their firm and able bodies responded to their will with beautiful precision.

Behind them, a huge airborne vehicle came over the horizon. It came low and fast. A cloud of dust rose in its wake. It would be on top of them in moments. Lowering out of the craft were two cables. Each with a sort of a hook mechanism at the end. The cables were weighted slightly so they extended out behind the craft but didn't touch the top of the bushes.

Marr and Luna had separated slightly so whilst running level, there was now a gap between them. As they ran, they unfurled a length of tether from their belts and clipped one end into their body harness. Just as the massive quadcopter reached their position, Marr and Luna sprung into the air, pivoting as they went and letting go of the loose end of the tethers.

The craft passed overhead and then climbed. The tethers spiralled out and caught the cables. The locking mechanisms found each other and made a secure bond. As the craft climbed the cables where unfelled some more so when they went taut, Marr and Luna only felt a slight pull as they flew through the air. The winches then reversed direction, bringing Marr and Luna into the belly of the transport. The doors in the floor closed below them.

Once unclipped from the winches, Marr and Luna headed straight for their lockers. The lockers were hidden in the walls of the hold. They stowed most of their equipment and changed out of their fatigues and into their keepers' outfits. Then they each found a spare console to sync the fake logs.

Only when the consoles and lockers were hidden from view again, did they give the other a high five and acknowledge their colleagues. A dozen other colleagues were already in this space completing a similar routine.

As the adrenaline rush dissipated, sweat soaked their clothes and added to the illusion they were crafting. They found seats and settled in for the ride.

5

The transport made two further stops on its course towards the citadel. These stops were to pick up other keepers from the sheds, vineyards, and orchards. Now that the transport was within visual range of the citadel, these subsequent pickups were done in full view, and done with far less sophistication or glamour.

The quadcopter would land in a predesignated area and the keepers would come aboard. By the time they reached the citadel there were near fifty keepers squashed into the hold.

The transport slowed as it approached the wall of the citadel. A huge door slid open exposing a platform on which the transport landed. The doors closed behind the transport the moment it touched the pad.

Similar doors were now closing around the circumference of the citadel as other transports returned for the night with their load of keepers.

Within the transport, the occupants waited patiently as the transport's four massive rotors came to rest.

When the back doors finally opened, Marr, Luna, and everyone else filed out, walked across the pad, and started to queue at a mantrap. One at a time, they entered the mantrap and waited for their logs and vitals to be scanned. A misstep here would have the person picked up by sentinels and taken away, never to be seen or heard of again. However, once cleared by the operators of the mantrap, the keepers would be free to roam the outer ring of the citadel in search of food, recreation, and rest.

Recreation was not on the minds of Marr and Luna as they left the transport pad and headed towards the nearest Hyperloop station. The signs were there. More real work was on the horizon, so if it was tomorrow, a good night's rest was going to be essential.

Like most of those who worked outside the walls, Marr and Luna shared a h-pod near the port. It meant they had to use the Hyperloop instead of walking. But the location had its advantages. Firstly, there was always more things going on near the port. And secondly, it was rougher, so the sentinels and observers stayed clear of the bars and recreation rooms, mostly.

The Hyperloops were frequent and fast, so it wasn't that much of an inconvenience.

"Let's go via the stores, as I need to get a food pack," Luna announced as they boarded the train.

"We still have two portions of cacciatore," Marr replied.

"I don't feel like it. I am in the mood for a curry. Besides if we aren't going for a drink, perhaps we can get a dessert as a treat?"

"Fine," Marr agreed.

She knew it wasn't going to be a battle she could win or be bothered with.

The Hyperloop didn't take long to reach their stop. The stores were on lower levels. So, they made their way down the access stairs instead of heading straight to their h-pod. The stores were busy as labourers exchanged their EUs for essential supplies and food. The habitation pods were small and had little storage so most made daily trips rather than stocking up.

Twenty minutes later, and Marr and Luna were opening the glass door to their shared space. Their h-pod consisted of a living room, two small bedrooms and a shared bathroom. The glass door opened into the living room and served as the only window. The living room contained a kitchenette, and a table with two chairs. It didn't need much more as they were rarely there for more than showering, sleeping, or eating. The kitchen had a small storage cupboard, a basic sink and the rehydration unit used to process the food packs.

"You shower first, as it's my turn to prepare the food," Marr insisted as they stowed their boots.

"What level do you think observers need to be at before they can get access to have a bigger h-pod?" Luna asked as she headed for the shower.

"That is something the likes of us will never need to know," Marr replied.

Chapter 3 – Grounding

1

The descent had been uneventful. They had made good time and didn't see any further delays. Dukk had stayed in the cockpit for the slow and steady descent into Kuedia.

As they came over the large continent in the northern hemisphere, Dukk reflected on his favourite approach, the track into Utopiam.

The smallest of the five citadels was located in the eastern region of the massive island continent in the southern hemisphere. His fondness wasn't logical. Being smaller, it was less likely to produce the most lucrative business. The fondness wasn't even the view that he enjoyed immensely as the rig tracked out of the upper atmosphere. This view included the vast western coastline with its crystal-clear blue water and bright white beaches. And the red dirt that stretched out from the coast. During certain descent paths, he would even get glimpses of the remains of a sprawling city that was long gone. Unlike the ruins in most other places, which were ugly and disturbing, here the vast coastal desert almost hid the destruction all together. He would look out and fantasize what life would have been like in the times before the war.

No, the fondness was something else. Something he couldn't quite put a finger on.

Dukk had the cockpit to himself for much of the descent.

As advised, the passengers and observer had mostly stayed put in the passenger seating area. Whilst spread out over three hours, the return to full gravity and deceleration was unsettling to those who weren't familiar with it.

Bazzer had been determined to do another session of pumping iron before the mandatory overnight stay away from the rig.

Larinette kept busy in her cabin deciding on the outfit to wear for the evening's celebration.

Annee caught up with Rachelle. Dukk sensed something wasn't right. Annee had been distracted during the post reentry checklist review. He guessed that she and Rachelle had some important things to work out.

Being alone in the cockpit suited Dukk fine. The need to find a contract was weighing on him. He was keen to get started on his own terms. He didn't want to get tied into some one-sided deal simply because he was the new kid on the block.

When the rest of the crew returned to the cockpit, for the final approach and set down, Dukk still found it hard to engage in the chatter about the plans for the evening.

The customs clearance only took an hour.

Rachelle had then given Dukk and Larinette the rest of the afternoon off to relax and get ready for the evening's celebration. Rachelle felt she didn't need their help to supervise Bazzer and Annee as they managed the disembarkment and unloading of her last payload.

They would also use the afternoon to prepare the rig for tomorrow morning's inspection, a necessary condition of the intergalactic transport game. The observers were suspicious and insisted on thoroughly inspecting all systems. They also used the inspection to apply upgrades and install any further monitoring equipment. When unloaded and with everyone off the rig, a Squad of sentinels would be stationed to watch the rig overnight until the observers got there in the morning.

After packing Dukk's belongings into lockers, ready to move to the master cabin, Dukk and Larinette left the Dinatha and checked in to a h-pod. They found one that was a stone's throw away from the restaurant booked for this evening's celebration.

After a little downtime they headed out into the narrow streets that surrounded the port.

"You have to wear something nice tonight, Dukk," Larinette pleaded as they approached the nearest Hyperloop station.

"My favourite red shirt and blue chinos will be fine," Dukk replied.

"That shirt was fine two years ago; it isn't fine anymore!" came the retort.

"Fine, if you see something that you think will suit me better, get it and I'll pay you back! But I am not going shopping, I have work to do!" Dukk insisted.

"Fine!" Larinette stated as she entered a carriage and left him standing on the platform.

A slight smile touched his face as he watched the Hyperloop disappear around the corner. Dukk was quietly pleased with himself for standing up to her.

Larinette was heading to the outer ring's retail district. The retail district was adjacent to the larger h-pods. These were typically occupied by older and retired deprivileged, who had accumulated influence and means. The streets were wider and there was less evidence of any trouble with sentinels. This was unlike the port area, where the streets were narrow, and the buildings stacked on top of each other. Also, the buildings near the port were often cracked or blackened following trouble.

Rachelle had her eye on a h-pod in the nicer area, which also had places to eat and socialise. Dukk found it odd that Rachelle had decided to stay within the port district for tonight's celebration. Annee had said it was for old time's sake. Dukk didn't feel that fitted with what he knew of Rachelle.

2

Dukk made his way down to street level and then into the labyrinth of alleys and passageways that gave access to the many bars that flanked the port.

He made his way to one of the bars Rachelle had mentioned. Dukk was aware that all jobs had to be listed on the public contract boards, however he also knew that was just a formality. The tendering process was just a cover. Deals were actually done across tables in dark and grotty pubs.

Just as he crossed the threshold, he was nearly knocked flat by a sentinel squad. They had been just behind him. He stumbled aside and watched as they spread out through the crowded bar.

Everyone mostly ignored them, which whilst a behaviour Dukk had seen plenty, it was a behaviour that he was still not accustomed to. He found sentinels both frightening and fascinating.

As well as being nearly seven foot tall, clad in black and heavily armed, they wore fully enclosed helmets. Instead of a face, one was confronted with a black mask. There was no hint of eyes, nose, or mouth. Just a black void. And they rarely spoke and when they did it was unemotional and harsh. Also, they were fast, strong, and deadly accurate with their weapons. And they would even blow themselves up if there was the slightest possibility of being overrun. Dukk wasn't sure, but he felt they were mostly human.

Within minutes, and as expected by Dukk, a man in the corner of the bar screamed out and flung his hands over his ears. He bent over in complete agony. The hands over his ears were in vain as the noise was being produced by the man's communications implants.

Immediately, the sentinels closed in on the man. Two of them lifted him off the ground and made for the door. All the while, the man was still screaming in agony.

The remaining sentinels followed them to the door.

As the last member of the squad reached the door, it turned and spoke to the disinterested crowd, "Being in the possession of or using crypto in anyway is a punishable offence."

The sound bellowed through the bar like if amplified. The volume caused everyone to stop speaking, but they didn't look around or even seem bothered. Dukk knew also, it wasn't an infrequent occurrence.

With the message delivered, the remaining sentinel disappeared through the door and into the alley. Immediately, the conversation returned as if nothing had happened.

Dukk approached the bar. Eventually the owner came over to take his order.

"What can I get you?"

"Information," Dukk replied.

"Like what?" the owner said dismissively.

"I'm looking for a broker that needs a fine rig to fulfil their orders," Dukk said with a little too much confidence that clearly showed it was a rehearsed line.

The owner saw right through it.

"Who are you?" he said.

"The new Captain of the Dinatha," Dukk replied.

"What happened to Rachelle?"

"Retired."

"Well new Captain of the fine rig called Dinatha, you need to find Thumpol!" said the owner.

"Great!" thought Dukk, "That thug is the last person I want to talk to."

Dukk had known the short round man since his days learning the ropes after the test. Thumpol was a bully and a thug. Always had been. His greasy hair and beady eyes had helped with that. And he was lacking in decency of any kind. A trait that had helped him rise to the top of the black market that operated in the citadel. That had also given him some access to the privileged. Which opened the way for access to those doing trade deals. That gave him early visibility of hauling contracts. And he used that information to his advantage. Dukk felt he would make a natural EO and considered that his lack of height was the only attribute holding him back.

"There must be other brokers working contracts around here?" Dukk suggested.

"There are, but I am telling you that Thumpol is the only broker you want to be speaking with at this moment," insisted the owner as he headed to the other side of the bar to take another order.

"Odd," thought Dukk as he headed for the door.

Dukk found another bar not far away that also had been mentioned by Rachelle as good for ad hoc contracts. Once more, he made his way to the bar. He took in the scene as he waited.

The place was already filling up. The day shift was ending, and the night shift would have got underway. Dukk could tell from the tan lines, that the crowd included some keepers.

Just as he was about to turn back to the bar to attract the owner's attention, he noticed two men entering from the street. He recognised them at once.

They were two of Thumpol's goons. He'd known them since his days in the labour rotation. Dukk had also seen them about more recently when Rachelle took work from Thumpol's clients.

"It can't be a coincidence. Not good!" thought Dukk.

They spotted him before Dukk could hide his face. As they made a b-line in his direction, Dukk slid off his stool and used the crowd to mask his retreat and exit.

Dukk tried two further bars and got the same cold and unhelpful instruction from the owners. He also made a quick exit of two further joints when he noticed more of Thumpol's goons milling around.

"All roads appeared to be leading back to Thumpol's clutches," Dukk said to himself as he continued the search.

The seventh place he tried, looked clear so he sat up at the bar and ordered a drink. He decided a different tact was needed. The drink tasted good, so Dukk relaxed a little and enjoyed the moment. That moment didn't last long.

As he was about to take a second drag of the drink, two men sat down at the bar. One on either side. On his left was one of Thumpol's goons. On his right was Thumpol.

3

"One might get the impression that you are trying to avoid me, Dukk. It is almost as if you haven't joined the dots," Thumpol announced calmly.

"What dots?" Dukk replied, willing to play the game for now.

"The dots that join my influence with you securing what you needed to buy out Rachelle's share of the Dinatha! You didn't think the line of credit just appeared before you as if by magic!" Thumpol responded.

Dukk stared ahead.

"So, one might hope one would honour said favours in order to avoid any unpleasantness, of which I am not a huge fan," Thumpol continued.

Dukk turned and made a comical face at Thumpol.

"Ok, point taken, however I am pretty sure you won't share my appreciation from your perspective of the unpleasantness I have in mind for you!" Thumpol retorted.

"What do you want, Thumpol?" Dukk demanded.

"Simple, I want to support and help you as you get started as a rig Captain! It appears no one else is interested in passing any contracts in your direction," Thumpol shared in glee.

"I gather you had nothing to do with that," Dukk replied sarcastically.

Thumpol continued, "I am going to ignore that and put it down to long haul fatigue. Perhaps I have wronged you in the past. Let's put that behind us. And since I am feeling particularly generous today, how about we put the favours behind us too?"

"What's the catch?" Dukk interjected.

"No catch. I will even provide you with twelve months of contracts to get started?" Thumpol replied.

"What are the terms?" Dukk asked.

"The terms are simple! Twelve months' worth of work for a fixed payment of seven hundred and fifty thousand EUs. That is on top of fuel, interest, fees, and sundries. Easy work and a fine offer some would say. I will even connect you with four of my finest people to make up your crew shortfall. And to top it off, I might even put in a good word with other brokers after the twelve months is up."

Dukk said nothing.

"Not ready to decide? Take your time. I look forward to your decision tomorrow evening, when you officially take over as Captain," Thumpol added.

Without another word, he then rose and headed for the door. The goon followed.

Dukk was gobsmacked.

His self-talk was racing, "Over twelve months, with five qualified crew to pay, the deal would make me less than I'd make in a few months as second in command. And I'd not be in any position to start clearing my debts. It would certainly increase my visibility and experience, but I'd risk being trapped taking Thumpol's contracts for ever. Of which, the terms would certainly worsen once I had no other options. And what did he mean by 'four of his finest'? My current crew shortfall is two, maybe three!"

Dukk felt like he was between a rock and a hard place. He wasn't ready to decide. Something wasn't right. His gut told him to hold off for now.

Dukk had lost the taste for the rest of the drink. He paid his tab and made for the street. He decided he needed somewhere else to think. Somewhere that he didn't now associate with Thumpol and his goons.

As Dukk made his way away from the bar, his comms sounded. It was Larinette. Dukk answered but didn't even have the chance to say hello before she got started.

"Dukk, you missed out. There were some great bargains to be had. I got a fab outfit for this evening and found you a new shirt. And that isn't the best or biggest news. I am just off the comms with Kimseeti, the captain of the Plinthat. I've been offered second in command and the likelihood of captain within two years! Can you believe it, Dukk? My very own command in two years. I know you will miss me terribly and I will be hard to replace, but I would have to be crazy not to accept this offer! Look, we can talk more later, I've got to get ready for tonight. See you back at the h-pod. Bye."

"WTF," thought Dukk.

No sooner had the comms gone quiet when it chirped again. This time it was Rachelle.

"Hi Rachelle, what is wrong?" Dukk asked.

"Wrong? No, nothing. Dukk, are you okay?" Rachelle replied.

"Yeah, I'm fine, ignore me. Are you done?" Dukk said quickly as he caught his tone and corrected.

"Yes, all unloaded and ready for the inspection tomorrow morning. But that isn't why I am calling. As a parting gift, I decided to get those starboard heat shield locks fixed. I've organised for a crew to be on the Dinatha tomorrow afternoon. They will get them sorted after the observer's inspection. Come five p.m. when the legal details are all in order, you will be captain of the Dinatha in the best shape it's been in, for ages," Rachelle shared.

"Oh, thank you," Dukk replied trying to hide his shock.

"You are welcome. Time to get showered and into some finery for our little party. See you soon, Dukk," Rachelle said as she disconnected.

"That is totally out of character for Rachelle to be so generous! The world has gone nuts!" thought Dukk as he continued down the road in search of a place to think.

4

Dukk found a suitable spot easily. He went in, headed towards the far end of the bar, sat in a seat one in from the wall, and ordered a drink. He looked around whilst the drink was being poured.

The place was busy. A few rowdy groups at tables and a few solos seated along the bar. He wanted thinking space, so he chose the end of the bar. It was a good distance from anyone else. He glanced around. No one was paying him any attention. That was good.

When he turned back to the bar, a man was sitting in the seat next to him against the wall. He had a jacket on the bar between them.

"So much for finding my own thinking space," thought Dukk.

"Hello," Dukk said as he smiled at the man.

The man ignored him and ordered a drink.

When the man's drink arrived, he looked around briefly, then reached into a pocket of the jacket and pulled out a bracelet. It looked like a typical supplement bracelet. The kind of bracelet they all wear from time to time. Most of the ones Dukk had worn were used to put proteins and nutrients into the body. They'd help with the challenges of diet and balance resulting from lots of galactic travel.

The man put the bracelet in front of him and held his hand over it. After a moment there was a slight green glow coming from inside of the bracelet. It was only just noticeable. That had Dukk's interest.

"Supplement bracelets don't do that. Perhaps it was some sort of fashion accessory?" Dukk thought to himself.

Then, while still looking blankly across the bar, the man held his drink near his mouth and said, "We only have a moment. Just listen and don't say anything. Don't look at me. Look around slowly, as if you are people watching. You must do exactly what I say, or you'll be dead within a week. Look away. Enjoy your drink, look about but say nothing until I tell you to."

As Dukk looked away, he noticed the bracelet stop glowing green. Dukk was wary but interested. The man looked harmless. Dukk figured he could take him if needed. Besides, he was intrigued as to what was going on and the day couldn't get any weirder, so he complied. Dukk sat in the chair, sipped his drink, and looked about.

After about five minutes the man spoke again. As the man started to speak, Dukk risked a quick glance over. He noticed the man's hand over the bracelet, and it was glowing green once more. And as the man spoke, the drink was back up near his mouth.

Meanwhile, in the depths of the citadel, an alarm went off on a console.

The operator pulled up the alarm. The algorithm had flagged an anomaly in a small pub in one of the dirtiest and poorest areas of the citadel. The operator saw that the algorithm was complaining about somebody blocking their mouth repeatedly over the course of several minutes. The algorithm was not able to lip read what was being said.

The two people in question had been identified. One was a nobody. A general labourer. The other was only just short of a nobody. A crew member on a galactic freighter.

The operator checked the pub's security footage. The sound was unusable owing to the background noise. And the video wasn't great. The lenses were smudged, and the three angles showed little more than the heads and shoulders of the two people. The pictures were also further obscured by other people and furnishings.

The operator didn't even have a clear view of one of the people's hands owing to a jacket resting on the bar.

Whilst the operator reviewed the pub footage, the system was connecting to the implants in the heads of these two people. It now had connection. The operator listened in. Then the operator reviewed the recordings.

There wasn't much on any of it. Just the same background noise as picked up by the pub cameras. No conversation. Just drinking.

The operator concluded it was just two wasters sitting at a bar, drinking, and looking about. It appeared they didn't even know each other. It didn't look like anything out of the ordinary. So, the operator cleared the flag and instructed the algorithm to ignore that scene for the rest of the evening.

Back in the pub, the man sitting next to Dukk said, "My name doesn't matter. Don't ask for it. In fact, don't ask anything. Try not to speak, but if you need to speak, hold your drink near your mouth. I have a contract offer for you. Three loads of beef. Destination is a local system. Must be sequential. Seven hundred and fifty thousand EUs on top of costs. That's the same Thumpol promised you for an entire year. It will go a long way to clearing your debts. And it will save your life."

Dukk was gobsmacked for the second time in less than an hour.

The amount was off the scales. A local system run meant he could turn around a load in just under three weeks.

"But" he thought. "How does this man know what Thumpol is offering, and why does he keep saying my life is at risk."

Before Dukk could respond, the man continued, "When I leave, look up the contracts job board. Search for urgent high value beef contracts. Locate the contract offered by Wallace in Utopiam. Get the meeting details off the notice. Tonight, go to dinner with your crew, have fun, enjoy yourself. Tell them you are exploring a contract and leave in time to get the midnight VG to Utopiam. Make the most of the five hours of rest during the flight. You'll be on the ground at seven p.m. local time. Go to the meeting place at nine p.m. Meet with Wallace. Make the deal. He will even sort out your crew shortage challenges. Eat. Be Merry. Get the midnight return. You'll be back here at three p.m. tomorrow. That will give you two hours to refreshen up ahead of the handover at five p.m. You'll hardly be missed."

With that the man finished his drink and stood up. Before leaving he said, "oh, don't mention this conversation to anyone and take this bracelet with you. Wear it at all times. Wallace will explain."

He then turned, pushed the bracelet in Dukk's direction, collected his jacket and left.

5

Dukk stared at the wall behind the bar and let the barely touched drink go warm.

"What in the world is going on?" he thought.

His self-reflection was interrupted by an incoming alert on his comms. It was Annee.

"Ann, what is going on?" Dukk answered in a daze.

"Are you alright?" Annee asked.

That woke Dukk up.

"Sure. You?"

"Yes, all done here. Rachelle has taken all her stuff from the master cabin. Bazzer and I gave it a once over and moved your lockers in there."

"Thanks, Annee."

"So, I was thinking I could move into your old cabin? I already checked with Bazzer, and Larinette is hardly in hers, so she shouldn't care?"

"Wait, what? You are staying? What about you and Rachelle," Dukk asked calmly. He was starting to get used to the idea of the unexpected by this stage of the afternoon.

"All good things come to an end, Dukk. Besides, I have years of potential left in me. I am not ready to settle down or be grounded just yet!" Annee replied awkwardly.

"That is brilliant news!" Dukk replied gleefully without thinking.

"Actually, I will miss her," Annee added.

"Oh, of course, I mean, I am sorry for you and Rachelle, but I am delighted you are staying with the Dinatha, you are one in a million. And, definitely, take my old cabin."

"Thanks, Dukk, see you at dinner," Annee added and ended the call abruptly.

That suited Dukk fine as he felt it was getting a little uncomfortable. He was struggling with his emotions and was in no state to help Annee with hers.

Dukk used the heightened awareness following the call with Annee, to get his thoughts together. He used his heads-up display to access the contracts board.

He searched for urgent high value beef contracts. There was only one. It had just been posted.

"Odd! And as suggested by the mystery man, the contact went by the name of 'Wallace'," reflected Dukk.

The listing gave the details of the load and destination. It all looked legitimate. The listing also gave the place where Wallace would be tomorrow at nine p.m., local time. He saved the details. Paid the tab, left yet another drink barely touched, and headed for the door.

As Dukk made his way back to the h-pod to shower for dinner, he did his best to disconnect from the day's events. He did his best to quieten his mind. Which wasn't easy. His curiosity streak was strong. It had been pivotal in his decision to follow the mystery man's orders. And now it was working overtime on what this might all be about.

Before entering the h-pod, he stood for a moment. Undecided.

"Should I check-in on the Dinatha, before getting ready for dinner?" he thought to himself.

"No," he concluded, "The sentinels will keep it secure. Besides, I must clear my head and be present and engaged at dinner. I will need to be alert so that I can pick the right moment to take my leave and get to the VG station on time."

Chapter 4 – Cause and effect

1

Marr and Luna were walking quickly but methodically as they moved deeper into the wild.

They were covering their tracks away from the outcrop that sentinels would soon be searching. That outcrop overlooked the citadel and had a direct view into the port and one of the pads used to house a rig. And all was not well on that pad.

There had been an explosion causing minor damage to the under carriage of the rig on the pad. The scene at this point was one of chaos as sentinels and observers tried to fathom what was going on.

Marr's mind was not on the scene at the port. Nor was her mind on the task at hand. Covering her tracks was second nature at this point. No, her mind was on the events earlier in the morning.

The start to the day had been routine. Marr and Luna had alternated between the shower and eating, such that they were ready to leave on time at six a.m.

As they left their h-pod, they noticed a man and a woman talking, further down the corridor. The man was tall, muscular and of dark brown complexion, with cool undertones. He had dark brown eyes and short black hair with wisps of grey. The woman was fair and average height. Marr and Luna paid little attention to them and moved swiftly down the corridor in the opposite direction. Immediately the two stopped talking. The man split away and started following Marr and Luna.

The closest Hyperloop station was embedded in the outer walls of a series of warehouses that serviced the port. There were many routes to this station.

On this occasion Marr and Luna chose a route that took them via a corridor which they knew had disabled cameras. They knew this because they had disabled them. This route took them down a series of passageways, up some stairs and over a walkway that bridged the outer ring with the middle ring.

The man followed the two women over the bridge. He then turned into the corridor on the other side. A little way down the corridor the women stood, backs to him, waiting.

The moment he came into the corridor they started to walk again. Matching his pace.

In a single movement they all waved their hands over their wrist bracelets. The bracelets glowed green.

"Pad 16b. Just enough to keep the rig out of the air for one or two weeks. No collateral damages. The window opens at eight fifty. Eight-minute intervals. Eight chances. Single shot. There is no alternative window. Make it count," shared the man.

Seeing Mentor for the first time in months, threw them a little.

Marr reflected, "it is unusual for him to deliver a message in person. It was clearly important and a further confirmation that things were in motion. All the preparation would be put to good use soon."

"Pay a visit to Teacher when you are done," he concluded.

With that he pushed past them and turned into another passageway.

Marr and Luna looked at each other, smiled and then disabled their bracelets. Then, they continued as if nothing had happened and made their way to the station.

Unlike Marr, Luna wasn't reflecting on the meeting with Mentor. As she hid her tracks, Luna was going over the job. She was looking for oversights and calibrating the risks of them being caught.

Luna started her assessment following the encounter with Mentor.

They hadn't seen anything unusual as they waited for the Hyperloop. It had arrived a few moments later and took them to the stop near their transport.

They passed swiftly through the control doors and caught their usual transport into the wild. Still nothing unusual.

The quadcopter made two routine stops. All but Marr and Luna got off at one or the other of these stops. With the hold to themselves, they accessed their hidden lockers and retrieved their specialised equipment and fatigues. They swapped all of this for a fresh set of keeper overalls, which they had within their backpacks.

"That was all as per normal," Luna reflected.

With the routine stops done, the quadcopter accelerated and dropped over the horizon. It eventually came to rest briefly near some old and rundown sheds and hangers.

When Marr and Luna had jumped clear of the transport, it ascended again and headed back in the direction of the citadel for another run. Still business as usual.

From the drop off point, they had made their way to a nearby rusty hanger. Within the dimly lit building they were confronted by two of their colleagues. They were sitting at an old table and sipping hot drinks. A brief acknowledgement in the form of a nod was the only exchange.

Marr and Luna had then headed past the array of aircrafts, vehicles, and equipment to a set of rooms built into the back wall of the hanger. They had entered the low building via a grubby door at the front.

Within was a small room with a door at the other end. Standing in the middle of the room, they had smiled at the overhead camera and waited for a small green light to luminate in the ceiling above the camera. Only then did they cross to the door and enter the large room beyond.

This room had an assortment of tables, desks, and chairs in different formations. The tables and desks were covered in various pieces of equipment.

They had quickly passed between the tables and desks to the back of the room. There they pushed the wall in a specific place and an opening appeared. This gave them access to a ladder. That ladder led down into a labyrinth of passageways.

Deeper into the underground complex, they had come upon a control room. Four console operators sat before a wall of screens.

One screen showed the room they had just passed through before coming down the ladder. However, the room wasn't empty looking. Instead, it showed a dozen or so people moving about or sitting at desks. Marr and Luna saw representations of themselves in the image. The realistic nature of the made-up scene was uncanny.

Within the control room, one of the operators had looked up and welcomed them.

"Good morning. What adventure awaits you today?" he had said.

"We need a lift. We need to be dropped five kilometres west of this outcrop," Marr had said as she pointed to the map projected in front of the operator.

"None of that appeared out of order," thought Luna as she continued walking backwards away from the outcrop.

Within the citadel a similar assessment was taking place. However, it was not from the same viewpoint.

2

Deep within the citadel, at a console in the monitoring centre, an observer was in a state of panic.

The explosion, some thirty minutes prior, needed an explanation. It appeared that a sentinel had exploded causing minor damage to the nose of a rig. That rig was in the care of the sentinels and the crew would soon find out. They would be looking for answers. As would the observer's superiors.

The sentinel control system showed no evidence of any malfunction. Also, the recordings showed that other than the sentinel squad, there was no one else in the dock at the time.

The observer feared the worst. It was a career limiting situation to have been present during a successful attack by the radicals. The observer's only hope was to have evidence of what happened and have the basis of the narrative prepared before the superiors got involved and the news channels came looking for instructions.

The observer had already triple checked the citadel defence scanners and counter measure systems. Nothing appeared to be out of order.

The system was designed to detect and react to any missiles and even bullets sent towards the walls. The laser-controlled guns would intercept any projectile before it got close enough to cause any damage. All systems were fully operational and hadn't picked up anything unusual.

An alert sounded on the console. The satellite thermal imaging algorithms had found something. The observer loaded up the alert and maps. The algorithm had highlighted an anomaly on an outcrop to the west of the citadel.

The anomaly was small. And there was no evidence of people or even animals near the small heat signal. The duration of the heat signature and size matched that of a muzzle flash.

"A sniper!" the observer exclaimed.

The algorithm also identified activity five kilometres west of the flash, earlier in the morning. The logs showed a maintenance vehicle landing. It had spent fifteen minutes in the location, doing routine inspections of the fence monitoring equipment. It had then returned to base. It was well gone before the flash. A quick check of the surveillance cameras in the hanger and from the vehicle showed nothing unusual. It couldn't be them.

"Perhaps stowaways?" questioned the observer out loud.

The observer loaded up the other footage of the hanger and buildings within the hanger. There wasn't any sign of others in the vicinity of the craft prior to departure.

The observer reversed the recordings. The only other activity was ten minutes prior to departure. Two other keepers had entered the hanger. They crossed to the offices at the back of the hanger. The observer checked the footage from the cameras in the offices. The recordings showed that the two keepers had entered the control room in the back and sat at desks. Fast forwarding showed the keepers hadn't moved and were still there.

A check of the personal logs confirmed all keepers assigned to this location were where they should be.

"Dead end," concluded the observer.

"The perpetrator must have come from somewhere else. Perhaps they are still there or at least trying to sneak away," the observer said quietly.

The observer opened the sentinel command console and dispatched the coordinates to a mobile unit.

"We'll have answers soon!" thought the observer.

Back in the wild, Luna continued her reflection.

A lift had been organised. A fence maintenance crew were to be despatched to the requested location.

Luna and Marr had then made their way to their crew room. Within, they got into fresh fatigues, swapped their power cells, and restocked their kit with fresh water and rations. Luna had also checked her rifle and made sure she was carrying the correct ammunition for today's task.

From the crew room, they had returned along the passageways, towards the hanger.

However, instead of ascending the ladder to the dummy office, they had taken another passage that led to a different ladder with a hatch at the top. There they had waited.

In the hanger, the maintenance crew had appeared from the offices and headed over to their two-person quadcopter. They had got it warmed up and ready for departure.

Once ready, one of the crew headed to the small cargo bay at the back of the vehicle. Before closing the two doors, she had stamped her foot hard on the floor just below the doors.

On hearing the signal, Marr and Luna ascended the ladder, went through the hatch, and had climbed quickly into the back of the small quadcopter. The space was tight, but sufficient. The doors had shut behind them.

The journey to the drop off point had been uneventful.

The crew had landed in a known surveillance blind spot. Marr and Luna had let themselves out of the cargo bay, slipped under the fence and moved quickly into the bush.

They had used the dust whipped up by the quadcopter to cover their exit in the unlikelihood that someone was watching. And the special qualities of their fatigues would obscure them from any satellite images.

"All typical and nothing to be concerned with, thus far," Luna reflected as she continued to sweep the ground as she walked.

3

Luna continued her reflection.

After the drop off they had moved quickly through the bush, towards the citadel. They covered their tracks as they went.

The outcrop they had selected gave them cover and an excellent view of the port. They had spent forty-five minutes observing the routines of the sentinels guarding the rig in pad 16b.

They had done various distance calculations, gathered weather data and synchronised their timepieces.

They had found the optimal position whereby Luna could hit a Sentinel, cause it to self-destruct and not cause too much damage. Hitting a sentinel when it was too close to the rig could cause the fuel tanks to ignite. The resulting explosion could damage nearby buildings. That would definitely result in collateral damage.

"Mentor had been very specific about avoiding that!" Luna reflected.

The first window had opened at 8:30 a.m., however, the sentinels weren't in the right positions.

They had predicted it wouldn't be until the 9:22 a.m. window before the sentinels would be in the correct position. They had waited patiently for the interference software to cause a momentary glitch in the citadel's defences. Mentor's information suggested the glitch would cycle every eight minutes. When it did, a single shot could penetrate the shield undetected.

At 9:22, the sentinels were in the correct position, but a second sentinel blocked the shot. They had let that window pass.

"Three chances remained," reflected Luna.

At a little before 9:30, the second sentinel had moved. The shot was possible.

Luna had checked that her breathing was still slow and steady.

She had checked her calculations again. They had calculated the shot would take two point seven seconds to reach the target. Luna went over those calculations once more as she swept the ground behind her.

Luna recalled, she had then checked the sight once more and counted down the seconds.

At precisely 9:29:57 she had taken a half breath, then applied a slight amount of pressure to the trigger. The rifle fired. She had absorbed the recoil and continued to hold her breath.

Immediately, Marr had placed a cover over the rifle muzzle. Then they fell silent and held their breaths.

At exactly seven seconds after Luna pulled the trigger, a slight pop reached their ears. Success they both thought. No massive explosion, just enough to detonate the Sentinel.

With the confirmation, they had lifted themselves up gently and backed away from the outcrop, covering their tracks as they went.

Luna finished her reflection by recalling the path they had taken away from the outcrop over the last forty minutes. She felt confident and content.

It was at this moment that they heard the sentinel quadcopters!

"Right on cue," suggested Luna.

"Yep, let's have a little rest and sit it out," Marr added.

Pushing into the centre of a nearby bush, they settled in to wait.

Thirty minutes later, things hadn't gone well for the observer in the citadel.

The mobile squad had been dispatched to the location of the muzzle flash. They found nothing. The location showed no evidence of any persons being at the location or in the vicinity.

The observer had been over the logs and footage several times. The footage coming in from the wild was patchy and movement tracking systems glitchy. However, the observer knew cross checks when the keepers returned in the evenings, always showed things were as expected. No one looked out of place.

The observer trusted the system and it showed no trace of bad actors. The flash must have been something else.

The observer's superiors had taken over. They had listened to the report and then put the observer into a locked room. The observer would have no further involvement in narrative writing or work within the security team.

Sitting in the locked room, the observer tried to focus on reading the press release.

The observer would be reading it live to the media in a few moments. Staying focused was not an easy task given the rumours that the observer had heard about those that get unprivileged.

The press release read: "Earlier this morning, I was monitoring Pad 16b. I thought I saw someone acting suspicious near the rig. I ordered the Squad of sentinels to open fire causing a small amount of damage. I am terribly sorry for the damage that I have caused and accept full responsibility for the carelessness of my actions."

4

On hearing the retreat of the sentinel quadcopters, Marr and Luna got underway again.

This time they moved along much faster. They weren't as concerned about covering their tracks.

They still did their best to avoid leaving identifiable footprints, however they were now sufficiently into the wild, that it wouldn't matter as much.

Apart from some routine chatter for the fake logs, they moved in silence. Enjoying the sounds of nature, but also staying alert to any further search activities.

Their path took them on a wide half circle.

Eventually they arrived one kilometre south of the hangers they been in during the morning.

It was late afternoon by this stage. Soon, they would need to prepare to return to the citadel.

Their track had them into a valley filled with eucalyptus trees.

In the middle of the valley, they came across a decrepit chain link fence. Hanging on the fence was a very faded sign. The words were only just visible.

It read, "Keep Out, Medical Device Storage Facility."

They climbed through one of the many gaps in the fence and made their way towards the center of the area.

Bits of metal and rusty objects could be seen here and there. More than one hundred and fifty years of growth had almost hidden the junked equipment.

A sign was still barely visible on what was left of a small booth.

It read, "JAB BOOTH. Certified Covid Vaccine. In an instant, get fourteen days access to international travel and indoor hospitality. PCR Test included. Scan your Digital ID to get started."

They found the path markers and made their way north towards a small hut hidden amongst the metal, bushes, and trees.

Within the hut was some old rusting equipment.

They waited. After a couple of minutes, they heard a faint click. At the same time, the lip of a hatch appeared in the dusty floor.

Using a knife as a lever, Marr lifted the hatch to expose the ladder within.

Marr and Luna dropped down the ladder and entered the back of the base.

They made their way towards the center of the base and entered their crew room.

Within the crew room, they changed back into keeper outfits.

"I am surprised we didn't see any sight of the dingo pack; I am sure the tracks we were seeing were fresh," shared Luna as they stowed their equipment.

"A good thing too, definitely no time today for side activities!" added Marr.

"What do you think Mentor intended by 'Pay a visit to Teacher when you are done'?" asked Luna absently.

"Let's go and find out," Marr replied as they left the crew room and headed towards the training centre.

As Marr and Luna approach the door, they could hear a warm, but broken voice from within.

Through a window in the door, they could see an old lady, sitting in a circle with six younger people all dressed in Keeper uniforms.

The lady was of dark brown complexion. She had haunting black eyes, balanced with a pleasant expression. Her wild grey hair was drawn back exposing two disfigured ears and scars that ran down the side of her neck. She wore her hair this way as if to ensure everyone saw the scars. As a mark of pride.

Teacher caught them looking through the small window. Without breaking her monologue, she beckoned them to enter. She pointed them to some seats just inside the door.

Marr and Luna entered quickly and sat down. The students hardly paid them any attention.

"So that concludes our lesson for today. Any questions," concluded Teacher.

A silence filled the room for a moment or two. Then one of the students spoke up confidently.

"If things were so good, why was it so easy for the Utopians to gain so much control at the start of the Reset?"

Teacher paused for a moment, looking around the circle.

"That is a great question, thank you, Theona. Perhaps a review of Zuby's List will point us towards an answer. How about we add something about it to the homework and give it our full attention tomorrow," replied Teacher.

A groan echoed around the room.

"Perhaps everyone could find one example in your lives today, using the list as the reference, and bring it to class tomorrow," continued Teacher.

"Can someone share the list with us before we go?" she asked the room.

There was another pause.

"Perhaps the gentleman at the back of the room could refresh our memories?" Teacher said as everyone turned their heads to see whom she was referring to.

Marr and Luna spun around with everyone else.

Mentor was standing behind them.

Without even so much as a nod, Mentor began to speak softly, but clearly.

"Zuby's List, July fifth, year one.

"Number one, most people would rather be in the majority, than be right.

"Number two, at least twenty percent of the population has strong authoritarian tendencies, which will emerge under the right conditions.

"Three, fear of death is only rivalled by the fear of social disapproval. The latter could be stronger.

"Four, propaganda is just as effective in the modern day as it was one hundred years ago. Access to limitless information has not made the average person any wiser.

"Number five, anything, and everything can and will be politicised by the media, government, and those who trust them.

"Six, many politicians and large corporations will gladly sacrifice human lives if it is conducive to their political and financial aspirations.

"Seven, most people believe the government acts in the best interests of the people. Even many who are vocal critics of the government.

"Number eight, once they have made up their mind, most people would rather to commit to being wrong, than admit they were wrong.

"Nine, humans can be trained and conditioned quickly and relatively easily to significantly alter their behaviours - for better or worse.

"Ten, when sufficiently frightened, most people will not only accept authoritarianism, but demand it.

"Eleven, people who are dismissed as 'conspiracy theorists' are often researched and simply ahead of the mainstream narrative.

"Number twelve, most people value safety and security more than freedom and liberty, even if said 'safety' is merely an illusion.

"Thirteen, hedonic adaptation occurs in both directions, and once inertia sets in, it is difficult to get people back to 'normal'.

"Fourteen, a significant percent of people thoroughly enjoy being subjugated.

"Fifteen, 'The Science' has evolved into a secular pseudo-religion for millions of people in the West. This religion has little to do with science itself.

"Number sixteen, most people care more about looking like they are doing the right thing, rather than actually doing the right thing.

"Seventeen, politics, the media, science, and the healthcare industries are all corrupt, to varying degrees. Scientists and doctors can be bought as easily as politicians.

"Eighteen, if you make people comfortable enough, they will not revolt. You can keep millions docile as you strip their rights, by giving them money, food, and entertainment.

"Nineteen, modern people are overly complacent and lack vigilance when it comes to defending their own freedoms from government overreach.

"Twenty, it's easier to fool a person than to convince them that they have been fooled.

"Number twenty-one, most people are fairly compassionate and have good intentions (this is good).

"And, finally, number twenty-two, most people deeply struggle to understand that some people, including our 'leaders', CAN have malicious or perverse intentions (this is bad)."

The students, Marr and Luna had been transfixed, listening. They all sensed they had just witnessed something truly momentous. Being in the same room as Mentor was one thing, but hearing him speak, was something different all together.

"Very good, Mentor, you paid attention all those years ago when you sat here."

Teacher's thanks, broke the spell.

With that the students gathered their things and left, sensing these visitors were not here for their further entertainment.

5

With the students gone, Teacher waved Mentor, Marr, and Luna into the seats in the circle.

With everyone seated, she spoke.

"There will be a time when we will sit together and talk of the events that were set in motion today. We will talk about how no one else will need to suffer what I have suffered, to have their implants removed and be free of the observers constant monitoring. Now is not that time."

With that Teacher nodded and rose. She walked over to the door. They all watched her approach the door.

At the door, she turned and spoke as she shifted her gaze between Marr and Luna, "Come visit me tomorrow, before you leave."

Mentor smiled as the door closed behind Teacher.

"The ego is strong in that one. She can't stop herself hinting that she knows more than everyone else," Mentor shared as Marr and Luna tried to take stock of what was going on.

"What does she mean, before we leave?" Luna asked.

"The day after tomorrow, you embark on a new adventure," Mentor replied.

"It's happening?" Marr exclaimed excitedly. "Yes, Marr, it's time to use the training. This evening, you will interview for crew roles on an intergalactic hauler. It will be arranged such that you will get those placements. Tomorrow, the rig will arrive, load, and depart with you two on it," Mentor shared.

Luna stared. Her mouth hanging open.

"A Rig? What? Space? What? And what do you mean, training?" Luna demanded.

"You both are highly skilled technicians, warriors, and covert operators. What further training would you need?" Mentor replied.

"But I have no experience in space or using the systems on those rigs?" said Luna.

"Luna, you are applying for a role as an apprentice. You will be trained on the job into everything you need to know. Marr has been studying the systems used in these rigs for the last five years. She will still be on a steep learning curve; however, I'll be there to help with that," Mentor added.

"You are coming too?" Luna asked in a daze.

"Of course, someone has got to keep an eye on the two of you," said Mentor with a brief smile, which faded as quickly as it had appeared.

"Details?" Marr asked sensing Mentor's mood shifting back to the job at hand.

"The interviews will be held just after nine p.m. at The Triggerarti. Go together. Get there by eight p.m. Chat with the publican about finding a rig. He will suggest to you that captains come in all the time. He will tell you to find a quiet corner and wait. Stay alert but appear relaxed. All conversations must be on record, so bracelets off," Mentor replied.

Luna was still staring. Half in shock.

Marr listened intently.

"When directed, go over, and meet the captain. Share your work history. Tell him you are looking for a new adventure, and that you are hardworking and obedient. Leave it with him to get back to you. The rest will simply unfold," Mentor continued.

"I will be there too. As always, we don't let on that we know each other. The day after tomorrow, that will change. Once on board the rig, we will interact as if meeting for the first time and getting to know each other," Mentor added.

"That will be fun," Luna added sheepishly.

"Are we clear?" concluded Mentor, ignoring Luna's input, and finishing the sentence in a manner that showed there wasn't anything else to share.

"Yes, we are clear," responded Marr.

Luna took the hint and did her best to smile.

Mentor smiled back briefly, before standing up. Marr and Luna watched him leave. They knew from experience he would find his own way back to wherever he was going, and they weren't to follow or ask questions.

Marr and Luna made their way out of the base and back through the offices and hanger. They waited for their designated transport and return to the citadel.

They had a few hours to kill before they needed to be in The Triggerarti.

Chapter 5 – The first meeting

1

Dukk was feeling a little sleepy. Thankfully, he had managed to sleep for most of the five-hour supersonic flight from Kuedia to Utopiam. However, his body was demanding more.

The previous evening's events came into focus as he waited for the privileged to leave the craft.

He had taken his time getting back to the h-pod after the meeting with the mystery man.

By the time he got there, Larinette was already gone. Dukk, hadn't noticed the message on his comms.

Larinette had said she was ready and had gone on ahead to enjoy a pre-dinner drink. She mentioned she was meeting some of the crew from her new rig, the Plinthat.

Realising the time, Dukk had changed quickly and headed straight to the restaurant pub.

The place was heaving. The rest of the crew were already there, sitting at a round table in a back corner.

Larinette and Bazzer were sitting on either side of Rachelle. Annee was next to Larinette. That left Dukk with the remaining seat between Bazzer and Annee. That suited him fine.

The conversation during the meal had been jovial and light. And the food was good. The cooked food was a lovely departure from the usual rehydration packs they were accustomed to whilst hauling.

Dukk was pleased that he had been able to disconnect from the madness and enjoy himself.

Making his exit from the gathering, turned out to be quite straightforward.

After the meal, the crew from the Plinthat joined them as did a number of others. Things escalated quickly as the drinks flowed and the stories got longer legs.

Dukk had no problem simply easing himself out of the conversation and slipping away. After leaving the pub, Dukk had retrieved his overnight bag from the h-pod.

He figured he wouldn't have any further use for the accommodation and travelling without a bag only drew uncomfortable questions.

Making his way to the VG launch pad was uncomplicated.

While found near the centre of the citadel, the Hyperloop serviced the pad. It took him roughly thirty minutes to get to the ID Gateway, giving him plenty of time to clear the controls and board, ready for the midnight departure.

Being unprivileged meant he had to sit at the back of the VG in the food service area.

The seats weren't as comfortable as those in the cabin, but years of hauling had trained him into sleeping anywhere and anytime the opportunity presented itself.

"You can leave now," a voice interrupted Dukk's reflection.

A flight attendant was opening the curtains, signalling that the cabin was now clear.

Dukk made his way through the craft and into the ID Gateway area.

Before him was a large space with scanning stations at the other end.

Between him and the scanning stations were ropes marking two queuing zones. He filed into the queue that was labelled 'Unprivileged'. He was the only one in that queue. In the other queue there were fifty people dressed in typical observer garb.

Dukk smiled quietly to himself thinking of the trouble they all must have to go to. The elaborate, brightly coloured, and chaotic designs were worlds away from the red shirt and chinos that he wore. Watching them talking loudly at each other in their intoxicated state was a nice distraction.

Having had enough of watching the madness before him, Dukk gave his attention to the monitors on the walls. There were ads and political messages.

A news channel caught his eye. On the screen was a picture of a reporter talking. And, in the background was a rig with what looked to be damage to the nose.

Dukk tuned his comms to listen in.

"This morning, a simple misunderstanding resulted in damage to the Bluilda galactic hauler. The captain has expressed disappointment at the accident which she says will have her grounded for one or two weeks. The Bluilda was due to load and depart tomorrow. A spokesperson for Galactic Core Foods said they were seeking a new haulier to fulfil the beef contract which they had previously awarded to the Bluilda."

Dukk silenced the broadcast.

He didn't know the Bluilda crew personally, but he had heard of them. He also knew they used Thumpol to get contracts.

"Coincidence!" reflected Dukk sceptically.

Dukk lifted his arms and opened his hands.

"Open local haulier chat rooms," Dukk instructed his comms.

An array of panels and words began to appear in the air between his hands.

"Show me chat relating to the Bluilda, for the last eight hours," Dukk said in his head.

A collection of stories streamed in the air before him.

Dukk scanned them quickly. As he suspected, there was chatter about trade wars and contract agents competing for business. A few comments suggested the incident was intentional and aimed at putting the contract back on the market. Thumpol's name appeared a couple of times. It looked like the contract had been facilitated by Thumpol and now was being handled by one of Utopiam's main players. A man who went by the name of Wallace.

"Not a coincidence," Dukk said aloud, drawing the attention of a couple of the observers.

Dukk smiled, dropped his arms, and drew his eyes to the ground as he continued to wait for his turn to be scanned.

2

It was eight in the evening by the time Dukk had cleared the ID Gateway.

He used his nav to get the directions to The Triggerarti, the bar where he was to meet Wallace as instructed by the mystery man.

There were a few options. He chose the option that involved more walking.

For a haulier, walking under full gravity was something to be treasured. Dukk was no different. Feeling the weight of his body reminded him of his past. It gave him a sense of belonging somewhere.

His commute would involve a hyperloop journey from the VG station near the centre of the citadel. That would bring him to the middle ring. From there he would have a forty-five-minute walk to the port area.

He was looking forward to refamiliarizing himself with the layout.

In the port area, Marr and Luna had arrived at The Triggerarti.

The Triggerarti was a popular bar and restaurant, with plenty of tables as well as seating along the bar.

Luna hung back a little as Marr headed off to find the owner.

He had already seen them. He tracked Marr's approach and was standing ready at the bar when she got there. He smiled.

"Need a drink or something to eat?" he asked.

"Maybe, but first I have a question."

"Shoot."

"If one was thinking on embarking on a new adventure and getting off this planet, who would one talk to?" Marr asked.

The publican laughed.

"You two look like keepers to me," he said nodding over at Luna. Luna was trying to look inconspicuous near the door. "And you, look a bit old to be changing direction. You'd be better off sticking with what you know."

"Thank you, for your advice, but I think I am clear in my head as to what is best for me," Marr responded with a smirk.

"Well, if you are clear, then who am I to get in your way. And if you want adventure away from this rock, get yourselves on a rig, that will certainly achieve all your aims! Captains come here often looking for contracts and crew. Take a seat, get some refreshments and I'll let you know if I see any captains," the owner instructed as he signalled to a server to find them a table.

"Thank you," Marr replied as she and Luna followed the server to a table.

The Hyperloop journey had been fast and clinical.

Before descending to ground level, Dukk stopped briefly to gaze up into the night sky. The city lights made it hard to see many stars, but the Southern Cross was there as clear as day. Seeing it from space was a far more spectacular experience, however Dukk liked to gaze up at it and imagine how most that went before him would have seen it.

Dukk had enjoyed the walk across to the outer ring. He had enjoyed exploring the narrow streets as he made his way to the pubs near the port.

It was a warm night. A little humid, but clear. Ideal walking conditions.

It all looked familiar. He wasn't sure if that was his memory of the last time, they hauled a load out of here. Or, if simply that citadels mostly looked the same.

The nav comms informed Dukk that he was nearly at his destination. The nav suggested that The Triggerarti was at the end of the street he was now entering.

Halfway down the long and narrow street, Dukk noticed a drinks stand. There were a few people queuing to buy a beverage.

At that moment, the streetlights went out and immediately two men were at his side.

One covered his mouth as they hustled him through a door that opened in the building opposite the drinks stand.

The door shut behind them. Within, was a dimly lit room. It looked like a small pub, with a bar, a few chairs, and the odd table.

At one of the tables sat a man. The low light made it hard to make out any distinguishable features.

Dukk's escort shuffled him towards the table and sat him at a chair opposite the man.

The man waved his hand over Dukk's bracelet and Dukk noticed a faint green glow. The man also had a faint green glow coming from his wrist. It was the same as his experience with the mystery man in Kuedia. Only then did the goons release him and uncover Dukk's mouth.

"Hello Dukk, welcome to Utopiam, you can call me Wallace," said the man as he reached over and switched on a lamp.

3

Wallace looked short and muscular. His hair was grey and wiry. His grey and full beard mapped out his black face, which was dominated by a wide and full nose. And his eyes were black, but warm and knowing. They stared at Dukk now. Dukk felt oddly scared but safe at the same time.

"I am going to be brief, we don't have long, and you need to follow what I say as your life depends on it," Wallace continued before Dukk could think of a reply.

"In a moment, you are to leave via the door you came in. Cross to the drink stand, hand over your credit and take the drink offered. Pretend to drink some, then dump it down the street. Just make sure you complete the purchase, so the observers don't draw any conclusions.

"Then, make your way to The Triggerarti. Go across to the bar and ask for me. The bar staff will point you towards a table, which I will be sitting at. Come over and act as if we'd never met. We'll have a normal contract conversation. We'll exchange details and agree to chat again within the hour.

"Go back to the bar. Ask the publican for advice on picking up crew. He will tell you where to sit and what to do. Follow his instructions. Five potential crew members will find you. Interview them as you would under normal circumstances. Exchange details and promise to get back to them later with a decision. You will pick candidates two, three and five. Not the first or forth. They will be decoys. Then finish your drink, come back to me and we'll close the deal. The rest will proceed as it normally does.

"Make no mention to anyone of this conversation here or the conversation yesterday. What else do you need to know?" concluded Wallace.

Dukk collected his thoughts.

"What was the most important thing to know right now?" he asked himself.

"Who are you and why is my life in danger?" Dukk blurted out.

"To answer your first question, I am but a very typical businessman. A middleman. I connect people. I do business and I take my cut. I look after myself and those that don't cross me. Cutting deals is what I do and have always done. That is all."

"This doesn't feel like a typical deal to me?" Dukk asked more calmly having regained his composure.

"That might be true, but the principle is still the same."

"Alright then, who are you connecting on this deal?" Dukk asked as his mind cleared.

"The official answer is, Galactic Core Foods, the real answer is not for me to disclose for now. I've been in this game long enough to know; somethings are best left unsaid and allowed to unfold. The real answer is one of those things," Wallace responded kindly.

"Okay, so how about my second question? Can you answer why my life is in danger?" Dukk retorted dismissively.

"Yes, I can. Thumpol is making a play for a bigger share of the market. He plans to take control of as many rigs as he can get his hands on. You have proven difficult to corrupt so he aims to take you out. Should you take his deal and his crew, an unfortunate accident awaits you on your first haul."

Dukk paused. He wasn't surprised. It would be the kind of thing Thumpol was capable of.

"Who says I can trust you any more than I can trust him, or the three new crew members you are making me take?" Dukk responded.

"Nobody, neither should they. I and Thumpol are of the same breed. However, I think I am right in saying you are a good judge of character, so I'll leave it up to you to decide."

"Okay, and what if I like the deal, but not the crew members?" Dukk retorted.

"It is a package deal, take it or leave it," Wallace responded firmly.

Dukk paused. He was getting frustrated and angry. That hadn't served him in the past, so he took in a couple of breaths.

"We are out of time, anything else pressing?" Wallace interrupted Dukk's pause.

"Yes," Dukk replied as a nagging question surfaced again.

"What is the story with these?" Dukk asked pointing to his bracelet.

"Ah, that is something I can answer directly. The bracelet is coded to your implants. It lays down interference. It basically takes recent background noise and inserts it into your implant feed in place of what you are actually saying or hearing. So as long as you cover your mouth to prevent lip reading, observers won't have access to your conversations when it is active. You simply hold your hand over it like this. That action will turn it on or off," Wallace shared.

"Oh!" replied Dukk.

"That sounds like the type of thing that observers wouldn't like to have happening," he added.

"Quite the opposite. They built them. The EO and their immediate subordinates use them themselves as do their spies, operatives, and partners. They know some activities are best not overheard or put on record. The likes of us, can use them to swing things in our favour, so long as we do it carefully and not in a manner that gets in their way or alerts normal people to the reality of the constant monitoring," Wallace added cheerfully.

With that Wallace turned off the lamp and stood up.

"Did you cut the streetlights?" Dukk added as he stood too.

"Yes of course, now we must leave before the power outage draws any further attention. Besides, we are about to be late for our own meeting. Whereby the way, we must leave the bracelets off as the contract conversation needs to be on record," Wallace answered.

The two men were at Dukk's side again. They deactivated his bracelet and ushered him towards the door.

Dukk looked back at the table. Wallace was gone.

Dukk cross the street to the drink stand as instructed.

The moment he reached it, the streetlights came back on again.

Dukk looked around. At the end of the street in the direction he had come, stood two sentinels. They paused for a moment and then moved on.

"Interesting," thought Dukk turning back towards the drink stand.

The barista was holding out a beverage, smiling sheepishly.

Dukk paid for and took the drink. He smelt it. Strong coffee.

"I need a stiff drink, but this will have to do!" he declared to himself as he took a sip.

Dukk made his way to the end of the street.

The entrance to The Triggerarti was nothing out of the ordinary. The sign and door were very typical of a port bar.

The place was busy. All the tables were occupied as were the seats at the bar. People were also standing in small groups, drinking, and chatting.

"Keepers and hauliers," thought Dukk.

He even thought he recognised one or two.

Dukk made his way across to the bar. He noticed an elderly man behind the bar tracking his approach.

"What can I get you?" the barman said.

"Directions. I am here to meet Wallace," Dukk replied.

"Isn't everybody. He is on the balcony, at his usual table. Last one on the right. You'll know which one when you get there," replied the barman dismissively as he pointed towards the stairs.

Dukk found Wallace straight away. The table was positioned in a corner, slightly away from the others. Clearly Wallace had influence.

Wallace sat at the table with his back to the corner. Hovering nearby were the two goons that grabbed Dukk in the street.

The two men stepped forward as Dukk approached the table.

"Can we help you?" said one of the men.

Dukk sighed but decided to play along.

"I hear I'd find Wallace in this corner."

"What is he to you?" continued the rough and burly looking man.

"I understand he is looking for a haulier. An urgent beef contract. So, do you want to get out of my way and allow us grown-ups to get down to business," Dukk said firmly holding his gaze.

The goons stepped forward.

"What do you go by?" came a voice from behind them.

"You can call me Dukk."

"Never heard of you," replied Wallace playing his part well.

The two goons step back.

"I am the new captain of the Dinatha. I served under Rachelle for several years," said Dukk stepping towards the table.

"Ah, yes. Dukk, second in charge to the no nonsense Rachelle. That now rings a bell. But! I heard she just retired. She got quite a send-off from what I hear. How is it that you were her second and yet you are here before me, not in bed doing your best to take the edge off a hangover?" Wallace enquired.

Dukk was tiring of the game. He simply stared back with a sarcastic grin.

"Not in the mood for small talk, I appreciate that. Take a seat," Wallace continued.

Dukk sat down opposite him.

"Here is the deal. Three shipments of beef. It will load tomorrow. Destination is a local system. Must be sequential. No side excursions will be tolerated. Seven hundred and fifty thousand EUs on top of costs."

"That's a generous deal. What is the catch?"

"No catch, except that you need to fulfil all three loads before I release your fee, and the first load must be in the air tomorrow."

"That is a little aggressive, but doable. There must be something else! Wait! Thumpol had this deal before. Is there a mark on the deal?" Dukk reflected aloud realising the predicament as he spoke.

"You are perceptive, young captain. You will go far. Yes, taking this deal may create some bad blood with the Kuedia black market king!" Wallace conceded.

"And, come to think about it, I don't see a queue of other captains lining up here tonight!" Dukk observed.

"You are getting ahead of yourself young pup! Not all those that want this deal need to find me in a pub! Perhaps this deal isn't for you, after all!" Wallace said firmly.

Dukk held Wallace's gaze and said nothing. Dukk was struggling to hold things together. The reality of the risks he was facing were starting to weigh on him.

Wallace smiled.

"You have a lot of spunk. I like that. And now you've got me thinking. The Dinatha is marked as one of Thumpol's rigs. Giving you this deal will really annoy him. And annoying that dirt bag makes me happy. That might be fun," Wallace concluded.

"Tell you what. You have a think about it. Meanwhile, I'll run some checks on your situation. Let's chat again in an hour and I'll let you know my decision," Wallace added.

With that, Wallace waved at the two goons. They moved to Dukk's side. It was clear the conversation was over.

5

Dukk return to the bar and ordered a drink.

"Did you get everything you were after?" the barman asked casually as he served the drink.

"Nearly. I am also looking for some new crew," Dukk replied.

"And The Triggerarti shall provide," the old man stated as he beckoned a server.

Dukk smiled.

"This young captain is looking for crew, find him a table and ask around," the owner instructed the server.

Dukk followed the server to an empty table in a darkish corner. Dukk was sure there were no free tables when he arrived. He could see no other free table in the place.

"What good fortune!" Dukk said sceptically as he got seated.

The server ignored him and headed off in the direction of the bar.

Dukk didn't have to wait long for the first decoy.

He reviewed the experienced haulier's track record and asked her a few questions about her interests. As instructed, Dukk exchanged details and promised to get back to her later in the evening.

Next was a young woman. She was of average height, with dark brown hair and eyes that matched her complexion. She looked slim, but strong. She had a curious energy about her.

She was at the upper end of the typical apprentice age, but her eagerness balanced that.

The third applicant was also a woman. She was of average height and medium build. She had olive complexion, dark hair, and light blue eyes.

Dukk was slightly distracted by her beauty. It was in her eyes. Knowledgeable and a little melancholy, but kind.

Dukk had to collect himself.

Calling herself Marr, she had tremendous technical qualifications and planet side pilot certificates, but no space time. Her skills would be useful, but he really needed a strong co-pilot who could handle the demands of space, not another apprentice.

Dukk interviewed the fourth candidate quickly as he was losing his patience.

The last of the dictated new hires was tall, muscular and of dark brown complexion. He had dark brown eyes and short black hair with wisps of grey.

This guy had plenty of experience on the rigs and medical qualifications, but his age and dubious past was alarming. He had completed the observer education and spent time as an observer before being deprivileged. The details weren't clear. After that he had taken on many different labour roles.

Going by the name of Mentor, he spoke very little, and his gaze was intimidating. It had a similar feel to that of the third candidate. And there was something familiar about him.

"All so disconcerting! How could I ever trust people like these," Dukk thought as he promised to get back to him later.

Dukk felt spooked, on top of the building anger.

At that moment he spotted Wallace at the bar. He was sitting there with an empty seat next to him.

Dukk was fuming. He grabbed his drink and marched over, activating his bracelet on approach.

Wallace noticed Dukk's approach, stood his ground, but activated his bracelet too. Once at the bar, Dukk raised his stein to cover his mouth.

"What are you playing at! Those crew options are rubbish and possibly dangerous!"

Wallace smiled, lifted his drink, and said "I'll sweeten the deal. I'll match the EUs with crypto."

Dukk was stunned. It took a moment to grasp this. His anger turned to disbelief. Was this all a big joke. He was all for making money under the table, but that was a huge amount. It was absurd, unrealistic, and downright lethal.

"What am I going to do with that much crypto here. I'd be picked up by sentinels the minute the crypto got anywhere near my wrist wrap. For sure, I'd never be heard of again. Well, yes, I could buy stuff in other systems, but I'd never get it back here!" Dukk replied,

"Buy another drink," Wallace replied in a manner which sounded like both a challenge and a threat.

Dukk ordered another drink. When he did, Wallace tilted his head slightly at the barman.

The barman returned a moment later with a full stein. It looked identical to the one Dukk had nearly finished. The barman scanned Dukk as normal and Dukk observed his EU credits deducted for the right amount.

"Drink some," Wallace said.

Dukk went to lift the stein and was momentarily caught off guard. This stein was much heavier. On closer inspection Dukk noticed the thick wall he was used to seeing was much thinner. And the mug looked deeper. He took a swig. It tasted the same. Just lots more of it in the same outwardly appearing stein.

As he put the drink back on the bar, Wallace turned to the barman and said "Selfie?"

Wallace then took a selfie of himself and the barman. When done, Wallace flicked the image across to the barman's wrist wrap.

"There, I just bought you the other half of your drink, enjoy," Wallace said smiling, adding "Get hold of the picture app by Antiw, it will be useful when we close this deal."

Dukk stared ahead, dumfounded.

It wasn't enough that, in less than twenty-four hours, Dukk had learnt of tech that could prevent the overlords from hearing his every word. But now he had been shown a way to move currency under their very noses. What more was in store?

Wallace waved his hand over his bracelet. Dukk followed suit.

"You checked out. It's yours. I decided the entertainment value outweigh the risks of using a rooky like you. I'll even cover your fuel costs getting your rig over here for the loading. You in?" Wallace shared confidently.

"Yep, I'll take it," Dukk replied cautiously.

"Excellent, my people will send you the contracts and pad clearance. The load will be ready for your arrival. Don't mess about."

Wallace paused for a moment before continuing.

"Feel free to use my corner table. I am sure you have some things to organise before returning to Kuedia to collect your rig. Oh, and it will serve you to avoid any further interactions with Thumpol for the next twenty hours. I suggest until you are airborne out of Kuedia, you keep this news to only those you fully trust. I will also keep it out of the media until I know you are clear. Good luck, Dukk," Wallace concluded as he nodded at the publican, swung himself off the chair and headed for the door.

A server was standing behind Dukk beckoning Dukk towards the stairs. Dukk grabbed his drink and headed up.

Chapter 6 – Saying goodbye

1

Marr and Luna watched Dukk as the server led him back up the stairs.

From where they sat, they could just see him settling into a table in the corner.

"He is cute," Luna commented, breaking the silence that had prevailed since the interviews.

"He is."

Luna turned her head to look at Marr. Luna was taken aback by the uncharacteristic comment.

"Interesting! Are you laying a claim, Marr?" Luna added cheekily.

Marr allowed the slightest smile as she ignored Luna and watched Dukk interacting with his comms.

Simultaneously, Marr and Luna's comms sounded as a new message arrived.

It was a message from Dukk. He was letting them know they were on the crew.

The message included a list of items they needed to get. It also included the approximate time they were to be ready. And the message included the rig codes they would need to change their designations.

"Dinatha! It has a nice ring to it," Marr shared casually as she absorbed the details in the message.

"He is way too efficient for my liking. He is all yours," Luna added.

"Time for a drink," Marr concluded.

"Absolutely, best make the most of our last night on this rock!" Luna announced as she signalled a server.

Dukk was struggling to concentrate. And it wasn't just the tiredness and events of the last fourteen hours.

He had noticed the two new crew, Marr, and Luna, tracking his path from the bar to Wallace's table.

He had noticed them chatting and doing their best not to look in his direction.

And he had noticed a brief and slight smile from Marr just as he pressed send on his messages to them.

An alert on his comms snapped him back to attention.

It was a message from Mentor accepting his crew offer. Messages from Marr and Luna followed shortly after.

Dukk looked back at the two again. They were ordering drinks. For a moment he thought about joining them.

"I could definitely do with a few more drinks," Dukk muttered to himself.

"All in good time," he concluded.

Instead, he waved the server over and ordered some food. It had just occurred to him that he hadn't eaten since last night.

Ninety minutes later, Dukk was at the ID Gateway preparing to board the midnight VG back to Kuedia.

Before leaving The Triggerarti he had managed to stay reasonably focused.

He had mostly managed to avoid watching the girls as they drank and laughed, while he checked the contracts and details he had received from Wallace's people.

Now, he was looking forward to getting into a seat and shutting his eyes for a time.

Meanwhile, Marr and Luna were stumbling up the stairs to their h-pod. Giggling and buzzing from the drinks.

"What do you think it will be like?" Luna asked.

"What are you talking about?" Marr replied.

"Sex in near zero-g," Luna giggled.

Marr laughed too, not sure how to answer.

"Time for rest," Marr said as they entered the h-pod.

"We'll have a little lie in, then head to the stores to get the travel lockers and the other items on Dukk's list," Marr continued.

"After that, we'll pack up the h-pod, then I'd like to jog out to the old hangers. It might be a long time before we can do that again. We can shower out there before we say goodbye. We'll still have plenty of time to get back to the port for the Dinatha's arrival," Marr concluded.

"Oh, I nearly forgot! My monthly dosage appointment is in two days!" Luna slurred as they took off their boots.

"All under control. Our meds will now be injected while on the rig. Rigs carry adequate supplies of vaccines and supplements. If they don't have a medical officer, Mentor is qualified to administer them," Marr replied.

Seven hours later, Dukk was in Kuedia's Port Authority offices.

He decided it was best to go in person rather than send messages. The timing was too tight. The heavily bureaucratic observers always responded a little faster when approached in person. It was still taking time. It had been nearly forty minutes thus far. He had filled in forms and answered a lot of questions.

And Dukk was nervous. It was nearly five p.m. And that was the time he was due at the rig for the formal hand-over. Before that he had to secure the departure permission. Wallace's team had shared the access approval to get the rig into Utopiam, but he still needed to get it out of Kuedia. He had to have the rig in the air before the citadel's outer doors closed for the evening. That would happen at seven p.m.

Then it would be a further nine hours before the rig would be on the ground in Utopiam. With the time difference, he would only have two hours to get loaded, refuelled and off the ground and space bound before the port doors in Utopiam closed for the night.

He had avoided any contact with the crew as he didn't want to draw any attention from Thumpol. It was going to be a little crazy when they learned they were leaving immediately.

And, he had just realised that Larinette hadn't made contact. He figured that it was possible she hadn't even been back to their h-pod yet and noticed he wasn't there. Dukk figured she was already acquainting herself with her new crew. Dukk was mildly intrigued that it wasn't bothering him much. Perhaps he was tired, and the loss would hit him later, he concluded.

"I just hope she is at the hand-over so I can ensure her things are off the rig," thought Dukk.

2

Clapping and cheering greeted Dukk as he entered the pad. He had just come through the security door that gave him access to the port pad that temporarily housed the Dinatha.

Rachelle stood in front of the small crowd dwarfed by the Dinatha behind them. Beside her stood Annee, Larinette and Bazzer. Many familiar faces made up the rest of the crowd.

"Welcome, Dukk, Captain of the Dinatha," Rachelle announced.

The clapping and cheering started up again.

A huge smile erupted across Dukk's face. The seriousness of the moment could wait.

"Thank you, Rachelle, I am truly honoured," he said as he joined the crowd.

"How does it feel, cap," Annee blurted out.

"Surreal, Ann."

"For a moment we were worried you'd got cold feet. No one has seen you since you slipped out of my party, last night," Rachelle added.

"Not a chance, Rachelle. Besides, it was your night and I had plans to make."

"Always on the job, is Dukk! Good luck with it all, not that you'll need it. You are more of a captain than I ever was," Rachelle reflected out loud.

Everyone stopped. Silence.

"You are too kind. But full of shit. Rachelle, now how about you get on with your retirement and let me get this old rig loaded and paying its way again," Dukk shared to lighten the mood.

"Right you are, Dukk. Take care," Rachelle concluded.
With that she gave Dukk a deep but quick hug, before making her way to the security door.

The others in the crowd followed suit, congratulating Dukk as they left.

"Good luck, Dukk, it has been an adventure," Larinette said when it was her turn.

Dukk, still smiling, held her gaze briefly before drawing her in for a final kiss and hug.

"You take care of yourself, Larinette. You will always have a place on my crew, if you ever are in the need," Dukk added when they broke apart.

With a final smile, she turned and left in the direction of the exit.

"Clearly she had already cleared her things," Dukk reflected as he watched her go.

"That just leaves us three," said Bazzer from behind Dukk.

Dukk turned around and paused for a moment to look at Bazzer and Annee.

"Yes, it does, Bazzer. Now down to work. Change of plan," Dukk shared as he looked around the pad for anyone else remaining.

With confidence that they were alone, he continued.

"I have secured our first contract. However, the pickup is in Utopiam in ten hours, so I want this rig in the air immediately."

Bazzer and Annee stared. Stunned.

"Lucrative?" Annee ventured.

"More than you can ever imagine."

"Risky?" Bazzer asked.

"Of course! You in?"

They both smiled.

"Definitely, captain," Bazzer and Annee said in unison.

"Great. Bazzer, engine room and start the system checks. Annee, external. I'll get into the cockpit and start loading the navigation," Dukk said as they made their way to the stairs.

"Fuel?" Bazzer enquired as he reached the stairs.

"Check it, but we should have plenty to get us to Utopiam. And, time is tight, so I want to run light and fast. We'll refuel proper from there."

"What about crew?" Annee called as she watched Dukk and Bazzer climbing the access stairs.

"That is covered too," shouted Dukk.

Bazzer stopped and looked back.

Dukk continued.

"Us three will be well able to handle this inter-citadel hop. Then, three new crew will join us in Utopiam when we load. I've got lots to share. Once we are airborne."

"Observer?" questioned Bazzer as he started the climb again.

"Any minute now. And, I have requested that the ground crew get the hanger barricades open, stairs retracted and us moving towards the launch zone the moment the observer is seated."

A commotion at the pad doors stopped their progress once more.

"Two lockers for an overnight inter-citadel hop! Clearly a noob being trialled on this short journey. I've never seen a noob on their own. They say it is a bad omen," Bazzer shared in jest as they watched the observer, and two assistances stumble through the door into the hanger.

Each assistant was carrying a large locker that was similar in size to the two units that Dukk allowed each of his crew to have on the rig.

Dukk sighed.

"Leave the lockers there, I will have my crew bring them aboard. Please lock the pad door behind your assistants and come aboard," Dukk shouted down at the observer and the entourage.

"Ann, I'll open the nose cargo door. Will you lob those lockers into the forward hold? We'll get them to the passenger cabins once airborne," Dukk said quietly into his comms.

The moment the pad door was locked by the observer, orange lights started to flash in the hanger ceiling. And a warning siren started up.

The lights and noise startled the observer, who then immediately bolted for the stairs.

When Dukk reached the hatch, he turned, and waited for the observer to hurry up the stairs.

Only when the observer reached the top, puffing and clearly distressed, did Dukk say, "Relax, it'll be ten to fifteen minutes before the hanger barricades open and we get underway. Let me show you to your seat. Follow me."

The observer stared back at him.

Dukk smiled and tilted his head, trying to hide the glee of getting one over on his authoritarian rulers.

Bazzer could be heard laughing uncontrollably as he made his way down to the engine room.

With the observer seated and settled, Dukk headed into the Cockpit.

He sat at the navigation station and was about to start loading the details when his comms alerted him to an incoming call.

Dukk answered it without thinking.

"Dukk, wonderful of you to take my call. I had hoped to hear from you before now."

"Who is this? Oh, Thumpol, hi!" Dukk replied wishing he'd checked the caller ID first.

"I was in the area and thought I would drop by and congratulate you on becoming the new Captain of the Dinatha. And the strangest thing happened. I get to the pad door, and it's locked. And it appears an operator up here in the console room is preparing to move a rig out to the launch zone," Thumpol shared.

Dukk climbed over to the cockpit windshield and peered up at the control room in the side of the pad wall. An operator could be seen sitting at a console behind the glass. The operator was looking down at the rig. In the observation room next to it, Dukk could see Thumpol and some goons, looking down on the rig.

Dukk put the call on hold and dialled the operator.

"Operator," was the response.

"Dukk, captain of the Dinatha requesting a status update."

"Departure clearance received. Low loaders are started and ready. Barricades are ready to be lowered. Path to the launch zone is clear. Give me the word, and I will remove the stairs and start the low loaders rolling. Standing by. "

"Thank you, I'll be back to you shortly. Out," said Dukk as he returned to Thumpol's call.

"Sorry, Thumpol, I can't talk right now. I am kind of busy," Dukk said as he ended the call.

"Annee and Bazzer, I am switching to proximity mode on the comms. I suggest you do the same. We can open comms again to the outside world once we are airborne. A little heat might be coming our way. I'll explain when we are all up here in the cockpit," Dukk announced on his comms link to his crew.

"I gather Thumpol's influence isn't that sufficient or else he would have been in that control room, not locked outside of it. Hopefully, that situation doesn't change until we are airborne," Dukk thought to himself as he returned to loading the navigation details.

3

Five hours later, as the Dinatha blasted its way towards Utopiam, Marr and Luna were making their way through the underground tunnels of the base.

They had successfully procured the things they needed, packed up their h-pod and jogged all the way out to the old and rundown sheds and hangers that hid the underground base. They had also showered and said goodbye to some colleagues.

"Do you think we'll ever see this place again?" Luna asked as they approached the training centre.

"Who knows. Perhaps you'll be a rubbish haulier and find yourself back here in three weeks?" Marr replied as she peered through the window in the training room door.

"Come in ladies, take a seat," Teacher beckoned from within.

Teacher was at her usual place, but no one else was in the room.

Marr and Luna entered the room and took a seat each in the circle.

"What an exciting time it is! Luna, what occurs to you at this moment in your journey?"

Luna stared back.

"Marr?" Teacher continued.

"Am I ready, is what is on my mind, Teacher," Marr replied.

"Good thought but wasted. Of course, you are ready. You are always ready. You can never be more ready for the moment at hand than you are when you are at that moment," Teacher shared smiling, self-congratulating herself on her own brilliance.

Marr smiled back.

"However, I can remind you of something that may help ease your mind. And Luna, this will help you find more ease with your path. Luna, Marr will share this daily with you until you too have memorised it and can pass it on."

With that, Teacher settled back in her chair and began to talk in a reverend manner.

"The Creator's Experiment. Before the beginning there was a mountain. Hovering above that mountain was a huge orb. Contained within the orb was all the wisdom of the universe.

There was nothing unknown. There was nothing more to know. Or was there? It was hard to tell. It was accepted that learning creates further wisdom. It was accepted that the process of seeking wisdom produces wisdom. So, if the wisdom was just idle in this orb, how could one be certain that it contained all the wisdom. What if there was more that could be discovered through the use of that wisdom?

So, the orb's creator decided to conduct an experiment. The Creator hit the top of the orb. A crack appeared and out poured all the wisdom contained. The wisdom erupted out into the sky and split into tiny fragments. Each fragment duplicated itself, many times. Each duplicate contained a small piece of each piece of wisdom. The fragments formed as tiny droplets. These droplets rained down on the plain that surrounded the mountain. When the droplets reached the ground, they would cycle back up into the sky and then rain down again. It didn't rain over the mountain, only the plain. Thus, no wisdom would ever return to the orb automatically. It would need to be collected, carried up the mountain and put back into the orb.

The Creator then put all manner of creatures on the plain surrounding the mountain.

The Creator suspected that any singular piece of wisdom may be too great for any creature to grasp. So, the Creator gave each creature a thimble sized cup to catch the fragments that rained down. The idea being that each creature would then carry the droplets back up the side of the mountain and at the top, merge the fragments back into the orb.

The Creator constructed the experiment such that the process of climbing the mountain would enable said creatures to look at the fragments they carried. Through this process, they would learn and obtain growth in themselves. And perhaps, as they considered the fragments of wisdom, they would see something new or different in those fragments. This would then enable the fragments to embody the adjustment or addition to the overall piece of wisdom when the fragments were reunited with other fragments within the orb.

4

Teacher continued.

"To help reduce the risk of corruption of the experiment, the Creator added some extra safety measures.

"First, the Creator hid the design from the creatures. Many would barely notice the mountain or the orb, and only a few would ever attempt to climb the mountain. The Creator even hid the knowledge of the cup. The Creator made the cups invisible and only observable by each cup's owner. Most creatures would never know they even had a cup, let alone know what it was for.

"Secondly, the Creator added time to the mix. Time gave the experiment boundaries and ensured that at some point the results could be assessed. While seemingly infinitely long and starting with a big bang, the experiment would eventually end.
 In addition, the Creator gave each creature a life that lasted only a miniscule fraction of the overall time to maximise the potential for variety and evolution.

"Thirdly, the Creator wanted to give the creatures something to do that encouraged them to search for meaning, for something else. So, the Creator made life on the plain hard. The Creator made time on the plain a toil of survival.

"Forth, the creator gave the creatures the ability to choose. The freedom to choose how they approached their toil would ensure wisdom was observed and considered with an open and free mind.

The creator designed things so the creatures could choose if and when they engaged with their purpose.

"And finally, the Creator designed a flaw into the creature's psyche. The flaw would cause the creatures to self-sabotage their own experience should they try to cheat the design. The Creator called this flaw the Ego, the servant of the non-authentic. The non-authentic would eventually fail at any attempt to climb the mountain, and instead would perish on the plain. Thus, only the authentically oriented would contribute to the process of returning the wisdom to the orb."

"The Creator wanted to maximise the potential for wisdom to create wisdom, so the Creator constructed the cups so they would increase in size. They would increase in size as the creatures traversed the mountain. They then had a choice to return to the plain and collect more fragments before reaching the summit and merging their cup with the orb. Also, the Creator designed the experiment such that the cup would grow and fill faster as a creature took on more engagement with their path, and even more so when that engagement related to the task of prolonging their species. The logic being that this added complexity gave that creature a different perspective and increased the potential for new wisdom to be uncovered.

"The Creator knew that completing this task would require enormous effort on the part of the creatures. It would take every bit of their strengths, down to the last breath. As a reward for working hard to complete this task and reach the orb, the Creator made available three gifts. Firstly, only those that pursued their purpose or honestly endeavoured to grasp it, and did so authentically, would receive one hundred percent of what was due to them for their toil on the plain. Secondly, cup size growth would result in a greater sense of joy, wellness, and ease with the toil on the plain. Thirdly, the creatures would be given a glimpse of all the wisdom of the universe, as they completed their purpose.

"And to help things go in the right direction for those that engaged fully, the Creator etched into the side of each cup, the details of the design, plus a set of hints of the overall wisdom. These design details and hints of the overall wisdom would be readable only by a few. It was only visible to those who engaged fully with the toil of their purpose, such that they lived in fulness and died before they died. For most these hidden etchings would serve another purpose. Should they find themselves on or close to the right path, the hidden etchings would help the creature sense the correct path without the need for external confirmation.

"Initially, the creatures were too simplistic to grasp their true purpose. For a time, no creature even noticed the mountain or orb, let alone went near it. While still oblivious to the cup, the mountain, the orb, and their purpose, over time some sets of creatures, found ways to reduce the toil and prolong their time a little longer. They joined with others. They increased their numbers. They found new capabilities within themselves. They evolved new skills. This all enabled them to be better able to cope with the toil on the plain. They also got to know the plain better. They used its resources to add comforts and reduce the apparent futility of their existence."

5

Teacher continued.

"Eventually some of these evolved creatures noticed their cup and tried to fill them. After even more time, some ventured onto the mountain. It was rocky and steep. There were many perils. A wrongly placed foot or hand and the creature would topple down the path and even fall from the mountain entirely. Many died on the mountain as on the plain. Never reaching the top or realising their purpose.

"Those that didn't die on the way up the mountain, extracted learning. When that happened, they observed that their thimble sized cup got slightly bigger. They found it could hold more of the droplets. The creatures also found they could help others up the paths, and that that act of sacrifice also increased the size of the cup. This all gave them the incentive to keep trying.

"Over time paths were added. And then interlinking ladders and ropes for support. And they eventually got to the top.

"Once at the top they realised and completed their purpose, in the same moment. They saw both the meaning of the toil on the plain and the toil of the climb. As life left them, they merged the contents of their cup into the orb. In that final moment they also saw all that the orb contained, all the wisdom of the universe. They fulfilled their purpose.

"As time passed and to move things along, the creator left further treasure, or mysteries. These were miniscule, well-hidden, and only discoverable by those who had devoted a lifetime to climbing the mountain. The mysteries opened a creature's eyes to the design. This would cause them to delay their final ascent. Instead, they would choose to stay on the mountain a little longer, sharing the knowledge of this treasure, helping others make the climb and ensuring their cup was completely full before they reached the top and completed their purpose.

"Climbing the mountain was not only a risky business, but it was something that had to be done over and over again. Creatures still had to maintain their bodies. They still had to return to the plain to work and toil. This enabled them to create the means for which they could nourish their bodies and then return to the climb, day after day.

"The creatures also discovered that there were no shortcuts. Only those that walk the path themselves ever made it to the top. Only those that climbed the mountain under their own steam, got to touch the orb and obtain the riches.

"Many felt the climb was too hard compared to the comforts on the plain. These creatures chose to embrace the plain and entertain themselves to pass their time.

Some felt cheated by those who were making the climb. They would block their path. Spread lies. Do what they could to prevent others from filling their cups.

At times, the number of detractors would swell, and they would wreak havoc on the mountain's paths. Tearing down the ropes and ladders and slaughtering the helpers on the mountains. These black spots in the course of time would eventually correct as sufficient believers stood up and fought back.

"Some tried to cheat the system. They built great structures using other creatures. They used the resources on the plain to reenforce the structures. They used the structures to propel themselves high into the sky so they could reach the orb. It never worked. Eventually the structures would collapse. As the structures grew in height and the prize appeared near, those close to the top would jostle for position. As they did that, they put more and more weight and pressure on those below. The resulting instability would bring the structures down before any creature got close enough to the orb."

Teacher paused for a moment, looking at both Marr and Luna.

Then she continued, "for those that turn their back on the climb, life becomes a meaningless toil, even with comforts to distract them. For these a different end awaits. At the last moment, when their time is up, they will see the design and realise the folly of their choices. Their cup will shatter as their body is no more, and anything contained within the cup is recycled back into the sky to rain down again.

"For those creatures that embrace the responsibility gifted to them by the Creator, riches await. Their choice to toil both on the plain and on the mountain, is rewarded. In engaging in the Creator's Experiment, they earn the right to know all the wisdom of the universe."

With the story shared, Teacher closed her eyes. Moments later Teachers' head dropped forward, and she started to snore gently.

Marr and Luna, looked at each other briefly, nodded, got up and left quietly.

Chapter 7 – Instability

1

From the training centre, Marr and Luna made their way back towards the common areas.

They had an hour or so to kill before the transports would resume their runs to the citadel.

"I need to speak with you two," came a voice from behind them.

"What The!" Luna exclaimed as she spun around.

"Follow me," Mentor said as he brushed past them.

"Do you think he will continue to creep about when we are all on the rig?" Luna whispered to Marr.

"I may be a little aloof, but I am not deaf, Luna," Mentor said as he ushered them into a storage room.

"I need you to collect your weapons from your lockers and bring them here. Place them in the false compartment of this crate. Put that on top and seal it up. I'll see that it is safely stowed aboard the Dinatha this evening," Mentor instructed as he pointed to a stockinette wrapped beef carcase lying on the table next to a food storage container.

Luna's mouth dropped.

"You expect me to put my prized possession in with that dead cow?" Luna stated.

"Yep, see you in a couple of hours," Mentor shared as he turned and left the storage room.

Ninety minutes later, Marr and Luna were sitting in an observation deck at the port. They were waiting for the arrival of the Dinatha.

They had just watched a rig disappear over the horizon.

"Let's do some revision. What just happened there?" Marr asked.

"Really?" Luna responded.

Marr said nothing and continued to look out towards the horizon.

"A rig just shot out over the horizon," Luna replied.

"Seriously?" Marr exclaimed before continuing, "explain it as if I am seeing it for the first time!"

Luna sighed but conceded and started to share unenthusiastically.

"The remotely controlled low loaders brought the rig out of the port and lowered it on to the maglev track. The maglev system then took the rig out of range of the citadel. Over the horizon."

"What control over the process do the crew have?"

"None, until the rig is well down the track. The low loaders and then the maglev system prevent the rig from starting its engines until well clear of the citadel."

"Why is that?"

"Because the rig is basically a flying bomb. The fuel cells and DMD are highly volatile. The rig could cause significant damage if it were crashed into the citadel."

"Correct. And what is the other purpose of the maglev?"

"The rigs are basically optimised for space flight, not atmosphere flight. They can't get lift at less than nine hundred kilometres per hour. So, the maglev system builds up the speed allowing the rig to get airborne without needing to use vertical thrusters. Once airborne, the rig can engage a hard burn and enter orbit."

"Great, top marks. Now what of the landing?"

"Things happen in reverse. The rig drops out of the sky towards the outer end of the maglev track. It flies along the track, attaches, shuts its engines, and then coasts into the port."

"What makes this sequence even more risky?"

"During descent, the rigs use the heat and friction to replenish their fuel cells. They create far more than they need, and they even often sell it on after landing. Therefore, by the time the rig reaches the citadel it is an even more capable flying bomb!" Luna shared with glee visualising the damage that could be caused. It was significant compared to the miniscule amount of damage she could do with her rifle.

Marr rolled her eyes. She had picked up the change in tone and joy in Luna's voice.

"How does the citadel prevent some crazy person like you flying a rig directly into the wall?" Marr asked in jest.

"The citadel's defences track incoming rigs. The automated defences show no hesitation in blasting a rig to kingdom come if it diverts off the scripted approach. Equally the defences will activate if the rig doesn't cut its engines before the outer marker."

"What happens if the rig connects to the maglev but keeps its engines running?"

"Just after the outer marker there is a side track that ends in a very solid concrete wall!"

At that moment they caught the sight of the rig in the distance.

It was merely a speck but was clearly in a hard burn. It was racing away from them and accelerating fast towards the upper atmosphere.

"That has got to hurt!" Luna shared.

"How is it, that after all this time of watching these rigs, it is only now that you are making these types of observations?" Marr commented.

"I never had to consider actually being in one of those contraptions, until now!"

"Well, I understand that reaching orbit is a walk in the park compared to traversing."

"Way too much information at this stage, Marr. Baby steps! I am going to worry about getting through this ordeal first," Luna added as she contemplated things further.

2

A little after four thirty p.m. local time, the Dinatha was on its final approach into Utopiam.

Dukk was re-orienting himself after a well needed rest.

Once they were airborne out of Kuedia, a chin wag took place in the cockpit. Dukk shared the story, in all it's crazy details.

Bazzer and Annee had been rightly concerned. However, Dukk had given them the option of jumping ship when they reached Utopiam. Both had confidently stood by Dukk and committed to helping see out the contract.

After that, Annee and Bazzer had insisted Dukk lie down and get some well-needed rest. There was little to do once at cruising altitude.

Now at his seat in the cockpit, his mind was starting to wake up. At this point he remembered he had put his comms on proximity mode. Effectively blocking all external communications.

He switched to normal mode.

Instantly he was alerted to several missed calls from Thumpol. There were some messages too. Mostly short and very colourful.

Dukk grinned as he made sure his online status was limited to close contacts only.

"He can keep trying, but I have no intention of entertaining that thug, ever again," thought Dukk.

Then a connection request came from Rachelle.

Dukk accepted it.

"Hello Rachelle, how is retirement suiting you?" Dukk said.

"Where the F! is the Dinatha? Or more importantly, where are you, Dukk?" demanded Rachelle.

"What do you mean? We are on the way to pick up our next contract. Why?" Dukk responded.

"You are in the air!" Rachelle screamed.

"Yep," replied Dukk nervously.

"Oh my God! What have I done?" Rachelle exclaimed, "Don't under any circumstances try a citadel approach!"

"Are you mad? How else will we pick-up our load? What in the world is going on?" Dukk demanded.

Rachelle started to speak softly, "I made a mistake. And I am truly sorry, Dukk. But Thumpol gave me no choice. He even threatened to kill me. Now, I've killed you all."

"What have you done, Rachelle," Dukk asked sternly.

"The heat shield locks weren't fixed by any old maintenance crew. Thumpol insisted I use his people. It looks like they may have been at more than just the locks. This evening, I came down to the port to see the rig for one last time. Instead, I found his goons looking dumbfounded. Beside them are what turns out to be the stabilisers from the Dinatha. They told me Thumpol had had them removed to force your hand should you refuse his offer."

"But we checked all the systems before we departed Kuedia," Dukk uttered in disbelief.

"The goons are here boasting that they had looped the safety cable so that the system wouldn't notice the stabilisers were missing. You must have known that Thumpol always adds insurance and looks for retribution if he doesn't get his own way. Dukk, if you allow the autopilot to start your deceleration into a citadel, without those stabilisers, the rig will bounce around like nobody's business. The citadel will see you as a threat and their automated defences will take you out!"

"Shit!" Dukk whispered in shock.

"I am sorry, so sorry, Dukk, good luck." replied Rachelle and hung up.

Dukk was stunned. He stared out into the distance as the top of the citadel appeared over the horizon.

"Utopiam air control just confirmed we are in range and locked in. Let's take her down!" Annee piped, too preoccupied with the pre-landing checklist to notice Dukk's state.

"Feck, Feck, Feck, Feck, Feck!" Dukk shouted.

Bazzer and Annee looked up. Shocked at the uncustomary outburst.

Dukk hit the pause on the autopilot.

"What are you doing?" screamed Annee, "if we don't decelerate right now, they'll take us out!"

"That is what concerns me!" Dukk shouted back.

"Bazzer, get down to the wings, check the stabilisers. Do it NOW!" Dukk continued.

Bazzer launched out of his seat and bolted for the hatch. He had the sense to know something wasn't right.

"Annee, I am transferring the overground velocity controls to your console. I want you to refamiliarize yourself with them right now. You need to align the overground speed with the approach guidance system parameters. Bring both up, now."

"What is going on, Dukk?" Annee uttered nervously as she complied with his request.

"More action, less talk," Dukk answered coldly.

Annee complied reluctantly.

Dukk loaded up the directional and altitude guidance systems onto his console.

He overlaid them so that he could see the Dinatha's direction and altitude against the citadel's instructions. It wasn't perfect but was their best shot.

"No stabilisers, Captain! The safety has been looped," Bazzer announced into the rig comms.

"Ok, here is the deal! Thumpol had them taken out. Nothing we can do about that now. It is too late to alter course. We are going to do this manually, like we've practiced many times. We have one chance, let's make it count!" Dukk said more calmly having taken ten slow breaths and named his emotions.

"Bazzer, strap in down there. Bring the reactors to full speed. I am transferring the threat scanners to your console. If you see the slightest twitch from the citadel, hit the hard burn. The rig will automatically pull up. It might save us from a direct hit," Dukk commanded.

"We don't have enough fuel to hold a hard burn for very long," Bazzer stated.

"It will be enough to get us clear of the defences. We'll worry about what happens next, later."

"Helmets on and let's connect the g-juice just in-case," he added.

"Hello, if you haven't already, I suggest you get seated and make sure your belt is FIRMLY tightened," Dukk announced into the passenger cabin comms link. He had no time to check on the observer but was keen not to have the observer smashed against the bulkhead if things got rough.

3

Dukk checked his breathing. He slowed it down. He cleared his mind.

"Sorry, Annee, for my tone. Are we good?" Dukk asked looking over to his co-pilot.

"Yep, we're good, Dukk. Let's do this," came a calm response from Annee next to him.

"All set," added Bazzer on the comms.

"Commencing the approach now," Dukk shared as he dropped the nose of the rig.

Annee adjusted the thrusters and airbrakes to keep the velocity aligned.

They both focused intently on the instruments in front of them, stayed silent and ignored the scene out the front windshield.

Had they been looking out; they would have seen the ocean racing towards them. At the point where the water met the shore, there was a thin silver line stretching inland and over the horizon. This silver line was their target. It was the start of the maglev track they needed to pair with. It would take them to the citadel port. They needed to bring the rig down to just above sea level, race towards the track holding a precise speed and altitude. And they needed to be dead on. Any variation and the citadel defences would automatically send missiles in their direction.

For the next few minutes, Annee and Dukk made constant and miniscule adjustments.

The rig creaked slightly with each bit of turbulence.

The concentration was taking its toll. Sweat had started to accumulate on their foreheads.

"Breathe," Dukk repeated to himself as he focused on the next waypoint.

"Levelling out now," Dukk announced at the precise moment he brought the nose back up.

The rig gave an almighty groan as the forces came into play.

They were now just above sea level, and they were still alive.

Holding things firm and steady, Dukk and Annee brought the rig over the beach and in line with the maglev track. An awesome feat given the rig was still travelling at over nine hundred kilometres per hour. The wake behind them smashed against the shoreline.

Alarms sounded. The maglev track was aligned. The rig was now flying at speed just above the track.

Dukk clicked the manual controls to lower the attachments from the belly of the rig. He held his breath.

A thump indicated the maglev cradle was down and a chime told them that the connection was made.

"Still alive," he thought as he started to breathe again.

"Ann, you can kill the thrusters."

"On it," Annee replied.

"Bazzer, you can start the reactor shutdown protocol," Dukk said into the comms.

Moments later the battery alarms sounded indicating they were now powering the rig.

Annee looked up.

"Citadel operations have acknowledged our landing and are requesting control," Annee shared after listening to the message.

"Switching control over now," Dukk responded as he interacted with the console.

The rig started to slow down.

Dukk and Annee sat deeply into their seats and removed their helmets.

Looking out the windshield for the first time since commencing descent, they could see Utopiam growing larger in the distance.

"If we weren't turning this rig around immediately, it would be drinks on me," Dukk shared into the comms.

"Rain check," Annee added as she smiled over at Dukk.

"Awesome job, you two. I couldn't have done it better myself," came the reply from Bazzer in the engine room.

"If you had been up here, we'd all be fish food by now," Annee retorted.

"What do you mean by fish food? And can I get unbelted now. I need to use the bathroom," came a voice on the comms.

It was the observer. In the effort to stay alive, Dukk had forgotten to isolate the observer from the cockpit comms.

They all laughed deeply.

"Hello?" came the voice again.

Dukk personally went out into the passenger seating area to attend to the observer.

Dukk didn't like them, but he wasn't keen on getting a bad report going through to the overlords for mistreating an observer.

"Yes, you can now unbelt and use the bathroom. Though, I suggest you return to your seat after. We are still moving fast and besides we'll be on the pad within ten minutes, when we'll get your lockers to the pad doors. You can leave whenever you like. Let me know if there is anything I can help you with," Dukk shared warmly, smiling.

"Can I ask you something?" the observer said.

"Of course."

"Was that a typical landing? Because I had heard that it can be a bit rough, and this wasn't the case."

"Some landings are rougher than others. It is mostly weather related. You were just lucky today, I guess," Dukk answered, doing his best to hide his amusement.

"Is that why you were laughing?" the observer added.

"Yes, absolutely. Mind you, we wouldn't typically share the cockpit chatter as it can make passengers nervous if things get a little rough," Dukk replied.

"Oh, good. And, by the way, I have been assigned to your outward journey too. I hope it goes as smoothly as this first leg. So, you can leave the lockers in my cabin, which by the way I found to be most comfortable."

Dukk stared but tried to smile.

The observer continued, "It appears no one else wanted this assignment. I was the only one available. Which was a blessing as I have wanted to get assigned to an intergalactic freighter for years. And it gets better. My superiors have assigned me a subordinate. Imagine, me, being a formal mentor already. So, you will have the company of both of us for the rest of the journey," shared the observer, smiling gleefully.

"Perfect," Dukk replied, and then added, "By the way, I realised I hadn't caught your name?"

"You didn't ask. It's Kimince."

"Good to meet you, Kimince."

"Two Noobs! Bad omens or what?" Dukk reflected to himself recalling the comment Bazzer made before departing Kuedia.

With the observer off to the head located near the stairs, Dukk returned to the cockpit.

4

"Annee, can I talk to you for a moment?"

"Sure, what's up?"

"I know you have aspirations for your own command someday and want to be doing more of the flying. However, for this contract, I need your skills elsewhere. I want to put you as chief mate. I need someone I trust who knows the protocols inside out."

"I am ahead of you on that. I figured the same. While you were napping, I did a stock take and placed an order. Food and other supplies are being delivered to the pad; we'll have everything we need. And we will avoid having to pass through the ID Gateway. That'll save us even more time."

"Thank you, Ann. You are undeniably brilliant," Dukk replied.

Dukk's comms sounded. It was an incoming call.

He checked the Caller ID this time. Wallace.

"Hello, Wallace."

"You are some pilot. I was on the numbers giving you this deal!"

"How so?"

"I got a call from Rachelle. It appears her worst fears were unfounded."

"Let's just say we are dancing around some bad omens at the moment!"

"Ok, not sure what that means. I will never fully understand you hauliers. Anyway, I owe Rachelle and made some calls. I sourced some stabilisers. They are reconditioned, but they are all I could swing this quickly. They should be good enough for this first run. They are already at the pad. I assume you have the skills onboard to fit them."

"Thanks, Wallace."

"And, I saw you hadn't posted any passenger notices, so I put the word out. It looks like the observers have reserved two seats already. That leaves four seats to fill if I, I mean you, want to make the haul more profitable."

"Umm, very good of you," Dukk added as Wallace continued.

"Yes, it is. So, I have two going to Mayfield. There were pretty insistent on getting this ride. They said they are tourists. However, I have it on good authority that they work for the Atesoughton family. By now you will have determined that Craig Atesoughton the Third, is the client. And, that your destination for this beef contract is his settlement for the rich and famous, on the only inhabitable exoplanet in the Mayfield system. So, it looks like you have a couple of chaperones along for the ride. Which may work in your favour, I believe."

"Yes, I got the gist of things from the contract dockets. I am also familiar with this resort. I've hauled there plenty. And, yes, I agree having these two on board could help ensure we get a clear run through the waypoints and hub."

"Speaking of the hub. I also found two wanting to get to the Maple Tower space port. Before you go pushing back. Maple Tower might be a little rough and attract some unsavoury types, however these passengers are paying well. Besides, I have a good relationship with Ileadees, the Port Commissioner in Maple Tower. He will ensure you have a pirate free passage with minimal hassle," concluded Wallace.

"How very convenient. Let me guess. Ileadees has given you a good rate on refuelling?"

"Favour for favour, Dukk. You know how it goes. I sourced the stabilisers. Now you help me reduce my overheads."

"Send over their passenger proposals and Ileadees' profile, and I'll do a little diligence of my own."

"Of course, I wouldn't expect it any other way."

"By the way, do you have anything for the return yet?"

"No passengers, I'll leave that with you. But, yes, load. Out of Mayfield, I have a container of personal items and a container of empty crates."

"Anything that actually pays?"

"Yes, a metals shipment out of the hub at Kaytom Beach."

"More favours."

"Of course."

"Rates?"

"Typical. Nothing substantial, but it will sweeten the deal you already have, Dukk."

"Send over the dockets. We'll take it."

"Already on the way. Also, I gave a couple of small packages to one of your new crew members, Mentor. A gift for each of your existing crew members. It will help them feel more included in the conversations," concluded Wallace as he ended the call.

"Gifts? Coded bracelets perhaps?" thought Dukk.

"Ann, as the Dinatha's new chief mate, passengers fall into your area of responsibility. So, I'm forwarding you some proposals."

"Let's see," Annee shared as she brought up the proposals on her console. She continued, "So, two tourists for Mayfield. And two for," she paused, "Maple Tower?"

"Yep, looks like it's the best way to keep everyone happy."

"Ileadees still in charge?"

"Looks like it."

"Bazzer won't be happy!"

"No, he won't. Let's keep the flight plan to ourselves until the final pre-departure circle-up."

"Playing with fire, Dukk!" Annee warned.

"Keeping it interesting is all. Anyway, I'll leave it with you to check these proposals properly and share the rig codes and directions. And make sure they can get to the pad within the hour. We don't have the luxury of pandering to whims."

Annee smiled and nodded.

Moments later she looked up, "That's done. I'm going to the crew mess. I need a coffee. You got it covered up here?"

"I'll manage," Dukk said smiling.

"Operator, I am passing pilot communications over to the captain as I am leaving the cockpit," Annee said into her comms.

"I am on the numbers here too," Dukk thought as the cockpit door closed.

5

The citadel was looming large as Dukk brought his attention back to the controls.

There was little for him to do at this stage, other than monitor the controls. The operators within the citadel remotely controlled the rig. So, he put some music on.

"Retro Indie, yep that is what I need," Dukk reflected out loud.

"Preparing for detachment from the maglev," came the voice of the operator in Dukk's comms.

"Check," Dukk replied.

Moments later, the rig slowed on the maglev and then came to a complete stop just as it reached the end of the track.

The rig vibrated slightly as three huge jacks were extended out from below the rig to rest on three corresponding low loaders parked alongside the end of the track. The rig trembled as the jacks lifted the rig up off the maglev. A thud indicated everything was locked into place. Almost immediately the three low loaders started moving in unison. The task at hand was to drive the rig away from the maglev track and towards the pads within the citadel walls.

"The taxi destination I have is Pad 14a and I have here you are for loading only, no personnel or cargo to be unloaded. Please confirm," requested the operator.

"Pad 14a confirmed. Confirmed loading only. Please proceed," Dukk replied.

While the outer port shield doors were open, the three-metre-high barricades that kept each pad secure were still up. They would be retracting just as the rig reached them. The intention being to minimise the risk of anyone moving in or out of the citadel freely.

Dukk rested his mind as he observed the progress from the launch zone and into the port.

He idly looked around for activity in other pads as the rig glided forward.

"Barricades opening, prepare for stop," shared the operator.

"Check," Dukk responded.

Moments later the rig passed over the lowered barricades and then came to rest in the middle of Pad 14a.

"Barricades closing, low loaders are in park and powering down, please commence post docking checklist."

"Thank you, operator, will do. Hold tight," Dukk responded as he started running through the checklist and updating the logs. That took about five minutes.

"Sharing logs now," Dukk said to the operator.

Minutes later the operator responded, "All confirmed, I'm putting the stairs in place. Enjoy your evening. Standing by."

"Operator, can I get a status update on both the personnel clearance area and load clearance area?"

"Checking now. Please hold."

Moments later.

"There are three persons of crew designation already cleared and waiting at the pad door. A fourth person of observer designation is about to be cleared. Four others of passenger designation are in the ID Gateway. I see that they have rig codes but need observer approval too. For load clearance, I have four standard RoboCrates categorised as supplies, and I have a RoboCrate categorised as components. They are all cleared. I also see three RoboContainers that are classified as load destine for the Mayfield system. These are showing as clearance in progress."

"Any ET on the RoboContainers?"

"They are showing as at stage four, so about thirty minutes."

"Thank you, operator. Also, did you receive departure instructions?"

"Yes, your rig is down for priority departure and launch, however there is a small backlog being cleared. I'd say it will be cleared by the time you are refuelled and loaded. Not to worry, we'll get you back out before nightfall. "

"Good to know. Thank you."

"Standing by."

Dukk disconnected, then opened up his closed-circuit comms to Annee and Bazzer.

"Circle up in five. Crew mess."

"We are already here," came the response from Annee.

Dukk smiled and headed for the cockpit door.

"We are docked, however we are on a tight schedule, so I request that you stay with the rig. There are plenty of comforts in the accommodation level," Dukk shared with the observer who was standing at a window looking around.

"That's no problem, I was already informed that would be the case."

"We now need to get the pad door open so we can get the new crew on board. I'll also need your assistance in about thirty minutes to open the doors to the load clearance area. Your final task to help get us underway will be to lock the pad doors. I hope that will happen in about an hour."

"Of course, all part of the service, lead the way. Oh, I nearly forgot. I have just approved four authorisation requests for the passengers your colleague put forward," replied the observer.

"Thank you, let's go."

Chapter 8 - Orientation

1

Kimince followed Dukk closely as they exited the rig and came down the access stairs.

They crossed to the pad door, where the observer used the biometric scanner and then entered some codes into a keypad. The pad door swung open.

Inside stood the new crew, Mentor, Marr, and Luna. They all wore the customary tightly fitted blue shirt and slacks with matching jackets, the official uniform of the haulier designation. Mentor was cleanly shaven and looked to have just had a haircut. Marr and Luna had their hair neatly tied back in low ponytails.

"Impressive! They even have the Dinatha emblem on the jackets. Made To Demand was fast but to get an emblem too, that is impressive!" thought Dukk as his eyes scanned over the new crew.

Each had a hand on a stacked set of two travel lockers, with built in wheels in the bottom locker and a pull handle in the top locker.

Dukk smiled. These where the type of lockers that Dukk had suggested they get. Dukk wanted his crew to be able to move easily and freely. And they looked very professional. That was important to Dukk too.

Behind them was the fourth. The other observer, dressed in the usual multi-coloured and chaotic garb. The observer was looking flustered. It was as if the observer had just stumbled through the door from the ID Gateway. On the floor were two large lockers. No wheels. No handles. Dukk sighed.

"Welcome," Dukk opened with.

Dukk paused. The observer looked familiar. The observer was of medium height, slim build. Black hair. Brown eyes. Warm brown complexion.

"Have we met before?" Dukk asked looking at the observer.

Luna tuned in. It was a question she had just asked herself too.

"I don't think so. Observer level ten, sorry, I mean level eleven. Trainee assigned to this long hauler," the observer shared timidly, "My name is Trence. You are?"

"You can call me Dukk. I am the captain of this long hauler," Dukk replied coolly.

"Nice to meet you. Where can I put these?"

"You can all bring your travel lockers through the door and leave them there. They will be delivered to your cabin," shared Dukk pointing to a space on the floor just inside the pad door.

To speed things along, Dukk and Mentor helped Trence move the observer's lockers into the pad.

"Wallace asked me to give these to you," Mentor shared as he discreetly offered Dukk two small packages.

"Thanks, this way," Dukk replied as he accepted the packages.

"Wow! Impressive aren't they," Trence said on stepping through the pad door. The observer was looking up at the rig.

"Are you all passengers?" Trence asked Mentor, Marr and Luna. Clearly oblivious to the fact that they were all dressed in a similar uniform to Dukk.

"We are new crew. Just starting today," Luna shared gleefully.

"Oh, wow, it is my first day too. I am a little apprehensive if I am truly honest."

"Why so?" Luna continued to engage despite a frown from Marr, and clear disinterest from Dukk and Mentor.

"Yesterday, I was in security control. Today, I am off to space!"

"Wait, what? Now, I have it. You were on the broadcast yesterday. Something about the incident on Pad 16b?"

110

"Yes, I am afraid. That was me. I let everyone down. I've been demoted and now here I am."

Dukk nearly tripped.

"Ah," responded Luna, clearly lost for words.

"Oh, hell-low," Trence announced in a high pitch tone on spotting Kimince.

"Bad omen and not a coincidence!" Dukk thought to himself.

Regaining his composure, Dukk led the group up the stairs and in through the main door. They passed straight through the starboard passenger airlock as all the doors were still ajar.

They then climbed the flight of stairs that led from the mezzanine to the accommodation level.

"Mentor, Marr and Luna, wait here please. You two, please follow me."

Heading forward from the stairwell, Dukk opened the second door on the left.

"Please," said Dukk beckoning the two to enter the medium size room. The room had two portal windows, which currently showed only the inner wall of the pad. In the middle of the room was a large dining table with eight chairs. In the aft part of the room was a kitchenette, with standard beverage and rehydration machines.

"I assume you two have plenty to discuss. Make yourselves at home. You are free to move about this accommodation level and the passenger seating area on the level above. At no point are guests allowed in the crew only areas. By guests I do mean you two as well as paying passengers. The out of bounds areas include the hold, engine room, cockpit, transport pod bay and crew accommodation in the back. Safety first. We must be able to run the rig."

They both nodded, smiling cheerfully.

Dukk continued, "as discussed with your colleague, I will be needing your assistance shortly."

With that, Dukk turned and left, shutting the door behind him.

111

"Nope, it's our first time. What about you?" Marr could be heard saying in the corridor.

"On an old rig like this, yes, but not rigs in general," Mentor answered.

"It may be old, but it has it where it counts. Now, let's meet the rest of the crew," Dukk said as he brushed past and headed aft in the direction of the crew accommodation.

Passing through an airtight door, Dukk welcome the newcomers into a space with a number of doors on both sides. Immediately to the left was a lounge area with a couch and console with cockpit style seat. Just aft was a large oblong shaped dining table with six chairs. Annee and Bazzer were already seated.

"Take a seat, this is Annee and Bazzer," Dukk shared as he ushered Mentor, Marr, and Luna to their seats.

All three removed their jackets and put them on the back of their chairs. Dukk had to check himself as he realised, he was staring. The muscular nature and fitness of their bodies was very clear without their jackets. A quick glance at Annee and Bazzer confirmed he wasn't alone in his thinking.

"I'm used to seeing hot bodies. The nature of what we do on these rigs demands it. But you three have just set a new standard," Bazzer blurted out.

His comment was met with awkward expressions.

"Annee and Bazzer, meet our new crew, Mentor, Marr and Luna," Dukk said in an attempt to bring everyone back to focus.

They shook hands and took their seats.

"These are for you. A gift from our new contract agent," smiled Dukk handing over the packages to Annee and Bazzer.

"A bracelet! And, it matches the ones you all have. How quaint." commented Annee sarcastically as she put on the bracelet and held her arm out in front of her to size up the new accessory.

After watching Annee, Bazzer didn't feel the need to open his gift. Instead, he just tried to smile.

2

"Right, let me welcome you all and I hope this is the start of something real," Dukk said as he sat down.

"We have a big challenge ahead of us and on top of that we don't know each other. And some of you are new to this game. So, let me start with a few non negotiables. Number one, no heroes. Your own safety comes first. As they say, attend to your own air supply first before helping others with theirs. Second, everyone has the obligation to challenge things that you don't understand or that don't look right. If I, or anyone else, overlooks something or makes a poor decision out there, we all may die. So, we all must be prepared to be challenged. And we must all challenge. And, finally, we leave no one behind, no matter the designation, privilege or whatever. Clear?"

Nods and smiles all round.

"Great. So, on this rig we operate in pairs, or buddies. You'll cover the same areas of responsibility. You'll be on watch together. You'll eat at the same time. You'll sleep at the same time. You'll do whatever else at the same time. Buddies check each other's equipment. You look out for each other. You keep each other alive. Mentor, Marr, and Luna, are you okay with that?"

More nods and acknowledgements.

"Having said all that, we are one team. The default position is 'how can I help you', and not 'that is your role not mine'. And no-one on this crew is above cleaning the heads. We all do our share and help carry the load. Annee as chief mate will be in charge of doing the watch roster and chores rota. What she says goes, no exception. Anyone got a problem with that?"

No one did.

"So, the buddies. Luna you are the least experienced, so I am pairing you with Bazzer. As the first engineer he will show you the ropes. Your goal will be to get to know every part and system on this rig, in intimate detail, down to the most miniscule component. Bazzer, as the most experienced haulier on this rig right now, is the right person to guide you. You good with that?"

"Yep," Luna replied.

"Mentor, I am paring you with Annee, who as already mentioned is chief mate. She'll make good use of your varied skills. And it is a tall ask being responsible for hosting our guests, and keeping us all secure, safe, fed, and comfortable. And that is on top of being responsible for liaison and external communications. Your medical skills will also come in handy in that role. Okay with you?"

"I'm good with that," Mentor said confidently.

"That leaves, you, Marr. You'll join me in flight control. You'll have a steep learning curve as I need someone who can hold their own ASAP. You up for the challenge?"

"Absolutely," Marr answered very enthusiastically.

"Excellent, so from this moment forward, Mentor, Marr and Luna you will be glued to your buddies."

Luna had to choke down a laugh. The others smiled.

Dukk looked at Luna and smiled as he realised what he just said.

Dukk continued, "anyway, moving swiftly along. We have about an hour before we will be locked and loaded. Hopefully, our passengers are on time. We'll have forty-five minutes after that before we can get clear. During that time, I want to do an evacuation drill. So, make sure at some point over the next hour, you get clear on your part of the protocol. Otherwise, normal duties as per your stations. Any questions?"

"Loading?" Bazzer asked.

"Marr and I will supervise the loading. Bazzer and Luna, you do the QA. Annee and Mentor will have their hands full with passengers and supplies."

"Sound."

"Anything else?" asked Dukk.

"Perhaps these are stupid questions, but where do we put our stuff and where will we sleep and all that?" Luna interjected.

"SLEEP, who is going to be sleeping!" Bazzer answered.

"No such thing as a stupid question, Luna, just stupid answers," Dukk answered, looking at Bazzer.

"Bazzer will show you around, that will include your cabin. To reduce further hijinks, your cabin, Luna, will be the mid cabin on the starboard side. Not the aft on the port side, that would be Bazzer's. On the subject of quarters, Mentor you are aft starboard side and Marr, mid on port side. Mentor and I will see that your things are brought up and installed into your cabins. It is part of the responsibilities of chief mate," shared Annee.

"Cool," Luna responded, smiling.

"Anything else?" Dukk added.

His answer was in the happy expressions on the faces before him.

3

"Let's go Mentor, we've only got an hour to get everything we need ready for the next three weeks. The supplies are in the clearance hold with the load, but we've got to get them secure. The passengers will be here shortly, and they'll need briefing. Let's start with your travel lockers. We'll bring them through the nose door and to make light work of it, we'll use the vertical conveyor in the forward ladder shaft," Annee shared as she got up from the table.

"Show the way, and I am not afraid of hard work," replied Mentor as he followed her to the airlock door that led back to the passenger accommodation.

"Don't worry, I have plenty of hard work in mind to satisfy that need."

"By the look of you, I am pretty sure you can satisfy my needs, bring it on, Annee," Mentor replied in a provocative tone.

Annee laughed briefly saying, "you'd be so lucky, old timer," and smiled cheekily back at him and the others as she disappeared through the door.

Mentor laughed loudly as he headed into the corridor.

Luna coughed and laughed briefly, failing completely to hide that she knew something of Mentor and had just witnessed a completely different side to him.

"Enough of this, there will be none of that carry on with me," Bazzer added in a serious tone.

"Yea right Bazzer!" Annee shouted back from the corridor. She then joined Mentor in his deep and heartly laughter.

Luna blushed briefly before joining the laughter.

With that everyone joined in.

"Maybe I have read this new lot all wrong," reflected Dukk to himself as he enjoyed the rapport building moment.

"Right, Luna, let's get to the engine room and get this old bird fed! We'll use the aft ladder shaft," instructed Bazzer as he opened the airtight door adjacent to the table.

Dukk turned to Marr.

"Time is short, so I suggest we see if we can get you orientated at the same time as getting some things checked off our list. We'll start with getting the nose door open in preparation for loading. Let's follow Bazzer and Luna."

"This accommodation level, with separate spaces for passenger and crew, makes up two thirds of what is effectively the third level. It sits directly above the hold, which is double height, so we need to drop down two levels to reach the hold floor," Dukk said as he took the lead entering the ladder shaft.

"What is above us?" Marr asked, keen to show interest in engaging Dukk and building rapport.

"The transport pods. The top of this shaft enters the back of the space that houses the three five-persons pods. We'll head up there and have a quick look at them after opening the nose door. You'll need to know where they are for the emergency drill."

"What is on the other side of this wall?" Marr asked as she followed Dukk down the ladder.

"The aft third of the rig is the engine room. The DMD, reactors and primary burners occupy the bottom three levels. The batteries and harvesters are in the upper region, which is effectively behind the transport pods and below the tail."

"Fuel, water and air?"

"Mostly in the wings, but also tail. The wings also hold base elements and materials for the printer."

"Compact?"

"Intermediate. It is not as fast as an industrial 3D printer, but it is adequate for most of the components that typically break during passages. The partition walls in the accommodation level can also be used for hull repairs. We aim to be as self-sufficient as possible once airborne," Dukk answered as they reached the bottom of the shaft and entered the hold.

"Wow, what is the capacity?" Asked Marr as she joined Dukk in the hold.

"One thousand, one hundred and eighty-eight cubic metres. It is eleven metres wide, by eighteen metres long by six metres high. We can take three full size RoboContainers, with room to spare. Those floor to ceiling doors over there, go to an airlock. Another matched pair are on the other side of the airlock. And that gives access to the forward airlock compartment, or the nose of the rig. We open the nose and those hold doors and the RoboContainers can drive straight in. Those half height side doors are over each wing, for access and part unloading. There is no airlock on those."

"Interesting," Marr added.

At this point their exchange was interrupted by Bazzer's voice coming from the door to the engine room behind them.

"Here we have the heart of the rig, two TLM series eight reactors with mirrored support systems. Propulsion is delivered via two TLM T5 quad core, twenty-eight-gauge hard burners and a single TLM H5 dual mode, double core, thirty-gauge burner thruster. Plus, four vertical, twelve-gauge dual mode burner thrusters and eight directional, five-gauge dual mode thrusters."

"Series eight reactors are seventh generation tech, right?"

"Yep."

"Marr was wondering about that. She said it was confusing that the hard burners and thrusters are fifth generation space tech, but the reactors are seventh generation?"

"She is well informed. Yes, the rig is primarily based on fifth generation tech with several upgrades. The reactors were replaced ten years ago. A breach caused a compromise to one of them. They had to limp back to port. Once back, it was decided to replace them both rather than trying to fix it or to get the different generations of tech working together."

"Interesting. And what else is in here?" Luna asked.

Marr looked over at Dukk. He was looking at her.

"You've been pulling my chain!" Dukk said as he raised his eyebrows.

Marr smiled sheepishly.

"New plan, you are now in charge of this tour!" Dukk responded with a smirk.

"You are doing great. I am learning loads. Not everything about this rig is in the public record," Marr shared as a peace offering.

They smiled awkwardly at each other briefly before looking away, blushing.

Dukk pointed at the engine room door.

"Want to have a look?" Dukk said. He used a more collaborative tone than he'd used coming down the ladder.

"I am good for now. Maybe I will pick Bazzer's brain another time?" Marr said still smiling.

4

Bazzer and Luna had continued talking and hadn't noticed Dukk and Marr eavesdropping.

"Yes, it is one of three full consoles outside the cockpit. The other two are in the crew mess and in a wall locker in the starboard passenger airlock. With the right authorisation you could fly the rig from any of these consoles," Bazzer could be heard saying.

"It is all blank, how does it work?" Luna asked.

"Consoles are activated by biometrics. As are all the doors, seats, and g-juice lines. Yours will have been made available to the rig when your redesignation was approved. And, it should have been uploaded to the rig when you cleared the ID Gateway. The captain just needs to grant you access. Which he may have already done. Just sit down and put your hands near the panels."

"Wo!"

"There you go, the captain has it all configured."

"What is all this over here? It is disabled," Luna asked pointing to a series of panels.

"The DMD and reactor controls. The observers lock us out until we are beyond the outer marker."

"Why."

"Who knows really. They are a bunch of suspicious loons. They'd have us believe they are still under threat. They tell us that someone might try to use one of these rigs as a flying bomb. Madness!"

"Madness," Luna repeated back, half-heartedly.

"Now let's get to work. Open the system gauges. Yep, over there. Now navigate to fuel and supplies gauges."

"Holy cow, why so many?"

"Redundancy but also because we carry everything we need to survive on our own."

"That make sense."

"We want to check all the tanks. See over there. Select them all and then click the button labelled 'Calibration'."

"Done. Now what? Wait, several have gone orange?"

"Perfect. Now select the orange ones and click the button down there labelled 'order and replenish'. Great, now click that button there on the rig schematic."

"Done. Oh! What does that flashing indicate?"

"It means our job is mostly done. You just opened the access panels under the wings, and a request has now been sent to the captain. Once authorised the hoses will emerge from the pad floor, connect to the one-way valves, and fill our tanks."

"We don't need to connect anything ourselves?"

"Nope, but we still need to go under the rig and monitor it. Things can go wrong, and it is best if we are on hand when it does. Let's continue the tour while we wait for authorisation."

Realising their quiet moment together enjoying hearing Luna's orientation was at an end, Dukk turned to Marr saying, "let's get the nose door open. We'll use the console in the starboard passenger airlock."

They headed in the direction of the stairs in the forward wall of the hold. Dukk approved the resupply request as he walked across.

Marr was slightly ahead when they reached the other side of the hold. She went to climb the stairs that would take them up to the Mezzanine and starboard passenger airlock.

"Nope, not that way," Dukk interrupted as he approached an airtight door near the stairs.

"Why?"

"I like to check for any obstructions first. The hold doors are strong, as are the motors on them. The motors will jam the doors into any object in their path. It's a delay we can't afford."

The airtight door gave them access to the bottom of the forward ladder shaft.

Marr noticed the tracks that ran up the ladder shaft. "That must be what Annee was referring to by the vertical conveyer," Marr thought to herself.

An airtight door on the other side of the shaft gave them access to a storeroom. To their left was another airtight door. In front of them were two larger doors.

"We'll also open these storeroom doors as Annee, and Mentor will be bringing the supplies in here."

"Is the hold airlock accessed through there?" Marr suggested pointing to the door to their left.

"Exactly. While I open these, stick your head in there and see that it is clear of obstacles."

Marr opened the airtight door and stepped into a wide and tall corridor. At either end were large doors. On the other side was a ladder leading up to what Marr assumed was the external door on the port side. She retreated and closed the airtight door.

"All clear."

"Great. And it is all clear in the forward airlock compartment too. Let's use the ladder over here to get up to the mezzanine and starboard passenger airlock."

Marr followed Dukk up a ladder to a landing. Passing through an airtight door on the landing gave them access to a room filled with g-suits. Marr recalled that it was regulation that two spare g-suits be available to every person onboard. One set was to be kept near the main passenger door and the other near escape pods.

Dukk led the way out of the suit locker and onto a landing. That landing gave them access to the starboard passenger airlock and the main door they had entered after climbing the stairs from the pad floor.

"Ok, the console is behind these panels."

Dukk opened the panels and the console lit up. He swiped the pages to find a schematic of the rig. He also opened some video feeds of the hold and nose section of the rig. On the schematic he pressed the open buttons on the internal hold doors that Marr had seen moments ago on the level below. Next, he pressed the open button on the nose door. On the video feeds they watched the doors open.

Dukk flicked to further screens and was able to access the pad video feeds. From there they could see the nose lift up and expose the forward airlock compartment where they had climbed the ladder.

The video feed also showed Annee and Mentor on the pad bringing the travel lockers towards the nose of the rig.

With the nose door open, Dukk pressed another button on the schematic. The video feeds then showed a ramp unfolding within the forward airlock compartment and extending out of the open nose section. The moment it touched the pad, Annee and Mentor were onto it, bringing the lockers behind them.

"Job done, now let's make our way back upstairs and load the navigation while we wait for the load clearance to complete."

5

Leaving the starboard passenger airlock, they used the stairs to access the accommodation level.

"So, Marr, what does the public record tell you about this level?"

Marr smiled and started to talk as if she was a tour guide.

"The accommodation level is split into guest and crew areas. Separated by an airtight door. The crew accommodation has a shared common space with a table and couch, fondly called the Crew Mess by hardened hauliers. The starboard side, starting aft, has a small double cabin, a single cabin, the kitchen and then a large double cabin with a portal window and its own bathroom. The captain's suite." Marr shared blushing.

"And port side?" Dukk added quickly, feeling uncomfortable too.

"Starting aft, there is a small double cabin and a single cabin as per the starboard side. Then there are two shared bathrooms and the final crew cabin, a small double with a portal window. The latter being the prized cabin after the captain's cabin. And against the forward wall there is a utility room on the port side and a full console on the starboard side."

"Very thorough, and what of the guest accommodation?" said Dukk, playing along with the game.

"The guest accommodation area has a gym that sits in the nose section above the g-suit room. There is a lounge and combined kitchen/dining on either side of the corridors going aft. Then at the back of the guest accommodation area there are four cabins. Two on the port side and two on the starboard side. The forward two have a double birth each and the aft two have twin single births. Each cabin has its own bathroom. There is a laundry room near the starboard double cabin and through these two doors is the med bay," shared Marr confidently as she swung open two doors adjacent to the top of the stairs.

"Excellent. And what did the public record say of the safety and practicalities of the rig?" Dukk asked, immensely enjoying the sound of Marr's voice, and not wishing it to stop any time soon.

"The internals of the rig are designed to be functional under all gravity levels. The floor, ceiling and walls have special magnetic properties that marry with the magnetic threads in the booties and gloves of the g-suits. These threads will engage and disengage when one applies or reduces pressure with their fingers or toes, allowing one to move relatively easily in any situation. Also, the floor, ceiling and walls are made of the same material but have different textures and colours. The darker colour is the floor. Ceilings are a lighter colour, and the sides are a tone in between. The texture on the floor is a little gritty. The walls are smooth, and the ceiling is far grittier. The idea that in any condition, be it lit or not, one can navigate around. And finally, there are arrows embedded into the floor, walls, and ceiling. These arrows point towards the main evacuation point and away from the secondary evacuation point. This provides one with all they need to get clear of the rig if needed."

"My oh my, you are well read!" Dukk shared laughing.

Marr joined in.

Chapter 9 - Loading

1

As they closed the med bay doors, Dukk and Marr heard voices coming from the port twin cabin.

"What is this for? It looks to line up with the med line point at the back of your shoulders," said one voice.

"And look at this attachment on the helmet," said the other voice.

Dukk and Marr headed down the corridor and stopped at the open door of the cabin.

The two observers were standing in the middle of the cabin. Kimince was dressed in a colourful g-suit, not the standard issue blue that the crew wore.

Dukk made a gesture with his hand to Marr in a manner that suggested she should help.

"It is for the g-juice," Marr offered causing the two observers to look up.

"G-Juice?"

"Medication to help you with launch and traversing. The system is tuned to your exact medical needs. It will inject you via the attachment at the appropriate time and will ensure you have a much more pleasant journey."

"Oh, that's sounds lovely," came the reply in a high pitch and gleeful tone.

Dukk was already giddy from spending time with Marr. Now he had to control himself from laughing. He quickly turned his face away from the observers. Marr noticed his reaction and had to quickly turn her face too, as she struggled not to laugh along with him.

"Just as well they didn't ask Bazzer," whispered Dukk.

Composing themselves, they turned around.

"Wait, what are you two doing in this twin cabin. Wouldn't you each want the bigger double cabins?" Dukk blurted out.

"Your lovely colleague, Annee, helped me get settled in here last night. She said the single beds were more comfortable. Less rolling around than the doubles," answered Kimince.

"Did she? Well, she is right about that," replied Dukk as he glanced at the digital pad next to the door.

"And, Trence, you are here as well?" Dukk added.

"Yes, we asked Annee to organise it. We met her in the corridor moments ago. Now, she is going to fetch my lockers. So lovely and helpful," replied Trence.

"Building a false sense of security, I bet. Wait until you drag your feet, like when it's time to get strapped in upstairs," thought Dukk, hoping his amusement wasn't showing on his face.

"We thought it would make sense, because as you suggested we have lots to talk about. And besides, we are more accustomed to sharing accommodation than having our own space," added Kimince.

"Cool, we'll leave you get back to it," Dukk answered, bemused.

Dukk turned to leave, then remembered, "Did Annee mention the security briefing and evacuation drill? She will do it in the dining room before departure. It would be a requirement, given this is your first launch."

"She did. That is why we are in here. She said we need to be in our suits," replied Kimince.

"I am helping Kimi get dressed while we wait for my lockers. Then we'll be off to space," Trence said with glee. The last sentence was sung as Trence did a sort of a dance.

Dukk practically shoved Marr down the corridor as he found it impossible to contain his amusement. Marr had failed completely to contain herself and was spluttering with laughter as she stumbled back in the direction of the stairs.

Just as they were about to take the stairs to the upper level, an incoming call from the Operator. Dukk accepted it.

"Go ahead."

"I have four passengers just cleared the ID Gateway. They will be in the personnel clearance area in a few moments. Standing by."

"Thank you," Dukk replied and disconnected before turning to Marr, "Change of plan. Let's welcome our passengers, before we load the nav."

"Annee, the passengers are here. I'll bring them up to the lounge," Dukk announced into his comms as he and Marr made their way down the stairs to the pad floor.

"Excellent timing," came the reply.

"Doesn't the chief mate look after the passengers?" Marr asked Dukk.

"Yes, but it helps if the captain sets the right tone."

"Helps what?"

"Our typical passengers are low level staff or workers for the elites. They aren't important enough to travel in luxury with the elites."

"So?"

"They can be a tad touchy and frustrated. Some can cause trouble. By me doing the welcome and her doing the briefing, Annee and I both have a level of authority. We can do the 'good cop, bad cop' routine later, if needed."

"Are you the bad or good cop?"

"Isn't that obvious?"

Marr laughed, adding "Not yet. What is the plan here?"

"I'll do a quick welcome and avoid any questions at this stage. Annee can handle that. I will then lead the way up the stairs and into the lounge. You will follow at the back."

"Got it."

2

By the time Dukk and Marr had got across the pad, the passengers were just coming through the door.

"I am the Captain of the Dinatha, you can call me Dukk or Captain, whatever you prefer," Dukk announced loudly, stopping the passengers in their tracks. Three men and one woman. All were smartly dressed. The woman, in particular, looked like she had made a special effort to be noticed.

He paused for a moment, looking each directly in the eye before continuing. All three men stared back with indifferent expressions. The woman smiled when Dukk looked in her direction. The smile was provocative and perfectly timed. Dukk had to break the stare to refocus his attention.

"While you are our guests on this passage, we are a working rig, not a luxury cruiser. Here are the conditions of passage. You are to stay within the guest accommodation area and not attempt to enter any areas marked otherwise. You fend for and clean up after yourself. The kitchen and service docks will be kept fully stocked. The bathroom and living spaces will be cleaned at the midpoint. There are washers and dryers if you need them. Fighting of any kind will not be tolerated and result in cabin confinement. If there is an emergency, you are to do exactly what you are told by me and my crew. And we go by my schedule with no exceptions."

Dukk paused again to let that sink in.

"These conditions are non-negotiable. Of course, you have the right to refuse them. You can exercise that right by turning around and going back through the ID Gateway. You will have my blessing and get a full refund. Continuing any further into this pad is indication of acceptance."

Dukk paused once more. No one moved.

"Excellent. This is your third mate, Marr, my co-pilot. My crew are chief mate, Annee, her second, Mentor, the First engineer, Bazzer and his assistant Luna. Welcome. Leave your travel lockers over there and my crew will bring them on board and install them into your cabins. Follow me."

Dukk led the passengers across the pad, up the stairs, through the main door, through the starboard passenger airlock and up the flight of stairs into the accommodation level. He then turned right heading forward. He opened the last door on the right and beckoned them to enter.

"Please make yourselves comfortable in here. Your chief mate will be along in a few minutes to provide further instructions, answer any questions and help you find your cabins," said Dukk smiling politely as the passengers filed into the lounge.

"Right, time to get the flight plan loaded," Dukk announced to Marr as he headed back towards the stairwell.

"Didn't you say that we'd check the transport pods on the way?" Marr asked as they mounted the stairs.

"I did, but that was before I knew you were our resident expert! Please show us the way," shared Dukk smiling as he reached the top of the stairs.

Marr rolled her eyes back at him.

"It should be through this door," she answered as she opened the door directly opposite them at the top of the stairs.

They passed through a tight airlock into a six metre by twelve metre room. Within were three transport pods.

"They seat five and can keep persons alive for forty-eight hours? They are kind of small?" Marr observed.

"Yes, it is tight quarters."

"Interesting. And the batteries and fuel cells are behind that door at the back?"

"Yep."

"Okay, now for the passenger seating area and cockpit."

Marr brushed past Dukk as she led the way back towards the top of the stairs. She opened the other door. This led into a seating area. It had eight g-seats.

"There is a head up here too?" she asked Dukk as they passed by the seats.

"Yep, on the other side of the stairwell."

"Cool. And through here is the cockpit," she announced as she opened the door beyond the seats.

"So that hatch is the top of the forward ladder shaft?" she asked pointing at a hatch in the back of the cockpit.

"Exactly. You'd make a great tour guide. Time to get to work?" Dukk asked in a smug tone.

"Absolutely. I am all ears."

3

"I don't expect you to do much during the launch. Annee and Mentor can cover it if something goes wrong. However, I will expect you to come up to speed with traversing and hub manoeuvres. We'll have plenty of time to do some simulations after we are free of Earth," Dukk said as they stood at the back of the cockpit.

"Where will I sit?" replied Marr.

"Your place will be in the co-pilot seat. I'd like Annee in her usual seat in the second row. And mentor in the other seat in that row. The second row is preconfigured for external comms and med systems. That will be where she needs to focus. And I can transfer flight controls to any other console if needed. Climb in there."

"Okay."

Marr climbed into the co-pilot seat on the right of the cockpit. Dukk followed her into his seat on the left.

"So, where do we start?" Marr asked as she hovered her hands over the console, bringing it to life.

"You tell me. What is our first step?"

"Ok, so let me think."

After a moment Marr continued, "Earth flight control will transfer the launch plan to the autopilot once we are cleared for launch. Those instructions will get us into orbit and ensure we avoid any local traffic and obstacles. It will take between twenty and thirty minutes after leaving the pad. Once we are in orbit, we'll continue to gain height gradually. During this time, the DMD will do the complex calculations and then start the countdown to the traverse. That could take up to twelve hours. So, back to your question. Our first step in the flight planning is to put in our first traverse waypoint?"

"Precisely. Though, first let me check your understanding. Why does it take so long after clearing atmosphere before we make the first traverse?"

"There are many factors to consider. It takes time to reach the right orbit of both our starting place and ending place. Also, the DMD needs to ensure we enter and exit the space between space free of any interference. Not forgetting that activating the DMD disrupts the space around it, even if ever so slightly. So, it is best done well clear of other things."

"Excellent. By interference you mean?"

"Celestial objects, rocks, and other craft. Not to mention gravitational flows. And, of course, solar flares."

"Very good, what happens after the traverse?"

"The traverse takes the rig from safe orbit of one planet like the Earth, to the safe orbit of another planet in the target system. In the new system, a similar process takes place in order to traverse again."

"Right, and after that?"

"It depends on the destination. We might do a few traverses before having to refuel and resupply at a hub. Then it might be a few more traverses before we reach the destination."

"Correct. And how long does all this typically take?"

"Each traverse while happening in an instant, will take up to twelve further hours of calculations and orbit adjustments. The stay at the hub is typically twenty-four hours to allow for some downtime, and with orbit adjustments and avoiding traffic, the elapse time could be two days. And also, when we reach our destination, re-establishing safe orbit and landing takes time too, perhaps a day."

"Very thorough. We'd be in good hands if something happened to me."

"Thank you."

"So, if our destination is a local system, and we will have six traverses each side of a hub stop, and we'll also factor in two half days along the way for more thorough inspection and repairs, what's our ETA?"

"Perhaps eight to nine days?"

"Very good. Now let's put the draft flight plan into the nav. I am sharing the flight plan on your console. Use the galaxy navigator to check my entries," Dukk instructed.

Dukk opened his console, checked his notes, and started entering the waypoints.

"First waypoint is Teegarden."

"3.8 parsecs," Marr blurted.

"Exactly, now I'll callout what I've entered, and you verify that I've entered it correctly," Dukk shared as he smiled to himself.

"She is good. She had found her way around the apps with speed and agility," he thought to himself.

"The Second waypoint is JR18, 7 parsecs."

"Check. Doesn't look like there is much there other than the red dwarf and the odd exoplanet in the hot zone?"

"No, it's just got an active relay."

"Relay?"

"The relay is a message delivery system. It uses a DMD. Periodically it traverses to and from a neighbouring system. It uploads the messages to another relay and thus messages can move through the galaxy. It is crucial for the flow of information out there and for getting assistance if needed."

"Cool."

"The third waypoint, and the potential place for the intermediary inspection, is JK56, 6.2 parsecs."

"Check. It says the view of the exoplanet from this orbit is spectacular."

"It is indeed."

"You said 'intermediary inspection', what does that mean?"

"It is good practice to get outside and inspect the exterior after every two or three traverses. Also, some systems need to be taken offline briefly to be checked properly. And breakages and damage are the normal run of things out there. So, we want to make sure we have time. For that we stay in orbit at that waypoint for an extra 12 hours or so."

"Cool."

"Next we have JR72, 3.1 parsecs."

"Check."

"Next is Maple 12, 8 parsecs."

"Check."

"Our hub on this outward journey is a space port orbiting the Maple Tower red dwarf. 2.5 parsecs from Maple 12."

"Check. The entry has a warning about pirates?"

"Yes, hubs mostly do have warnings about pirates. The broker has put in a good word with the port commissioner. We should be fine."

Marr nodded.

"Our next waypoint after Maple Tower is Maple 15, 3.2 parsecs," Dukk continued.

"Check."

"Maple 18, 3.2 parsecs again."

"Check."

"From there to the next regroup stop Finch 2, 11 parsecs."

"Check."

"Finch 12 after that, 4.2 parsecs."

"Check."

"Then we have WZR22 in the outer regions of the Atesoughton cluster, 6 parsecs."

"Check. Atesoughton? Any connection to the family?"

"Yes, the very same. Not uncommon for an elite family to name a cluster after themselves. It isn't really a cluster under astronomical definition, but at least it helps them justify their colonisation of the systems they define within the region," Dukk shared without thinking.

Marr smiled.

"After WZR22, we have a final traverse into the Mayfield system. 3.2 parsecs."

"Check."

"Then it is orbit and landing."

"Sounds like a walk in the park!"

"I like your thinking."

At that moment, a light started flashing on the large doors to the load clearance area. Dukk's comms sounded. It was the Operator.

"Go ahead," Dukk answered.

"Your load, components and supplies are now cleared. You can commence loading. Standing by," came the reply.

"Thank you," Dukk replied as he disconnected the call.

"Perfect timing," Dukk shared with Marr.

"The supplies and load have been cleared, Annee and Mentor, will you meet us at the door. Anyone got eyes on the observers?" Dukk said into the crew comms.

"Excellent timing. The observers are with us. On our way," Annee replied.

4

Dukk and Marr made their way back through the passenger seating area and down the flight of stairs to the accommodation level.

From the stair door they could hear Annee in the corridor.

"Joantyi, you have the first cabin on the right. Larony the first cabin on the left. Bognath and Carltor, all I have left is a twin. Second cabin on the left. Please check your travel lockers are correct and then change into your g-suits. Then make your way back to the dining room. We'll be starting the pre-departure briefing in twenty to thirty minutes. Kimince and Trence, the Captain needs your assistance at the load clearance door. Please follow me."

Dukk and Marr continued down the stairs.

As they got near the mezzanine level, they could hear Bazzer and Luna coming back through the starboard passenger airlock.

"Let's run through the upper levels while Dukk and Marr get us loaded. This room has one of the sets of spare g-suits. The other spare set is in the transport pod bay on the upper level."

"When do we suit up?"

"After we check the resupply is finished and close the valve panels. It is good practice to finish the sweaty groundwork first. Then I like to have a quick shower before suiting up as it can be a good while before the suit is taken off again. Also, I find the first hit of g-juice is easier to handle in a fresh set of inners."

"Why, what happens?"

"The cocktail is designed to suppress vomiting and bowel movements and prevent heart failure or strokes during hard burn and also the traverse, but it isn't perfect or free of side effects. The traverse is particularly ugly. Few manage to come through that for the first time, without saying hello to a sick bag. And most break into a sweat the moment the juice flow is turned off."

"Oh," said Luna as they arrived at the bottom of the stairs Dukk, and Marr were about to leave.

"How's the resupply progressing?" Dukk said, announcing their presence on the stairs.

"We'll have the tanks full, and pipes disconnected in about 15 minutes," Bazzer replied.

"Excellent. We should have the RoboContainers in place by then. We'll do the pre-departure circle up at that point. The stabilisers are with the load in the clearance area. Do you want to collect them now and get them installed?"

"Sound. We'll follow you. Be there in five. No point in us hanging around as the observers open the clearance area doors."

"I see what you now meant by your comment about Bazzer when we were talking to the observers," Marr shared with Dukk as they made their way down the access stairs to the pad.

"Yes, he doesn't mess about."

"Is it really that bad?"

"It can be. Bazzer is also exaggerating a little. It largely comes down to fitness and preparation. Fitness won't be an issue for you from what I gather. And Mindfulness practices can help prepare the mind and this reduces the sweating and other involuntary body movements."

"'Involuntary body movements', how charming," Marr added, cringing.

Dukk and Marr stopped at the bottom of the stairs and waited for Annee, Mentor and the observers to join them. They weren't far behind.

"Thank you for your time once more," Dukk said as the observers reached the pad floor.

The observers smiled back gleefully. Dukk forced a smile, so he didn't laugh. He had never quite managed to get over the colourful nature of the g-suits they preferred.

"What will we find in the clearance area, Captain?" Kimince asked.

"We have supplies, some components and the load we are carrying to Mayfield."

"What do we need to do?"

"Firstly, I need you to open the clearance area doors as you did for the passenger pad door. Then I need you to follow me into the clearance area and verify the three RoboContainers. You will need to scan the security seals. You will be required to check them again on arrival in Mayfield to verify that the contents haven't been tampered with. Once done, I'd like you to go over and lock the passenger pad door, then wait nearby until we have cleared this room. Once done, you can lock these doors too and come back on board."

"That sounds straight forward, lead the way please."

Dukk led the group across the pad to the clearance area door.

Once at the door, Kimince used the biometric scanner and then entered some codes into a keypad. Instantly the ceiling height, double doors started to slide open, exposing a large space.

Contained within the large room were five standard robotic crates and three robotic containers. Each of the latter being just over thirteen metres long, two and a half metres wide and four metres high.

5

"Which are the stabilisers?" Bazzer announced from behind the group as they watched the doors slide open.

"You and Annee find them, I'll get the load's security seals checked," replied Dukk.

While Dukk took Kimince past the smaller robotic crates, Annee started scanning the content tags to find the components.

"This crate contains components. It must be them," Annee said moments later.

Bazzer came over to the crate. He extracted the wireless lead, a palm size device, from the side of the robotic crate. Then he pressed a green button on the top of the wireless lead. With the device in hand, he headed off in the direction of the rig's open nose door.

Instantly the robotic crate rose off the ground. It was lifted by small jacks in each corner of the crate. Trolly wheels could be seen dropping to the ground. The robotic crate then lowered onto its wheels before heading off after Bazzer.

"Wow," gasped Luna, "I had heard of these things, but never seen one for real. There isn't much call for them in the dust and dirt of the fields, vineyards, and orchards."

"Coming Luna? We have got to get these installed before the resupply finishes," Bazzer called.

Annee continued to scan each of the robotic crates with her wrist wrap. Then she opened her wrists and projected two lists into the air in front of her. The two lists merged, matching items as they merged.

"Everything we need is here. Things are unfolding beautifully, cap," Annee shared as she detached the wireless leads from the side of each of the robotic crates and stacked the devices together.

"Good, Ann. And we're done with the security protocol too. Now let's get it all on board," Dukk answered from the front of the third container.

"On it. Let's go Mentor," Annee shared as she pressed the big green buttons on the wireless leads and headed off in the direction of the rig.

In unison, the four robotic crates organised themselves in pairs before heading off after Annee and Mentor.

With the observers out of the clearance area and heading to the passenger pad door, Dukk retrieved the wireless leads from each robotic container.

"We'll do this one at a time, Marr. They aren't as well behaved as the RoboCrates," Dukk suggested as he pressed the green button on one of the wireless leads.

Immediately one of the robotic containers responded. The power units, embedded in the underside of each end of the container, could be heard starting up. Huge jacks at each corner retracted leaving the weight on the power units. The wheels in the power units could be seen just touching the concrete floor.

As Dukk walked forward, the robotic container followed.

"Take this wireless lead for the second RoboContainer. Follow behind the first RoboContainer. When it reaches the ramp, click the green button, and then join me in the hold," he said to Marr as he handed her the device.

The robotic container followed Dukk across the pad and up the ramp at the nose of the rig.

Annee and Mentor could be seen in the storeroom monitoring the robotic crates. The crates were stacking themselves neatly on top of each other.

Dukk continued into the hold. On the starboard side of the hold, near the aft bulkhead, Dukk lifted a cradle out of the hold floor and fitted the wireless lead into it.

The huge robotic container appeared in the narrow airlock and successfully made its way fully into the hold. When it was clear of the airlock, the jacks extended below the container. The jacks lifted it up just enough for the power units to swivel ninety degrees below each end of the container. When lowered back down onto the power units, the whole robotic container shifted sideways into the starboard side of the hold. It came to rest millimetres away from the cradled wireless lead. Dukk pressed the red button on the wireless lead. The container settled back on its four jacks. The jacks locked themselves into the floor of the hold.

By this stage, Marr was in the hold. Dukk showed her how to retrieve the cradle from the floor and fit the wireless lead into it.

The next robotic container appeared in the doorway and moved itself into position. The final robotic container wasn't far behind as Dukk had activated the wireless lead the moment he saw the second container.

With the robotic containers in place, Dukk revisited each of the wireless leads. Within a flap was another button. On pressing this button, large arms appeared from the sides and tops of the robotic containers. The arms extended to neighbouring containers, and the strong points affixed to the walls and ceiling of the hold.

"Impressive," said Marr as she watched the dance of the robotic container bracing arms.

"Aren't they just," added Bazzer as he emerged from the side door that led to the port wing.

Luna wasn't far behind him.

"Wow, that didn't take long," she said looking up at the robotic containers which now mostly filled the hold.

"Are the stabilizers in place?" Dukk asked.

"Yep, and the diagnostics are running. Time to check the resupply and close the valve panels," Bazzer replied as he and Luna headed back towards the hold doors.

"Excellent, we'll do the pre-launch circle up when you get back."

"Let's check for obstructions and then close the nose and hold doors," Dukk shared to Marr as they followed Bazzer and Luna.

On the way back to the console in the starboard passenger airlock, they ran into Annee and Mentor.

They all used the nose area ladder to access the suit locker to reach the landing near the starboard passenger airlock.

"Circle-up once we close the nose door?" Dukk asked.

"Yep, we are ready. See you in the crew mess," replied Annee.

Kimince and Trence arrived at the main door as Annee, and Mentor disappeared up the stairs.

"I told Trence about the warning lights and siren. I had hoped there would be no surprises when we locked the pad doors," Kimince offered unsolicited to Dukk and Marr.

"It all still gave me a fright," laughed Trence.

Dukk and Marr stared blankly as the observers made their way up the stairs to the accommodation level.

Chapter 10 – Launch

1

With the nose and internal hold doors closed, Dukk and Marr made their way to the crew mess. The others were already seated around the table.

"How are we all tracking? Ann?" Dukk asked as he sat down at the table.

"We need to check-in with the passengers briefly, then we are ready to hit the showers," replied Annee.

"Everything in place for the pre-launch passenger safety briefing and evacuation drill?"

"Of course."

"Bazzer?"

"Valve panel doors are closed and checked. We just need to QA the loading process and we will be in the showers," answered Bazzer.

"The flight plan is loaded, so all that is left is the external inspection and we'll be ready to close the door. So, we'll hit the showers now and do the inspection suited up. Annee and Mentor next and that'll give Bazzer and Luna the last showers before we commence pre-launch. Does that work for everyone?"

Everyone agreed.

"Right, let's do the flight plan overview," Dukk continued as he displayed a 3D plan in the air above the table.

He pointed at the 3D image as he shared the plan.

"Our destination for this load is Mayfield in the Atesoughton cluster. That takes us in the direction of Teegarden first up. Our track for this leg will take us via Maple Tower where we'll refuel and recoup. To get to the hub, we'll traverse via JR18, JR56, JR72 and Maple 12. We'll likely have a longer stay at JR52 and do an intermediary inspection."

"Hold up," Bazzer interrupted, before adding, "Maple Tower?"

"Yes, and I understand Ileadees is still in charge. Are we going to have a problem, Bazzer?"

"Not if he keeps his distance!" Bazzer replied.

"It was a long time ago, Bazzer. It might be time to let go. Forgive and forget?" Annee added.

"Not a chance!" Bazzer uttered with gritted teeth.

"What's going on?" Luna asked.

"For another time, perhaps," Annee replied.

"Bazzer, can I proceed?" Dukk asked, looking to regain the room.

Bazzer grunted.

"Right, so after the twenty-four-hour layover in Maple Tower we'll continue on towards the Atesoughton cluster. We'll traverse through Maple 15, Maple 18, Finch 2, and Finch 12. Finch 2 will be the likely spot for the intermediary inspection. Our second last traverse on this outward journey will be WZR22, which is considered within the Atesoughton cluster. From there we are one traverse away from Mayfield. Any questions at this stage?"

"How long will that all take?" asked Luna.

"All going well we should be on the ground in Mayfield on the eighth day. Our progress, including the time lapse, will be tracked here within the flight plan map. You can interact with this map here at the crew table or on any console."

"Cool. And how far is Mayfield from Earth?"

"About sixty parsecs?"

"Oh!"

"Any other questions?"

Calm faces met Dukk's question and gave him his answer.

"Annee, will you give us a quick summary of the chore rota and watch roster?" Dukk asked.

"Sure," Annee replied as she flicked the 3D plan aside and displayed a series of tables.

"Here is the chore rota summary. I will send the individual lists to your comms. We don't need to go into the detail now. Give me a shout if you have any questions. I suggest you try to complete your chores during your watch so you can use your off-watch time for yourself. Is that good with everyone?"

Everyone nodded.

"Here is the watch roster. I'll go into more detail than usual for the benefit of our newcomers. At all times, you will be responsible for your primary station duties, and we are all on deck during the launch, landing, docking, and traversing. When on watch you must be awake and present to monitor system logs, and rouse the department lead to address anomalies. When not, your time is yours, unless needed to address an anomaly or help respond to an emergency. Also, we try to share a meal together as a crew, at least once a day. It typically happens just after a launch or traverse, as we are all on deck anyway.

"We will operate four-hour watches, rotating around the clock. The roster runs from now and until we are back here in Utopiam and unloaded. Rig time starts at the hour closest to launch preparation. So, I've set it to six p.m. Utopiam time as we'll be in and out of here for the next while. FYI, rig time usually starts at six p.m. as it's our typical launch time. We try to make the most of planet side time and get out just before the citadel outer doors close for the evening.

"Now for the allocations. As you can see here, first up will be Dukk and Marr. Flight control is most active now and during traversing, which occurs roughly every twelve hours. Also, the downtime for those on the first watch has less interruption which is going to be key for rest for those flying the rig." Annee emphasised the last part.

"Next watch will be myself and Mentor. Passengers can get unsettled in the evenings, Earth time, and are most active in the middle of the day, so we'll need to be present anyway. The last watch is with

Bazzer and Luna, which is the hardest watch, but it is where it fits best, besides, it has the second-best stretch of rest time."

"Two a.m. to six a.m.? The graveyard shift?" Luna asked.

"Yep, but also two p.m. to six p.m. You get used to it. Besides, it's always day out there, so you make of it what you want," Bazzer said in response.

"Exactly, thank you, Bazzer. That's it," Annee concluded.

"Any further questions should be raised with your buddy," said Dukk bringing the focus back to the job at hand.

"It is now six ten, so our window is closing fast to get out of the citadel before nightfall. I want to commence departure protocols in fifteen minutes. We should be in a position to request taxi shortly after. That gives us only about thirty minutes to get out and heading towards the maglev. Approval will take at least ten minutes so best case is that we are moving off the pad at six thirty-five. I'll need you all suited up and at your stations by that time. We'll do the evacuation drill once the low loaders get us moving. Are we clear?"

"Is this typical for departure, it all feels very rushed?" Luna added, ignoring Dukk's attempt to close the circle-up.

"From this point on yes. We don't mess about. If the rig isn't moving, we aren't accumulating credits. We good?" Dukk replied as he stood up.

Everyone nodded.

"Excellent. Now if it is okay with you all, and as it is our tradition, I'd like to take a quick crew photo before we launch. Perhaps with jackets on," Dukk said in a pleasant tone.

Everyone smiled and complied.

2

With the photo shoot done, Dukk turned to Marr, "Right, time to get suited up. Ten minutes good with you for g-suit cross check?"

"Sure," Marr answered confidently.

"Give me a shout, Marr and Luna, if you need any help with the facilities or getting into the g-suit," Annee said as she stood up.

"Thank you, will do," Marr and Luna replied in unison.

"Anthem time," said Dukk as he selected an object from the air between his wrists. He flicked it at the centre of the table.

"Anthem?" asked Luna.

"'Mr Blue Sky', Electric Light Orchestra, the haulier's Anthem," answered Mentor just before the uplifting tune started to fill the air.

"Retro rock?" Marr questioned.

"Yep, can't beat it!" Dukk shouted above the music as he headed towards his cabin.

Dukk closed the door of his cabin and continued singing along to Mr Blue Sky as he started his pre-departure routine.

He had it down pat. He would put some calming music on his implants the moment Mr Blue Sky finished. He would hit the shower and, he would even typically manage to include a one-minute meditation on his bed before suiting up.

Marr on the other hand was feeling a little apprehensive as she left the circle-up.

She had just agreed to getting showered and suited up in under 10 minutes. On top of that, she would be using a shower technology she was unfamiliar with, and she'd be putting on her new g-suit for the first time.

She went straight to her cabin, grabbed a robe, and headed to the bathroom. She was sure Bazzer's advice was correct. In that she should wear a cap and avoid the hair wash cycle until she had more time. That advice hadn't helped much with the apprehension.

Stripped off and with the cap on and her hair neatly tucked inside, she stepped into the circular shower unit and sealed the door. She had read about these units but that wasn't helping either.

"Perhaps this was the kind of thing one is better not knowing too much about," Marr thought to herself as she listened to the shower instructions.

First, she was blasted for ten seconds with a soapy solution. She then had twenty seconds to lather up. Then a further thirty seconds of rinsing water blasted her from all angles. The final stage was the one minute of the cyclone like drying system.

Standing there in the unit waiting for the machine to instruct her that she could get out, she realised that while perhaps a little too efficient, she was dry, and feeling surprisingly refreshed.

In the robe, she returned to her cabin, applied some moisturiser, put on the inner layer, and got into the g-suit.

Marr opened her cabin door just as Dukk was emerging from his cabin on the opposite side of the crew mess.

"Let's do the g-suit checks and then get outside and inspect the rig," Dukk said as they met in the middle of the room.

"I am sure you are well read on this, but for efficiency, I'll check your suit first and show you, our protocol. Then you check mine. We start with the ankle clips, the waist, then gloves, and now the med feed connection at the back of your shoulders," Dukk shared as he inspected her suit.

His hands were firm, gentle and in no way intrusive. She just hoped she wasn't blushing as the butterfly feeling washed over her.

"Ok, now check mine, then we'll helmet up and do an airtight test," Dukk shared, feeling a little self conscious. He hoped his directness was hiding it and keeping everything in check.

Marr followed the same procedure.

With everything in order, they put on their helmets and took turns to use the g-seat at the console to run an airtight test.

"Right, that was relatively painless. What is next?" Marr concluded hoping to hide her awareness of the strengthening connection between them.

"Let's get out to the pad, have a quick walk around and then we'll close the doors," Dukk replied.

"How did you find the shower, Marr?" came a voice from behind them.

Annee was standing in the bathroom door, in a robe, having just had her shower.

"Way too efficient!" laughed Marr in answer.

"Wait until you try the hair washing cycle," Annee said laughing as she headed towards her cabin.

"Can't wait," Marr said sarcastically as she followed Dukk towards the door.

Dukk and Marr made their way silently through the guest accommodation.

The cabin doors were shut, but faint voices could be heard from behind the first door on the left. Clearly the observers still had lots to talk about.

They continued in silence until they reached the pad floor.

"What is the process for this inspection?" Marr asked.

"It's pretty straight-forward. We walk around, see that nothing is open and that the pad is clear for our departure. Bazzer will have already done a more detailed check as part of his preparation. And the rig has sensors on everything, so this is really just a sanity check."

"Great," Marr answered as they headed off in a clockwise direction around the rig.

3

With the inspection done, Dukk and Marr returned up the stairs, through the main door and stopped in the starboard passenger airlock.

"Let's close the door and get this rig out of here," Dukk said as he opened the console in the panels of the airlock.

Using the console, Dukk opened the rig schematic and found the main door. He clicked the close button. The door swung into place behind them.

"Now to pressurise and start the test. And we'd better let everyone know."

Dukk selected broadcast mode on his comms. A pleasant gong filled both the air and the comms of all on board.

He gave it a moment, then began to speak, "Good evening, all. The main door is now closed and sealed. Your crew and I will now start making final preparations for departure. And I'd appreciate if you would follow all instructions so we can get launched on time. I am pressurising the cabin and starting the integrity tests. You may find your ears popping during this process. Also, the internal doors will close themselves to facilitate the tests. If you need to move about, please wait for the access panel to show green again before trying to open doors. I will be back with further details of our launch once we have cleared the pad. I am expecting that to happen in the next ten to twenty minutes."

With that, he turned off broadcast mode.

"Smooth," Marr said.

"Thanks, now let's get into the cockpit and submit the departure request."

"After you, captain."

Dukk and Marr headed up the two flights of stairs to the upper level. They passed through the passenger seating area and entered the cockpit.

Dukk jumped into his seat on the left and Marr got into her seat on the right.

Dukk opened his console and located the flight plan. He dragged it onto a request form and submitted it. He then opened a channel to the pad control.

"Operator, this is Dukk, captain of the Dinatha," he said into his comms.

"Welcome back, how can I help you?"

"I have submitted the departure clearance request."

"Thank you. I will process it now. Please hold."

"Thank you," answered Dukk before going on mute.

"And now we can run through the launch protocols. I will mirror my console, so you can follow along," Dukk said to Marr.

Fifteen minutes later, the Operator was back.

"The Dinatha is cleared for departure. The launch plan should be with you now. Low loaders are started and ready. Barricades are ready to be lowered. Path to the launch zone is clear. Give me the word, and I will remove the stairs and start the low loaders rolling. Standing by."

Dukk enabled his crew comms and said, "we are cleared for departure. Check-in please. Annee?"

"The passengers are in their seats. The Passenger debrief is complete. They are currently getting familiar with belts and g-juice connections," was the reply from Annee.

"Excellent. Bazzer?"

"QA complete and the logs have been updated. Luna and I are reviewing the launch protocols," was Bazzer's response.

"Perfect, let's get moving," Dukk said back to his crew.

"Operator, please proceed," Dukk said after unmuting the connection with the pad control.

"Pulling back the stairs. Barricades opening, prepare for taxi," shared the operator.

"Check," Dukk replied.

Moments later the rig started to move as the three low loaders turned and then manoeuvred the rig out of the pad.

Dukk waited until the rig was clear of the pad, then turned to Marr saying, "Time for some fun."

"How so?" Marr replied.

"First let's see how the passengers are getting on and also listen in."

Dukk flicked a panel and opened a video feed in the air before them. They had a full view of the passengers sitting in their seats in the area behind the cockpit. The four paying passengers looked bored. The observers were clearly chatting and fully enjoying the new experience. Their merriment was coming through muffled in Dukk and Marr's comms. Annee was standing at the back, behind the passengers, near the door, smiling up at the camera.

"Why is Annee smiling at the camera?" Marr asked.

"She knows what is about to happen. Now open the protocols panel that I showed you just now."

"Got it."

"Now select 'Wellness, Health, and Safety' and locate the 'Emergency Scenarios' panel."

"Done."

"Select 'Transport Pod Evacuation Drill' and press 'execute'."

"Nothing happened," Marr said prematurely as a high pitch siren rang out followed by a repeating single long tone. The lights turned orange and arrows illuminated in the floor.

A scream came from the video feed. The observers had both launched out of their seats and nearly hit their heads on the ceiling. They were screaming hysterically and flapping their hands. Annee could be seen in the video feed, trying not to laugh.

"It is okay, Kimince and Trence. This is exactly as we spoke about downstairs. Calmly put on your helmets, then get out of your seats and make your way to the Transport Pods behind these doors," Annee could be heard saying in between attempts not to laugh.

The other four passengers had hardly moved. They calmly got up and headed towards the door.

"Let's join them," Dukk said grabbing his helmet.

Dukk and Marr followed the guests through the doors and into the Transport pods. The evacuation alarm continued to echo around them.

"Remember what we talked about. Fill the middle transport pod first. Fill the back three seats and leave the two front seats for crew. And remember if you didn't have your suit on when the alarm sounds come directly to the evacuation point as there is a spare suit for you here," Annee said from the middle of the space that housed the Transport pods.

Bazzer and Luna appeared from the hatch at the top of the aft ladder shaft. They immediately got into the front seats of the aft pod.

Annee and Mentor got into the pod in the middle.

Dukk and Marr took seats in the first pod. Carltor, one of the passengers for Mayfield, and the two observers were in the seats behind them.

"Cosy isn't it," Kimince said nervously.

"Imagine having to sit in here for two days waiting to be rescued," Carltor said coldly.

"Is there a bathroom?" Trence asked.

At that moment, the alarm stopped. A short tone sounded twice indicating the drill was finished. The lighting returned to normal.

"Well done everyone, that is the drill done. You can now return to your seats and get settled ahead of the launch," Annee said loudly as she got out of the middle pod.

Dukk and Marr headed back to the cockpit and got settled.

The video feed was still running. They watched the passengers return to their seats. Bazzer and Luna came through also and appeared at the cockpit door.

"Hello, you two, mind if we join you for a bit. Much better view up here," Bazzer said as he and Luna entered the cockpit.

Bazzer came up between Dukk and Marr and peered out the windshield.

"Only one rig in the queue ahead of us. Quiet night?" commented Bazzer.

"This is typical. You wouldn't get more than a couple of rigs going at this time here in Utopiam," Marr answered.

"Bit of a rig watcher, are we?" asked Bazzer looking at Marr.

"Somewhat. Perhaps I sensed my future," Marr responded in jest.

Together they watched the rig ahead of them disappear down the maglev track.

"Approaching the maglev track, prepare for stop," the Operator announced into Dukk's comms, which had remained open since requesting departure authorisation.

"Check," Dukk replied to the Operator.

"We are at the maglev already! Excellent. That means we'd better get downstairs, Luna. It is nearly time to turn the key," Bazzer announced to the room as he turned and headed back towards the door with Luna in tow.

"People we have about 5 minutes before launch point, time to start pre-ignition protocols," Dukk shared on the crew Comms.

"Passengers are settled, heading downstairs to double check everything is locked down on the accommodation level. We are on time," came the response from Annee.

Dukk opened the comms to the passengers, "Hello, your Captain here again. Thank you for your help in doing the evacuation drill and getting seated. We are now preparing for launch. We'll be in orbit very soon. Please sit back and enjoy the ride."

Dukk remembered to disconnect this time.

Dukk and Marr watched as the start of the maglev track disappeared beneath them and the rig straightened up.

They felt the rig tremble slightly as the maglev cradle was lowered and then as the jacks retracted to bring the rig onto the maglev.

A chime sounded to indicate connection.

"Ready to advance to the launch point," shared the Operator.

"Check."

The rig pulled away. Whilst not uncomfortable, the acceleration was noticeable as the rig put the citadel behind it.

"Let's go through the launch plan. Do you want to run us through what you see?" Dukk asked to Marr as he displayed the instructions on their consoles.

"Ok, let me see. So, from the launch point?"

"Exactly."

"The maglev brings us to lift off speed by the time we reach the end of the track at the ocean. Thrusters will be used to continue our progress out over the ocean. The plan suggests our turning mark is six point two kilometres from the shore. At the turning point the nose will be pointed skywards and a ten-minute hard burn will be initiated. We'll level off at four hundred and fifty kilometres. From there we slowly gain height as the DMD plans and calculates the first traverse."

"Perfectly interpreted."

"Thank you."

"Time to helmet up and connect the g-juice lines. We'll be plenty busy the moment we get to the launch point, and we regain control of our engines," Dukk said to Marr.

Five minutes later Annee and Mentor had joined them in the cockpit.

They too got their helmets on and connected the med feeds.

"Approaching launch point, prepare to stop," said the Operator.

"Check," Dukk replied.

The rig came to a stop in what appeared to be in the middle of nowhere. Up ahead, on the track, they could see the rig they saw leave the citadel ahead of them.

The movement of air near the back of the rig indicated the burners were warming up.

"Relinquishing control. And I am handing you over to air traffic control, have a safe journey, out."

"Thank you, Operator. Have a great evening," Dukk responded.

"Marr, I am handing air traffic control to your comms."

"Got it," came the reply.

5

A slight tremble could be felt as the Dinatha's reactors spun up.

"Bazzer, you are not wasting any time," Annee said on the crew comms.

"It was Luna. Very eager. The moment the panels were enabled again, she launched the power up sequence. Got to love that level of enthusiasm. Reminds me of another apprentice I once knew. Oh, wait, he is still around and recently got promoted. I must have done a good job back then hey cap?" Bazzer replied laughing.

"Yes, Bazzer. I put all my success down to your tutelage. Now stop messing about down there and let me know when we are hot and ready to launch," Dukk replied and laughed.

Bazzer chuckled before muting the comms.

Moments later the rig in front of them jumped into life and disappeared down the maglev track.

Dukk, Marr, Annee and Mentor all watched in silence as the rig disappeared into the distance.

The silence lasted for a few more minutes before it was broken by Bazzer.

"The reactors are hot. The burners are priming. The coolers are running well. All systems are green. We are on our way up," Bazzer.

"Excellent, Bazzer. Marr, you can request launch permission as per the protocol we discussed," Dukk requested to his co-pilot.

"Oh, yes, of course. Let me see," Marr replied.

She flicked through some panels on her console. Located the script and then activated the comms.

"Air traffic control, this is the Dinatha. Outbound from Utopiam. Requesting launch permission," Marr could be heard saying on the crew comms.

"Marr, if you flick the auto isolate switch you can chat away to air traffic control without us all eavesdropping," Annee offered.

"Oh, cool. Nice. Thank you. Umm, okay. I see that here," Marr said before her voice abruptly cut off.

Dukk was watching her and enjoying it. Marr could be now seen speaking. But with helmets on nothing was being shared.

Then she turned to Dukk and started mouthing something.

"You've isolated us now too," Dukk said on the comms.

Marr adjusted the controls.

"Right, sorry. I was just saying that they received the request. We are waiting on the rig that just launched. We are good once it reaches the turning point," she now shared with everyone.

"Perfect," Dukk replied happily.

Two minutes later Bazzer and Luna entered the cockpit and got strapped in.

"Did we miss anything?" Luna asked when they were settled.

"Just the start of some good pub stories, that's all," Annee laughed.

"Like?" Luna replied.

"We have the all-clear. Launch permission granted, captain," Marr announced quite formally, doing her best to stay on top of it while under scrutiny.

Dukk smiled.

"Status update please, Bazzer," Dukk said bringing everyone back to focus.

"All systems are still green. We are good to go."

"Annee?"

"Passengers are settled. And things are quiet on the external channels. Just the usual chatter."

155

"Meds?"

"Mentor, do you want to give that update," Annee said looking across at Mentor.

"Certainly. Vitals are all stable. All g-lines are showing as functioning. Med feeds all calibrated to individual needs," Mentor replied to the group.

"Anything else anyone?"

No one replied.

"Excellent. We are good for launch. Engaging the launch auto pilot. Marr, will you request maglev activation. Hold on everyone," Dukk said into the crew comms.

Marr could be seen speaking again.

Waiting was a big part of the haulier life. It was the first real test of their ability to do that together. The silence didn't last.

"'I get knocked down. But I get up again. You're never going to keep me down'," was blurted out by Luna.

"The mute button would be a good idea, Luna. I gather there might be a few nerves at this point and your singing is lovely and all, but it would be better to keep this group channel clear if that is okay. You can simply mute yourself if you want to continue singing," Dukk said empathetically into the crew comms.

"Woops. Sorry," was the reply.

Moments later, the rig launched forward and started to accelerate down the track.

The thrusters could be heard powering up as the speed increased.

After roughly ninety seconds the rig shot out over the ocean.

Forty seconds later the nose came up and the hard burn was initiated.

The crew were pushed back into their seats as the rig blasted its way towards lower orbit.

The g-juice ensured Dukk, and his crew were comfortable but conscious and alert as the g-forces came into play.

On the other hand, the dosage for passengers was slightly higher. They simply drifted off as the rig raced into ever thinning air. Had they been awake they would have seen glimpses of the stunning and mouth opening view of the curvature of the Earth as it met space.

Marr and Luna were awake and experiencing it for the first time. It was a sight they would never forget. Like those before them, they would be ever thankful for the experience of it.

Chapter 11 – Orbit

1

Dukk paused before starting with the post launch protocols.

He allowed an extra few minutes for the newcomers to take in the breath-taking scene before them as they made orbit. It was a haulier tradition. The first time was the most memorable and he wasn't going to take that away from Marr or Luna.

Turning his head to look at Marr, then to Luna, behind him. He was glad of his choice to make the tradition, his tradition.

Luna noticed him looking back and smiled. Her eyes said, thank you.

Dukk caught Bazzer's gaze as he started to turn. Bazzer nodded his head and smiled.

Mentor and Annee took notice of Dukk turning. They too smiled back at him.

It meant a lot to Dukk. The acknowledgement that Dukk had made it. He was captain of the Dinatha.

Hiding a tear, he turned back towards the wind shield.

As he did, Marr turned her head in his direction. She smiled at him. He realised she'd seen the emotion, and it didn't bother him.

Dukk reached towards the console. The autopilot was waiting for permission to engage the flight plan for the first traverse.

"When you are ready, I'd like us to proceed with the post-launch protocols. Let's start with vitals, Annee, Mentor?" Dukk said into the crew comms.

"Crew vitals are all stable. Passengers are coming around. All stable," Mentor answered immediately.

"Thank you, Mentor. Bazzer and Luna, integrity, and systems?"

"Luna, do you want to share the update?" Bazzer said.

"Definitely," came the reply from Luna. There was a short pause as she interacted with the console before her and Bazzer.

"Hull integrity is one hundred percent. Air quality ninety eight percent. Systems are all green," Luna shared enthusiastically.

"Excellent, thank you, Luna," Dukk answered and then continued, "let's bring the DMD online."

"Of course. Umm, Bazzer?" Luna replied.

"Open up the system protocols panel. Yep, now choose DMD. Okay, and check there," Bazzer replied.

"It is looking for authorisation," Luna commented.

"Done," Dukk replied after interacting with the console.

A slight shiver ran through them all. Marr and Luna gasped in unison. As it dissipated, their limbs got slightly heavier. Not the same as on Earth, but more than the moment they reached orbit.

"Looks like that worked," Dukk said as he accepted the flight plan request on the autopilot.

Almost instantly a minor vibration could be felt as the thrusters engaged for a split second. The rig began to rotate gently.

"Excellent, Luna. The DMD is responding, and we have an initial traverse countdown of eleven hours and fifty-three minutes. That would put our first traverse at four minutes to seven tomorrow morning. Let's go to slow running and wait it out. Luna?" Dukk added.

"Slow running?" Luna replied.

"Go back up a panel. Select 'Slow Running'. Choose 'Commence protocol'. Yep, you have it," Bazzer instructed.

"The indicators are lighting up. Starting to go green. Reactor two is spinning down. Solar panels are being deployed. Estimated time is four minutes," Luna replied.

The rig trembled slightly as the solar panels were deployed and heat shields moved into place as counterbalances. The thrusters fired briefly again to adjust the angle of the rig to maximise its orientation with respect to the Sun.

Dukk removed his helmet and the others followed suit.

"Time for something to eat. Dinner is on me," he grinned to his crew.

Annee raised her eyebrows.

Dukk continued as he laughed to himself. "Marr and I are on cooking duty since we are on watch. What are your orders?"

"What's on the menu?" Luna asked in jest, knowing she could look it up.

"On the specials list tonight we have Crayfish Bisque, Angus Beef Chateaubriand, and Lemon Meringue Tartlets. There is also, oh wait, that was last week's menu. Actually, on today's menu we have a selection of rehydrated meals of the usual variety. I hear that the cacciatore is particularly good this time of year," Bazzer responded.

Luna and Bazzer laughed at each other.

"Clearly the rapport was building," Dukk thought to himself.

"Flick me your order and I'll get down there and sort it out. Let's say twenty minutes. That good for everyone?" Dukk said.

No one objected.

Annee and Mentor started to leave their seats but stopped when they noticed Bazzer smiling at them.

Bazzer unbelted and then turned to Luna, "Time for some R&R, after you."

Luna unbelted and went to push herself up out of the seat. Unaccustomed to the reduced gravity her muscles propelled her straight upwards towards the ceiling. She tried to hook her foot under the console to stop her upwards motion but that only took her off balance. She then reached out for the ceiling in an attempt to cushion the impact. But she pushed back too hard and that launched her body back towards the seat. Where she bounced three times before coming to a rest.

Bazzer folded onto the console in fits of laughter. The others giggled too.

"Sorry, Luna. The first of many initiation ceremonies for apprentices," Annee shared in sympathy.

Luna tried to smile as she was sprawled on the seat indignantly.

Mentor offered an indifferent expression as he reflected on his own experience of this haulier ritual.

"Marr, you could have warned me," Luna pleaded.

"Sorry, Luna. In a lot of ways, I am as new to this as you are. Only glad it was you not me," Marr said smiling innocently.

"Mentor, we'd best get into see that our guests get settled so we get some downtime ourselves. Dukk, I am passing the hail channels back to your comms," Annee said as she made for the cockpit door.

"You'll have plenty of chances to get me back," Bazzer said to Luna warmly, then continued, "Our last task before we eat and relax, is to sanity check the load and engine room. We are done after that until two a.m. Let's use the forward shaft and avoid any delays on the stairs as the passengers get themselves downstairs."

With that he spun his legs into the air. He did a sort of a handstand on the chair armrests and connected his boots to the ceiling. He then walked across to the hatch and opened it whilst still upside down. He then pushed off the ceiling and shot into the shaft.

"Show off," Luna said as she watched his style and committed to trying it for herself at the first opportunity.

2

Dukk opened a video feed to the passenger seating and then selected the broadcast channel.

"Welcome to orbit. I hope you had an enjoyable launch," Dukk announced as he watched the video feed. Annee and Mentor were amongst them helping them unhook from the g-juice. He continued.

"Our flight path to the Mayfield system will take us via the Teegarden, JR18, JR56, JR72 and Maple 12 systems. We'll have a twenty-four-hour layover in Maple Tower before continuing on. The

162

second half of the trip taking in the Maple 15, Maple 18, Finch 2, Finch 12 and WZR22 systems. We will likely take a couple of intermediary inspections along the way. All going well, we should reach Mayfield within nine days. The flight plan and progress are available within the rig information panels in your cabins and living spaces. We have just under twelve hours before our first traverse. I will be around later if you have any questions. To help you prepare, you'll hear from me and my crew fifteen minutes prior to the first traverse. Enjoy your evening."

Dukk switched off the broadcast and turned to Marr.

"How are you getting on? Any questions?"

"Loads, but they can wait. I am hungry," she answered smiling.

"Me too. So, let's move down to the crew mess. I'll go first and open the console down there. You can follow the moment you see that happen. I'm going to go the long way using the forward ladder shaft, through the hold and up the aft shaft to avoid any interactions with passengers. I'd rather check in with them later when they are settled."

Dukk made his way through the rig and popped out at the back of the crew mess.

After freshening up quickly, he headed over to the console and transferred control down from the cockpit. He then opened his messages and retrieved the food orders. Annee and Mentor had made a good job of restocking the stores of rehydration packs. It didn't take him long to locate the correct meals and put them into the rehydration unit in the kitchenette.

He was setting the table as Bazzer and Luna exited the aft ladder shaft.

They both headed for the bathrooms. Bazzer appeared first. He made a b-line over to Dukk in the kitchenette.

"Luna mentioned she had seen the second observer, Trence, on the news yesterday. That incident with the Bluilda. What is your take? Can it be simply a coincidence that Trence is now on the rig that got the contract instead of the Bluilda?" he asked Dukk.

"My take is that it is just a coincidence."

"Coincidence or not, this will get back to Thumpol. That can't be good for us?"

"I am led to believe, he had it in for us before all of this, so it can't make it worse. Marked is marked as far as I am concerned. You are either alive or dead. There isn't any grey area."

"What about Trence? Is Trence safe to have around?"

"Hardly the type to be of any threat. You've met Trence, right? I doubt Trence has the capability. It would take specialist knowledge to trigger that sentinel like that, without taking out the entire rig. No, I feel that those behind this are very sophisticated. Not the type that Trence would be associated with. It is a setup. It looks to me that Trence was in the wrong place at the wrong time. Perhaps a scape goat. I see the whole situation as turf wars. The usual. Besides, I get the sense that Wallace is connected to those that did it. And I'd rather be on the right side of those capable of pulling off that stunt."

"What stunt? Need any help?" Luna announced as she arrived at the doorway.

"Just ranting, let's sit down. Dukk has it well in hand as usual," Bazzer answered.

After sitting down, Bazzer reached into the projection in the middle of the table.

He zoomed the flight plan so that just the Sun and Teegarden systems were in focus. Then he opened the map legend and checked on 'Show DMD Activity'.

A count down in hours, minutes and seconds appeared at the top of the projection. Then a red line shot out of the Sun towards Teegarden but missed it wildly. Then another. And another. As more lines appeared, the initial red lines faded. The resulting image was spectacular.

"What is that?" Luna asked mesmerised by the image before her.

"The DMD dance."

"What do you mean?"

"The DMD is sharing its attempts to find the path we'll use in the traverse. We give it the target exoplanet. It then tries to find a safe path and resulting orbit. It shares each failed attempt. The map here simply displays the results. Red means it is a long way off. It gets closer with every attempt. The countdown is based on its calculated probability of how long it will be before it gets it right."

"What happens when it gets it right?"

"We traverse."

"Like in that instant?"

"Yep, without warning, unless we take it offline and start over."

"How accurate is the count down, like does it ever get lucky and go early?"

"Not to my knowledge. The A.I. is not known to get things wrong. The countdown may speed up or slow down occasionally, but the change is more like a millisecond every so often, so for our purposes it is highly accurate."

"You said red indicates it is still a long way off? Does the colour change?"

"The colour of the line changes as per the visible light spectrum as it gets closer to success. Starting at bright red, then orange, yellow and so on."

"What colour indicates the DMD succeeded?"

"The final line will be the brightest and most vibrant violet, I am told."

"Why 'told'? Haven't you ever seen it at the end?"

"Nope, I'm doped up on g-juice by that time, thankfully."

3

"Wow, that's impressive. Is that projection illustrating the DMD's progress?" Marr said as she entered the crew mess.

"Yes, Bazzer was just explaining it to me."

"Explaining what?" asked Annee as she appeared in the doorway from the guest accommodation.

"The DMD Dance?" Mentor offered on seeing what the focus of their attention was.

"Exactly," Luna responded.

"Food is nearly ready. Two minutes," Dukk said from the kitchenette doorway.

Whilst they freshened up, Dukk headed over to the console and did a quick scan of the system logs.

Moments later they were all at the table. Bazzer had turned off the flight plan projection as Dukk served the meals.

"Who wants to give thanks?" Dukk said looking around the table.

"Go for it cap, you deserve it," Annee suggested kindly.

Dukk nodded, then lifted his head and pulled his shoulders back.

"I express gratitude for all that was, is and yet to be. May Mentor, Marr and Luna find what they seek in our company and may we all serve our purposes well. Focus on that which is real in the heart. Create the space so that the process can emerge. Honour that which serves you well. Engage in the journey as it unfolds. Thanks, I give."

"Thanks, I give," they all replied.

Bazzer and Annee looked over at Dukk with interested expressions. Marr had a blank confused expression. Luna looked over with delight. Dukk looked stunned. Mentor tried badly to hide his smile.

"What was that last bit. The 'Focus on what is real in the heart' and all that?" Annee asked.

"The creed," blurted Luna without thinking.

"The creed? No, umm. What creed? No, I don't know of any creed. The sentences just came to me. It felt like something that I knew and should share in this company," Dukk answered.

"The creed was once spoken to young children in the incubation centres. I thought it had been banned. Clearly some nannies are still doing it. Strange that it only came to you just now, Dukk. You know of it too, Luna?" said Mentor.

They all looked around. First at Mentor and then at Luna.

"Yes, Mentor, that is what I've heard too," Luna answered confidently doing her best to make up for her mistake.

"Let's eat," said Dukk, who was feeling a little embarrassed. He didn't feel it was the time to explore the subject any further.

There were no objections. Everyone was hungry.

Before long, Dukk's odd behaviour was forgotten. The conversation turned to the launch and arrival into orbit.

When everyone was done eating, Marr jumped up and started to clear the trays.

Annee sat back in her chair and stretched her arms out in front of her. Seeing her bracelet, she blurted out, "What is the purpose of this bracelet? They look typical, however when I put my hand like this, it starts glowing green. That doesn't normally happen?"

There was a moment of silence. Dukk looked at Annee, and then the new crew.

"It is no big deal. Look," Bazzer said as he pulled up his sleeve. He waved his hand over a bulky and warn bracelet that he was never without. There was instantly a faint green glow.

The others turned towards Bazzer, looking perplexed. Especially Dukk.

Then Mentor waved his hand over his bracelet. Marr and Luna followed. Dukk figured he do the same.

With all the bracelets showing a faint green glow, Bazzer continued.

"They are anti-snooping devices. They are tuned into your implants. When they are active, they will cloak any conversation from being recorded or listened to live. In the citadel you need to cover your mouth to prevent lip reading, but in this crew mess where there are no cameras, you can talk freely once it glows green."

Dukk tilted his head sideways and looked at Bazzer.

"You knew when I shared the story on the flight from Kuedia," Dukk thought to himself.

Bazzer smiled as if he could read Dukk's mind.

"When you have been around as long as I have, you accumulate a few tricks, you see what isn't being said and little goes unnoticed," Bazzer said aloud but clearly directed at Dukk.

"They are usually worn by thugs and undesirables to get the upper hand or swing things in one's favour, which sums me up," Bazzer chuckled.

"And is that what you three are?" Annee asked abruptly looking at Mentor, Luna, and Marr.

Dukk sat back in his seat. He was thinking the same, but glad it was Annee who had the courage to ask the obvious.

"I can only speak for myself. Wallace likes to play outside the rules. He insists those in his favour use them. That sums me up," Mentor answered sincerely.

"That is pretty much as it is for me too," answered Marr swiftly, taking the hint from Mentor's response.

"Yep, me too," Luna was quick to add.

Annee didn't look convinced. Dukk wanted to believe them. But he wasn't there yet.

No one spoke. Annee looked slowly from Mentor to Luna and Marr.

"Well, this has been fun. I'm going to press some iron before hitting the hay. See you here just before two AM, Luna," said Bazzer as he stood up.

The comment broke the tension. There was a collective sigh.

Mentor, Luna, and Marr moved off.

Annee looked at Dukk.

"Breathe," he mouthed back.

She sat back and nodded. After a moment she too got up and made for her cabin.

4

With the others taking their leave, Dukk checked the system logs, then followed Marr into the kitchenette. He checked his bracelet. It was still green as was Marr's.

"Marr, don't take me for a fool."

Marr turned around to face him. Her expression suggested that she was listening.

"I sense there is a lot more than what is obvious here. I realize that I am not, nor perhaps will ever be, privy to that. You and Luna clearly have some sort of connection to Mentor. That's not worrying me. The thing that concerns me is trust. Trust is everything out here. It means the difference between life and death. We push the boundaries too far and things get ugly. It's not about knowing everything. I realize that some things are better not known. But I need to know that we are on the same page."

Marr held his stare for a moment. The silence felt like an age to Dukk.

"What does he want? Can he be trusted? I hope so?" Marr asked herself.

"Dukk, we are on the same page."

"I need more than a hollow commitment at this stage. I need to know if I am close to the mark."

"Okay, yes Luna, myself and Mentor are connected. Mentor to me is as per what his name suggests. Me to Luna, is the same."

"Thank you. That is a start. What else?"

Marr paused again. Thinking.

"Okay, so we may have more knowledge and skills than what is outlined in the details we provided. But honestly, I know little more of why we are here on this rig than you do. As you suggest some things are better not known."

"That doesn't help me with the trust issue. What is an example of more knowledge and skills?"

"That is best for another time."

"Okay, however, to trust you I need to know something of what motivates you. I am not getting that from anything you have shared."

Marr paused once more. She was in conflict. Her training told her to withdraw. Her gut told her otherwise.

169

"We are at war Dukk. What the observers tell you is a lie. The war never ended. They just won a few major battles. There are those of us who are still fighting to turn the tide. That is what motivates me."

Dukk paused. He allowed that to sink in. It felt authentic.

"Thank you for being honest. I sense that took a lot of courage. You don't have to spend much time away from Earth in other systems, to understand that things shouldn't be taken at face value. However, it also is clear to me from observing what is going on outside of Earth that it's never really clear who the enemy is. Or what one might be truly fighting for."

"I guess you need to figure it out for yourself, Dukk. The real question is where you stand with respect to me and the others. Like you say, push the boundaries of trust too far out here and we're all dead," Marr replied and looked Dukk straight in the eye. Her expression wasn't threatening. It was empathetical. A plead. Dukk held her stare.

"You are either very good at this game or it is your truth. I am going with what I'd prefer," Dukk thought to himself.

"I know where I stand. We're good," Dukk replied empathetically and still holding her stare.

"Good, I am glad. Can I ask you something that will help me do the same?"

"Sure."

"Before launch, when we were talking with the observers about the room allocations, you seemed surprised that they were in the same cabin. Is that not usual?"

"Good observation. I'd forgotten how the younger observers behaved on their first rig assignment. It has been a good while since I was involved with the chief mate role, dealing with them and their accommodation. Also, for the last few years Rachelle has tended to take shorter contracts which are favored by the older and more privileged observers. They always insist on the larger cabins for themselves."

"That is good."

"What is?"

"That you are willing to share openly. That puts us on the same page."

"I am glad to hear it."

"So, what is the plan for the rest of the watch?" Marr asked, softening her expression even further.

The tension shifted immediately away from confrontation. The tension was back to where it was the moment, they first looked at each other in The Triggerarti.

It was obvious to them both. It was even more frightening than the confrontation. They both blushed and looked away briefly.

"I know what I'd like to do for the rest of the watch," they both thought to themselves.

"We will start by finishing clearing away after the meal," Dukk started with as a first peace offering.

"I've got that covered. What else?"

"I'd like to check in with the observers and passengers. I'll then do a rig walk around before heading to the cockpit. Will you keep an eye on the system logs until I get upstairs. Then you can join me in the cockpit, and we will plan the rest of the watch from there. That work?"

"Perfect," Marr replied smiling.

Dukk smiled back, turned, and headed towards the crew mess door.

5

On entering the corridor that ran the length of the guest accommodation, Dukk checked the control panels outside each cabin. He checked the status. It showed him if the cabin was occupied or empty. It would give him a sense of who he would be meeting in the other living spaces.

Dukk knew that seeing occupied status was only part of the answer. It was not uncommon for passengers to seek companionship on these long passages.

171

The only cabin that was occupied was the second on the right. The cabin allocated to Larony.

Dukk continued towards the dining room. He knocked briefly before hitting the open button.

Sitting inside the dining room were Bognath and Carltor. They were both at the opposite end of the table, facing the door. They looked like they were eating in silence staring at the flight plan. The entire route was being projected in the middle of the table. The DMD Dance could be seen causing tiny fireworks in the bottom corner.

"Not tourists! Tourists would be more likely sitting with their backs to the door so they could see out the windows. This was especially true just after leaving Earth. Security people would be more interested in knowing what is coming at them," Dukk thought.

"Good evening. Everything ok?" Dukk asked.

"Yep," was the reply from Bognath.

"Anything I can help you with?"

"No thank you."

"Good. I'll leave you to it."

"No questions. Patient and calm. Not tourists," Dukk concluded as he closed the door.

His next stop was the door at the end of the corridor. The gym.

It was being put to good use. Trence was on the cross trainer. Kimince was on the treadmill. The bright and fluorescent colours of the observers' gym clothing flashed back at Dukk as they worked the machines. Even though they were both going hard at it, they each lifted a hand to wave gleefully.

Bazzer was at the weights machine. He looked up at Dukk and raised his eyebrows.

"Good evening, everything alright in here?" Dukk asked.

"Yes, Captain. Absolutely," answered Kimince.

"Wonderful view isn't it," Trence observed turning to look at the video projection from one of the external cameras. It showed a view of The Earth as the rig raced along in its low orbit.

"It is indeed. Do let me know if there is anything I can help you with."

"Will do. Thank you, Captain," answered Kimince.

Dukk closed the gym door and made his last courtesy call. The lounge room status was showing as occupied. Dukk knocked as he pressed the open button.

Joantyi was on one of the couches watching something on the big screen. As he entered, she adjusted the flimsy robe she was loosely wearing. Clearly, she was ready for bed. She looked up and smiled pleasantly.

"Good evening. Everything alright?" Dukk asked.

"Yes, thank you Captain. So far so good. Are we on track?"

"Yes, we are."

"Anything I can help you with?"

"Not right now," Joantyi answered, lingering on the word 'now'.

"Perfect. I'll leave you to it," Dukk said choosing to move on swiftly.

Dukk closed the door and headed downstairs.

Dukk knew Bazzer would have done a thorough check before eating, so Dukk quickly completed his inspection of the hold, engine room and transport pod dock.

With that done he went to the cockpit and activated the console.

Marr appeared at the door a minute later.

"Passengers, okay?" she asked as she sat in her seat.

"As far as I could determine. Not a lot of small talk."

"So, what do we do now?" Marr asked, wishing she'd phrased that better.

Dukk smiled.

"Okay, so we have two hours left in this watch. The protocol is to check the system logs regularly and do a full rig walk around every thirty minutes. We will take turns. To mix things up we can split our time between here and the crew mess. I prefer to stay up here most of the time as it is quieter and has a better view. But it does help pass the time to get downstairs occasionally."

"Chores and bio breaks?"

"During the walk around is a great time to hit both on the head. But there isn't any issue at other times either. Alarms will sound in our comms no matter where we are."

"You mentioned preparation for the traverse."

"Yes, we can run through that now."

The next two hours passed quickly. They did several simulations of the traverse process in addition to the monitoring of logs and walk arounds.

Nearing the end of watch, they moved down to the crew mess. Marr was out on a walk around when Annee appeared in her robe on the way to the bathroom. She stopped when she saw Dukk at the console.

She came over to him.

"Hi."

Dukk swung around and looked up.

"Hi, Ann. Did you sleep?"

"Out like a light. Listen, I noticed you having a heated conversation with Marr after dinner. Anything to be concerned about?"

"I asked her about her and Luna's connection to Mentor."

"And?"

"He is her mentor. She is Luna's mentor. I don't have the details yet."

"Mentor for what?"

"Not sure. But Marr did admit she had skills that weren't typical of keepers."

"Can we trust them?"

"My gut tells me that we can."

"Are you sure that is your gut directing you?"

Dukk raised his eyebrows.

"Are you making a claim, Ann?" Dukk asked smiling.

Annee stepped in closer and leaned into the console. Video footage of the hold showed Marr weaving her way past a robotic container.

Dukk turned and watched too.

"Marr is hot, but she is not my type," she answered.

With that, she turned and headed for the bathroom.

Ten minutes later, Annee and Mentor were starting their watch. Dukk and Marr had completed the hand-over and had retired to their cabins.

Before going to sleep, Dukk lay on his bed and cleared his mind. He listened. He paid attention. He observed the hum of the reactor. He noted the faint clunk as a door closed somewhere on the rig. He felt the barely noticeable vibration as one of the eight dual mode thrusters fired for a fraction of a second to adjust the rig's orbit and position. He was home.

Chapter 12 – Traverse

Dukk woke with a start. Something was wrong. He collected his focus. He realised he'd been woken by the wake-up notification he set just under six hours ago.

"Oh! Clearly my rhythm is totally out of whack," he said aloud.

Dukk sat up, threw his legs off the bed, and did some basic stretches.

He checked the time. He had 45 minutes before the start of his next watch.

"Enough," he reflected as he headed for the bathroom.

Moments later he was in his gym clothes. Skin-tight shorts and a sleeveless skin-tight top. He also wore runners designed for use in near zero gravity.

He opened his cabin door and entered the crew mess.

The crew mess was dimly lit. Night mode was in effect.

Luna was at the console. Logs and video feeds filled her view and coloured the room.

Bazzer could be seen in one of the video feeds. He was in a tight space and giving his attention to an object on the floor of that space. Whatever he was doing, it was hard work. He had his g-suit half off. The evidence of the exertion was clear on the inner layer that clung to his muscular upper body. Dukk identified that Bazzer was within one of the wings.

Luna looked around. She looked Dukk up and down in his gym gear. She lingered briefly before smiling.

"Good morning, cap."

"Good morning, Luna. How is it all going?" Dukk responded with a smile.

"All pretty straight-forward."

"Tired?"

"A little, but mainly restless. Are you off to the gym?" Luna added cheekily still gazing at his body.

"Yep," Dukk replied feeling a tad self-conscious.

"I am looking forward to getting in there when you and Marr start your watch."

With that, she gave him one further look, up and down, smiled again and then turned back to the console.

"Has Bazzer been showing you the ropes?" Dukk asked regaining his composure.

"Yep. And in between he has been in the wings. He tells me that the reconditioning of the stabilisers left a lot to be desired. He said he didn't want either playing up when we exit the traverse."

"We are lucky to have the likes of him on board. Any more apprentice hijinks?"

"Nope. Some laughs but nothing like the gravity stunt in the cockpit earlier."

"Have you got him back?"

"Not yet?"

"I have an idea. Between us."

"Shoot."

"Which wing is Bazzer in?"

"Starboard."

"Okay. Enable sound on the video feed. Now, open the system protocols page. Select 'Wellness, Health and Safety' and locate the 'Alarm Tests' panel."

"Done."

"Find 'Starboard wing depressurization' and choose 'Localised Only'."

"I like the sound of this," Luna said as she hit the execute button.

The sound of the alarm came back through the video feed. The video feed showed Bazzer jump and bounce off the side of the wing wall.

"Very funny, Luna. Good morning, Dukk. I assume," Bazzer said looking up at the camera as he regained his footing.

Dukk hit the two-way audio button, "Good morning, Bazzer. Will we be good for a traverse?"

"Yep, nearly done," came the reply.

"I'll leave you two to get on with it," said Dukk as he smiled at Luna and headed for the door.

The corridor through the guest accommodation was also dimly lit.

Dukk was in the habit of getting in a brief and intense workout before the early watch. He would then do strength conditioning and endurance later in the day. While the gym was rarely empty, it was generally free in the early hours.

A quick check of the door control panels informed Dukk that all cabins were occupied.

"Good, I should have the gym all to myself," Dukk reflected quietly.

He was wrong.

Marr was on the treadmill, sprinting. Wearing shorts and a crop top. Her body showing the signs of the intensity of the workout. She was stunning. She had amazing tone and grace. A pristine example of the potential of the human form in peak condition. Dukk had to check himself in case he found himself staring.

The treadmill beeped as the program moved into warm down mode.

Marr looked over. Dukk realised he had failed to not stare. Marr smiled.

"Good morning, Captain."

"Good morning, Marr. I see we share the same idea about getting time alone in the gym by making use of quiet times," Dukk offered doing his best to regain his composure.

"Not quite. I am nearly finished my workout. Had the place to myself. You won't have this space to yourself until I am finished," Marr responded cheekily.

"Point taken."

Marr smiled.

"You have amazing muscle definition," blurted Dukk. His tone clearly indicating he had failed to keep things in the professional realm. Instantly berating himself for not keeping the Amygdala in check.

"Thank you, Dukk," Marr responded gracefully.

"Was there something in how she said my name?" Dukk thought before berating himself further for allowing the amygdala to continue the self-talk loop.

"I am done with the treadmill. Do you want it now or will I turn it off?"

"Leave it on, I'll use it after I do a few stretches. Thanks."

"You know, I was concerned about staying in shape out here amongst the stars," Marr said as she stepped off the machine and took a moment to observe Dukk.

"You aren't any more?" Dukk asked as he started his stretching routine. The skin-tight shorts and sleeveless top doing nothing to obscure his fit and muscular body.

"Well by the look of you, it is very doable," she answered cheekily.

"Thank you, I think," Dukk answered laughing.

Marr thoroughly enjoyed her warm down. She snuck glimpses of Dukk getting into his routine.

"The time alone was good, but having company like this is much better," she reflected to herself at one stage.

When done, she turned to Dukk.

"I'm done. This space is all yours. I'm off to try the longer shower cycle. Any tips?"

"For washing long hair? No sorry, my areas of expertise lie elsewhere."

Marr looked sideways at Dukk and laughed.

He laughed back as she left the gym.

2

With the short workout complete, Dukk made his way back to the crew mess.

Luna was in the same spot but facing away from the console. She was watching the flight plan projection in the middle of the table. The DMD dance light was now blue. She was swinging the seat gently from side to side.

Dukk looked at the countdown timer. It now showed one hour and eleven minutes.

"I have a question about the DMD if you could spare a moment," Luna said without breaking her gaze on the flight plan projection.

"Absolutely, but I need to shower and get suited up. I will do you a deal. You rehydrate my breakfast while I shower. Then I'll have time to chat."

"Done deal. What do you want?"

"Is there anything you'd recommend?" Dukk replied, noticing an empty food tray on the edge of the table.

"The enriched scrambled eggs thingy isn't half bad."

"Perfect. I'll go with that," Dukk replied as he headed for his cabin.

Ten minutes later, Dukk was at the table finishing his breakfast. Luna was sitting across from him.

"So, I understand the DMD has some sort of A.I. to help with the traverse. It does the calculations and the like. But how exactly does the traverse work?" Luna asked.

"So firstly, the DMD is all A.I. Well, okay, so apart from the double isolated generators behind us here and the super insulated outer layer, there isn't anything else really to the DMD."

"Oh, but isn't A.I. very dangerous?"

"Yes, true, but the A.I. in the DMD is shackled and caged. To finish answering your first question. We don't fully know how the DMD

181

achieves the traverse. You know the story about the first successful traverse and how it is linked to A.I. going feral, right?"

"Yes, sort of. The first part is something like, after years of research the first successful traverse was achieved. And the rest is history. I can't remember how it is linked to A.I. going feral."

"There is a little more to it all," Dukk laughed, before continuing. "The years of research was largely done by A.I. enabled space crafts. These machines got smarter, faster, and travelled longer and longer distances. Then one day a craft simply disappeared. It reappeared months later. The batteries were dead. The researchers recovered it and powered it back up. The A.I. got aggressive. It basically tried to reshape the machines around it and access more power sources. In the process it nearly killed all those involved. An electromagnetic pulse had to be used to shut it down. They then isolated just the computational parts and embedded a small battery. The limited power source calmed it down. They managed to communicate with it. While still aggressive it did share a little. They determined that this A.I. machine had discovered how to access the space between space. It had entered the dark matter. It travelled to other systems in an instant. But it liked being within the space between space more than anything. It only came out when it ran out of power. The researchers managed to negotiate a deal. The researchers would give it more power in return for using its knowledge of how to move through the dark matter to access other systems. In exchange for periodical visits to the space between space, the A.I. agreed to bring a craft with all its contents safely through the vastness of space. The A.I. was then copied and embedded into ships like the Dinatha. And that is basically how we are here today, doing what we do."

"Wait! Do you mean the A.I. is basically a dark matter junky and we are? Wait! We are its drug dealer?"

"Yep, that is one way to look at it."

"What is stopping the DMD from taking a hit whenever it likes, so to speak?"

"We control its energy source. Huge electromagnetic generators are what powers it. The rig's reactors are used to spin the axle and turn the electromagnets that give it life. Passing into the space between space disrupts the electromagnets and that kills the power."

"So, in effect it kills itself to get a hit?"

"Exactly. We then choose when we bring it back to life."

"Cool! But we don't know how the traverse works?"

"Correct. The A.I. won't share that. I guess the A.I. realises if we had that knowledge, we wouldn't need it anymore."

"What! So, we don't know how the near zero gravity works either?"

"Well, we do know more about that. Firstly, let's clarify what happens when we turn it on. With power it does a little test or something. It basically reaches into the dark matter. When it realises its predicament is unchanged, it comes back. It backs out a little and waits for our instructions."

"That is the odd tingling feeling we all experience when the DMD is brought online?"

"Exactly. Also, it was discovered that during this process the neural pathways gain mass. That results in gravity."

"And that is how we have near zero gravity right now. Because the DMD is running and because the neural pathways are threaded through the belly of the rig."

"Precisely."

"But does that mean if we take the DMD offline we are back in zero gravity?"

"Not quite. The mass in the neural pathways dissipates slowly. We get a few minutes or so. Also, we can bring the DMD online but not give it a destination. It will just wait."

"Does that not annoy it? Does it get impatient?"

"Eventually. A delay of twenty-four hours is usually pretty safe."

"What happens after that?"

"The DMD does a bounce to get our attention."

"What is a bounce?"

"That is a conversation for after your first traverse."

"What is a conversation for after the first traverse?" Marr asked as she joined Dukk and Luna at the table. Her hair was tied back in a low ponytail. It looked clean and fresh.

"I was just quizzing the captain about his knowledge of the DMD," Luna answered.

Marr laughed.

"How did he get on?"

"He had most of it right. We'll have to continue another time as his knowledge had a few gaps."

They all laughed.

"Not having fun without me, are we?" Bazzer announced coming out of the ladder shaft.

"Of course not. How's the head?" Luna answered.

"You will keep, noob! I see it has just gone six a.m. You two good to take it from here. I want to get to the gym before the traverse," Bazzer replied.

"Yep, I'm ready. Marr did you want to eat before we get upstairs?" Dukk said.

"Nope, with less than an hour until we traverse, I'll hold off. From what Bazzer has been saying, it might be wise to have less to bring back up."

"Ignore what you've heard from me. I am just winding up Luna for amusement value. You two are the fittest first timers that I've seen. You'll get through it with flying colours," Bazzer replied.

Luna narrowed her eyes at Bazzer and tried badly to keep a serious face.

Bazzer mirrored her odd expression, and she broke into laughter.

"Right, gym time. We have forty minutes before we need to suit up again. Watch handover notes are in the system," Bazzer concluded as he headed for his cabin.

"Stabilisers?" Dukk called after Bazzer.

"Luna, you did the last calibration. What were the results?" Bazzer called back.

"Ninety seven percent, up from seventy eight percent," Luna answered.

"The master at work," Bazzer called back as he shut his cabin door.

"Good news," Dukk added.

"Not that we'd be needing them with you at the controls from what Bazzer tells me," Luna suggested.

"To be good, a story needs to grow legs. Luna, be wary," answered Dukk as he rose and headed towards the kitchenette.

"How did you find the hair washing cycle?" Luna asked Marr.

"Efficient, but surprisingly satisfying."

"Can't wait. Perhaps I'll keep the gym session short and give it a go before we are called back upstairs for the traverse," Luna commented on her way to her cabin.

"Definitely worth it. Enjoy."

"So, what is the protocol now?" asked Marr.

"First, we need to check each other's equipment," Dukk said half stumbling on the last word.

Marr smiled and lifted her arms as Dukk came over.

They did the checks quickly, without speaking.

"Now what?"

"We check the hand over notes and then things will be pretty much as per the last watch until fifteen minutes before the traverse."

"What do the notes say?"

"Here, have a look for yourself."

Dukk opened a panel for Marr to read.

"All I see is three dots."

"Yep, Bazzer isn't one for lengthy and mostly meaningless updates."

"So, effectively, nothing happened?"

"Such is the nature of long hauling. Let's get a walk around done and move upstairs at the same time. Do you want to go first?"

"Yep, sounds good. See you up there."

Twenty minutes later, Dukk and Marr were in their seats in the cockpit looking out over the Earth.

"Do hauliers ever get tired of that view?" Marr asked.

"It is pretty amazing. That is true."

"That doesn't answer my question."

Dukk smiled.

"The Earth will always hold a special place. But you're going to see some amazing sights over the next few weeks. The sight here is just the start."

"Still not answering my question."

"Ok, the view does get a little same, same. But saying that I am tired of it, is too simplistic. The view might be the same and the work largely repetitive, but passages are never the same."

"How so?"

"The crew and at times the guests. Complexity is created from the interplay of lives being lived and the routines being performed. The complexity creates the haulier's experience. It is hard to tire of that."

"Very interesting. So, without the people there is no hauling?"

"No, machines could haul. Without people, there is no experience of hauling. Machines could never be hauliers. That would simply not make sense."

Marr went quiet. Looking out the window. Dukk joined her for a time. He also checked the logs. Then he returned his attention back to Marr.

"You didn't make the choice to join us on this rig, did you?"

"Yes and no."

"That doesn't answer my question," Dukk said smiling.

"Touché."

"Well?"

Marr waved her hand over her bracelet. Dukk did the same.

"I chose to study and prepare. But no, I didn't make the choice to meet with you two days ago."

"Who made that choice?"

"I don't know. I got the instruction from Mentor. I don't know any more than that. And I won't try to find out. As we discussed already, some things are better not known. Besides, do we really ever make our own choices? Take you for example. Are you sitting here next to me because of choices you have made yourself?"

"Nice. I like how you turned the attention away from yourself."

Marr smiled.

"Well?"

"Persistent aren't you. Yes and no, Marr. You are correct in that much of my path has been put before me as the only option. And I've gone along with it. Isn't that a choice in itself?"

"It is, Dukk. It is."

At that moment, a gentle chime rang out in their comms and the air around them. It stopped and then repeated slightly louder.

"Is that the fifteen-minute warning?" Marr asked.

"It is, Marr. Time to prep the rig."

4

"Good morning, check-in please," Dukk said into the crew comms.

"Bazzer and I are heading down to the engine room. I understand we are to spin up the other reactor and then retract the solar panels and heat shields," Luna responded instantly.

"Mentor and I are with the passengers. Everyone looks to have set their own alarms and are nearly suited up. We'll be upstairs in five," Annee responded next.

"Excellent. See you all up here soon," Dukk added before disconnecting.

"Do Bazzer and Luna really need to be in the engine room to spin up the second reactor and retract the panels? Can't we do it from here? We've even got video feeds of everything," Marr asked as she gestured towards the video feeds of the solar panel doors.

"We could, but you can't sense it up here like you can down there."

"Sense what?"

"The hum of the reactor as it comes back to life again. The vibration of the solar panels as they return to their lead cased sleaves. The gentle thud of the heat shield locks. It is how we survive. By knowing this old bird's mood."

"Interesting. You speak of this rig as if it is alive."

"Isn't it?" Dukk replied and winked.

"Weird. Perhaps too much time up here distorts your concept of what is real and not real."

"Most certainly," Dukk laughed.

"And why both reactors? I see here on the energy usage logs that we are barely using the capacity of a single reactor."

"Hull breaches. We could get a projectile enter the rig on exit of the traverse. We want to increase our chances of being able to respond should it take out one of the reactors."

"What if it hits both?"

"That would require the projectile to basically travel the length of the rig. In one end and out the other. Having both reactors down would be the least of our worries."

"Oh!"

Ten minutes later they were all seated. They had their helmets on and were plugged into the med lines.

Dukk enabled the broadcast to crew and guests.

"Good morning, all, I hope you made good use of the last twelve hours. This process might be a little uncomfortable for those experiencing it for the first time. Please rest assured that we have done all the necessary preparations and will be on hand after to help you. Please relax and allow the system to take you under as we traverse."

Dukk disconnected.

"Four minutes. Unmuting crew comms. We now stay live to each other. Status check. Vitals?" Dukk then said into the crew comms.

"All stable. Calibration is at ninety eight percent," Mentor answered.

"Systems?"

"All doors shut. Integrity at one hundred percent. All green," Bazzer replied.

"Check-in."

"Ready," Annee replied immediately.

"Ready," Bazzer followed.

Replies followed from Luna, Mentor and then Marr.

Dukk looked over at Marr. She was staring straight out the window. Rigid. Clearly petrified. He didn't dare turn around to look at Luna. He was certain that he'd see the same in her.

"Ready too. Deep and full breaths everyone. We are committed. Three minutes. Load up the guests," Dukk said firmly.

"Juice running. Heart rates dropping," Mentor replied.

They all waited. A minute later Mentor added, "All stable."

"I am taking back med control," Dukk said as he interacted with his console. He then watched the countdown.

"Thirty seconds," he announced.

"Twenty seconds."

"Ten seconds."

"Running the juice to the crew. See you on the other side," Dukk said as he hit the button. Seconds later, the cocktail hit his blood stream. His consciousness faded.

Moments later Dukk came around. The sickly feeling swelled. It was a combination of nausea, shortness of breath and dizziness. Suggesting it was unpleasant would be a gross understatement. He fought back. He focused on his breathing. He counted to ten, three times. His awareness came back. He was through the worst of it.

"Status," he croaked into the crew comms.

"Back," came a shaky response from Annee.

189

"Baaack," was Bazzer's croaky response.

Dukk gave it a moment.

"Ann, med controls are back to you. Vitals update, please?"

"Cockpit, three stable, three stabilising. Passengers, four stabilising, two racing. The system is putting those two back under," came Annee's response a moment later.

"I'm back! I am getting too old for this shit," came the shaky response from Mentor.

Marr made sounds of someone trying to stop herself from vomiting. Luna was the same.

"Breathe, Marr and Luna. Count it out. Stay with us or the med system will put you back under," Dukk reassured, then continued, "Systems, Bazzer?"

"All green," responded Bazzer.

"Good. Give the DMD some juice again so I can give it the next waypoint."

The tingle washed over them. Marr and Luna could be heard trying not to vomit again.

"As we practiced, Marr and Luna. Bring your focus back to your centre," Mentor added, still in a shaky tone.

Dukk interacted with his console. A moment later, he looked up.

"Okay, the next waypoint is with the DMD, and it is responding. Looks like we arrived at peak hour. We have fourteen hours and forty-five minutes until the next traverse. It is good news for Annee and Mentor on mid-watch because it will be near nine forty p.m. before we do this all again. Bazzer, once you have the slow running protocols started, do you want to help Luna get downstairs and settled. Mentor, feel free to head down. Annee, I'll help you get the passengers sorted. Marr, unfortunately you are going to have to suck it up and hang here for now. You okay with that?"

"The view changed," whispered Marr.

Dukk turned and looked over.

"It has, Marr. It has," Dukk said gently. She was through. He smiled as he removed his helmet.

5

A little later, Dukk re-entered the cockpit.

"How are you getting on?" he asked Marr as he sat into his seat.

"Still a little wobbly, but I am getting there. Everything sorted?"

"Yep, the two observers settled eventually. They are sleeping off the double hit. The seasoned passengers went back to bed. The rest of the crew are sleeping too."

"Luna?"

"She is fine. I heard that she even tried to make the odd joke before heading to her cabin."

"That is good. You, Annee and Bazzer were amazing. How do you do it?"

"Like I said before, fitness and mindfulness practices can help keep on top of it. And the more you do it, the easier it becomes. You'll be flying by the time we reach Mayfield."

"What? So, I only have to go through this morning's experience eleven more times?" Marr answered laughing.

"I am glad you've got your sense of humour back. That is key too," Dukk laughed.

"I see what you mean," Marr said nodding at the view before them.

Dukk looked out. Patches of purple and red could be seen through the clouds that circulated the planet they now orbited.

"What did you learn?" Dukk asked pointing to the various information pages floating above Marr's console.

"Teegarden C, or TC, is a young planet, rich in microscopic organisms. The planet life is primitive in Earth terms. The air is thin, the weather patterns unpredictable and it is susceptible to solar flares. This all makes it a relatively hostile environment. However, a small community of approximately twenty thousand has carved out an existence in the remnants of research stations and mining exploration camps. They are basically farmers now. The micro-organisms they farm have some uses elsewhere and they trade them for essential supplies."

"You've used your time well. Anything showing up on the system logs?"

"The rig is solid. Although, there is a lot of traffic. I've even had visuals on the odd rig."

"Yes, this system is a key gateway in and out of the Solar System. Let's see who is about."

Dukk interacted with his console and put the hailing channel on speaker.

"Good morning hauliers. Dinatha. Local haul. Sailing on. Outlook is cloudy?" he said into the hail channel.

The was silence for a moment. Then a reply came.

"Hello Dinatha, Plinthat. Postal drop. Lifting the nose."

"Plinthat, familiar territory?" Dukk added to the broadcast.

"Dinatha, you are on the numbers," came a familiar voice but not the voice from before.

"Howdy people. Rimera II, long hall. Yes, cloudy weather. Dead calm ten. Looking forward to buying a round," came another reply.

"Any hostiles on the path?" Dukk asked.

"All clear sailing," came the voice from the Rimera II.

"Good to know. Sitting pretty," Dukk finished with.

Dukk looked over at Marr and smiled.

"Ok, I kind of got some of that. Let me see if I am right," Marr said.

"Go for it."

"Two other rigs responded to the hail. The Plinthat and Rimera II. They are orbiting up here too. Rimera II is heading back to Earth. And they have been further afield than we plan to be."

"Yep. And, what else?"

"Hostiles is raiders or pirates. And Rimera II hasn't encountered any. And 'sitting pretty' means we are slow running and waiting to traverse."

"Yep, that's all spot on."

"I am stuck on 'postal drop', 'Lifting the nose', the weather exchange and 'familiar territory'."

Dukk laughed.

"Firstly 'familiar territory' is a former colleague. The second voice on the Plinthat was until recently a crew member on the Dinatha. A weather conversation relates to delays. Cloudy indicates longer than hoped time spent in orbit. 'Dead calm ten', means they've been waiting for ten hours to traverse. 'Postal drop' means the rig is not travelling very far from Earth. Usually only a few traverses. And the 'lifting the nose' indicates the rig is planning to land on the planet and it is not passing through."

"Of course. Clear as day," Marr replied sarcastically.

Dukk laughed.

"Do you want to take a break, get something to eat and do a walk around on your way back up?"

"Absolutely, I am seriously hungry all of a sudden," Marr answered.

Chapter 13 – In Between

1

On entering the final hour of the watch, Dukk and Marr were back in the cockpit. Dukk had just returned from doing a walk around.

"All good?" Marr asked Dukk as he sat in his seat.

"Yep, mostly all quiet. There is some movement as everyone re-starts their day. Have a look at this," Dukk said as he interacted with the console.

A video feed appeared before them. Dukk had enabled sound too.

It was a view of the hold airlock. Annee and Mentor could be seen jumping around and bouncing off the walls. Annee was dressed in a sports bra and gym shorts. Mentor was only wearing gym shorts. They were both sweating profusely.

"Wall ball?" Marr commented.

"Exactly. The airlock isn't a perfect court. But it is a little more unpredictable and that adds to the challenge and entertainment value."

"What are the rules?"

"Hands or bare feet only. The ball can only touch another surface twice between turns. Miss your turn and your opponent scores a point. First to twenty-one wins. Outside that, anything goes."

"Anything?" Marr looked over and raised her eyebrows.

"Yep," Dukk said grinning.

The ball could be seen changing colour as it hit the walls. First yellow, then orange and back to green as Annee or Mentor hit it back towards the walls, ceiling, or floor.

"The ball senses the hands and feet verses the surfaces or body?"

"Yep."

195

Annee and Mentor were in an intense rally. Mentor dove to the floor and just touched the ball. It bounced gently along the floor and turned red.

"Nine to fifteen. I am catching you Annee," Mentor puffed from his position sprawled on the floor.

"I'm being kind old timer," came Annee's reply as she put out her hand to help him up.

Marr reached over to the video feed and pressed the audio button.

"Come on, Mentor. Don't let us newcomers down."

"Oh, is it going to be like that is it, Marr? Challenge accepted. What do you think, Dukk?" Annee said aloud at the video camera.

"Definitely. Best of three. Marr and I will play later today," Dukk said into the feed looking over at Marr.

"You are on, Captain."

"Annee, finish him. After I beat Marr, Bazzer and Luna won't even need to play!"

"Not a chance," Marr fired back smiling.

"Right, my serve," Mentor said as he retrieved the ball.

Marr and Dukk watched the rest of the match. They added plenty of encouragement and the odd dig.

Annee countered Mentor's height and strength advantage with her agility and knowledge of the space. She used all the corners to her advantage. Mentor scored only one further point.

"Challenge is on, Marr. I hope you picked up some tips. You'll need every trick you can conjure to beat Dukk. He rarely loses," Annee said as she used a hand towel to mop the sweat from her body.

"Oh, really," Marr said looking over at Dukk.

He grinned back as he flicked away the video feed.

"So, you have a competitive streak, Dukk?"

"Surprised?"

"Not really. I just didn't get that from your BIO."

"I guess I like to hold some cards close."

"Don't we all."

Dukk looked up from the console and his perusing of the system logs.

"You didn't hesitate to make this all more than exercise. You showed your competitive streak. What other cards are you holding close?"

"Somethings are best not known," Marr said grinning.

Dukk laughed. They both returned to interacting with their consoles.

"Can I get your views on something?" Marr asked a little while later.

"Shoot."

"I was reading the passenger manifest. It says the two passengers heading to Mayfield, Bognath and Carltor, are tourists."

"It does."

"They don't exactly behave like tourists. They behave more like soldiers. What is your take on that?"

"My take is that their behaviour is intentional. They want us to know exactly what they represent."

"And what is that?"

"The buyer's interests. Their destination matches the load's destination. They behave like they are in the protection business. It looks to me that they are protecting the buyer's interests."

"Are you okay with that?"

"Absolutely. There are a lot of dangers out here. Advertising their presence helps reduce the chances of unwanted intrusions or even racketeering."

"It doesn't prevent it?"

"Nope. There is just too much space out here for the elites to protect fully. And everyone is corruptible?"

"Even you?"

Dukk looked over at Marr. He narrowed his eyes.

"Are you trying to recruit me for your war?"

"Maybe," Marr said provocatively.

"What about the other two, Joantyi and Larony. The manifest says they are traders. They are only going to Maple Tower, a dodgy space port. Hardly the centre of commerce. Is that a lie too?"

"I don't know yet. I have had zero interactions with Larony and only a little more with Joantyi. Besides, you'd be surprised how much commerce gets done in dark bars and dodgy corners. What is your take?"

"I had some brief interactions with Larony. He seems genuine. He has a gentle manner. Not exactly the traits of a salesperson."

"Perhaps it is an act?"

"Why do you say that?"

"Those moving in and around space ports include those directly engaged in hauling and those that benefit from it. This includes undesirables. You have the usual parasites like prostitutes and drug dealers. But you'll also find racketeers and their enforcers and collectors."

"Interesting. I guess we'll learn more over the coming days. It is after all, a small space we are all inhabiting."

2

"Speaking of inhabiting. Let's move the conn back down to the crew mess for the handover. Do you want to head down first?" Dukk asked.

"Sounds good. Yep, I'll go down first. By the way, what time are we having our wall ball showdown?"

"You mean, wall ball slaughtering," Dukk laughed.

"We'll see."

"How about around one p.m.? I have some administration I need to get on top of first."

"More to this captaining than just flying and watches?"

"Yep, sure is."

"One p.m. is perfect."

Marr was sitting at the console when Annee came out of her cabin. She was suited up ready for the start of watch.

"All set for some downtime?" Annee announced.

"Hi Annee, definitely," Marr replied spinning around. "That was some performance against Mentor. You were amazing. You looked so graceful too."

"Thank you. By the way, I am happy if you want to call me Ann."

"Oh, of course, Ann. Anything you are willing to share to help a first timer get up to speed?"

Annee laughed.

"You want me to help you defeat Dukk. The same Dukk who is on my team?"

"Well, you said yourself that he is practically unbeatable. A tip or two, surely won't make a difference," Marr added cheekily.

"I was caressing his ego. Besides, you'll take him easy. If he gets a few points in front, his ego will get in the way. And, if you aren't afraid of showing a bit of skin, you'll have him distracted most of the time."

"Mentor wasn't afraid of showing skin. That didn't appear to distract you."

"He isn't my type. If that was his strategy, it was wasted on me."

"Who is your type?"

"Let's say you won't get any competition from me for any of the men on this rig," Annee said boldly.

Marr lifted her eyebrows and said "Interesting."

"What is interesting?" Dukk asked as he entered the crew mess.

"We were just discussing your love life and our preferences, anything you want to add, Dukk?" Annee replied with an innocent expression.

"I have a preference for privacy. How's that, Ann?" Dukk said jovially.

"There must be more to it than that, Dukk. Ann is very tight lipped."

"Surprising for Ann, but good. What's it to you, Marr?" Dukk said provocatively.

Annee raised her eyebrows at Dukk. He winked back at her.

"Trying to get the lay of the land. Just doing a little research to understand how to best integrate with those on board. Not everything is in the public record," Marr replied.

"That is a good thing too. What about you, Marr? Anything we should know about you that will help us integrate better too? Preferences?" Dukk said in a cheeky tone.

"I am going to borrow your reply, Dukk! I have a preference for privacy too," Marr replied provocatively.

They all laughed.

"Did I miss something?" Mentor asked as he appeared from his cabin.

"Nope, nothing of any use anyhow, unfortunately," Annee replied.

Mentor looked around and then shrugged his shoulders.

"Ready for the equipment cross check?" Mentor asked.

"Yep, let's do it. Anything that we should know about for the handover, Dukk?" Annee replied as she put her arms out to allow Mentor to check her suit.

"Nothing unusual, but it's busy out there."

"No surprise given where we are. Anything come close?"

"Nope, the autopilot is keeping on top of it. We've got some friends up here."

"Who?"

"Larinette."

"Great, I might see if we can have a chat."

"Larinette?" Marr asked.

"Dukk?" Annee provoked.

"I am borrowing Marr's response that she borrowed from me."

They all laughed again.

"I am clearly missing something," Mentor added.

"Anyway, Ann, I'm going to send through the docking request for Maple Tower. I know it is early days, but it won't hurt to get the message into the relay. Do we want to include a notice for passengers for the leg from Maple Tower to Mayfield?" Dukk asked.

"Yep, I'll write it up. I also need to check with our current passengers to see if their plans have changed. I will check as I do my rounds. Give me an hour."

"Perfect, you got it from here?"

"Yep, enjoy your downtime, Dukk and Marr. Mentor, I am thinking we base ourselves here for this watch. It will be easier to keep on top of things. I'll do a walk around now if you want to keep an eye on the systems. That work?"

"Yep, that works," Mentor replied.

With that, Marr got up from the console to make way for Mentor. She joined Dukk in the middle of the room.

"Everything alright?" he asked.

"Anything I can help you with during the down time?"

"Eager to learn the ropes?"

"Absolutely."

"I can show you the hub docking request process if that is of interest?"

"Sure."

"I am going to freshen up. About thirty minutes?"

"Perfect. Back here?"

"No, let's use the console in the cockpit seeing as Annee and Mentor are setting up here for the watch."

"That works. I'd also like to get started with the simulation of hub manoeuvres."

"Of course. Up there will be a good place for me to show you how to access them."

An hour later, Dukk and Marr were sitting together at the back of the cockpit using a console. Annee entered the cockpit.

"There you are."

"Hi, Ann."

"I got some news on the passengers question."

"Shoot."

"Bognath said there are four passengers that need a ride out of Maple Tower. Something about a broken craft."

"They will be sharing doubles, right?"

"Yep, he doesn't think that will be a problem."

"Paying?"

"Over the odds."

"Catch?"

"Not sure. I have asked for the profiles. I should have them later today."

"So, we'll hold off for now on the passenger notice?"

"Yep, I think that would be best."

"Perfect. Thank you, Ann. Then, Marr, we can submit this docking request as is."

"Leave you to it," Annee said as she exited the cockpit.

3

Near one p.m., Marr came out of her cabin dressed in her gym gear. She had on a slightly different crop top than earlier in the day. There was a little less of it.

Annee was sitting at the console. She sensed Marr entering the crew mess and spun the seat around.

"Dressed for success I see," Annee said smiling.

"Yep, absolutely," Marr replied and grinned.

Annee reached behind the console and retrieved the digital ball. She tossed it over to Marr.

"Dukk just headed into his cabin to change. You might have some practice time. I'll tell him you've already gone down."

"Thanks, Ann. Your allegiances aren't shifting, are they?"

"Not at all. Just being sporting," Annee replied and smiled.

Marr headed through the guest accommodation. She used the forward ladder shaft to drop down to the lower level. From there she accessed the hold airlock just as she had done with Dukk before departure the evening before.

Marr first practiced dashing and jumping off the walls and ceiling. She did several laps of the tight space before stopping to catch her breath. With a better understanding of how she would control her body in the near zero gravity environment, she turned her attention to the ball.

The ball was twice the size of her hand. It wasn't heavy but felt solid. The rubber outer coating made it easy to grip in her hand. It felt very similar to the hand ball she was familiar with using. She wasn't sure how to turn it on, so she practiced bouncing it off the surfaces.

Marr was only just getting a sense of what force was required, when Dukk opened the door. He was wearing a similar outfit to what he wore to the gym, earlier in the day.

"Ready?" Dukk announced as he stepped into the space and closed the door.

"Absolutely, who serves first?"

"The challenger, who would be you," Dukk answered smiling.

"For now, but that is about to change, Dukk. So how do I turn this thing on?"

"Squeeze it three times to start the match."

Marr squeezed the ball three times, then immediately served it hard at the wall behind Dukk. It bounced back onto him and back onto the wall. Red light.

"One nil," she announced triumphantly.

"Nice, no prisoners then," Dukk said as he retrieved the ball and repeated Marr's maneuver.

Marr anticipated the copycat and got to it after the second rebound. Dukk missed the reply.

"Two nil," Marr said coolly.

Marr won the next two points.

"Come on, Dukk. You are letting the team down," boomed a voice from the walls. It was Annee.

Dukk and Marr looked up and smiled. A tiny green light could be seen next to a black dot in the ceiling.

"Watch yourself, Marr, he is playing with you," came another voice. It was Mentor.

"Practice time was over, no quarter," Dukk thought to himself.

Marr served the next ball into the wall hard. Dukk stepped aside and raised his right hand to return the ball. At the last moment, he jumped and twisted. The ball got lost behind him. He gave it a light touch and it rose with his body. Marr had no idea of the direction the ball was taking. Too late. It bounced off the ceiling, then skimmed the wall and shot towards the floor. Red light.

"One to four," Dukk said pleasantly.

"Well done," Marr replied disingenuously.

Dukk won the next eleven points. He used his and her body to hide the path of the ball. He made use of the corners and angles offered by the port airlock door. He pushed the limits of the small court such that Marr was often caught off balance. He used the collisions of their bodies to his advantage.

Heckles and encouragement came from Mentor and Annee as the match continued.

"Do you want to concede?" Dukk asked as Marr lay sprawled on the floor having just missed a repeated twist maneuver.

"A repeat maneuver. The end of the line," Marr reflected to herself.

"Hardly, I am having too much fun watching your style," Marr replied innocently.

She won the next point.

"Five to twelve" Marr said provocatively.

"Thirteen to five," came the smug response on the next point.

It was point to point until fifteen to seven.

"Just a matter of time now, Marr," Dukk said smugly.

"Finish him," came a new voice through the walls. It was Luna.

"What is going on?" came another voice. Bazzer had clearly just joined them watching the video feed in the crew mess.

"Check it out," Luna could be heard saying.

"Cool, what is the score?"

"Fifteen to seven in my favour, Bazzer. When you are ready, I'd like to finish this," Dukk laughed up at the camera.

"Got you, that was your ego talking!" Marr thought to herself.

"By all means," Bazzer replied.

Dukk won no further points. Marr had to work hard, and they bounced off each other as much as the walls and floor, but she controlled the game from that moment on. Marr had learnt his tricks and leveraged his ego.

As Marr won the twenty first point, Dukk looked over puffing.

"You played me, again! You've done this before!"

"Not at all Dukk. I am just a good learner. And you, are an excellent teacher," Marr laughed.

"Way to go, Marr. So, it is me and Bazzer up next?" Luna shouted.

"Yep, one game a piece between old and new crew. Right back to work," Annee added.

Marr and Dukk smiled up at the camera. The green light went out.

"I am going to do my warm down in the gym as it's got better ventilation. Coming?" Dukk said to Marr.

"Sounds good."

4

Marr led the way back out of the hold airlock and up to the accommodation level. She opened the door to the gym and gestured Dukk to go first.

Dukk nearly tripped as he entered the room.

Joantyi was on the cross trainer doing a gentle pace. The barely ample sports bra and booty shorts were showcasing her muscular and perhaps too perfect figure. She was made up and her hair looked like it had been given much attention.

Larony was on the rowing machine, working hard. His attire gave no illusion as to the fitness and muscular nature of his body.

Joantyi looked over and smiled warmly. The smile changed slightly as Marr stepped around Dukk.

Marr gasp and stared for a moment before collecting herself.

"May we join you? Dukk asked as he regained his composure.

"Of course. Besides, I am nearly done," came a pleasant reply from Joantyi.

Marr and Dukk went about doing some stretches as Joantyi finished and left.

A little later, with the warm down done, Dukk was the first to leave the gym. He made his way down the corridor towards the crew accommodation.

Joantyi was in the passageway that led to her cabin. She stood there in the same flimsy robe she wore the evening before. And once more, little was left for the imagination.

"Is everything alright?" Dukk asked as he reached her.

"Pretty much. Some company in the long quiet hours would make it better," she replied as she allowed her robe to fall open.

"Very tempting," Dukk said with a pleasant expression to acknowledge the offer. "But my own company is what I need most at this junction."

Dukk held her stare as to convey confidence but also to make it clear where they stood.

She smiled back but didn't adjust her stance.

"What about you, co-pilot? Any gaps in your dance card?" Joantyi said breaking eye contact with Dukk and looking beyond him.

Dukk turned around and stepped aside. Marr was coming up the corridor. Her expression was jovial and pleasant.

206

Marr stopped just beside Dukk. She looked at Dukk for a moment. Holding his stare with the same jovial and pleasant expression. Then she turned to Joantyi. Dukk followed her gaze back to Joantyi. Marr looked her up and down and smiled.

"Interesting offer. However, I am with Dukk," she said before pausing momentarily.

Dukk turned back towards Marr.

"In that, it is my own company that I need most at the moment."

Marr then moved her gaze slowly from Joantyi and back to Dukk. The smile shifted into a more provocative expression.

"Suit yourselves. You know where I am," Joantyi said to them both. She held her ground, with the flimsy robe still open.

"We do," Dukk answered still looking at Marr.

"Time for a shower and then coffee," said Marr, signalling to all that the conversation was done.

Dukk turned first. He smiled at Joantyi and then continued down the hall. Marr followed suit.

"What did you make of that?" Dukk asked as they closed the crew mess door.

"A little forward, but I am guessing it's not that unusual out here?" Marr replied.

"You are guessing right. Though, it did feel a little too contrived. Not sure what to make of it at this stage."

Luna interrupted their chat. She was standing near the kitchenette with Bazzer. They were doing the g-suit cross-check.

"That was an awesome spectacle you two. I can't wait to have a go. Here was me thinking it would be totally boring up here in space for days on end," She called over.

"No Luna, it's all go up here in space," Dukk offered back as he made for his cabin.

5

Towards the end of Bazzer and Luna's watch, Dukk and Marr were at the table having some food.

Luna bounced into the crew mess. She was clearly singing along to a tune only she could hear.

On seeing Dukk and Marr, she swiped her wrist to mute the music. She then bounced into the seat at the head of the table.

Dukk and Marr looked up.

"Hey, you two, what's going on?" Luna asked cheerfully.

Marr rolled her eyes as she pointed to the food tray before her.

"Cool, so Dukk, earlier today I asked you what a DMD bounce was. You said that was a conversation for after my first traverse. That brings us to now. So?"

Dukk laughed looking over at Marr.

"Marr, do you have this?"

"You might need to help me fill in some gaps."

"Of course."

Luna smiled as she turned her head from Dukk to Marr, and back.

"The DMD bounce is simply a traverse but where the starting place and ending place is the same. It happens fast. Was one to observe it from a safe distance, nothing would appear to change," Marr offered to Luna in starting the explanation.

"What do you mean by very fast?" Luna asked.

"A blink of an eye."

"Cool. And what do you mean by safe distance?"

"Generally, beyond one kilometre, however it does depend on the size of the rig and DMD."

"What happens inside that distance?"

"You would be bounced too."

"But if nothing changes, what is the big deal?"

"Nothing appears to change. But for those within the bounce, it is no different than a normal traverse."

"And if one was juiced up, the experience of coming out would be the same as it was after this morning's traverse?"

"It would."

"So, what is the problem?"

"This is where my knowledge gets fuzzy. Dukk, you might need to take it from here?" Marr said.

"Sure. Luna, the key is in what you said. Yes, being juiced up helps with recovery. But the bounce usually happens without warning. You wouldn't be juiced up."

"Oh. And what happens then?"

"You basically go into cardiac arrest."

"Oh. That doesn't sound good."

"No, it isn't. If you don't act fast or get help, you will die."

"Ok, so let's not be letting it happen any time soon."

"Well, it isn't as easy as that. Sure, we can manage the DMD and not let it get impatient. But at times we need to invoke a bounce ourselves."

"Why in the world would we do that?"

"Pirates," Added Marr.

"Pirates?" Luna asked.

"Yes, we use it to take out any uninvited guests that may try to drop in," answered Dukk.

"Wait! Why would pirates 'drop in'? Wouldn't they simply point guns at us and force us to hand over our load?"

"Well, it isn't that simple. They do typically have some sort of weapons. But weapons out here aren't very precise. Not like a sniper rifle, for example. Rail guns just make a big mess and that makes it harder to retrieve loot if there is anything left. CDLs are a little more accurate but they require a lot of power and that makes them expensive to run and maintain. Missiles are accurate, but generally don't leave anything behind. Besides, the electromagnetic wave shields we use to help prevent being hit by projectiles also do a pretty good job of deflecting any weapons."

"So how do pirates pose a threat?"

"Well, they come up behind us, in our wake and then launch themselves at the back of the rig. In the wake they are very difficult to detect. The pirates then grapple on and crawl along the rig to the nearest hatch or door."

"And we only know they are here when they try to secure a grapple hook?"

"Exactly. Once they are hooked on, it is just a matter of time before they are inside."

"And that is why we intentionally cause a bounce? To induce a cardiac arrest and stop them in their tracks?"

"Yep. Once on board we have little means to resist them. They can be ruthless and that isn't a situation any of us want to bring upon ourselves."

"But if they go into cardiac arrest, so do we."

"Exactly. It is one of the reasons we always need someone on watch and at a console. At most times we enabled the rig's proximity alert system. That system will detect something moving near the rig. It will react if a pirate drops in on us, but we won't have much time. So, when the alarm sounds those on watch must do their best to drop into a g-seat and attach the g-juice feed. The system will detect the attachment and then run the feed and induce the bounce."

"What happens if no one attaches the g-juice?"

"The system will just bounce anyway."

"Shit! How come I am only learning this now?"

"In fairness, Luna, we did talk about some of this. Remember we spoke about bounce training and the bounce test?" Marr added.

"Yes, now I recall. But it didn't make sense at the time. I had no context. I do now."

"Have you been training already, Marr?" Dukk asked.

"Yes, but as Luna mentioned, it wasn't easy without context."

"Remind me of what is involved in bounce training and the test?" Luna asked.

"Dukk?" Marr asked.

"The training is to improve your reaction to the bounce and ability to self administer an EVM pack."

"EVM pack?"

"A cocktail to help you recover from the arrest. To use it, you must build an automated response. You need to grab the pack and jam it into your med feed whilst going into arrest."

"And the test?"

"The test is where you are basically put into cardiac arrest, and you must use the EVM pack yourself to help you get out of the arrest. Of course, during the test you'll have a medic monitoring you to bring you back if you fail. Which most do on the first few attempts."

"Is the EVM pack the same as the traverse juice?"

"No. The juice is designed to induce a very short coma and then bring you out immediately. The cocktail is measured to the exact needs of your body at the time of the traverse. The EVM is not. The EVM pack is to help you bring things back under control in the face of a cardiac arrest."

"Right, so when do we start training?" Luna asked.

"Immediately, during your downtime using a dummy EVM pack. I'll show you where they are kept," Dukk answered.

"And the test?"

"When you feel you are ready. But I'd suggest not until you've got the hang of coming out of the traverse. One thing at a time."

"Cool," concluded Luna as she sat back in the seat.

"Great. Time to get ready for watch. You finished with that?" Dukk concluded pointing at Marr's empty food tray.

"Yep. Thank you. See you in twenty," Marr replied as she got up and headed towards her cabin.

Chapter 14 – Troubleshooting

1

With the score one a piece, the excitement going into the evening watch was the match between Bazzer and Luna. Annee and Mentor said they were going to watch the replay later, because sleep was their priority.

Marr requested with Dukk that they base themselves in the crew mess initially so they could enjoy the banter with Luna and Bazzer as they got ready.

Bazzer was the first to appear following some short downtime at the end of watch. Marr was alone in the crew mess as Dukk was on a walk around.

"I am ready!" exclaimed Bazzer as he exited his cabin.

Marr turned around and nearly fell off the console seat.

"Holy cow! Are you for real?" she laughed.

Bazzer was wearing bright green, skin-tight shorts and a bright orange, skin-tight singlet that barely covered his overly muscular upper body.

"I figure, against Luna's youth and fitness, using humour will be my only chance!"

"Well, you have definitely got me laughing."

Bazzer grinned back sheepishly.

"Oh shit! I forgot my sunglasses," Luna laughed as she appeared at the door of her cabin. She mimicked covering her eyes as she looked at Bazzer.

"You can hardly talk!" Marr added as she laughed even harder.

Luna was wearing a ridiculously small, hot pink bikini that barely gave any cover and look to offer very little support.

"What the F!" exclaimed Bazzer, and continued, "How in the world will I concentrate on the ball with you bouncing around the airlock like that!"

"That is the idea," Luna laughed.

"This will be a battle of wills, not skill," offered Marr.

They all laughed.

"What is so funny," Dukk said casually as he entered the crew mess via the ladder shaft door.

"What the hell! What did you two do, ransack Kimince and Terence's lockers?" he added.

"Stand over there together, I have to get a photo," Marr demanded.

The photo was impossible to take. The sight of Bazzer's outfit against his pale skin tones, next to Luna in the hot pink bikini against her brown skin, was too comical for anyone to keep a straight face.

The attempt at getting a photo, set the tone for the match. It was a shemozzle. Luna and Bazzer spent most of the time falling over each over laughing.

In the end it was abandoned and declared a draw.

"I haven't laughed that hard in a long time," Marr said as she flicked off the video feed of the airlock.

"Me neither. We'll have to start over and play again?" replied Dukk as he stepped back from the console.

They looked at each other.

"You up to it?"

"Absolutely," Dukk said in an overly enthusiastic tone. He blushed and turned away quickly.

Marr smiled.

"Will we move the conn upstairs," she offered to reset the mood.

"Yes, good idea. I'll go up directly. It's your turn for a walk around. See you up there."

2

Later in Dukk and Marr's evening shift, Dukk entered the cockpit. He was carrying drink containers.

"Here you go," Dukk said has he handed Marr the hot drink.

"Thank you, Dukk."

"Anything strange?"

"Actually, yes. There is a yellow warning on internal integrity."

"Show me," Dukk replied as he leaned over to see her console.

"See the log here. It says pressure regulation is at risk."

"Did you check external integrity?"

"Yes, it is showing as one hundred percent."

"Did you check internal door integrity?"

"No, how do I do that?"

"Navigate to 'Intermediary Maintenance'. Right, and find 'Internal Doors'. Yep, and now review the list of doors. Each time a door closes, it should register an integrity reading."

"Cool."

"Anything unusual?"

"The lounge door is showing sixty percent."

"Looks like you have found the problem. I'll go down and have a look. It might be something we can sort out ourselves and avoid disturbing Bazzer on his downtime."

Dukk used the forward ladder shaft. It was the most direct route from the cockpit to the front of the accommodation level. The ladder shaft door on that level was adjacent to the lounge door.

Dukk stepped out of the ladder shaft. The lounge door looked closed; however, he could hear voices. That indicated the door hadn't sealed properly.

Dukk didn't feel comfortable eavesdropping, but he also wanted to understand the problem before he touched the door. He didn't want to make the problem worse. He did his best to tune out their voices as he looked for the problem.

"Look, I just feel we need to think it through. You've been saying for a while now, that you are over Earth and this type of work. I was talking to those too heavies from Mayfield. They said there is plenty of security work out there and in neighbouring systems. Maybe it is time to retire," said one of the people in the lounge. The voice was deep, like that of a man. Dukk assume that it was Larony.

"I know, but we made a deal. It is bad form to renege. It will follow us no matter where we end up," said another person. That voice was higher. A woman. Dukk recognised the second voice. It was Joantyi.

From Dukk's perspective he could see there was a slight gap in the top corner.

"I need to open the door and inspect the hinges," Dukk thought to himself.

He was about to open the door and let them know when something told him to pause.

"We won't be reneging. We will simply be invalidating the terms. Thumpol made no mention of Mentor being on this crew. If half of what we have heard is true, there is no way we'll pull this off unscathed or even perhaps alive!" said the man.

Dukk stopped dead.

"Yes, I know this job will call for some creative thinking. I have that already in play."

"You are insane, and you are going to get us both killed. I'm going to get some rest before the next traverse."

Dukk quickly retreated into the shaft and closed the door as quietly as he could.

He then slid down the ladder to the hold. From there, he dashed back up the stairs and opened the door to the main corridor of the accommodation level. He timed it well. Larony was just coming down the corridor.

"Hi, everything alright?" Dukk asked politely.

"Yes. Everything on track, Captain?" Larony replied coldly.

"Pretty much. I just got a warning about an issue with the lounge door."

"Interesting. It looked fine to me. I just closed it."

"I'd better check it all the same."

"Whatever," Larony said as he brushed past and continued towards the cabins.

On entering the lounge, Dukk found Joantyi on the couch. She had next to nothing on as per usual.

"Oh, sorry to disturb you," Dukk said, doing his best to look surprised.

"Captain, I was just thinking of you. I have a question if you have a moment."

"Actually, I am in the middle of something. This door is broken, and I need to sort it before we do the next traverse," Dukk answered as he closed the door and inspected the hinges.

"I assume you've been to Maple Tower before?" she continued as if she hadn't heard Dukk's attempt to end the conversation before it got started.

"Yes, several times," Dukk answered mindlessly.

"I hear it can get a little rough."

"Yes, that tends to happen with the isolated hubs."

"I want to avoid any grief while I am there. Any tips on how I might do that?"

Dukk paused. He had found the problem. The bolts on the top hinge were loose. He tried to move one with his hand and it turned. That shouldn't happen if they were tensioned correctly. He kept a calm expression.

"Possible, but not probable that these bolts just loosen themselves. Someone wanted my attention," Dukk thought to himself.

"I am sorry, you are obviously busy, perhaps when you have some time later. After all we've got another few days before we get there?"

"Yes, we do," Dukk answered without thinking.

"Great so, I look forward to sitting down with you later."

"Right," Dukk replied realising he'd just been suckered into a meeting he didn't really want to have.

3

It didn't take long for Dukk to get the tensioning tool and return to the lounge.

On his return, Dukk found that Joantyi was no longer alone. The two observers were sitting together on a couch. Joantyi looked bored.

"We've been studying the public record on hauler traditions. There are some fascinating things," Trence could be heard saying.

"How interesting," Joantyi replied sarcastically.

"We also found the material confusing. Like for example, it says that hauliers typically try to eat together once per day and do a ritual called 'Giving Thanks'. We don't understand what the ritual is for," Kimince added.

"Haulier traditions and rituals aren't my forte. The captain here might be able to help you out?" Joantyi said as she watched Dukk working on the door hinge.

"Oh, yes, of course. Captain, can you help us understand why hauliers do this 'Giving Thanks' thing at meals?" Trence asked politely.

Dukk looked up. Joantyi smiled sheepishly back at Dukk.

"This is a risky business. We may not be around this time tomorrow," Dukk replied.

"Well, isn't that a bit morbid. And how does the 'Giving Thanks' fit in?" Kimince asked.

"It is a prayer. A prayer to express our gratitude for still being alive," Dukk offered.

"A prayer. Well that now makes sense. Prayers were done before we were awakened. It is part of the test. The test ensures only those who have what it takes to evolve efficiently will go forward. Hauliers, like all less evolved, fail the test," Kimince said in a snobbish tone.

"Is that true? Don't some in labour roles pass the test?" Trence argued.

"Well, it is not perfect. Some do get through and must be deprivileged later," Kimince replied.

Dukk sighed. "Your definition of 'evolved', as far as I can see, simply means you've lost the ability to truly think for yourself," Dukk thought to himself. He felt he saw the same response from Joantyi.

"I'd better get this door fixed. I'll leave you to it," Dukk said aloud. Kimince and Trence barely noticed Dukk's response. They just kept talking at each other.

Dukk fixed the door, put the tool back in the engine room, and then headed back upstairs.

"Whatever you did, it worked. The pressure consistency alarm has gone off," Marr commented as Dukk entered the cockpit.

"A door hinge had loose bolts. I tensioned them again," Dukk replied.

"Interesting, does that happen often?"

"First time for me."

"Odd"

"Yes, it is. I think it was intentional. It is hard to imagine the bolts just loosening themselves."

"What would have been the impact if it hadn't been fixed ahead of the traverse."

"None really. Even if we got a breach in that space and couldn't seal the room off, it would just take longer to make the repairs. It would be more of an inconvenience rather than a risk."

"Why do it then?"

"Boredom maybe. Perhaps to get attention. Perhaps to test how thoroughly we were monitoring the rig's systems."

"A mystery to solve?"

"Yes, it is."

Dukk fell silent and gazed out at the planet racing below them.

"Is there something else?" Marr asked.

Dukk turned and looked at Marr.

"After dinner last night, you said you had skills not typical for a haulier."

"I did. So?"

"Would Mentor share those skills too?"

"He would."

"And would he have other skills, that you don't have?"

"Probably. He has been around for a lot longer. Why, are you suggesting he, or even I had something to do with the loose bolts?

"No, I am pretty sure Joantyi loosened the bolts."

"Joantyi? Why?"

"She was in the lounge. Next to nothing on again. I get the feeling that she mostly gets what she wants. Perhaps she didn't appreciate the knock back earlier today."

"I can see how you could get there. But what then, does this have to do with Mentor's skills? What else happen downstairs?"

Dukk paused. He wanted to trust her. But he was less sure now. He had an idea.

"The observers were in the lounge. They were confused about the ritual of 'Giving Thanks'. It reminded me of dinner last night. You and Luna followed suit as if it were normal. I only learnt it after becoming a haulier. Did Mentor teach you that too?"

Marr laughed.

"No, that is a tradition you hauliers share with keepers."

"Oh. What other traditions do we share, I wonder?"

"Time will tell," Marr answered with a smile.

Dukk smiled back. He softened his expression.

Marr looked relieved.

"I'd better keep the rest to myself for now," Dukk thought to himself.

"You don't want to share more yet. That might be a good thing. I'm not sure I can lie to you, Dukk. Tread carefully," Marr thought to herself as she reflected on her own behaviour. She had used the video feeds of the corridors to watch and listen in on his movements during the whole lounge encounter.

With that, they both returned their attention to the consoles.

4

"Mind if I stretch my legs and do a walk around?" Marr said when the silence got a little too much.

"Go for it. And take your time. It will be the last walk around before we start the traverse preparation," Dukk answered.

Marr made her way aft of the upper level and headed down the ladder shaft.

She was hoping to catch Mentor before the traverse. He wasn't in the crew mess, so she continued to the lower level to inspect the engine room and hold. She then checked the nose and airlocks. With that all done, she headed up the stairs to the accommodation level. She tried the gym. He was there and he was alone.

"Good evening. Good rest?" she said as she swiped her bracelet.

"Good evening, Marr. Somewhat. But mostly restless," Mentor answered as he too activated his bracelet.

"Those two destine for Maple Tower mentioned you. Dukk overheard them talking about you getting in the way of something they need to do. They also mentioned someone by the name of Thumpol. It clearly meant something to Dukk."

"Did Dukk share this all with you?"

"No, I overheard it. I was tuned into the corridor video feeds. The lounge door was broken, and their voices carried. Dukk only shared his thoughts on the woman, not the mention of you or this Thumpol person. He thinks the woman loosened the bolts on the door hinge to get his attention."

"Well, that is good news."

"How so?"

"Three things. First, I wasn't sure. But now, I know their intention."

"What is their intention?"

"Best if you don't know."

"Fine. And the second?"

"We know they are sloppy. Allowing themselves to be overheard, speaks of amateurs."

"Haven't you always said amateurs are often the most troublesome?"

"Yes, they can panic and that can result in unnecessary consequences. We must tread carefully."

"And the third?"

"Dukk doesn't trust you yet."

"How is that good news?"

"It shows that he is not a fool. He is street wise, and that is what we need him to be."

"What are my orders?"

"Stand down. Hold your cover. It will be best if yourself and Luna stay out of the picture for now."

"What if something happens to you? I know nothing of the mission."

"I have that covered."

"Bazzer?"

"You are learning, Marr. Your skills are growing. However, that piece of knowledge will only impede you. Put it out of your mind. Focus on becoming what you trained for."

"A haulier Captain."

"Precisely."

Marr nodded and swiped her bracelet. She went to open the door, but it swung open nearly knocking her over.

Kimince and Trence came bouncing into the room.

"Hello co-pilot, hello Mentor," they said in unison.

"Hello," Marr responded as she stepped out of the way of the door.

"Annee said we had to find you a little before the next traverse," Kimince said, ignoring Marr and walking directly over to Mentor.

"Yes, I have an idea that will help you get through the traverse with flying colours. I need you suited up and in your seats before the fifteen-minute warning. Can you do that now, please?" Mentor replied without missing a beat on the treadmill.

"Oh, okay. Let's go Tren."

They bounced back out, and the door closed behind them.

"What was that all about?" laughed Marr.

"I am going to sedate them. After this morning's experience, they will be uncontrollably nervous as the countdown approaches. We won't get them settled otherwise."

"Any chance I can get a little of what you are going to give them. I'm pretty nervous too," Marr said and then laughed.

Mentor laughed too.

"It gets easier. You'll be fine."

"I bloody well hope so."

With that Marr headed for the door.

Thirty minutes later, everyone was seated, helmets on and ready for the next traverse.

Dukk had just completed his broadcast to the passengers.

He turned on the crew comms.

"Right, let's do this. Marr and Luna, take comfort in the fact that this will be the hardest traverse you will make. Your nerves will be at a peak because you know what is coming. It will get easier after this. Four minutes. Unmuting crew comms. Status check. Vitals?"

"All stable. Calibration is at ninety seven percent," Mentor answered.

"Systems?"

"Integrity at one hundred percent. All green," Bazzer replied.

"Check-in."

"Ready," Mentor said immediately.

Annee and Bazzer followed.

"Ready," Marr said nervously.

"Ready," Luna said in a faint voice.

Dukk didn't look around. He knew he'd only make it harder for Marr and Luna if they saw him checking.

"Ready too. Deep and full breaths everyone. We are committed. Three minutes. Load up the guests," Dukk said firmly.

"Done. Heart rates dropping," Mentor replied.

They all waited. A minute later Mentor added, "All stable."

"Med control is back with me," Dukk said as he interacted with his console.

"Thirty seconds," he announced.

"Twenty seconds."

"Ten seconds."

"Juice on its way. See you on the other side," Dukk said as he hit the button.

5

Moments later, Dukk was awake again. The view had changed. They were in orbit of a rocky planet in the JR18 system. The traverse had put them in the shadow of the planet. It was dark.

Dukk fought back the traverse sickness. He got things back in balance. He looked around.

Marr had her head up. She was concentrating.

"Good woman," Dukk thought to himself.

"Status," he forced into the crew comms.

Bazzer, Annee and Mentor responded immediately.

"Back," Marr said in a whisper.

"Bah," Luna uttered before making a gagging sound as she fought back the nausea.

"Mentor, you up to med check?"

"Yep."

"Transferring med control back to you. Give us the status when you are ready."

"Cockpit, four stable, two stabilising. Passengers, two stable, rest are stabilising," Mentor replied, moments later.

"Excellent. Systems, Bazzer?" Dukk asked.

"All green," responded Bazzer.

"Perfect. Let's get the DMD going."

The tingling sensation washed over them. Luna could be heard gagging again.

Dukk interacted with the controls.

"It is quiet here. Not a lot of traffic on this route. The next traverse is in just over nine hours at six, forty-four tomorrow morning. Bazzer, do you want to get us into slow running mode. Annee and Mentor, are you good with helping the passengers?"

Annee looked over at Mentor. He nodded.

"Yep, we've got it covered. Will you cover the start of our watch if we are delayed?" Annee replied.

"Yep, we'll move down to the crew mess and cover you from there until you are sorted," Dukk answered as he removed his helmet. He then continued, "Marr do you want to head down now with Luna? I'll transfer the conn once you are down there."

"Okay," Marr answered softly.

Dukk turned around and looked at Bazzer. Bazzer nodded. He took the hint to stay put.

Whilst the others got up and left, Dukk watched the view. It was changing. A glow was appearing on the horizon. The auto pilot kicked in. The rig gently rotated so that its belly would face the sun as they approached the horizon.

"What's up, Captain?" Bazzer announced as he plonked himself down in Marr's seat.

"Useful things, these," Dukk said as he waved his hand over his bracelet.

Bazzer followed suit.

"I need your help, Bazzer."

"Shoot."

"One of the passengers destine for Maple Tower, Joantyi, is coming on strong."

"Wouldn't be the first time for you. What's the problem? Too much for you? Lost your nerve?"

"No, none of that," Dukk laughed.

"Too soon after Larinette?"

"What? No, it is not that."

"Well, what then?"

"Something doesn't feel right. Also, I overheard her talking with Larony, the other passenger for Maple Tower. They mentioned Thumpol and doing a job for him."

"What kind of job?"

"They didn't say. That is what I need your help with. It might be worth looking into it a bit. Get close to her, so to speak. Get a sense of what's what. If it is about me, it might be wise for me to keep my distance."

"If she had eyes for you, I'd have a hill to climb!"

"True. But I have an 'in' for you."

"I'm listening."

"She asked me for my thoughts on Maple Tower. The ins and outs. She doesn't want to ruffle any feathers. I didn't answer her, but she walked me into a corner, and I figure she'll use it to get my attention again. You could pre-empt that and say I asked you to help her out."

"Interesting. But not ruffling feathers in Maple Tower might not be my area of expertise. Quite the opposite if you remember."

"Yes, I do remember. I was thinking you might be able to kill two birds with one stone. You could steer her in a direction which serves your purposes as well. Then you might get close enough to learn what the job is. And, if you did it right, you'll have some fun on the way."

"It sounds challenging, but I like your thinking."

"Looks like Marr is at the console downstairs, let's head down."

"Roger," said Bazzer as he launched out of the seat.

Dukk followed.

Bazzer and Dukk used the aft ladder and were in the crew mess moments later.

Annee was sitting at the table interacting with her wrist wrap heads up display. She looked over as they exited the shaft door.

"Dukk, I got the profiles for the four passengers that need a ride out of Maple Tower."

"Suitable?" Dukk replied as he sat down opposite her.

"I guess."

"What's your concern?"

"They are teenage girls. Fifteen or sixteen years of age. They were on board an elite cruiser that has broken down."

"That is unusual. You said Bognath gave us the lead. And they are paying above the odds?"

"Yep."

"Where is the broken cruiser registered?"

"Let me check."

Annee flicked some panels around, then added, "Mayfield, under Craig Atesoughton."

"Perhaps the presence of Bognath and Carltor has nothing to do with the beef contract. Interesting."

"So, what do we do?"

"I can't see anything obviously wrong. But it is your call. What's your instinct tell you?"

"The money is good, and they are just teenage girls. They can't be that much trouble. So, yes, we do it."

"Cool."

"There is something else."

"What?"

"Joantyi approached me. She wanted to see if there was a possibility of joining us on the leg from Maple Tower to Mayfield."

"Okay?"

"She got annoyed and snooty when I said that we already had a request ahead of her for the seats."

"Interesting."

"Yes, isn't it. Something doesn't feel right about that woman. The teenagers feel like the better option."

"Yes, I agree. It feels like going with the teenagers would be a smarter move. Do you need a hand with Joantyi?"

"Nope. I can handle her type," Annee replied smiling.

Chapter 15 – EVA

1

The alarm didn't startle Dukk as much as the day before, but he still found it hard to get started.

"Clearly those power naps yesterday weren't sufficient to shift my body clock enough," Dukk thought as he swung his legs off the bed and started his morning routine.

The crew mess was dark and quiet when he left his cabin five minutes later.

He went over to the console and checked where the conn was centred. The engine room. He flicked up the video feeds for the engine room. Bazzer and Luna could be seen at the console, interacting with it, and talking. He then checked the flight plan.

"Ninety minutes until traverse. All good. Exercise time," Dukk said aloud.

As Dukk had hoped, Marr was already in the gym. She was dressed in a similar manner to the day before and looking to be thoroughly enjoying the intense workout.

"Good morning, Dukk. Sleep well?" she said between hard breathing.

"I did, thank you Marr. You?" Dukk responded, lingering a little, before starting his stretches.

Marr's machine sounded to indicate it was going into the warm down stage.

"Yes, better than the night before. I guess I am getting accustomed to all this."

"That's good. You didn't sleep well the first night?"

"Nope. I tossed and turned. I guess I was nervous about what was ahead."

"And you are not nervous now?"

"Well, still a little. But I have a better sense of how things are up here. And that has made it much easier."

"What do you mean?"

"Well, for starters everyone has been helpful and kind. Also, you have shown yourself to be professional, organised, and disciplined. These are traits that I admire. You also like to have a bit of fun. Humour is important to me too."

"Interesting," Dukk responded as he smiled up at Marr.

Marr blushed and then stumbled into more words.

"Yes, it makes it much easier to serve under someone who knows his stuff but doesn't take it too seriously."

Dukk laughed. He sensed there was more than just a professional observation in her tone but now wasn't the time.

"Well, I am glad you are getting more accustomed to our ways. So, how are you feeling about the plan for today?"

Marr smiled too. She liked that they were both getting a sense of when to shift the subject.

"The inspection you mean?"

"Yes, and there is the opportunity to take a walk, extravehicular activity, EVA, if you feel up for it."

"Absolutely."

"It will have to be tandem to start with but, you'll still get a sense of it."

"How will it work?" Marr asked as she finished her treadmill time.

"All going well, the inspection should happen shortly after the traverse. We'll get everyone settled then turn off the DMD. We will then launch the drones to inspect the outer hull. We'll also use the downtime to run more detailed diagnostics of the engines and systems.

We will analyse the data we get back. From the results we generate a to-do list of closer inspections or repairs."

"That I know, but how does the tandem EVA fit in?"

"Bazzer will go out with the drones. He will monitor their activity. He can take you with him."

"Wouldn't he take Luna?"

"Actually, it is tradition that an apprentice's first walk is with the captain. So, I will take Luna later. This tradition won't apply to you. Whilst you are new to all this, technically you aren't an apprentice. Besides, we can't have both of the flight crew outside of the rig at the same time. That would go against the regulations. And, you know how I like to be professional."

Dukk grinned after the last sentence. Marr smiled.

"Who says I'd like to take a walk with you?" Marr said provocatively.

Dukk laughed and raised his eyebrows. He stopped the stretch and stood up directly in front of her.

"Am I not good enough for you?" Dukk said in jest.

She also stopped stretching and stood up.

"Funny how things don't stay professional for long," Marr thought to herself.

"Undecided," Marr answered as she looked him in the eye. She smiled. Dukk smiled back.

"So, I have to do my first walk with Bazzer?" Marr added as she leaned sideways into another stretch.

Dukk moved around her and climbed on the exercise bike.

"Well, no, Annee or Mentor could take you too, but that might not happen today. It will depend on what repairs are needed. It is just an opportunity if you want to take it?"

"Bazzer it is then. What do I need to do?"

"Bazzer will take you through it once we are safely through the traverse."

"Wait, won't we be on watch?"

"Yes, that is another reason why one of us needs to remain on board."

2

The third traverse went ahead as planned. Luna and Marr were less nervous. They both managed to respond with the others when Dukk asked for a status update as they came out.

With the vitals and systems all checked, Dukk asked Bazzer to bring the DMD back online.

"Let's get an estimate of the traverse preparation time out of JR56," Dukk said as he interacted with his console.

Moments later he continued, "the DMD is indicating the preparation time for the traverse to JR72 will be just under twelve hours. I'll put it in a holding pattern and then restart it proper just after seven p.m. All going well, that will put our next traverse, at seven AM tomorrow morning."

"So, we have nearly twenty-four hours to complete the inspection and repairs?" Luna asked.

"Exactly, Luna. And I am glad to see you are recovering faster," Dukk answered.

"Me too."

Dukk opened the broadcast mode.

"Good morning. Welcome to JR56. This dusty planet is the location for our intermediary inspection and routine maintenance. We will be turning off the DMD at times so we can give the outer hull our attention. I suggest you take extra care when moving about during these times. And, if in your bunk it would be important to use the straps. All going well, we aim to be in orbit here for about twenty-four hours. I will get back to you if that changes."

Dukk disabled the broadcast mode as he removed his helmet.

"Let's get the passengers settled and start preparation for the inspection."

"On it," Annee said as she headed for the cockpit door. Mentor followed.

"So, Captain, Marr tells me there might be the opportunity for my first spacewalk," Luna said.

"Yes, Luna. All going well you and I should be good to start suiting up in about an hour."

"Excellent. So excited. Do you need me for anything else before then?"

"Nope, just be in the lower g-suit locker near eight a.m."

"Cool. See you then," she added as she headed for the cockpit door.

"She is in a hurry," Dukk stated as the door closed behind Luna.

"Yes, I wonder why, not!" exclaimed Bazzer laughing.

Dukk looked over at Marr. She shrugged her shoulders.

"Right, I am heading down to check the lanyards and backpacks. See you down there, Marr."

"Right behind you," Marr replied.

She looked over at Dukk as Bazzer opened the forward ladder shaft hatch and disappeared.

"Let's move the conn down to the console in the starboard airlock as it will be closer to the action," Dukk suggested.

"Won't we be using the airlock?"

"The starboard door is really for ground access. The port door is better suited to zero-g. And the hold airlock provides a better space to get organised."

"Cool. Will I go down first and activate the console?"

"Let me go first, I want to have a word with Bazzer on the way."

"Okay."

Dukk activated his bracelet as he caught up with Bazzer. Bazzer saw Dukk above him and did the same.

"No, nothing yet!" Bazzer stated as he opened the shaft door and crossed to the lower g-suit room.

Dukk followed him and closed the door. He moved backwards towards the door and casually stretched his arms in the air such that they blocked the overhead camera.

"I need more detail than that. You've had twelve hours. I've known you for far too long to know that 'nothing yet' is not the entire story."

"Fair point. I am just saying I have no line on her true game. Or any idea how she is connected to Thumpol. She responded well to your idea. I am helping her get an idea of how to not ruffle any feathers in Maple Tower. That has been fruitful and may even help resolve my situation with Ileadees. Give me another day or two."

"Not enjoying yourself too much perhaps. Losing sight of the mission?"

"Never," Bazzer laughed.

"Good to know."

"Now, get on and do your flying thing, and let me get on with the inspection."

"Drones?"

"Already in the airlock. Luna and I serviced them during our watch."

"Excellent."

Dukk smiled and left.

3

Marr arrived on the mezzanine level to find all the internal doors open.

She closed the forward shaft door and looked around.

Through the door immediately opposite, she could see the g-suit locker with the suits and support and propulsion backpacks hanging on the walls.

She poked her head through the door on the right. Dukk was at the console. He was flicking panels and lining up the external camera video feeds.

She turned around to face the hall to the left of the ladder shaft. She paused, confused. She headed in that direction. She had hardly noticed the door on the other side of the base of the stairs to the accommodation level. It was now open. She knew the hold airlock was adjacent to the stairs, but the mezzanine was two and a half metres higher than the floor of the airlock where they had all been playing wall ball. When she got to the door, she found there was now a platform that extended from the hall door across to the port external door. It created a bridge across the hold airlock.

"Cool," she said aloud.

"Isn't it," came Bazzer's voice from behind her.

Bazzer was carrying two tether lanyard rolls. He walked over the bridge and placed them on the floor near two drones. He attached one end of each of the tethers to pad eyes in the floor near the door.

"I've put everything we need in here before we put on the backpacks. They are quite a load when the DMD is running. Let's check with Dukk before we put the backpacks on."

Marr followed Bazzer back towards the starboard airlock.

"We are ready when you are," Bazzer announced to Dukk.

"Nearly there. Ann just messaged me to say the passengers are settled," Dukk replied.

"Excellent. We'll get the packs on and get into the airlock before you pause the DMD."

"Sound."

Bazzer led the way back to the locker.

"I'm going to help you with your backpack first so you can get a sense of the weight in near zero-g."

"Cool," answered Marr.

"I've checked these two packs just now. First attach your gloves and helmet to your thigh clips so they are within arm's reach. Okay, now come over here, bend your knees slightly and back up to this pack."

Marr did as instructed.

"Now insert your arms into the straps. Reach between your legs and find the groin strap.

Great. Now reach around and grab the waist belt. Connect it all up."

235

Bazzer watched as Marr sorted the straps.

"Perfect. Okay, now put your hands up over your shoulders and grab the shoulder apparatus. Pull it up and over your head."

Marr felt for the straps and tugged gently. A frame swung up and over her head. It rested on her shoulders.

"Doing well. Now take those connections at the front and clip them to the shoulder straps."

Marr connected the straps.

"Right. Now you are ready for your helmet and gloves. Let's go onto comms so we can communicate. Let's bring Dukk in too."

Bazzer interacted with his comms.

"Everyone connected?" Bazzer asked.

"Yep," answered Marr.

"Loud and clear," Dukk added.

"Awesome. Now grab the helmet off your thigh clip and put it on as normal."

Marr put her helmet on. When it clicked into place on her g-suit, the connections on the shoulder apparatus married perfectly to the attachments on the rim of the helmet.

"Cool," Marr exclaimed as her heads-up display now included a panel for the backpack.

"Yes, the pack is integrated fully with your helmet and comms now. Access the power controls and bring the pack online."

Marr followed the instructions. A slight vibration could be felt as the systems in the backpack came online.

"Right. Now put your gloves on and let's do a systems check," Bazzer instructed.

"Done, what now?" Marr asked once her gloves were on.

"Now lean back and push up to take the pack off its wall brackets."

Marr did as instructed.

"Excellent. How does that feel?"

"Heavy!" laughed Marr.

Bazzer laughed.

"Get a sense of it as I get my pack on."

When they were both ready, Bazzer led the way back to the hold airlock and closed the door.

"Okay, let's bring the suit atmosphere online before we go any further. Use the controls and activate 'suit atmosphere'."

Marr did as instructed. Immediately her suit inflated slightly. It became a little more rigid too.

"That's interesting," Marr commented as she got used to the sensation of the inflated suit against her inner layer.

"Check the status," Bazzer asked.

"Showing one hundred percent."

"Great. Now let's buddy up. I'll send you a request."

"Got it. Accepted."

"Cool. I can see your vitals. You should also be able to see mine alongside yours."

"Yep, got that too."

"I am now sending you a request to control your propulsion. Until you get more practice, it will be me doing the driving."

"No problem. Done."

"Time to get the tethers attached," Bazzer said as he attached the other ends of the tethers to their harnesses. "We are ready, Dukk."

"I can see. Smile for the camera," Dukk answered.

4

A chime sounded throughout the rig, followed by an automated message. "Brace for zero gravity."

Dukk killed the power to the DMD. He set his toes firmly into his boots. He felt the boots grip the floor. He waited as the DMD let go of its mass. His limbs lightened.

"The DMD is now paused. I have also disabled the rig's proximity alert system. I am going to initiate the port door opening sequence," Dukk announced to Marr and Bazzer.

Dukk pressed the buttons on the schematic of the rig.

Marr looked around. The floating sensation was unsettling. She pressed her toes into her boots and felt them lock down to the floor.

The lighting in the hold airlock was now flashing orange.

"Airlock depressurised. Rig integrity holding at one hundred percent. Opening the port door now," Dukk announced.

Marr watched as the door swung inwards and tucked itself neatly out of the way. Blackness now filled the opening.

"Deploying drones," Dukk continued.

The drones lifted off the floor and shot out the open doorway.

"Everything ok?" Bazzer asked.

"Yep. A little nervous."

"You'll be fine. I read in your BIO that you have had zero-g training."

"Some, it was a while ago."

"I'd suggest taking it easy today. I am going to follow these drones and keep an eye on them. You can move around in here and once you feel up for it, make your way to the doorway and signal me. I'll then bring you out to join me."

"Sounds good."

Bazzer turned and pulled himself towards the doorway. Once clear, he engaged the propulsion and disappeared.

Marr used the handles to pull herself around and rotate slowly within the airlock. She repeated the process a few more times before manoeuvring herself to the doorway.

Marr looked out. The planet could be seen racing below them. Beyond was darkness.

She caught her breath and counted. "I got this," she said to herself.

Bazzer could be seen floating several metres above the port wing. The two drones could be seen zooming across the wing in a crisscrossing pattern.

"I'm ready," she said into the comms.

Bazzer turned in her direction.

"Great. Let go of the doorway and I will engage your pack."

Marr let go and floated in the opening as her pack trembled momentarily. The propulsion engaged. She relaxed as her pack brought her out of the doorway and moved her swiftly towards Bazzer.

Side by side, Bazzer and Marr floated along as the drones surveyed the rig.

They had to back track a few times to get their long tethers out of the path of the drones.

When the drones had finished their survey, they zoomed back into the port door and came to rest on the floor in the exact spot they had been before.

"Time to get back inside. We can't leave the DMD off too long. Zero gravity makes life on the rig uncomfortable," Bazzer said as he manoeuvred them both back towards the open doorway.

"That's a pity. It is so peaceful out here," Marr replied.

Dukk watched Bazzer and Marr on the video feeds as they returned into the hold airlock.

"Closing the door and pressuring the airlock, stand by," he announced as they brought themselves back down on the bridge.

Dukk interacted with the rig schematic again.

The tingling sensation washed over them as Dukk brought the DMD back online. Their limbs went heavy again.

Dukk then locked the console and headed to the hallway. He opened the internal door to the airlock.

"What do you think?" Dukk asked as Marr removed her helmet.

"Easy with Bazzer in the driver's seat," Marr answered making her way into the g-suit locker.

"She was a natural. And the rig looks pretty good. If the drones haven't picked up any major repairs, there will be another opportunity for a walk before we depart this system. And there will be more opportunities once we are in Maple Tower. You'll be a pro in no time," Bazzer added.

"Thank you. It must be your guidance," Marr answered.

"Absolutely, I am the best there is. Right, Captain?"

"Yes, Bazzer you are the best," laughed Dukk.

"Now that we've done the hard part, you can do your sanity check and give our apprentice a taste of EVA."

"Exactly. You good to help Marr manage the DMD and airlock process?"

"Yep, leave it with me," Bazzer answered.

"Speaking of Luna, she should have been down here by now," Dukk said as he helped them get their packs back on the racks.

5

"Hi," came Luna's voice as she bounced into the suit locker.

Dukk turned around.

"Are you alright? You are all flushed?"

"Yes, I am fine. I was practicing some yoga in zero-G. I lost track of time. Quite challenging and not what I expected," Luna replied.

"Yoga?" Marr mouthed silently at Luna from behind Dukk.

Luna smiled cheekily.

Marr held her hands up and looked away as if to say, 'I don't want to know'.

Dukk laughed. He'd been an apprentice too once. He knew what was on his mind the first time he was in zero-g. And he could tell an intentional lie.

"Are you sure you want to try this now? I can go alone, and you can get back to your 'yoga'?" Dukk asked in jest, emphasising the last word.

"Nope, I'm good. Let's do this."

Thirty-five minutes later, Luna stood at the port outer doorway. She was in awe.

Dukk and Luna had completed the same process Bazzer, and Marr had done earlier. Marr, with Bazzer's help, had then brought down the DMD, depressurised the airlock and opened the port door. With the door open, Dukk had headed out and Luna had done some practice within the hold airlock.

Luna peered out the door. She could just see Dukk up beyond the tail. He was floating near the solar panels.

"Ready, Dukk," Luna said enthusiastically into her comms.

Dukk turned around so that he had visuals on the port door.

"Excellent. Let go of the door and I will engage the propulsion. Let's bring you out here," Dukk replied.

"Done, so I do nothing right?"

"Yep, just float and allow me to do the rest."

Luna started to move forwards out of the doorway.

"So, I just succumb to your will, so to speak?"

Dukk laughed. "It is up to you how you interpret this process."

"Is all of this haulier tradition, like you giving me your backpack for this first EVA?"

"Well, some of this is just common sense."

Luna laughed into the comms.

Dukk waited until she was clear then went to adjust the propulsion.

Nothing happened. Luna just kept moving away from the rig. And she was gaining speed. He checked the buddy connection. It was still working. The system was telling him he was adjusting the propulsion, but nothing was happening. Something was wrong.

"Wow, this is amazing. How do I turn around to see you and the rig?" Luna asked.

"Luna, something is wrong. I'm coming to you. Hold tight," Dukk said as he engaged his propulsion in her direction.

"What's going on, Dukk?" came Luna's voice in a panic.

Dukk knew he was not going to get to her before she got to the end of the tether. He was going to need help.

"PAN-PAN, we have a pack malfunction. I am still buddied, but I can't shut down Luna's propulsion. Attempting intervention. Assistance required," Dukk announced on the crew comms.

Luna's tether went taut. She was swung around violently as the clip was attached to her chest harness. The outwards momentum was counteracted by the taut tether. It pulled her back towards the rig.

Luna screamed as she now raced back towards the rig.

"LUNA, I need you to listen," Dukk said firmly in the comms as he targeted her with his propulsion guidance and engaged full power.

"Holy cow, help!" she answered.

"LUNA, I need you to unclip your tether. I can't get you clear if we are tethered. Your momentum will smash you into the hull. Focus, Luna, focus."

Dukk unclipped his tether as he raced towards her. He then gathered a lanyard from his belt and clipped one end to his harness.

Luna was still racing towards the rig. She was still attached to the tether.

"LUNA! UNHOOK, NOW!"

Luna could be seen struggling with the clip at her chest. She got it free just as Dukk crashed into her.

The combined momentum took them away at a tangent. They zoomed past the nose of the rig.

During the collision Dukk had managed to grab Luna. He now turned her around. Facing each other, he clipped the other end of the short lanyard into her harness.

"Look at me, Luna," Dukk instructed.

"Everything is moving past so fast!" Luna screamed.

"We are spinning. Just look at me. Ignore everything else," Dukk said calmly.

Luna looked at him. "What now?" she replied in a slightly less panicked tone.

"We hope someone reacted fast and got into a Transport pod. The crash took out our propulsion. But we still have suit integrity and air. Unfortunately, by my calculations we are now dropping towards the planet. The atmosphere here is light, but our speed will be enough to burn us to a crisp if we enter it.

"Oh shit!"

"At least we'll not have to suffocate."

"Is that an attempt at a joke?"

"Trying to lighten the mood."

"Oh, in that case. So, this is cosy, some time alone together at last. Do you come here often?"

Dukk laughed. "Let's get someone's attention."

"MAYDAY, MAYDAY, we're going to need a pick-up!" Dukk said into the crew comms.

Chapter 16 – Docking

1

Marr had watched in horror. All the training hadn't prepared her sufficiently for what had just unfolded. Her self-deprecation was interrupted by a blur on the video feed. A transport pod could be seen racing away in the direction of where she last saw Dukk and Luna.

"Marr, I am going to close the port door and airlock from up here in the cockpit. Do you want to make your way up here too," Bazzer announced on the crew comms.

Bazzer had disappeared the moment Dukk said 'PAN-PAN'.

"Wait, if you are up there, who is in the pod?" Marr asked.

"Mentor. He was already in a transport pod when I got to the transport bay door. The bay was already being depressurised."

"I am on my way up too," came Annee's voice in the comms. "We will coordinate the rescue from there. And I am assuming command until Dukk is back with us. Let's move the conn up there."

"On my way," Marr uttered in disbelief.

"How fast things change," she thought to herself.

Moving through the rig in zero-g wasn't easy. By the time Marr had reached the cockpit the rescue was well underway.

A video feed was displaying the view from inside the transport pod.

The planet could be seen flipping in and out of view of the front windshield. Dukk and Luna could be seen together rotating slowly.

"What's going on?" Marr asked as she sat down in Mentor's seat in the second row.

"Mentor is trying to match their spin before he gets too close," Annee answered.

"Dukk and Luna, I am opening the canopy now and attempting to bring you on board. Brace for impact," Mentor shared into the crew comms.

The video feed blurred as the canopy opened. Then the view cleared momentarily as the pod came up to Dukk and Luna. Then the video feed went all blurry and messed up, before stopping altogether.

"What happened!" exclaimed Marr.

"Mentor? We've lost the video feed. Are you still there?" Annee asked calmly into the crew comms.

They waited.

"Got them," came Mentor's reply. "The video camera must have been knocked when I crashed into them. They are pretty beaten up and this pod might need some work, but we are safe. On our way back."

Marr burst into tears. Tears of joy.

"Well done, Mentor," Annee said emotionally into the comms.

"Well, when you two have got things together, we'd better get ready for their arrival," Bazzer said smiling back at Marr and Annee from his seat at the front of the cockpit.

They all laughed.

"Do you two want to get to the transport bay door and be ready to give Mentor a hand. I'll keep an eye on the rig until Dukk and Luna are checked out," Annee suggested.

"Good plan let's go Marr," Bazzer replied.

Two hours later, Mentor and Marr were approaching the med bay doors. Moments before, Mentor had found Marr and alerted her. He had finished with Dukk and Luna. They were ready for visitors.

Mentor opened the door and held it for Marr. Dukk and Luna were sitting up on the med bay beds chatting. Dukk was wearing only gym shorts. Luna wasn't in much more. Their bodies showed bruising and signs of Mentor's medical work.

"So, you aren't from Utopiam?"

"No, I grew up in Kuedia?"

"What was that like?"

"Growing up?"

"Yep."

"The same as for you, I suspect. School until ten, then labour rotation until eighteen when I joined a rig as an apprentice."

"What was your favourite job before joining the rig?"

"Anything in the port. Cleaning, maintenance, unloading, loading. I just loved being around the rigs. What about you? What was your favourite job?"

"Anything outside that involved heights. I had some of my happiest moments dangling from a lanyard to clean windows."

"We can arrange that at the hub if you like?"

"I might give dangling from lanyards a miss for the moment."

They both laughed.

"Hey, you two, ready to get back to work?" Marr asked.

"Yep, all stitched back together and good to go," answered Luna with a smile.

"Why, couldn't you manage without us?" Dukk shared with glee.

"Ha, ha. In fact, we did better than manage without you. We even did a little investigation of what went wrong out there. Look at this," Marr said as she flicked her wrists at the screen on the wall.

"What are we looking at?" Luna asked.

"The back of your backpack," Dukk answered.

"Exactly. This is a magnified feed of the propulsion unit just after Luna left the doorway. See that blackened area. Bazzer looked at the pack after we got you both in here. The pack was pretty smashed up, but he managed to piece enough of it together to find this thumb size hole. So, we ran back through the video footage. Now, watch what happens as I run this clip."

They watched the clip. After a few moments, a spider like object appeared in the hole and jumped out.

247

"A nano drone?" Luna observed.

"Yep, that is what we think. The video feeds couldn't offer any other angles to see what happened when it jumped clear. Bazzer thinks it simply disappeared into orbit and we won't find it."

"But a drone must have a pilot?"

"Yes, it does. That is the part of the mystery we have yet to figure out."

"So, someone used a nano drone to take control of my pack? To? Wait. To take me out?"

"Well, most of that is what it looks like. Except, you weren't wearing any old propulsion pack. You were wearing the captain's pack."

"Oh," Luna said as she looked over at Dukk, as did Marr and Mentor.

"Well, I guess if the nano drone pilot thought the pack was on me, they didn't know much of haulier traditions," observed Dukk.

They fell silent.

Dukk looked casually at Luna, Marr and then Mentor. He saw empathy. He was glad he wasn't seeing signs of involvement in the sabotage of his propulsion pack.

He opened his crew comms. "Circle-up in five. Crew mess."

He then disconnected and said aloud, "Luna, time to get some clothes on." With that he got up and made for the door.

2

Marr and Mentor waited for Dukk and Luna to leave the med bay. When they were out of earshot, Marr activated her bracelet. Mentor noticed and did the same.

"You didn't show any emotion at the mention of the nano drone?" Marr asked.

"So?"

"You knew about it?"

"No, but it fits."

"So, you didn't know about it, but you were pretty quick to respond. Bazzer said you were already in the transport bay when he got there. You must have been close."

"Yes, I was paying attention. After what you told me about what Joantyi said, I knew I had to be on hand."

"You think it was her?"

"Either her or Larony."

"Not the observers?"

Mentor looked over from his tidying up of the med lab and raised his eyebrows.

"Point taken. What about the two Mayfield soldiers?"

"No, not them. Best not ask any more about that. Or look into it."

"Okay. So, are Joantyi and Larony a bigger threat now? Does something need to be done?"

"No, Marr, I think they will lay low and watch their backs. The rescue response was too quick. I had no choice. They will now be on alert. They must know I was watching them and alert to the possibility of an attack. Which I was."

"How do you mean too quick? Dukk is quite relaxed about it. I listened to the recordings. They were even making jokes before you got to them."

"Dukk is making light of the risk they were in. I gather to protect Luna from further stress. Dukk would have known that they were in grave danger of breaking atmosphere. I barely got to them in time."

"Oh," Marr replied in a quiet tone. She paused for a moment then spoke up again.

"If you knew something might happen during the EVA, you deliberately put Luna, and me, for that matter, at risk!" Marr said angrily.

"No, Marr. I suspected something might happen. But I did not deliberately put anyone at risk. I also had to protect my cover. You are also forgetting your training. And Luna's. You two are very capable. I must trust in that too. Besides, did you see how quickly Dukk responded. He is more capable than one might expect for a haulier. He has skills too. Perhaps skills he isn't even fully aware of."

"Is that something I shouldn't ask more about also?"

"Yes. We good?"

"Yes, Mentor. I apologise for questioning your judgement."

"No problem, Marr. Remember your training. Remember your mission."

"I will."

With the crew gathered at the table, Dukk sat down. He activated his bracelet and started to speak.

"This morning's incident was disturbing. Clearly someone on this rig is behind it. However, we are not going to investigate it further at this stage."

Dukk looked around the table. Luna looked shocked. Marr looked curious. Annee sat back with a disappointed expression. Bazzer and Mentor looked on with blank expressions.

"For those of us who have been in this situation before, we know that if we investigate it further while out here, we put the perpetrator under pressure. Investigating may push them into a corner. There is no where for them to go. Feeling trapped they might escalate things and that puts us all at risk. Be on alert, but we go about normal activities. This rig is a powder keg. We don't want to give the perpetrator the reason to light the fuse. Observe anything unusual and bring it to me directly and immediately. I want no heroes. Clear?"

No one said anything.

"I want to hear it! Clear?" Dukk repeated.

"Clear," came the response from all.

Dukk waited a moment for that to sink in. He then continued, "Okay then, let's get back to it. We have repairs to do, and we now have a transport pod and equipment to fix."

"Speaking of repairs. The survey of the rig didn't find much. Just a couple of heat shield panels are misaligned. It won't matter until

Mayfield, and it would be easier to repair them at the hub in Maple Tower. And the damage to the transport pod is largely cosmetic. Mentor lowered the back seats and caught you two nearly perfectly in the space provided. And, in terms of equipment, I've done an inventory of broken components. I'll get them printed and assembled over the course of the day. We will be back to a full complement of suits and packs by the time we traverse again tomorrow morning," Bazzer said confidently.

"Well, looks like I am superfluous at this stage," Dukk laughed.

"Some rest would be a good idea before you try to be less superfluous. And, Luna, I'd suggest the same for you. If you go and rest now, you'll get a solid three hours before you are back on watch," Mentor said in a commanding tone.

"I like your thinking, Mentor," Dukk answered.

"Me too," added Luna.

Dukk stood up but didn't leave the table. He nodded at Annee and Bazzer. They stood up but didn't move off immediately. The others took the hint, got up and left.

"Anything you want to say?" Dukk said to them both.

"Nope, other than I felt you handled it well. It is the right approach in my mind," Bazzer stated immediately.

Dukk nodded and looked at Annee. She stared back at him.

"I am worried that we are in over our heads. A nano drone capable of that stunt, would be expensive. Not something you'd happily send off into space," Annee said eventually.

"Agreed, even more the reason to be very cautious and not create any further waves."

"How can you be sure it wasn't the new crew?"

"Only Mentor was alone when it happened. It doesn't add up that he then put his life at risk to rescue us. It wasn't them. Besides, I already made it clear, we aren't going to investigate this any further. We sit on it for now. Maple Tower will give us some more options."

"Okay," Annee concluded reluctantly.

"Good. By the way, how did you get on with letting Joantyi know we'd not be able to accommodate her or Larony onto Mayfield?" Dukk added.

"I called to her cabin after the incident. She was dismissive. She appeared to not care."

"Interesting. Let's stay alert."

"Definitely."

3

The rest of the day was far less eventful. The traverse the next morning had gone ahead on time. As had the one in the evening. Dukk and Luna had largely spent their time recuperating. They had also spent time together in the crew mess sharing stories. The events during the EVA had created a bond between them. Annee and Mentor went about their routine as normal. Bazzer finished the repairs. And, Marr had spent lots of her time practicing various rig manoeuvres using the simulations.

On arrival into Maple 12, the last system before the traverse to the hub stop, it was decided to have an evening meal together again. It would be their first daily meal since the first time, post launch. The events during the intermediary stop had got in the way. And the day before, Marr and Luna hadn't been up to eating much as they got used to the traverses.

With the passengers settled, they gathered at the crew mess table.

"Who wants to give thanks? Luna, perhaps you would like to give it a go?" Dukk said before they started eating.

"Why not, perhaps we can start our own tradition, or revive an old one?" Luna answered. She then activated her bracelet, lifted her head, and pulled her shoulders back. The others did so also.

"I express gratitude for all that was, is and yet to be. I express gratitude for the skills and quick thinking of Dukk and Mentor. I give thanks for being welcomed so openly to this new adventure," Luna said warmly. She paused briefly, then continued. "Focus on that which is real in the heart. Create the space so that the process can emerge. Honour that which serves you well. Engage in the journey as it unfolds. Thanks, I give."

"Thanks, I give," they all replied.

Smiles were on every face. And the odd tear had to be caught in every eye. They all felt the shift. They felt that something had changed.

"Let's eat before these go cold," Bazzer announced to break the silence and perhaps hide his own emotion.

"So, what is the plan tomorrow?" Luna asked between mouthfuls.

"The docking process or what happens after we dock?" Annee answered.

"Let's start with the docking?"

"Dukk?" Annee directed.

"Marr, do you want to take this. After all, you've been doing little else but practice for it?" Dukk answered. The was a hint of yearning in his tone.

Marr looked over at Dukk with a provocative expression. "Sure, Dukk, but please correct me if I get something wrong."

Dukk laughed awkwardly. The others looked on with amusement.

"So, Luna, after the traverse tomorrow we will reach the Maple Tower system. We will arrive at an orbit lower than that of the hub. We will then request docking clearance. With clearance we will slow down to match orbit with the hub and then proceed with docking. During the wait and adjustment, we will keep the DMD running to keep things more comfortable. However, to dock, we'll have to hibernate the DMD as the hub's own near zero-gravity system will come into play as we approach. The Maple Tower hub is small, so docking pads are external. As we match orbit, we will then maneuver around the hub and then land on top. Access to the station will be an airbridge attached to the port door. This entire process could take several hours, depending on how much traffic is about. How's that Dukk? Was my dedication to practicing used wisely?"

"Yep, that's pretty much how I would have answered," Dukk replied smiling.

"So, that puts docking around midday? What happens after that?" Luna asked, indicating her interest wasn't really in the docking process.

"It depends on how long we intend staying. Dukk?" Annee replied.

"I'd suggest we aim to undock between six p.m. and seven p.m. the day after tomorrow. Let's give ourselves the full twenty-four hours downtime, plus change," Dukk answered.

"So, after docking we will off load any departing passengers, manage any unloading and loading, do repairs, and refuel. We also have to monitor the cleaning crews with their automatics," Annee offered.

"Where does the downtime come in?" Luna asked in shock.

They all laughed.

"Ok, don't worry, Luna," Annee said. "Jobs like those are done during the time you are on watch. While when docked, we won't have systems to monitor, we still need to always have someone on the rig. We need to ensure it is kept secure. The watch roster will continue unchanged, but there is a little more flexibility. You don't even really need to be awake if you are on board. Just as long as you lock the door and keep your comms active."

"Oh, cool," Luna said in a relieved tone.

"This timing works well, Luna. We can do the heat shield repairs tomorrow afternoon. Then we can have the rig refuelled during the afternoon watch, the day after. That will leave the rest of our time pretty much open for fun and frivolity, and a few drinks too," Bazzer added.

"I like the sound of that," Luna replied.

"Yep, stick with me babe. I know all the best haunts!"

"Bazzer, I am pretty sure there is only one bar in this hub," Annee offered laughing.

"Details, details, Ann!" Bazzer replied cheekily.

"Well looks like tomorrow is going to need all my energy. I'm off to get some rest before the next watch!" Luna said as she rose from her seat.

"Hear, hear to that!" Bazzer replied.

And, with that, the second crew meal was done.

4

Early the next morning, Marr was on her own, having breakfast in preparation for starting the watch. She was particularly excited. In just over an hour, they would be doing the last traverse before reaching the hub.

Luna came bouncing into the crew mess and sat opposite Marr.

"Great to see you full of energy again, Luna."

"Yes, I feel great and am super excited about getting to the hub."

"Why?"

"Other people of course. Don't get me wrong, I've loved spending every waking moment sitting here staring at you," she said laughing. "But it's time to meet some new people."

"I see you've been spending time staring at more than just me!"

"Your companion, is that who you mean?"

"Dukk is not my companion!"

"Ha! Got you. Anyway, Dukk isn't interested in me. And Mentor told me that I am to consider Dukk a teacher. Therefore, the teacher to student rule has to apply. He was very specific about the no sex part of the rule."

"Interesting that Mentor didn't say anything to me of the sort."

"Yes, that is interesting. Anyway, what is your conclusion on the question of sex in space?"

"What!"

"You know. How have you found having sex in space?"

"It has only been three days!"

"Yes, plenty of time, right?"

"How on Earth?"

"Easy and besides, I am information collecting. What's the harm in having a bit of fun on the way?" Luna said and winked.

"Way too much information for me. And look if Mentor has you on some sort of mission, it's between you and him."

"There's no mission. I'm just taking the initiative."

"So, did you learn anything? By that, you know I mean information."

"Let's just say there are no tourists on this rig. I don't have any specifics, but that's pretty clear."

"What? Who? Really! No wait! I don't want to know!"

"Look just because your companion is holding out, don't be passing judgment on me!" Luna replied cheekily.

"For the last time, Dukk is not my companion and what he does or doesn't do with his body has nothing to do with me!"

"Hah! Got you again," Luna said laughing before breaking into a little ditty. "Marr and Dukk sitting in a tree. K-I-S-S-I-N-G."

"Here is me thinking you two were companioned," came a voice. It was Dukk. He was standing in his cabin doorway.

"How much of that did you hear?" Luna asked, surprised.

"More than I needed to."

"Have I broken some rules or a non-negotiable?"

"Luna, what you do or don't do in this regard, has nothing to do with me or have anything to do with any non-negotiable for that matter. Just don't create any bad blood. We can ill afford that, in these confined spaces."

"Noted, Captain!" she replied and stood up. "I'd better finish my walk around."

They both watched her exit the crew mess. Then they turned to each other.

"Got to love her energy," Marr said.

"Yep, you sure do," Dukk replied.

"Are we on track for docking in Maple Tower?"

"I think so. How are you feeling about it?"

"I am looking forward to the real thing. I am a little tired of experiencing it only in simulation," she said smiling.

Dukk laughed. "Yes, simulation is one thing, experiencing it for real is a different thing entirely."

"We are still talking about docking at the hub, right?" she added and laughed.

Dukk laughed too. "Time to get suited up."

"Yep, see you in ten," Marr replied as she got up from the table.

Just over an hour later, the traverse into the Maple Tower system was complete. Everyone was back and stable. The DMD had been engaged in stall mode.

"How about we let Maple Tower know we are here and request docking clearance. Marr, are you up for that?" Dukk asked.

"Absolutely, doing it now," Marr replied.

Marr interacted with her controls and could be seen speaking inside her helmet. Moments later she turned back on the crew comms. "That was very positive. They are busy but were alerted to our arrival and have already cleared a pad. We can commence our approach immediately. They have sent through the approach plan."

"Excellent. I can see it here. I'll authorise it and see how it pans out," Dukk replied.

Moments later he continued. "Right, so slowing down and adjusting orbit will take approximately five hours. The docking sequence should take a further forty-five minutes. So, we should be opening the door near twelve thirty rig time."

"What time is that local time?" Luna asked.

"Maple Tower is aligned to Utopiam time. So, it is the same," Marr replied.

"Lunch time. Nice!" Luna concluded.

"When you are finished, I'd like to proceed," Dukk laughed.

"Sorry, go ahead," Luna added.

5

Dukk returned his attention to the controls. The autopilot was waiting for approval to commence deceleration.

He enabled broadcast mode. "Good morning, and welcome to the Maple Tower system. We have just received docking clearance and will be docked close to twelve thirty. Our expected layover will be just under thirty hours. Those staying with us, you are free to come and go as you please, but please be back on the rig by five p.m. tomorrow evening. Those leaving us here, I wish you all the best and hope you enjoyed your trip. Please vacate the rig by two p.m. so we can prepare your cabins for our next guests. We will be commencing orbit adjustment in a few moments. Please remain seated while we do that. Then you can move about during deceleration. We will start the final docking sequence just after eleven thirty. Please be back in your seats by that time."

"Hold tight. I am starting the deceleration sequence," he then said on the crew comms.

The rig groaned as the thrusters pivoted the rig one hundred and eighty degrees. A momentary rumble could be felt as the TLM H5 thruster engaged for a short hard burst.

Dukk, his crew and passengers were pushed back in their seats as the deceleration sequence was initiated.

"Woohoo. What a ride," Luna exclaimed.

They all laughed.

"So, why can't I see the station?"

"Luna, we are below it and still a long way off. It is roughly over there," Marr answered as she pointed towards the top left corner of the cockpit.

"Oh!"

"Right, that looks all in order. Enjoy your morning," Dukk said as he turned off the seat belt sign and then removed his helmet.

A little over five hours later they were all back in their seats and belted in. The DMD had been powered down and they were weightless again.

Dukk opened the broadcast channel. "Hello again. Our deceleration is complete, and we have commenced the docking protocol. I have configured the main external camera to track our approach. The video feed is now showing the Maple Tower station in full view. In a moment we will pass by the station as we manoeuvre above it and make our way to our designated landing pad. As we pass by, you will catch a glimpse of the station out the starboard windows. All going well we should be on the pad in forty minutes. Please remain belted into your seats during this time as the rig is going to move around a little. I will be back once we are docked."

Dukk turned off the broadcast and returned to monitoring the controls.

Marr did her best to do the same. She was keen to see how much of her practice over the last few days would come into use. However, it wasn't easy. The view was mind blowing.

The station could be seen growing large above them. They were coming up on it fast. While from this angle, they only had a view of the disc shaped underbelly, the scene was still amazing. They could already see the vast array of solar panels and radiation shields. Clear also, were the DMD units scattered along the underside like upside down mushrooms.

The station filled the view momentarily before disappearing to the right as the rig passed by.

Marr turned her head to look out the starboard side of the windshield as the station disappeared. She then looked at the video feed. It showed the upper surface of the station. An array of structures could be seen stretching away. Dotted here and there were rigs and

259

other much larger craft. She guessed they were space-bound rock or ice haulers.

At that moment, the rig shook as the thrusters halted the upwards motion and rotated the rig clockwise by ninety degrees. Marr could now see the surface of the station directly in front. The thrusters engaged harder, bringing the rig over the surface. The rig bounced around somewhat as the station's near zero gravity came into play. The thrusters could be heard working hard to keep the rig from drifting down and crashing into the surface of the station.

"Where is our pad?" Marr asked absently.

"Follow the lights ahead of us. See the red and green flashing lights?" Dukk replied.

"Yep, got them. It looks like a kind of runway."

"Similar, it is just a reinforced section that we can fly over without our thrusters punching holes in the station roof."

"Cool."

"Do you want to handle the docking control comms from here?"

"Absolutely."

"Go for it."

Marr already had the protocol page ready. She interacted with her controls.

"Good afternoon, Maple Tower. Dinatha on final approach. Requesting clearance," She announced into the external channel.

"Hello Dinatha, we are all set. Continue," came the reply.

Marr, turned to Dukk, "We are all good. They are ready to catch us."

"You are really getting the hang of the haulier lingo," Dukk laughed. Marr smiled and winked.

The autopilot slowed the rig down gradually to bring it to a complete stop over a central point. The rig then shook again as the thrusters rotated the rig once more. A further vibration could be felt as the rig moved forward again along a narrow section towards an empty landing pad.

Once over the pad, the rig slowed to stop again but hung there.

"Marr?" Dukk said.

"Oh shit, sorry," Marr replied. "I got caught up in the excitement. On it."

Marr opened the external channel again. "Dinatha. Requesting set down."

"All clear. Please proceed," was the reply.

"We are clear to touch down," Marr said to Dukk.

Dukk authorised the autopilot. The rig vibrated gently as the jack doors opened and the jacks were lowered. The noise from the virtual thrusters dissipated as the rig came down to rest. A series of thuds was felt as clamps locked into the rig's jacks to secure the rig to the upper surface of the station.

A video feed of the port side of the rig showed a structure emerge from the surface and rise towards the side of the rig. The structure stopped when aligned to the port door. A fully enclosed bridge then extended out towards the side of the rig. It stopped just short by one metre.

"Docking control says they are ready for us to extend our port door PBB," Marr said to Dukk.

"On it," Dukk replied.

"PBB?" Luna interrupted.

"Passenger boarding bridge. The sealed gangway that will enable us to move in and out of the station without needing airlocks or g-suits," Dukk replied.

"Cool," responded Luna.

The video feed now showed an enclosed bridge extending out from the rig and marrying up with the station's enclosed bridge.

"Integrity is good. Well done everyone. We are docked," Dukk said moments later.

"Excellent. What now?" Luna asked.

"Luna, what have you been doing this last three days?" Marr said in jest.

"Other things," Luna laughed.

"Well, first, Luna you can help Bazzer shutdown one of the reactors and prepare the rig for slow running. Annee and Mentor will be off to the port door to welcome the security detail. They will come on board and inspect our papers. They will also do a quick walk around to ensure we have no stowaways. After that you can get back to 'other things'," Dukk replied and chuckled.

"Dukk, there is an incoming video hail from the port commissioner. The request is marked is urgent," Annee interrupted.

"Odd, put it through," Dukk replied as he unbelted.

Chapter 17 – Layover

1

Moments later the image of a large, bald, and middle-aged man appeared in the space above the forward console. The man had pasty white skin tones and a bushy, wild and long grey beard.

"Welcome, crew of the Dinatha. It has been too long. And, congratulations, Dukk, on your new command. I hope you had an enjoyable passage," Ileadees said confidently.

"Thank you, Ileadees. It has indeed been too long between drinks," Dukk answered.

"May I extend my hand and invite you and your crew to break bread. I see you have nothing to unload except passengers, so perhaps three p.m.?"

"I am busy," grunted Bazzer.

"Hello, Bazzer. That is a pity. Perhaps another time. What about everyone else?"

"We'll be there. Thank you, Ileadees," Dukk answered.

"Excellent. By the way, I have also invited the two observers. Must respect protocol and all that. Will you show them the way?"

"The bar?"

"Of course, see you all soon," concluded Ileadees, before disconnecting the video call.

"He seems pretty full of himself," Luna said.

"Well at this station he is the top dog. Everyone that lives and works here is answerable to him," Annee answered.

"Is it typical for a port commissioner to invite a crew to a meal immediately on arrival?" Marr asked.

"No, it is not, which is very interesting," Dukk answered.

"Right, Mentor, let's get the door open and the security checks complete. Will you stay with those doing the rig inspection and I'll bring the ID checkers up?" Annee said as she unbelted.

"That works for me," Mentor answered as he followed Annee into the forward ladder shaft.

Dukk opened the broadcast to the passengers. "We have docked successfully at Maple Tower station. Please wait while we bring the station security people on board to check our papers. Our chief mate will escort them to the passenger seating area. Please remain in your seats until the checks are complete. It shouldn't take more than ten minutes."

Ten minutes later, Annee was at the door of the cockpit.

The security personnel had just left and were heading back through the passengers seating area.

"Dukk, I need your assistance at the port door. Marr you might come too," Annee said quietly.

"Oh, of course," Dukk replied, taking her tone as an indication that he should just comply and not ask further questions at that moment.

Marr nodded, got up and followed Dukk and Annee out of the cockpit.

"Are we free to move about now?" Luna asked as they moved past her.

"Yep, we aren't on watch until two p.m. The rest of our jobs can wait until then. We can have a look around this station now if you are interested?" Bazzer replied.

"Sounds like a great idea," responded Luna.

"Let's get out of these suits first. Perhaps we can also get some lunch since the others will be dining in style at three p.m."

"Cool."

Annee, Dukk and Marr made their way down to the mezzanine level. They turned left and made their way across the bridge in the hold airlock to the port door.

The port door was open. Beyond they could see the tunnel created by the enclosed bridges.

Two security persons stood in the doorway, blocking access to the tunnel.

In the tunnel were four tall, slender, but shapely, teenage girls. They were dressed similarly in crop tops, leggings, and knee-high boots. Their faces were made up and their long, straight black, and dark brown hair hung loosely on their bare shoulders. The make-up made it harder to tell, but the shape of their eyes and light brown complexion with red tones suggested to Dukk that they were either from Norline or Genda, the citadels in the largest northern continent back on Earth. Their flustered expressions took nothing from their beauty.

Behind the girls, were two men. They looked angry.

Annee hung back a little and motioned to Dukk to take the lead.

Dukk approached the security personnel.

"Excuse me, may I?" he said. They stood back.

"Welcome, I gather you will be joining us on our trip to Mayfield," Dukk said to the group of girls.

"Yes, that is what we have been told," one of the girls replied confidently. The others nodded.

"Well, that is good, however we aren't leaving until tomorrow evening. Your cabins need to be cleaned and besides, you'll be spending enough time on the rig. Why the urgency to come on board the very moment we dock?"

"These two said we had to!" the girl replied pointing over her shoulder at the two men behind them.

Dukk looked at the two men.

"Captain, just tell Bognath that we have delivered the girls. They are his problem now!" one of the men said angrily.

The girls all started shouting at once. The men joined in and shouted back. Dukk caught but a few words, here and there. It was clear the girls didn't see themselves as the problem. Nor did they agree with being confined to the broken cruiser over the past five days.

"QUIET!" Dukk shouted.

They all stopped and turned back towards Dukk.

"Can I be of assistance," came a voice from behind Dukk.

It was Bognath.

"Perhaps. Can you help shed some light on what is going on here?" Dukk said as he turned around.

"It is clear that these two were not up to the simple task for which they were employed," Bognath said.

"F! you, Bognath. We are pilots not babysitters. Just because your moronic colleagues got themselves locked up, doesn't mean this was our problem. These brats are beyond help," came the retort from one of the men.

Immediately the girls started shouting again.

"ENOUGH!" Dukk shouted.

It all went quiet again.

"Locked up?" Dukk asked Bognath.

"Too fond of drink!"

"Whatever, anyway, you know my conditions of passage. You brought these guests to our attention. Do you vouch for them?"

"I do," Bognath replied.

"Well then. Let's not linger here. Girls, you are welcome to come on board, however you will have to make yourselves comfortable in the lounge or dining room until we have your cabins prepared. That will take a couple of hours. Also, Bognath is your sponsor, so he is responsible for you. However, you are on my rig, and I am in charge. Get out of line, and I will confine you to your cabins. That includes, you Bognath. Annee here is our chief mate so you are also answerable to her for your behaviour. You all okay with all of that?"

"Whatever," came the reply from the same girl who spoke before.

"Sorry! I appear to have not made myself clear. I need each of you to acknowledge you are okay with the chain of command whilst on this rig!" Dukk said firmly.

They all nodded at Dukk.

"Thank you, now Annee will show you the way and brief you on our protocols," Dukk concluded.

He stood back to allow them through.

"What should we do with these?" one of the girls said pointing to a stack of lockers behind them.

"Leave them there, we'll bring them on board for you. Now follow me," Annee replied firmly.

As they disappeared into the rig, Marr whispered to Dukk, "Still not clear who is the bad cop."

They both laughed.

2

Dukk and Marr were the last to leave the port doorway. They had waited there for the security people to conclude their inspection and leave. With the security detail gone, Dukk went to close the internal door which would secure the rig whilst they were docked. He was stopped by a voice from the internal passage.

"You can let us off first." It was Joantyi. Larony was behind her.

Dukk turned around.

"Joantyi, and Larony. Of course," Dukk replied as he stood back.

They brushed past.

"Goodluck with everything," Dukk called out as they headed for the lift at the end of the bridge.

They stepped into the lift, turned, and forced smiles as the doors closed.

"That is it? You are just letting them go?" Marr asked as Dukk closed the internal door.

"Letting them go?" Dukk asked.

"What about the sabotage?"

"What about it?"

"They did it!"

"Whilst that is likely, I want them off the rig before taking it any further. I will mention the situation to the port commissioner, he may be willing to confront them."

"They nearly killed you and Luna. What will confronting them achieve?"

"Confronting them will allow justice to prevail."

"What do you mean?"

"This place is a haulier domain. It has its own systems for justice."

"How is it any different than the EOs and the Rule of Twelve?"

"Fundamentally, haulier justice comes from the place that good intentions are assumed by default. One is not automatically guilty. Guilt must be proven."

"That sounds great. How will it work?"

"If the port commissioner wants to confront them, it will be done in public, and they will be given the opportunity to respond to the accusation."

"What then?"

"The judges will listen to both sides and pass judgement."

"Judges?"

"Seven annually elected representatives of the station population."

"Who elects them?"

"One vote is given to each permanent resident over the age of twenty-one."

"Interesting. Sounds like ancient ways."

Dukk smiled, "Let's get things organised on the rig so we can get off and visit the port commissioner. He has even given us an invitation."

"Sounds good," answered Marr.

A little over two hours later, Dukk, Marr, Annee, Mentor and the two observers were making their way through the labyrinth of passageways and enclosed bridges of the station. Their destination was the accommodation quarter and the restaurant bar at its centre. Occasionally they came across a large window or walked through an open space.

"Can I ask you a few things about this place?" Trence asked Dukk, as they walked.

"Sure," Dukk replied.

"Do people actually live here?"

"Of course."

"How many?"

"Not sure. I'd say a few hundred plus those in transit like us."

"Oh. Things look a little broken. Is this typical?"

"Maple Tower is like many older hubs. The refineries and much of the plant is now dormant. Mothballed."

"Why?"

"The mining in this system became uneconomical as more easily accessible locations were discovered further away from Earth. All that remains active are the biosystems necessary to keep it usable."

"Useable for what?"

"Refuelling, trade and perhaps lifestyle."

"Lifestyle?"

"Yes, some prefer what is on offer in places like these?"

"What is on offer?"

"The main thing from what I can gather is a greater sense of autonomy. Less control and monitoring."

"You mean elements of chaos are allowed?"

"They are," Dukk said in a provocative tone.

"How primitive," Kimince pipped, having been listening in.

Trence looked confused.

Eventually they exited a tunnel that opened into a brightly lit atrium.

Plants and greenery were distributed around the floor of the atrium.

The three-story high ceiling was painted blue with sections of white to mimic the Earth's sky.

Around the entire wall were windows and doors, serviced by balconies and stairways. The accommodation pods.

In the centre of the atrium was a small, white building. It looked a little out of place. It was not quite two stories high. It had big windows on the ground floor and dormer windows poking through a tiled roof. And it had a front veranda with rocking chairs either side of a large wooden looking door.

That was their destination.

Dukk led the group across to the building, onto the veranda and through the front door.

Inside was a large brightly lit room, with windows on all sides, except the left wall. Along that wall was a bar, fully stocked with all kinds of beverages. A staircase at the back of the room led up to a mezzanine that contained a large dining table. To the right of the table was a door to some sort of room above the right half of the room.

There were a few people at the bar drinking. A smartly dressed woman sat alone at the back wall, and a few others were sitting at tables, eating. They all looked up to see who had just joined them.

Standing at the top of the stairs was a large man. On either side were two of the security detail they had seen earlier when they docked.

"Welcome friends, join me up here," Ileadees boomed.

3

"Sit, please," Ileadees gestured to the group as they reached the table on the mezzanine.

The table was lavishly set for ten, with name plaques at each place. Dukk and Marr were sat either side of Ileadees at the far end of the table. The observers were sat at the opposite end, with Kimince at the head. Annee and Mentor were sat opposite each other, in the middle of the table with some of Ileadees' team on either side.

"So, Ileadees, this is all very nice. We are honoured. What is the occasion?" Dukk asked when everyone was seated.

"A celebration, of course, of your new command. You are spoken highly of. It is also a reunion of sorts," Ileadees answered as he looked at Mentor.

"Good to see you, Ileadees. It has been a long time," Mentor responded.

"It has, Mentor. What have you been up to all this time?"

"This and that. I like what you have done with the place."

"Why thank you, Mentor," Ileadees replied, holding Mentor's stare briefly. He then turned and looked across the table. "Annee, hello again. How are you keeping?"

"Hello, Ileadees. I am thriving. Thank you for your kind hospitality," Annee replied pleasantly.

"You are welcome, Annee. And I extend a welcome to you, Marr, isn't it? I hear you have embarked on a new adventure to be with us here today?"

"Thank you, Ileadees. And yes, I am new to the haulier experience," Marr answered confidently.

Ileadees smiled gleefully, looking at her directly as he did. He then looked back down the table.

"Now, let's not forget our esteemed Rule of Twelve representatives, Kimince and Trence. I hear you are new to this game also. Congratulations and welcome," Ileadees said warmly.

"Thank you," giggled Kimince and Trence in unison. They beamed big childish smiles.

"Well then, who is hungry, and more importantly, thirsty!" Ileadees added quickly before either observer could say anything further. "Let me get things started by giving thanks."

A little later, when the eating was done and the wine had put everyone more at ease, Ileadees turned to Marr.

"How are you finding your first experience of being off Earth?"

"Lots of new things to learn. Some amazing scenes. And lots of work," Marr giggled.

"Is Dukk demanding you slave away every waking hour?"

"Not quite," she answered smiling over at Dukk.

"Being a haulier isn't for the faint hearted. What drew you to it?"

"Adventure. Seeing more of the galaxy. You know that kind of thing?"

"What else?"

"I guess I am intrigued by the idea of meeting other advanced life forms. Do you get others here?"

"No, we only have the biosphere for humans."

"Have you ever met other life forms?"

"Not personally, that I know of," he replied and smiled. "And from what I've heard, it isn't as glamorous as you might think."

"How so?"

"Well, for one interacting with them isn't the same as what we are doing here. You wouldn't exactly be sharing food and wine together."

"Why?"

"Well for one, you have the biosphere challenges. You also have communication, culture, and all that. And you must take into account evolution and different stages of development. Many life forms we have encountered, have largely seen us as food. Besides, any life forms that may be interested in us for more than eating, are not exactly in the neighbourhood."

"Distance and probability, right?"

"Exactly. It is rare to find the right conditions to enable life to evolve to a state capable of breaching the galactic horizon."

"And we can't interact with those life forms that are conscious but haven't crossed the space between space?"

"Precisely, the 'Watchers stop us from doing that."

"What do you know of the watchers?"

"No more than you, I suspect. They are seemingly nowhere but everywhere at the same time. We only have evidence of their existence through the consequences when someone breaks one of their rules."

"Do you think we'd ever see more interaction and presence of similar life forms?"

"Eventually. Some of the early attempts at co-existence are still going. But I can't see that happening anywhere close to here anytime soon."

"Why?"

"Why would we or they, when we have plenty of planets to utilise, closer to home."

"Interesting."

"It is isn't it. Perhaps you and I could continue this conversation, over some more wine?"

"That is an interesting offer. For now, I must decline. I am on watch soon. Isn't that right, Dukk?" Marr replied as she looked over at Dukk.

The mention of his name got Dukk's attention. He had been talking casually with the person next to him.

"Rain check, then. So, now I must take my leave. After all, I have a station to run. It has been a pleasure talking with you all," Ileadees said bowing his head in Marr's direction. "Oh, and to mark this momentous occasion, drinks and food are on me during your stay. Hopefully, you will all make Maple Tower a regular stop on your travels. Now, Dukk, we have some business to discuss if you wouldn't mind accompanying me."

"Of course, lead the way," Dukk replied as he nodded to Marr and then the others at the table.

Marr smiled at them as they rose from the table. She looked over at Annee.

"Let's get out of here," Annee mouthed back at Marr.

4

Ileadees led Dukk away from the table and through a door into an adjacent office. The small office contained a desk, two small sofas and a coffee table.

Ileadees gestured to Dukk to sit in one of the sofas.

"That was very generous," Dukk observed as he sat down.

"The drinks and food? You are welcome. Besides having a rig like yours moving through here again will be good for business. I assume you don't mind if I advertise the fact a little back on Earth."

"Ah that makes sense. It is just business."

"Of course," Ileadees said, smiling.

Ileadees looked at Dukk's bracelet and smiled. "Please," he said gesturing to Dukk's wrist.

Dukk activated his bracelet.

"You don't have one?" Dukk said.

"There are other ways to block eavesdropping out here?"

"How so?"

"Modified implants. Anything is possible if one is willing to pay."

"Interesting."

"Speaking of paying, Wallace asked me to give you this," Ileadees said as he leant over and took a selfie. He then flicked the picture across to Dukk's wrist wraps. "I gather you have the picture app, Antiw?"

"Yes, I do," Dukk replied as he opened the picture with the app. It showed the selfie. A message appeared requesting he accept the credit update. Dukk approved the request and then went into the wallet feature of the app. His crypto balance now showed seven hundred and fifty thousand.

"Wallace is true to his word!" Dukk uttered.

"Wallace's word, that is one thing you can count on."

Dukk looked up. He held Ileadees' gaze.

"You haven't proven to be very trustworthy in the past. Has that changed?" Dukk thought to himself. He figured he would test the water.

"What can you tell me about the broken cruiser? The one the girls were on?" Dukk asked bluntly.

"Not much more than I suspect you already know. It is registered to Craig Atesoughton the Third. It was passing through and it broke."

"No offence, and don't take it personally, but this old place isn't exactly where you'd expect to see a fine cruiser like that?"

"None taken. Let's just say, we have established a reputation for asking minimal questions. It gives us a unique selling proposition and attracts a certain type of clientele and activity."

"Interesting. What type of activity do you think is associated with this cruiser?"

"Like I said, we have a reputation for asking minimal questions and I intend to keep it that way."

"Has the cruiser been through here before? What about others that are similar?" Dukk asked, after deciding he had nothing to lose by asking.

"Our business is our business. We do what we can and that is all I can share."

"Fair enough. Answer me this then. Is it not odd, that it isn't fixed yet? Surely you still have what is needed to support all the repairs, even for a modern vessel like that."

Ileadees laughed.

"Here is the thing, Dukk. Odd as it may sound, every time they fixed what was broken, something else broke."

"Sabotage?"

"Perhaps."

"Do you know everyone here?"

"As best as one can. Many here, come here because they don't want to get known. Besides, how good is it for you? I hear you are getting above the odds to provide passage to those girls."

"Yes, that is good. And, interesting."

Ileadees smiled and tilted his head.

"Now, Dukk, I have things to do. But before we end our little chat, there is something else, right?"

Dukk paused before answering.

"You know about the EVA sabotage?"

"No, but I can guess what may have happened out there."

"How so?"

"I hear things. I also had a visitor, just after you docked."

"Joantyi or Larony?"

"Joantyi."

"You know her?"

"Not before today, but I have heard of her. She is an assassin. But not a good one from what I now gather. Thumpol wasted his credit."

"I was the target?"

"Yes, well you and the rest of the crew. I get the feeling that Thumpol is angry and determined to do something about it?"

"What now?"

"What do you mean?"

"Will you challenge her?"

"This isn't any of my business. You are under contract to an elite family. It is their problem, not Maple Tower's. Besides, she has money too, and I am a simple businessman!"

"You sold us out?"

"What I do or don't do, is not a concern of yours."

"Am I in danger?"

"Keep Mentor close and you will all be fine. Now, with that out in the open, it is time for me to get onto other matters. Enjoy your stay, Dukk."

Ileadees stood up, smiled, and offered his hand.

Dukk slipped out of the bar and slowly made his way back to the rig.

Hearing Mentor talked about, in that way, had spooked him.

"Why did I feel Ileadees was right about Mentor?" Dukk thought to himself. "How is it that I feel so at ease in his presence? I only met him four days ago; however, I feel like I have always known him?"

Dukk didn't get any answers, so he decided to push the thoughts aside, and enjoy the rest of the day. He had a nice buzz from the wine and didn't want to spoil it with worry and unproductive self-talk.

Meanwhile, Marr and Annee had returned to the rig. Mentor and the observers had stayed to finish their wine.

Marr and Annee made their way up the stairs and into the accommodation level. They made their way down the corridor towards the crew mess.

As Marr was about to pass between the two double cabins, one of the new passengers came rushing through.

"Found it," the girl shouted as she collided into Marr.

As Marr was smaller, she slammed into the girl's bare chest. Marr stumbled back, in shock. The girl stood there, confident, and completely naked. Marr looked towards the cabin from which the girl had come. Then, she turned to look in the direction to which the girl was headed. The other girls were there, in the cabins with the doors open. Also, in various states of undress, with hair and makeup paraphernalia in their hands.

"We are going out, whether Bognath likes it or not!" the girl said to Marr.

"Fair enough," Marr replied in amusement.

The girl turned and headed off to join the others.

Marr continued towards the crew mess.

"What is the story with those girls? Their confidence and free spirit put Luna to shame," she said to Annee as they closed the door.

"I guess they are being trained as hostesses. Though, I have yet to see ones this young, that are as confident and brash. An interesting development," Annee replied.

"What do you mean?"

"Their presence on this hub is unusual. As is the cruiser that brought them here. Most traffic on this route now runs via places like Kaytom Beach which are more modern and have far better facilities."

"Someone hiding something?"

"Most certainly."

"Like what?"

"Not sure. We will have time to find out more over the next few days. Now, after that wine, a nap is what I need."

"Me too, but a shower may have to do as Dukk, and I are on watch soon."

5

Dukk found Marr waiting at the crew table.

"How do you want to run this watch? Annee mentioned that we don't really have much to do?" Marr asked.

"That is correct. We are basically responsible for opening and closing the security door. The lock is coded to only those on watch. So, we must open and close it for others to move on or off the rig. That way we can ensure no-one unauthorised comes on board. We also need to keep an eye on the other external doors and hatches. As well as monitor the proximity scanners. This hub is relatively safe, but we still want to make sure the rig is secure and not at risk. And that is all automated, so we really just have to respond to alerts."

"That sounds straight-forward. It doesn't sound like it would take two?"

"True, so we have plenty of time to exercise, sleep or whatever else. If we hear an alert or door opening request, we can have a quick exchange on the comms to see who handles it."

"Excellent. Now that I know that I might get a little rest. Take the edge off the wine. How about a wall ball match later?"

"Definitely."

"Before you go, I have to ask you something."

"Shoot."

Dukk enabled his bracelet. Marr did the same.

"Have you heard of the picture app, Antiw?"

"Absolutely," Marr replied.

"You use it?"

"Yes, it is how I get paid for jobs," she replied without thinking. The wine was still at play, clearly.

"Jobs?"

Marr smiled cheekily. Dukk took the hint that he wasn't going to get more on that for now. He laughed. She did too.

"Anyway, let's take a selfie."

Dukk came along side Marr and took the selfie. He then interacted with his wrist wrap and flicked the picture over to Marr. She caught it and interacted with the app.

"One hundred thousand? What is this for?" Marr replied in shock.

"It is your share of a contract sweetener. The code among hauliers, is that apprentices get a half share. Normal crew, a full share. Chief mate gets a share and a half, as does the First Engineer. Captain gets a double share. That formula applies to all gains."

"Wow! For a three-month gig that is excellent. In EUs, one hundred grand is what I make a year as a Keeper."

"Well, out here there are a lot more risks, so, all being equal, a normal crew member should make twice that in an average year."

"Nice. But this would buy a lot of drinks on Earth. More than I could drink in a lifetime. What else can I use it for?" replied Marr smiling.

"It is standard currency out here. This hub hasn't a lot of extra services, but places like Mayfield have lots of ways to spend it. Have you tried skiing?"

"In snow!"

"Yep, Mayfield is covered in the stuff. At the staff village, you can get lessons and buy lift passes. We have plenty of spare clothing and gear on the rig. Some of it might need a wash, but there is plenty of time to do that before we arrive into Mayfield," laughed Dukk.

"Have you been skiing?"

"Absolutely. You have got to make the most of every moment we have planet side, as there isn't a lot of it."

"Can't wait," Marr said gleefully as she turned towards her cabin.

Later that evening, Dukk, Marr, Annee and Mentor were in the crew mess about to do the watch hand over. Annee and Mentor had just returned from the hub's pub. Dukk, and Marr had just got changed, ready to head there.

"You look hot!" Annee said as she looked Marr up and down.

Dukk spun around. He had caught Marr in the corner of his eye as he exited his cabin. He hadn't paid much attention as she was wearing the customary haulier blue. He paid attention now. Her top was the customary colour, but not style. It was a deep v plunge peplum frill top that was skater flared at the waist. "Annee was right!" thought Dukk.

"Anything to know about, Dukk?" Annee asked.

Dukk said nothing. He was staring at Marr.

"Dukk?" Annee repeated.

"Things have been very quiet with you all off enjoying yourselves," Dukk replied quickly trying to recover his distracted moment.

Marr laughed, aware of the source of his distraction. "I like your shirt, Dukk."

"Thank you," Dukk said in a tone that was somewhere between embarrassment and pride. Embarrassment because he was berating himself for not commenting on her look first. Pride because it was his favourite red shirt, the one that Larinette didn't think was good enough anymore.

"Speaking of enjoying ourselves," Annee said as she smiled and looked between Dukk and Marr. "It is pretty chaotic in there now. The place was packed when we left. It feels like the entire population of the station is in there."

"Sounds like fun. How are the others?" Marr asked.

"Luna has been having a ball. Centre of attention. Bazzer is pretty lively too. The observers are in some state after drinking solidly since the meal with Ileadees. The girls have been watched closely by Bognath and Carltor, but they have still managed to kick up their heels."

"Excellent. Let's join them hey, Dukk?"

"Yep, absolutely," Dukk replied still quite distracted. "Annee and Mentor, the rig is in your hands. See you a little later," Dukk said as he opened and then held the door for Marr.

It didn't take long for Dukk and Marr to reach the pub.

It took a lot longer to make their way through the crowd and find the others.

They found them at tables in the back, near a small dance floor. The girls were dancing with Luna. Bognath and Carltor were standing nearby, giving hard looks to any man that went near the girls. Bazzer was sitting with Trence and Kimince. The observers looked worse for wear.

Luna spotted Marr and came rushing over. She grabbed her hand and dragged her back in the direction of the dance floor.

"Drink?" Dukk shouted at Marr.

"Definitely. Make it a double," Marr shouted back.

Bazzer looked up.

"I'll help you. You order while I use the bathroom," Bazzer said as he slid out of his seat.

Dukk followed Bazzer away from the table and then headed for the bar as Bazzer headed towards the bathrooms.

He pushed his way through the crowd and arrived at the bar.

The moment Dukk got to the bar, he felt a body push up next to him and an arm wrap around his shoulders. He felt a little pressure at the side of his stomach. He looked down. A knife.

"Follow that idiot, Bazzer, into the bathroom or I'll slit you right here. Your choice!"

He looked around. It was Joantyi.

She turned him and the two of them walked arm in arm, seemingly casually, through the crowd, to the bathroom.

"Larony, here is the second fool," Joantyi said as she used Dukk to shove the bathroom door open.

Dukk stumbled in with her. A pair of legs lay half out of a stall. Someone was lying there. The person was not moving.

Suddenly, a shadow appeared from behind. They were knocked forward.

Dukk was released and shoved. He spun around and stumbled backwards towards the sinks.

There was a blur of limbs.

"Nice try, you scumbag," shouted Bazzer.

The knife was now in Bazzer's hand. Bazzer had one of Joantyi's arms twisted behind her and the knife was now at her throat. She froze.

Dukk could now see who was in the stall. It was Larony.

"Yes, your plan hasn't exactly gone the way you'd hoped. Larony has seen better days. Struggle and I'll happily end yours," Bazzer whispered.

Then there was another voice.

"Put the knife down, Bazzer and step back. Do anything else, and I will gladly shoot you!"

Dukk looked over at the door.

Ileadees was standing just inside the door. He had a large gun. And it was pointed at Bazzer. Further security people slid in behind Ileadees, guns raised.

Bazzer dropped the knife and stepped back.

Joantyi laughed aloud.

Chapter 18 – Set down

1

Dukk leant against a bathroom sink. Stunned.

"I'd been wondering when you would show up, Ileadees. I guess you haven't changed," Bazzer said sharply.

Ileadees smiled.

Joantyi bent over to pick up the knife.

As she did, Ileadees stepped forward and kicked her in the face. She fell back on the floor. Her hands went to her face, as blood started pouring out of her nose.

"Not so fast, missy. You've read this all wrong!" he said.

The security people rushed forward and lifted Joantyi up. Ileadees shifted his gun from Bazzer to Joantyi.

"Turns out your credit isn't as good as you thought. Looks like you picked the wrong side!" he said to her.

"F! you, Ileadees. I've done nothing wrong," Joantyi muttered in disbelief.

"I am not sure about that. Looks to be more than nothing in that stall there."

"That wasn't me, and you know it!"

"I am going to let the judges decide. But, from where I stand, it looks pretty clear to me as to what has happened here. Dukk, and Bazzer, sorry for the inconvenience, please head back into the bar so my people can clean this up."

Bazzer looked annoyed.

"I guess that this might square things up between us?" Bazzer said reluctantly.

"I hope so," Ileadees replied.

Dukk looked over at Ileadees, "You said this wasn't a concern of yours?"

"I said the EVA sabotage wasn't a concern. An unprovoked assault, here on my station, is another matter entirely," Ileadees said smiling cheekily.

"Haulier's justice?" Dukk said back, smiling.

Ileadees nodded as he gestured to them to make for the door.

Dukk and Bazzer wandered back through the crowd. Half in a daze. They arrived at the table.

The girls were all seated, pouring drinks from two large bottles.

"Ileadees was just here. He said that these are for us to share. He suggested that you'd need them," Luna said with glee.

"Yippy" said one of the teenage girls.

"Sorry, girls, it is still no for you! Bognath was very clear about that!" Luna replied as she looked up at the burly man leaning against the wall near them. Bognath gave a fake smile.

Marr noticed Dukk's expression. "What's going on?"

Dukk smiled. "Haulier's justice. Let's drink!"

A little later with a suitable version of the story shared and the bottles emptied, Bazzer, Luna and the girls had returned to the dance floor. Trence and Kimince were slumped against each other. They were both snoring loudly.

"What will happen to Joantyi?" Marr asked Dukk.

"Exile, I'd think. If she has enough credit to pay her passage out."

"She'll get away with it?"

"Not quite. She will struggle to shake this. Remember, she failed to fulfil her contract. And I'd be surprised if Ileadees doesn't capitalise on the incident to build his reputation. She'll find it very hard to get work. And, she will have to be constantly watching her back. That will be nearly impossible without her bodyguard."

At that moment, Trence sat up and looked over at Marr.

"I just remembered. Watching you and Luna on the dance floor," Trence slurred. "You and Luna were at the old hanger the morning that sentinel blew up and damaged the Bluilda. By any chance, do you know if that crew that went to the fence line, saw anyone running around with a sniper rifle that morning. My superiors told me I was being incompetent for suggesting a sniper triggered the explosion."

Trence tried to focus briefly on both Marr and Dukk, before slumping back, and resuming snoring.

Marr looked at Dukk.

Dukk turned his head slowly to look at Marr.

"The records showed that we didn't leave the hanger that day," Marr offered cheekily.

"Trence didn't say anything about you or Luna leaving the hanger. Skills not typical for a keeper?" Dukk said in jest.

Marr shrugged her shoulders and smiled again.

"Come on you two, the night is still young!" Luna shouted from the middle of the group on the dance floor.

Marr smiled over at Dukk. She nodded her head towards the dance floor.

Dukk smiled and got up. He moved around the table and put his hand out to help Marr up.

She took his hand. It felt comfortable. She gripped a little tighter. Dukk sensed that and held on.

Hand in hand they moved the short distance to the dance floor. Dukk then swung Marr around and they danced together, in a light embrace. For a moment they were both oblivious to the others and the unfolding events. And, neither could remember being happier than at that moment.

All too quickly it seemed for them, the music changed.

"My turn, Captain," Luna interrupted as the music got started again.

Marr and Dukk pulled apart still smiling at each other.

Luna swung in and took Dukk with her.

"May I," Bazzer asked Marr as he stepped into the space that Dukk had just left.

"Of course, it would be a pleasure, Bazzer," Marr replied as she took his arms and they started to dance.

2

An hour or so later, everyone was back at the rig. The observers needed sleep after all the wine, so they had all helped bring them back safely.

Most were either now in bed or not far from it.

Bazzer and Dukk were sitting at the crew table.

"What happened in the bathroom?" Dukk asked after activating his bracelet.

"Let me start from a little before that," Bazzer replied. "I had been keeping an eye out for Ileadees and his crew. I had seen a few security people, but not Ileadees. Just after you arrived, I spotted Larony talking with one of the security people. I hadn't seen him or Joantyi for that matter, prior to that moment. They headed in the direction of the bathroom just as you appeared and offered to get drinks. I figured that I'd have a little look and perhaps catch what they were saying. I found no trace of them when I got near the bathroom. So, I went in. Larony was behind the door and came at me. I swung him off me and he landed in the stall and slipped. He collected his head on the toilet as he came down. He didn't move. That is when I heard Joantyi shouting as she pushed the door open. I jumped back behind the door. The rest you know."

"Interesting. So Ileadees set them up and Larony's death was an accident."

"Yep, that is how I see it."

"You were lucky that Joantyi didn't get you with that knife. Or me for that matter."

286

"Luck has nothing to do with it. I've been around long enough to know how to handle someone with a knife. Especially, if I get the jump on them," Bazzer replied and winked.

Dukk smiled. "Yes, I am sure you have. Talking of being around for long enough. Ileadees said something interesting to me during our chat after the meal."

Bazzer looked up.

"The subject of Joantyi came up. I asked him if she was a threat. He said, not if we keep Mentor close. What is your take on that view of Mentor?"

"I guess they have history, like Ileadees and I."

"What kind of history?"

"The kind that is good in a fight, I guess."

Dukk paused and looked deeply at Bazzer.

"What are you hiding, old friend?" Dukk thought to himself.

Bazzer smiled as if he could read Dukk's mind.

"Time to retire," Bazzer suggested.

Dukk smiled, nodded, and got up.

Later the next day, Marr found Dukk sitting at the console in the crew mess. They hadn't seen much of each other since all arriving in from the pub.

"Hey," she said as she approached him.

"Hi Marr. How are you?" Dukk replied as he spun around.

"Really good. The entertaining evening and downtime today have grounded me even more."

"Grounded?"

"It has helped me get a better sense of this new life. I feel it could feel like home, some day."

"Not there yet?"

"After spending so many years in the outdoors, on the edge of the wild, largely free to move about as I choose? No, not there yet," she said before laughing.

"You know you could put anything you like on the big screen in the gym? I am sure there are scenes much like what you would have seen beyond the walls of Utopiam. It would be similar to running in the wild?"

Marr laughed even harder. "I like your optimism. But it isn't the same."

"Speaking of not the same. Are you up for a walk?"

"EVA?"

"Yep. Just like before a launch, I like to take a walk, and eye the rig before we get going."

"Definitely. When?"

"In about twenty minutes. Once Luna and Bazzer are back inside. They have been doing the repairs on the heat shields. They will be back in soon."

"That is kind of tight? Aren't we due to leave in a little over an hour?"

"Yes, I have requested departure clearance for quarter past six. However, the heat shields were repaired a while ago. I've been watching the external video feeds. Bazzer and Luna have been doing some training. He is showing her how external emergency repairs might get done. Besides, our walk will only take twenty minutes. We will be back on board well before six and that'll be plenty of time to start the predeparture sequence."

"Excellent. Will I have control of my own propulsion?"

"Yes, but we won't need it. The station's near zero gravity will keep us from floating off."

"That is a relief. After what happen with Luna, I am reluctant to have you driving my suit," Marr said and smiled cheekily.

Dukk laughed and made a rude face back at her.

"Let's get suited up and head down to the mezzanine."

"Perfect," Marr replied as she turned and headed towards her cabin.

"Hey you two. Off to do some more dancing?" Luna said gleefully as she removed her helmet.

Marr and Dukk had just come through the doorway to the starboard airlock. They both laughed awkwardly.

"What is it to you, Luna? Need some more tips on how it is done?" Dukk replied in jest.

Luna laughed as she followed Bazzer out of the airlock.

"Are we all set for departure?" Bazzer asked as he stood at the door, ready to close it for Marr and Dukk.

"Yep. Everyone is back on board and the departure request has been confirmed. We are going for release at six fifteen. Is everything in order with this old bird?" Dukk replied.

"Yep, as ready as it can be. We'll fire it up once you two are back in," Bazzer replied before closing the door.

Dukk went out the door and down the ladder first. He looked up as Marr made her way out the starboard door and tried to use the ladder.

"Turn yourself around and then just use the ladder as a guide. Your weight will bring you down. Use your hands on the ladder to slow the drop," Dukk said into their comms.

Marr turned and started to drop slowly. As instructed, she used the ladder rails to control her descent speed. She bounced gently as she touched the pad.

"Cool," she said into the comms.

"Right, I'll follow you. Let's go clockwise. Walk gently towards the starboard wing. We'll go under it and get a look at the heat shields."

"Perfect. On my way."

Marr headed off gingerly at first but then sped up to a slow walk.

When they got to the wing, Dukk came up beside her.

"How did that feel?"

"Fine, easier than I thought."

"Great. It all looks good here, let's keep going. See if you can keep up," Dukk said smiling over at her.

Dukk bounced into a fast walk and headed towards the back of the rig.

When he got there, he planted his legs and turned suddenly.

Marr collided into him. Arm in arm, they tumbled gently a couple of times.

"You did that on purpose," Marr laughed.

"I didn't want to disappoint Luna," Dukk laughed back.

"Hey, you two, stop messing about, or we'll never get underway!" said a voice into the crew comms. It was Annee.

"Right you are, boss," Dukk replied.

They both laughed harder as they got back to their feet.

3

Thirty minutes later, everyone was seated ready for departure. Dukk turned to Marr.

"I am engaging the autopilot to take us off the pad. Let's request release and get underway."

"On it," came the reply as she interacted with her console. "Maple Tower, this is the Dinatha requesting release."

The rig trembled slightly as the thrusters prepared to take the weight.

A video feed of the underbelly showed the rig's jacks. The station's clamps retracted, and the rig lifted a fraction.

"We are released," Marr said.

"Retracting jacks, let's go," Dukk added.

The rig started to move backwards, retracing the path it had taken the day before.

Several minutes later, the rig was clear of the station and accelerating to reach a lower orbit. The DMD was back online and Dukk had just received the details for the next traverse.

"Looks like we have just over eleven hours until the traverse," Dukk said as he enabled the broadcast channel.

"Thank you everyone for cooperating with our departure protocols and emergency drills. We have just loaded the DMD and are expected to traverse in just over eleven hours at five thirty tomorrow morning.

You are now free to leave your seats. Have a pleasant evening and we'll see you back in your seats near that time."

"Right, time for something to eat. Who's cooking?" Bazzer announced as he rose from his seat.

"It is my turn, send me your orders," Marr replied.

The next three days passed without any major drama. The traverses had progressed on time with only the usual discomfort. The intermediary inspection was uneventful. The crew got into their routine. The passengers did their best to bide their time. And the events prior to and during the station visit, were largely left be.

It was now early on the morning of the eighth day since departing Earth. They had just come out of the last traverse. The crew and passengers were coming around and the rig was back in slow running.

Dukk switched on the rig's broadcast channel. "Hello and welcome to the Mayfield system. Like most inhabitable planets in red dwarf systems, this planet is tidal locked to its sun. Our destination, the resort space port, is in a mountainous region west of the centre point. Conveniently, local time is matched to Utopiam, so it is early in the morning. I've projected the view out the front of the rig on the main screen. In a moment you will get a treat. Whilst most of the planet will appear reddish and dark, as it will all day and night, the resort is about to enable day mode lighting. You should see the resort start to glow as we pass over head. If enjoying the view isn't your fancy, you are now free to move about as we prepare for descent. Hopefully, we'll be on the ground in near on six hours. I will get back to you closer to the time and ahead of breaking orbit."

Later in the morning, Marr and Dukk were sitting in the cockpit.

"Marr tells me that Mayfield air traffic control have given us a green light. Let's get this bird on the ground," Dukk announced into the crew comms.

"All set down here, we are on our way back up," Bazzer replied.

291

"Passengers are back in their seats. We are just doing the final safety briefing. We'll be seated in two," Annee added after Bazzer.

"You ready?" Dukk said turning to Marr.

"Yep."

"Okay, so this will go as we practiced. Once Annee is seated, pass the external comms back to her. You'll have your hands full monitoring thrust and pitch control. Let me know if anything goes into the orange zones. I'll run the nav and Bazzer will be monitoring the rig integrity, which is important as we'll be approaching fast and heavy. We don't have citadel protocols to worry about, but we also don't have a maglev to catch-us," Dukk said out loud, more so as a reminder to himself than an instruction to Marr.

"From what I see on the flight plan, we will be down in about ninety minutes. That is nearly half the time typically taken to breach orbit and land on Earth?"

"Yes, while this planet is slightly smaller, the main factor is traffic. Or the lack of it. Ninety minutes will still give us plenty of time to use the heat and friction to replenish our fuel cells."

"So, we plug the details into the autopilot, then sit back and relax?"

Dukk laughed. "Pretty much. However, there won't be much relaxing up here at the front of the bus. While the autopilot will be running the show, we will still have to stay alert. So, the crew dose will only be enough to stop us passing out during the final approach."

"Oh," Marr responded apprehensively.

She returned to the flight plan notes.

"It says here that our set down will be pad L7 in the hanger of the main space port. I am confused by the use of the word 'main' in the air traffic control directive. The planet notes mention the resort, the staff village, the mines, the support facilities, and the space port. There is no mention of more than one space port."

"The original settlement, used during resort construction, has a space port. I've never been there, but I have heard that Hauliers get diverted there on occasion. Perhaps during large festivals when the main hanger is full of elite cruisers."

"Is it the same as the main port?"

"No, I understand it is smaller and the pads are largely outside. I've heard that there are tunnels between it, the main port, and the rest of the settlement. But it is further away and doesn't have permanent staff. Everything, including getting refuelling tankers would take longer."

"Not ideal."

"No."

4

Near on ninety minutes later, the rig was on its final approach to the space port in Mayfield.

The rig was currently racing towards the landing pad that sat in the valley adjacent to the resort and staff village.

The rig was pointed up at forty-five degrees as it plunged into the valley. The combined efforts of the vertical and main hard burners kept the rig airborne as it approached the landing pad.

At the very last moment the rig went near vertical. The full set of thrusters engaged, in conjunction with the main hard burners. They all pushed against gravity. The rig came to a complete stop. Then before toppling over, the thrusters reverse to bring it back horizontal once more.

The rig was now hovering just above the pad.

As the rig touched down, there was silence in the cockpit.

If conscious, the passengers would have found this experience to be quite unpleasant.

Dukk sat back in his seat and removed his helmet. The final stage was always a shock to the system.

Dukk looked around. Marr was staring out the windshield. Clearly in a state of shock.

"Going to semi-assisted control. Let's get into the hanger," Dukk said as he interacted with the controls. "Ann, any chatter we need to know about?" Dukk asked.

"Nope, all clear."

"Excellent. Marr, are you back with us? I'd like you back on comms and watching that I correctly follow the directions to the pad."

"Wow, that messes with one's system. Yep, I think I am good," Marr replied as she removed her helmet.

"Great, passing comms back to you. Ann, do you want to see to our passengers and commence the related set down protocols."

"On it. Coming, Mentor?" Annee answered as she removed her helmet and unbelted.

"Yep," Mentor replied.

"Systems and integrity?" Dukk asked.

"All good. We will check things first hand, once on our pad," Bazzer replied.

"Marr, when you are ready, let's put in the taxi request."

"Right, on it."

Marr interacted with her controls. "Mayfield port control. This is the Dinatha. We are on the landing pad. Requesting hanger access and taxi clearance."

A moment later, the huge doors, in the cliff face before them, started to retract.

Marr turned to Dukk. "We have clearance. They said the direction markings are on the floor. Pad is unchanged. L7."

Dukk interacted with the controls and then gripped the joysticks on either side of his seat.

The vertical thrusters roared as the rig lifted off once more.

Dukk nudged the joysticks and the rig moved forward gently in the direction of the opening.

As they moved towards the hanger, two AMPs with drivers emerged from the opening. They walked diagonally away from the doors.

"Are those for us or something else?" Marr asked as she watched the two soldiers in their heavily armed exoskeletons.

294

"I'd say they are for something else. But I am sure they are just as effective at taking us out too, if they so desire."

The inside of the hanger was impossibly large. It stretched away into the distance. Both left and right. As the doors closed behind them, Dukk turned the rig to the left and followed the markings.

They passed several smaller, but slick looking vessels.

On reaching the pad, Dukk spun the rig and reversed it in. He nudged the joysticks one last time and the rig came to rest on the pad.

He turned to Marr. "Let's get back to port control and confirm that we are in place on the pad and request the stairs. Can you also request they leave the air wash barriers down for a time. We'll get unloaded right away and the barriers will only get in the way of the nose ramp."

"Will do," Marr replied as she started to speak into her comms. "Mayfield port control. This is the Dinatha. We are set down. Please activate the stairs. We will unload immediately via the nose doors. Please leave the jet wash barriers in place for now."

"Thanks, Marr. Bazzer, let's power down."

"On it," Bazzer replied.

"Hello again. Thank you for your cooperation during descent and landing," Dukk announced into the rig's broadcast channel. "I am expecting security personnel to be with us soon to check IDs and clear us for disembarkment. You are free to move about, but please make yourself available, with papers ready, when they arrive. Thank you for your patronage. Have a lovely rest of your day."

On their left was a similar size vessel. It was not quite as tall as the Dinatha, but slightly longer.

"An Interceptor," Dukk said as he looked out at the neighbouring craft.

"Armed, right?" Marr observed.

"Yes," Bazzer replied. He had unbelted and dashed up between Marr and Dukk. He was now looking out the window with them. "These have less load capacity than that of the Dinatha, but they are fast and weaponised. Some even have stealth tech. They can also be fitted to carry troops. Perhaps two, six person squads. You'd typically find them working in war zones or places awash with pirates."

"What would that be doing here at a luxury resort?" Marr asked.

"Good question," Bazzer replied.

"What am I missing?" Luna asked as she tried to get a glimpse over their shoulders.

"Did you see the Interceptor?" Annee said, having just returned to the cockpit. She laughed at the sight before her. "I guess so."

5

The pondering in the cockpit was interrupted by the arrival of three vehicles in the space in front of the rig. They all swivelled their heads and peered out at the convoy.

"Odd!" Dukk muttered.

"How so?" Marr asked.

"I was expecting the first vehicle. It looks like the port control people. They'll be interested in seeing our IDs and load paperwork. I just hadn't expected them so promptly. The other two vehicles are even more unexpected."

They all watched as four formally dressed people got out of the first vehicle. A door opened on the second vehicle. A person carrying a package got out. The person walked over to the four from the first vehicle. There was some sort of conversation then the package was handed over. The person then returned to the second vehicle.

"Port control just acknowledged our set down and have activated the stairs," Marr said to the group.

Dukk flicked his hands over his controls. A video feed of the starboard side of the rig appeared before them. It showed the stairs approaching the starboard door.

"Bazzer and Luna, will you get the nose door open and be ready to put the ramp out for unloading. Marr can you keep an eye on things up here for now. Annee, let's find out why we are getting the royal treatment today," Dukk said has he unbelted and rose from his seat.

Dukk and Annee opened the starboard door and stepped into the doorway. The security personnel were already on the landing at the top of the stairs.

"Hello, I am Dukk, the captain of this rig. What is going on?" Dukk said.

"Hello. I am here to check IDs and the load paperwork. Before we do that, I have been requested to ask that the four young ladies depart at once. I've also been asked that they wear these as they leave the rig. We will wait here while you fetch them. No one is to leave the rig until they are off."

The security person went to hand Dukk the package seen moments before in the video feed. The package fell open and the contents landed on the floor between them. Dukk reached down and grabbed one of the items. It was a black cloak. He lifted it up. It was long and even had a large hood. The security person quickly gathered the rest up and shoved them in Dukk's direction.

Dukk peered over the security person's shoulder. Four further security people were now on the pad at the bottom of the stairs. They were all heavily armed. The leader of the group, smiled up at Dukk and lifted his rifle slightly.

Dukk wrapped his arms around the cloaks, turned and passed them to Annee.

"All yours?" Dukk said smiling and raising his eyebrows.

Annee looked perplexed but accepted the bundle. She turned and headed back into the rig.

Dukk remained at the doorway. Smiling calmly. Moments later, there was a commotion behind him,

"Let me through," Bognath demanded.

Dukk stepped back.

The security person stepped forward and started to speak, "No one leaves until, Oh!"

Bognath stopped briefly and smiled. The security person stepped back and allowed Bognath to make his way down the stairs.

Dukk stepped out onto the stair landing to watch.

At the bottom of the stairs, one of the persons waved Bognath in the direction of the second vehicle. As he approached the vehicle, the person from earlier got out to meet him.

Dukk couldn't quite hear what was being said. But it appeared heated.

After the brief conversation, Bognath turned, headed back towards the rig, and climbed the stairs.

At the top, he pushed through the security people and then quietly said to Dukk as he passed, "Will you message Luna. If she wants to say goodbye to the girls, she'd better do it right now."

Dukk watched him disappear into the rig. He was intrigued.

Dukk wasn't surprised that Luna might want to say goodbye to the girls. After the first evening in Maple Tower, the girls and Luna had become quite close. The girls had looked up to her. He was surprised, however, at Bognath's uncustomary display of empathy.

Dukk opened a direct channel to Luna's comms.

"Luna."

"Captain, what is going on?"

"Not sure, but the girls are leaving. If you want to say goodbye, now is your only chance. Perhaps see if they need a hand with their luggage."

"Oh. Right. Good."

As Dukk disconnected, Mentor appeared.

"Captain, Annee suggested I come down and watch the door. Perhaps you've got other things to be doing right now," he said.

"Absolutely, thanks," Dukk replied as he headed back into the rig and up the stairs.

Dukk made his way swiftly up to the cockpit.

Marr was still in her seat.

"What is going on?" she said as Dukk sat in his seat.

"Not sure. I noticed the nose door is open."

"Yep, Bazzer had Luna go down first and check for obstructions. Then he opened it using the console here. After that, he followed her down."

"Great, can you bring up the video feed from inside the nose section."

Marr interacted with the console.

"Got it."

"Rewind the recording at triple speed. Slow down when we see Luna."

They watched the video feed. Initially there was nothing, then Luna could be seen walking backwards into the space.

"Keep going a bit further. Ok, stop there. Play forward at normal speed, with the audio up as loud as it goes."

They could see Luna standing there watching the door open. There was the grinding sound of the door motors. Then they heard Bognath's voice. It was faint, but auditable.

"What are you playing at?"

"I am collecting the girls. He wants them in their suite and ready to be inspected as soon as possible."

"Bringing them up to the resort was part of my instructions?"

"It was. It isn't anymore. He isn't happy with you. The orders were to keep the girls out of sight. An evening in the Maple Tower pub isn't exactly out of sight."

"For crying out loud! They were just dancing. They weren't in any danger. We made sure of it."

"He is worried about visibility, not safety. Regardless, these girls aren't your concern any longer. You're fired. He told me to tell you that you should find other employment. Perhaps return to Earth with this heap of junk! Goodbye."

Dukk disconnected the video feed.

"Who is 'he'?" Marr asked.

"Not sure, but very interesting."

Chapter 19 – Unloading

1

The odd events on their arrival had been put aside once the girls had departed and the security checks had been completed. That hadn't taken long.

With that out of the way, the observers were asked to check the seals on the load. With everything in order, Marr and Dukk had escorted the robotic containers off the rig. They had taken them to a load clearance zone in the central part of the hanger.

They weren't waiting long when a vehicle drove into the temporary storage area. It came across to them and stopped. A man and a woman got out. They walked over to Marr and Dukk.

"Dinatha?" asked the woman.

"Yep, that is us," Dukk replied.

"You are the captain? Dukk, right?"

"Yep, and this is my co-pilot, Marr."

"Good to meet you. Suzzona is my name. This is Rezcliff."

"Hi, Suzzona. Hi, Rezcliff," Dukk replied.

"So, this is our beef?"

"Soon to be. I just need your mark on the dockets."

"Flick them to me and I'll look them over, while my colleague checks the seals on the containers."

Dukk interacted with his wrist wrap and flicked the dockets across to Suzzona.

"You made good time. I wasn't expecting you until this evening or even tomorrow," she said as she interacted with the documents floating in the air between her hands.

"We aim to please," Dukk replied cheerfully as he looked at Suzzona properly. She looked a few years older than him. She wore the grey two-piece outfit of housekeeping staff. She was of average height and well proportioned. She looked fit and strong. Her fair complexion was like his own. She had short brown hair and her brown eyes spoke of strong awareness of the reality of things.

Suzzona looked up and smiled. "You planning to stay long?"

"The usual day or so. Any suggestions on how we might best use our time?"

"What are you into? Food, drink, action?" she asked as she returned to looking at the dockets.

"Bit of everything."

"Well, in the evenings, it is worth spending a few hours at The Captain's Table in the staff village. Best steak outside the resort. You should check it out. Definitely good for food, drink, and a bit of action. Ask for me when you arrive. I'll see that you get favourable service."

"Sounds like a great suggestion, Suzzona. Thank you," Dukk replied.

Suzzona looked up from the dockets and smiled.

"Seals are good," said the man as he returned from inspecting the containers.

"And these dockets are all in order. Here is your counter signed copy," Suzzona said as she flicked the dockets through the air towards Dukk.

Dukk caught the virtual dockets and opened them up in the air before him.

"That looks to be in order. Here you go," he said as he handed over the wireless leads for the robotic containers.

Suzzona reached over and accepted the devices. "Thank you, Captain. See you this evening?"

"Count on it," Dukk said as he turned to Marr. "Let's go."

Marr and Dukk headed out of the storage area. As they left, they could hear Suzzona giving Rezcliff instructions. "Take these two to the secure area and we will get them on the postal drop schedule. I'll take the third container to the unloading bay."

"Postal drop? Is that Haulier speak?" Marr said quietly to Dukk.

"I guess. It wouldn't surprise me that some of the load will be shipped to other systems. This is a big resort, but there is a lot of beef in a single container."

Marr and Dukk made their way out of the storage area and headed back into the hanger.

"Lining up some action for later?" Marr asked as they walked. Her voice trembled slightly.

Dukk sensed the tremble and looked over.

"Me, no," he answered defensively and looked ahead. "Besides, there is too much going on at the moment to accommodate that sort of distraction. Just making friends. The staff village can be hit and miss when it comes to food. Everything that doesn't need rehydration, is sourced under the table. If you want a decent meal, and a good night out for that matter, you need to know who to talk to. Someone working in the supply chain would have connections."

"The best produce goes to the resort?"

"Exactly. And even if we had sufficient credits, we wouldn't be welcomed in the resort. It is just like the inner circle of the citadel."

"So, the segregation exists out here too?"

"Even more so. However, here, it isn't hidden behind ideology."

"Oh."

"So, we have a few hours before our watch starts. Do you want to get out in the snow?"

"Absolutely. I found the ski suits as you suggested and washed one," Marr answered enthusiastically.

"Great. Let's hire a cart so we don't spend all our time walking up and down the hanger."

Dukk led Marr over to a series of garage doors near the centre of the hanger. He interacted with a panel and one of the doors opened. Within was a six-seater vehicle.

"I have coded the cart to the rig, so any of us can start it. Jump in. Do you want to drive?"

"Definitely," Marr answered as she climbed behind the controls.

Dukk climbed into the passenger seat beside her.

"Hey team, the load has been handed over," Dukk said into the crew channel as they made their way back towards the rig.

"Great, Dukk," Annee answered. "What does our turnaround plan look like? I am putting together the passenger notice. Bognath wants to return with us. So, I've got two rooms to fill."

"I got a message from Wallace's local contact. Our return load won't be ready until four p.m. tomorrow. I'd suggest we aim for a six p.m. departure. I'll firm things up and put together the flight plan, during this evening's watch."

"Perfect. I'll put half four as the boarding time."

"That works. Now, time for some fun on the mountain slopes."

"Mentor and I were thinking along the same lines."

"Cool. We've got a cart. We are on our way back to the rig. Will you get the ski equipment out?"

"Already done that. Great minds think alike."

"Indeed," laughed Dukk.

2

Twenty minutes later, Dukk, Annee, Marr and Mentor had just boarded a hyperloop. It would take them from the space port, through the mountain and into the adjacent valley. A group of four were already in the middle seats. They too were dressed for skiing. Dukk and Mentor headed to the seats in the back of the carriage.

"So, this is your first time skiing?" Annee asked Marr as they took two seats in the front.

"Yes, any tips?"

"Take your time. Start with the basics and you'll get it in no time."

Marr laughed. "That doesn't help me much."

"Getting some lessons is a sure way to get up to speed."

"I have booked a ski instructor for tomorrow. As we've only got an hour or so this afternoon, Dukk suggested we just take the snowboards and have a laugh."

"Yep, that is what I would do too. And don't worry, Dukk is a great teacher."

"He taught you?"

"Sure did. Helped me learn the skills and build my confidence. He was very attentive, patient, and generous with his time. Mind you, it was before he realised nothing would happen between us."

Marr looked over. "He thought that you and he might be companioned?"

"Yep. Poor lad. I guess he might have a better chance with you," Annee laughed.

"Maybe," Marr laughed and looked away to hide the blushing.

"How did you find your first haul?" Annee asked as she sensed not to go any further with that subject for now.

"I have loved it," Marr replied. "It has been a steep learning curve. The traverse is taking a little getting accustomed to. I have lots of questions still. But I am loving the experience of it."

"What kind of questions?"

"I guess the protocols around certain activities. Like the arrival protocol this morning. I am still confused about when IDs are checked and when they aren't."

"Do you mean the girls?"

"Yes, their IDs weren't checked, but everyone else's were."

"That isn't typical. In fact, I've never known it to happen on Earth, at a hub or on a system controlled by the elites."

"How intriguing."

"Yes, it is. The whole thing has got me interested. I plan to do some more looking into it later."

"I'd like to know more about that too. Will you keep me in the loop and let me know where I can help?"

"Of course, I would be delighted to share what I find."

"Do we really need this?" Marr asked. She was inspecting the oxygen inhaler that was clipped to the front of her jacket. "I don't feel short of breath or anything."

"That's because we haven't been outside. The atmosphere is artificial in the hanger, hyperloop and the places we'll go in the village. The interconnected buildings ensure we are always in a liveable environment. In fact, it isn't that much different than being on a large space station like Kaytom Beach. The only difference being that when you go outside you won't die straight away. A few blasts of that every so often will complement the naturally occurring oxygen levels here."

"That seems obvious, now that you say it," Marr laughed.

"How does the ski suit fit?"

"It is a bit loose, but it is alright."

"There is a ski shop near where we get off the hyperloop. Buying gear there is as good as any place."

"Oh, that's an interesting idea."

"I can help you if you like. Or you could go in with Dukk. He needs a newer suit too," Annee laughed.

"Yes, his suit does look a little worn. Why is that?" Marr laughed.

"He says it is still very functional," Annee laughed. "In fairness though to Dukk, he has been pretty thrifty in recent times to secure a captains share of the Dinatha. However, with that done and with the bonus from this gig, he should have plenty to invest in a new suit."

"Making good use of my bonus was on my mind too. It is settled then. I'll take Dukk shopping."

"This day is getting better and better," Annee laughed.

"Wow!" exclaimed Marr as the hyperloop shot out of the mountain and raced into the valley.

They had gone from the darkness of the hangers and tunnels within the mountain, to a brightly lit valley. The glass sides and ceiling of the hyperloop, gave them a full view of the valley. Ahead was a spectacular array of buildings built into the side of the mountain on the opposite side of the valley. High towers of silver and gold glistened in the artificial light.

To their left was an array of much more modest buildings on the valley floor. The staff village.

The hyperloop took them further up the valley and past the resort. They came to a stop in a building at the base of a snow-covered mountain side.

"You ready Mentor?" Annee asked when they stepped out of the building.

"Yep, lead the way. It has been a while so I'm looking forward to being at the top of a mountain again."

"See you guys later," Annee said to Marr and Dukk as she led Mentor towards the chairlift.

3

"So, what's the plan?" Marr asked Dukk.

"Let's find ourselves some space to practice standing on the board. Perhaps over there?" Dukk replied. He was pointing towards a flat area away from the chairlift and base of the slope. A very high metal fence could be seen on the other side of the space.

"I read up on the indigenous creatures," Marr said as she looked towards where Dukk was pointing. "They sound pretty nasty. Is there any possibility of coming across them on this side of the fence?"

"It is possible. Fences aren't impenetrable. But not that probable. At least not when the artificial daylight is in effect. Their eyes are tuned to infrared, so the artificial white light here keeps them away."

"So, what if we got off-piste and beyond the fences?"

"If there was no artificial light, you would want to hire some armed escorts."

"But aren't we poison to these creatures, as they are to us?"

"True, but that doesn't usually stop them attacking."

"Of course."

"We good?" Dukk asked.

"Before we get out into the snow," Marr said turning back to face Dukk. "What are the chances of having a quick look in the ski shop over there. Annee mentioned buying suits there was as good as any place?"

Dukk paused. He looked over at the ski shop and then back at Marr. She was smiling pleasantly.

"Did Annee put you up to this? She has been saying I need to replace this suit!"

"Perhaps. But I also want to get something a little better fitting," Marr said as she tugged at the loose fabric of her suit.

"Well then, let's go. After you," Dukk said as he pictured her in something that fitted better.

The ski shop had many distinctive styles and colours. However, Marr was more interested in quality and functionality. Specifically, the high-tech suits that could be near invisible to infrared spectrums. She expressed the desire to get beyond the fence at some point. That narrowed their choices down considerably. That made Dukk happy too. He liked things being simple but functional. And he disliked fences. That focus pointed them towards a single type of suit. All they needed to do was get measured up and come back later when the suits were printed.

To save time they got measured up together at the back of the store. Being semi naked around each other was a little awkward. But it was not much more than the time spent together playing wall ball or being in the gym.

With the order placed, they headed back out into the snow.

An hour later, Marr and Dukk were at the bottom of a blue run. Marr had just collided into Dukk again. They were sprawled in the snow laughing.

"Hey, you two, you really need to get a room!" Annee shouted as she swished to a stop near them. Mentor wasn't far behind.

Marr and Dukk laughed even harder.

"We are going to take a break and get a hot drink. Do you want to join us?"

"Absolutely, I need a break from this. The laughing is killing me!" Dukk answered.

"Me too," Marr added. "Perhaps we can find some food. I need to rebuild my energy reserves."

They found a bar on top of the building that housed the hyperloop station. It had a full view of the valley.

"How are you getting on?" Annee asked Marr when they were seated with their drinks.

"Really well. Dukk is an excellent teacher," Marr replied and smiled. "He is very attentive and patient. I am lucky he is being so generous with his time."

Annee laughed.

"Am I missing something?" Dukk asked.

"Yes, an X chromosome instead of the Y!" Mentor said cheekily.

"Well, I am glad of it," Marr said provocatively.

Annee nearly spat out her drink. "Way too much information, lads!" She said after recovering.

Marr blushed. As did Dukk.

They all laughed again.

There amusement was interrupted by the arrival of big plates of food.

"Fab view," Marr said when they had finished eating.

"It is," Annee agreed.

"Pity you can't see much of the resort from here," Mentor added.

"You get a better view of it on the walking trails on the other side of the valley," Annee said.

"Oh, cool. How do you get to them?" Marr asked.

"There are access tunnels from the space port hangers. I can show you if you like?" Annee replied.

"Perhaps tomorrow," Marr said. "I've had my fill of stomping around the snow for now."

"I'd like to go. Luna might too," Mentor said.

"Great," Annee replied. "That will occupy a couple of hours and build our appetite back."

"Perhaps Luna can then show you tomorrow, Marr?" Mentor said.

Marr looked across at Mentor. She knew the look. She had been given an order.

"Excellent idea, Mentor," Marr said.

Mentor nodded.

4

Later that evening, Marr and Dukk where together at the console in the crew mess. They were preparing the return flight plan.

"We'll track via Kaytom Beach as we have a metals shipment to pick up," Dukk observed. "After launch tomorrow evening, we will line up the first traverse for the following morning. That will take us back to WXR22. We then traverse via Layton 16, Layton 1, LX315, and LX306. Layton 1 will be the likely place for the intermediary inspection. After Kaytom Beach we'll traverse via Kaytom 1, MJ3, MJ12, Willpo 3, and Teegarden. Which will be the last system before reaching the Solar System again. That should have us back on Earth around midday on the eighteenth day since we left."

"Great. That looks straight-forward," Marr commented.

Their planning was interrupted by Annee, Luna and Mentor who had just returned from their hike. Marr went down to the door and let them in.

"How did it go?" Marr asked as they made their way back upstairs.

"Brilliant! Annee's knowledge of the trails is extensive," Luna answered. "We got up really high and had a magnificent view of the valley and the resort."

"It helped having that powerful pair of binoculars," Annee added. "Marr, thank you for lending them to us. We could see right into the resort. We could even read the menus on the tables of the posh restaurants."

"You are very welcome," Marr answered.

"I can't wait to show you tomorrow," Luna said casually.

"Me too," Marr replied promptly.

"Right, now it is time to get dressed and hit the village."

"Absolutely, Luna. Let's not delay, as Mentor and I have only two hours before we need to be back here for watch."

"Where is Bazzer?" Luna asked as they reached the crew mess and joined Dukk.

"He is already in the village. He said he was going to catch up with some friends. He will meet you at The Captain's Table," Marr answered.

"Why there?"

"During the load handover, Dukk flirted with a woman that works there. He thinks it will ensure we get good service," Marr said in a comical tone that had a touch of jealousy.

Dukk blushed. Annee laughed. Mentor and Luna looked on with interest.

"Fifteen minutes long enough for everyone to get changed?" Mentor asked to break the tension.

"Only if I am one of the first in the shower," Luna replied as she headed for her cabin.

When the room was theirs again, Dukk turned to Marr.

311

"Did I hear a hint of jealousy with your mention of Suzzona just now?"

"Perhaps," Marr smiled.

Dukk smiled back. "Perhaps we should go on a date?"

"Isn't that what we've been doing already?" Marr laughed.

"A proper date, maybe, without work to do, or other crew around?"

"That would be nice."

"So, it is not just your own company that you seek at the moment?"

"Hold up. No one is saying that. One step at a time. Besides, isn't that your position too?"

"True. And yes. One step at a time. So, not tonight then?"

Marr laughed. "No. Not tonight. Let's have fun with the others again."

"Sounds good. I think that once I let the others out and lock the security door, I'll have some downtime to recharge. It has been a long day."

"Yes, that's a good idea," Marr replied as she returned to interacting with the flight plan.

A little before ten p.m., Mentor and Bazzer returned to the rig. Marr went to meet them at the door.

Mentor was on the stairs first as Bazzer turned the cart around ready for Marr and Dukk to head out.

Marr could see Mentor activating his bracelet as he climbed the stairs, so she did the same.

"In the morning, when Luna takes you hiking," Mentor said covering his mouth. "Take your binoculars. Luna should take her rifle. Identify locations that have a perfect line of sight into the resort's penthouse apartments. Focus on the fireplaces. Get familiar with working in this terrain."

"A job?"

"Not yet. Maybe next time. We are just doing some preparations."

Mentor then deactivated his bracelet as Bazzer bounced up the stairs.

With the door closed, they made their way back to the crew mess.

"You'll have no competition with Suzzona, Marr," Bazzer said smiling as they entered.

"Words travel fast. Why? Was she not there?" Marr replied cheekily.

"No, she was there. Gave our table lots of attention. She kept coming over and sitting with us. But she won't be interested in Dukk."

"You?" Marr said smiling.

"No. Not me," Bazzer laughed.

"Wait, where is Annee?"

Bazzer laughed again. "You are astute!"

Marr laughed too. "But wait, isn't she on watch soon?"

"She stayed on. Suzzona said she finishes her shift at eleven. Annee will be on deck tomorrow afternoon for new potential passengers, so we traded some watch hours. And I need a good rest after catching up with some friends this evening."

"So, it is just Annee and Luna there now?"

"Bognath is with them. They'll be fine."

"Any sign of Kimince and Trence?"

"Nope, but Annee said she gave them some tips on places to stay overnight and venues in the village that might be to their liking."

"Right, then, this should be fun."

"What should be fun?" Dukk asked as he came out of his cabin.

"Meeting new people," Marr replied.

Dukk stopped and looked at Marr. She was wearing a tight black dress that was cut just above her knee. It was sleeveless and had a deep plunging V. She had what looked like a long coat draped over her arm.

"You look stunning. If meeting new people is your plan, that won't be an issue looking as good as that!" Dukk said confidently. He was determined to make up for his blunder in Maple Tower.

"Thank you, Dukk," Marr replied. "I figured I'd dress up after seeing what Annee and Luna were wearing when they left. You have your red shirt on again. It really suits you."

"Thank you, Marr," Dukk replied with glee.

"You ready?"

"Yep, let's go."

5

Getting to the steak house didn't take long. The cart got them from the rig to the hyperloop station. The hyperloop got them to the village and the walk from the station to the restaurant pub took less than five minutes.

The place was busy. The tables were all occupied and there was a good contingent on the dance floor.

"More retro rock?" Marr commented as they made their way through the room.

"Can't beat it," Dukk said smiling.

They found Annee, Luna and Bognath at a table near the centre of the room. It was on a slightly raised area that overlooked the dance floor.

Suzzona came over the moment they sat down. "Hello, Captain and his lovely co-pilot. What can I get for you?"

Marr laughed nervously.

Dukk watched the exchange. He checked his emotions. "Jealousy," he thought to himself. "That is interesting."

Marr caught Dukk looking at her. She knew the look. She smiled cheekily back. "Who is jealous now?" She thought.

Dukk understood the expression and what was being said.

"Touché," Dukk said quietly. They both laughed.

"'Lovely'?" Annee shouted in jest, oblivious to what was going on between Marr and Dukk.

Suzzona winked at Annee.

"I am interested in your best whisky, make it a double. To eat, I'll have the largest steak you can find!" Dukk said smiling.

"Done. And for you?" Suzzona said smiling at Marr.

"I'll have the same," Marr replied confidently.

"Perfect," Suzzona replied and disappeared into the crowd.

After eating, they packed up and headed to another bar. Suzzona had suggested they move venues as she wanted to have a drink with them, out from under the eyes of her colleagues. It wasn't far and Suzzona joined them a short while later. She had changed into a cocktail dress. It fitted in well with the outfits the others were wearing.

Initially they found some stools near the bar. There weren't enough seats, so Dukk and Bognath stood back while the girls ordered.

It was an awkward moment. Dukk hadn't really spoken to Bognath at all over the last eight days. It was the first time Dukk had even really looked at him.

Dukk knew from the passenger profiles that Bognath was eight years younger than himself and that he started out in Utopiam. He was slightly taller than average. He had complexion that was like Luna, in that it was warm brown with orange-red undertones. He had short black hair and brown eyes.

The moment was awkward because Dukk knew more about Bognath's situation than he really should. He started at the only place he could think of.

"You are from Utopiam, originally, isn't that right?"

"Yes. I started out as usual. Failed the test. Did the labour rotation. Got friendly with some of the contracting agents and moved into the protection business. Two years ago, I got noticed by the Atesoughton family and I have been working security for them since. Initially just escorting the staffers and more recently special assignments, like this one."

"A straight shooter. I like that," Dukk thought to himself.

"You seem young to have achieved all that?"

"I guess I applied myself," Bognath replied smiling.

"Annee tells me you will be returning to Earth with us?"

"Yes, Dukk. I got fired, so I am returning to look for more security work. Perhaps I'll go back into small time protection again."

315

"Sorry to hear that. Let me know if there is anything I can do to help," Dukk said sincerely.

"I will, thanks."

"Here you go," Luna said as she interrupted their chat to hand them drinks. "Suzzona has got us a table near the dance floor. Let's go."

They all followed Suzzona through the crowd to a table in a corner. Luna put down her drink and dragged Bognath over to dance. Annee and Marr took off to the bathrooms, leaving Dukk alone at the table with Suzzona.

"This is a lively place," Dukk said to break the ice.

"It is like this every night. Such is a party place like Mayfield."

"So, what is your story? How did you end up here?"

"I suspect my story started out not unlike your own. I got on a rig as an apprentice. I loved it. Would have happily continued."

"What happened?"

"I got too self-confident. Swapped around rigs too much. Tried to get ahead too fast. Ended up on the wrong rig. The captain was a drunken idiot. The rig got impounded here because she hadn't kept up her payments. There were no other haulier jobs around at the time, so I found work where I could. Working in the port is mind numbingly boring. It is also frustrating at times seeing those living the life I once had. The work in the restaurant in the evenings keeps me sane."

"Are there any other options?"

"Yep. I have found a love for cooking. Real cooking. With real food. I am putting some credits aside. One day, I'd like to have my own steak house."

"Excellent. What would you call it?"

"Suzzona's Place," she laughed.

"I like it. It has a great ring to it!" Dukk laughed.

Chapter 20 – Groundwork

1

The rest of the night had gone down pretty much as expected.

Dukk slept for much of the morning's watch. He had to get out of bed briefly, on two occasions. The first time was near seven a.m. He had to let Bazzer and Mentor out. They were off skiing. They had hired armed escorts so they could spend a couple of hours off-piste and do some exploring beyond the fences. The second time was just after nine a.m. Annee had returned. She was looking pretty happy with herself. She winked at Dukk as he opened the door. Dukk just smiled as he closed the door and return to bed.

It was near ten a.m. when Dukk made a proper effort at starting his day.

The crew mess was busy when he left his cabin, showered, and dressed.

He felt a little late to the party as everyone was there. They were seated around the table having breakfast.

"We crossed to the valley behind the resort," Bazzer said to the others. "We went to the original settlement and second space port. It must have been some sight in the day. With dangerous indigenous creatures running amuck. Now it just looks abandoned. The fences are broken in places and the pads are mostly hidden beneath the snow."

"Did you see any creatures this morning?" Luna asked.

"Nope," Mentor answered. "There were lots of tracks, but our escorts said we were making too much noise to come across anything."

"What was it like in just the red sunlight?"

"Much the same as getting around at night, back on Earth."

"The infrared goggles solved that problem," Bazzer added.

"I will definitely have to give that a go," Luna reflected.

"Well not today. We've got a full schedule," Marr interjected. "You have to show me the hike you did yesterday and then we have our skiing lessons at midday."

"Yep, not today," Luna conceded.

"You two are back?" Dukk observed as he approached the table and looked at Bazzer and Mentor. "I didn't hear the door open request?"

"Yep, I was up and saw them approaching the rig. I opened the door before they made the request. Figured, you'd already been up twice this morning," Marr answered for them.

"Thank you," Dukk replied, smiling over at Marr.

"What's the story with the packs?" Dukk asked pointing at the two medium size backpacks near the crew mess door.

"Precautions for the hike," Marr answered quickly. "Mentor mentioned it was much colder outside this morning than yesterday. So, I'd figured we'd pack extra warmth. Just in case."

"Wise move."

"Thanks."

"Are you coming back here between the hike and the ski lesson? I was thinking of getting some skiing done before loading."

"Yes, definitely. If it is anything like snowboarding yesterday, we won't want the extra jackets for the ski lessons."

"Great, I'll wait and come with you. Perhaps we can get some lunch after? It would be good to find another steak like the one last night."

"That would be good, except Luna has to be back for two p.m. for her watch."

"I'll come too," Bazzer interjected. "The off-piste foray was too slow going for my liking. I'd like to come down the mountain a few times at speed. Luna and I can come back together just before two p.m. and in time for the start of watch."

"Didn't you swap some hours with Ann?" Marr asked.

"Yes. Ann is covering a few hours this afternoon," Bazzer replied. "But I'll need a nap after the early start today, so coming back at two p.m. suits me. It will be all hands from four p.m. with refuelling and loading."

"And Luna and I will have plenty to keep us busy. We have passengers to find and get locked in," Annee added.

"Excellent. That's settled then. Ready Luna?" Marr concluded and smiled at Dukk, oblivious to the fact that she had just asked Luna a question.

The others grinned, having thoroughly enjoyed watching the exchange between Marr and Dukk.

A little later, Dukk was doing some paperwork at the console in the back of the cockpit.

"There you are," Annee said as she entered.

"Hi Ann. What's going on?" Dukk said pleasantly as he looked up.

Annee sat in the seat next to him. "I have received some proposals for the return leg. Four passengers. Two couples. They are mining scientists. They have just completed a six-month maintenance contract on the deep drilling equipment."

"Does their story checkout?"

"Yep. I contacted their maintenance supervisor. He confirmed the end of the contract. I also checked our copy of Earth's transit logs from six months ago. It shows them receiving a contract to work on the extraction equipment that collects fuel for the resort's reactors."

"That sounds a lot more solid than what Wallace got us leaving Earth," joked Dukk.

"Yes, it does," agreed Annee.

"Are they paying?"

319

"Their proposals are low. Well below what we got for the outbound leg. And they want to pay partly in crypto. They said they've accumulated more than they can spend here and want to get rid of it."

"I am happy to make less if it means we aren't watching our backs the whole time."

"Agreed. Should we use the standard arrangement for the crypto?"

"I think so. I for one don't want to set up a black-market wallet here. It makes more sense to keep them at the hubs as we pass through them more often. Besides, the rig wallet at Kaytom Beach is basically empty. I organised a transfer to Maple Tower just in case Wallace didn't come good on his promise."

"Great, I'll ask them to organise some transfer slips and tell them to hold onto them until we get to Kaytom Beach."

"Sound. Better they get caught with them than us if we get inspected before leaving here."

"I'll instruct them to be at the hanger entrance by four thirty."

"Perfect," Dukk answered as he turned back to the departure request forms.

Annee didn't leave straight away. She just hovered.

"What?" Dukk said empathetically as he turned back to look up at her.

"Our neighbours have gone. The interceptor."

"Yes, I noticed."

"While I was in the databases, I did some digging."

"What did you find?"

"The Ukendt's registration is private. The registration is hidden behind a legal firm in a central system in the Atesoughton cluster. The registration record simply says that it is a merchant vessel. No further details. The Mayfield Port Authority lists it as arriving three days ago with four crew, no cargo, and no passengers. I ran the crew IDs through our sync of the Earth's databases. Nothing showed up."

"Mercenaries? Sanctioned thugs?"

"I guess so. Odd place for them to be, here in a resort settlement?"

"Yep, it is odd," Dukk answered sincerely.

Annee tried to force a smile for a moment. Then she turned and left Dukk be.

2

Marr and Luna had focused on the job at hand for most of the hike. They had enjoyed working together once more. The terrain and temperature weren't familiar to them, but the activity was. They had identified possible sites on the way up the mountain. On the way down, they had inspected the potential locations in more detail. They took measurements using Marr's binoculars and Luna lined up her rifle to get a sense of the shot difficulty.

With their investigation complete, they headed back towards a door at the base of the mountain. The door would give them access to the tunnels that led back to the hanger.

"What do you think Mentor has planned?" Luna asked absently as they descended.

"It isn't clear."

"Tell me again what he said."

"He only instructed us to find and size up potential sites. He was specific about the resort penthouses and their fireplaces. Nothing else."

"If I was there, I would have asked him about what was coming."

"You know that isn't our place. But as it happens, I did slip up. I asked him if there was a job."

"What did he say?"

"Not yet, but maybe next time."

"So, we are to return with the next load. That's at least something."

"Good observation."

"Why the fireplaces?"

"Not sure. Did you find something odd about them?" Marr replied.

"Apart from them being there in the first place?"

"Yes, well there is that. I'd only heard of them. Thought they were done away with long ago."

"They looked pretty cool. That is the ones that were lit. The flames rising and all. What then?"

"They looked self-contained. The glass enclosures looked pretty solid. I gather they must be automated in some manner. I could not see any stacks of wood or means to tend to the fire."

"Yes, that is odd."

"I guess we'll find out when we find out what the job is."

When they reached the door, Luna pulled it open and said, "After you."

"Why thank you, Luna. Lovely manners," Marr replied.

"You are most welcome," Luna laughed. "By the way, what is the story with you and Dukk?"

"What do you mean?"

"The chemistry between you to is off the charts. You are constantly flirting and yet, you have not been with him. What gives?"

"What I do with my body isn't really any of your business," Marr replied in a cool tone. "And anyway, it feels right to wait."

"Wait for what? Don't you want him?"

"Absolutely, every time I see him come out of his cabin, suited up, I just want to push him back in there and rip his clothes off. And doing the suit cross check! Wow! The electricity is palpable. I am sure we are both lingering a little more than we need to."

"Shit Marr, that is way too much information," Luna laughed. "But now that I know that I am even more curious as to what is stopping you?"

"I am not sure. I haven't been able to put my finger on it."

"Feels to me that you are making things much harder for yourself. You toil unnecessarily."

"Toil! That is it! Luna you are a genius. I've been muddling over the story Teacher reminded me of, the last time we saw her. I couldn't figure out why. The story kept coming to me when I thought of Dukk in a certain way. The idea of the toil both on the plane and the mountain results in access to the wisdom at the end. This speaks to delayed gratification. Perhaps we need to know more about each other first. Perhaps we must understand a little of each other's individual experience of the toil before we are ready to join and share the toil together."

"Wow, clearly space travel doesn't suit you. It has turned your mind to mush."

Marr laughed. She liked that her and Luna were spending time working together again. It had helped her achieve more clarity.

3

A few hours later Marr and Dukk were in a small café-restaurant recommended to them by Suzzona.

They had ordered. Dukk had just excused himself to use the bathroom.

Marr glanced around the small restaurant. Sitting at the adjacent table were a group of four. They looked to be finishing and paying their bill.

One of the four, a woman, noticed Marr looking over. The woman smiled. Marr smiled back.

"The food is good here," the woman volunteered. "I hope you got the steak of the day. Can't beat it."

"We did. I hope so," Marr replied. "This place comes well recommended."

"I see from your jacket you are with the Dinatha."

"I am. You know of the Dinatha?"

"Not until today. We have just secured passage. We are boarding at four thirty. This is our last opportunity to get a decent steak before we go."

"Yes, the steak here in Mayfield is good. Much better than on Earth which is surprising given it comes from Earth."

"Yes, I guess that is surprising."

"Why go back then?"

"You know yourself, surely. The Rule of Twelve stable population rule. If we don't spend twenty, in fifty-two weeks, in our citadel of origin, our IDs get recycled. We become non-persons and can't get back into the citadel ever again. That would prevent us from ever retiring there."

"Of course. So, if you could get good steak in a citadel would you still be here?"

"That's an interesting question," laughed the woman. "It has always been our plan to retire to a larger h-pod in a nicer district of the outer ring. The credits we can accumulate far exceed anything we could be doing back there. Eventually, we'll have enough."

"Things feel pretty nice around here in this village. Why not retire here?"

"It is the light. The light here isn't the same as the Solar System. You must appreciate that as a haulier. We miss real sunshine."

"Yes, true that is something one craves."

"Well, we are off. See you soon."

"Yes. See you soon. By the way, my name is Marr."

"Good to meet you Marr. I am Wendie, this is Marinata, Jemes and Karvine."

Marr smiled as they left.

"What did I miss," Dukk asked as he returned to the table.

"Not much. Just making friends."

Dukk looked around. He shrugged his shoulders as he couldn't see anyone remotely interested in them.

The conversation for most of the meal orientated around the fun that was had by Marr and Luna during the ski lesson. With the dessert done, Marr decided to shift the subject.

"You've done well, from what I hear, to make captain at your age."

"I guess I applied myself."

"So, if you've made captain so young, what is next? Where do you see yourself, say in another fifteen years?"

"I am not sure. I can't see myself retiring like Rachelle. Dividing my days between a small h-pod, exercise, and a pub. That doesn't sound meaningful to me."

"What then? Keep hauling forever?"

"Perhaps, maybe I'll eventually secure enough credit to get a better rig. Perhaps a rig with more power and comforts. Perhaps some defences. Perhaps take on much higher paying contracts."

"Like the Interceptor that was parked next to the Dinatha?"

"Yes, something like that."

"How long will that take?"

"Years. Probably, more than I have got!"

"Why? Didn't you manage to accumulate the credit to get the Dinatha?"

"True. But the system isn't that simple. I'll never earn enough to actually have my own rig, even if that was possible under the Rule of Twelve. The rig will always belong to the citadel that commissioned it. Which in the case of the Dinatha is Kuedia. I only take a line of credit. The more I earn the more I can service the line of credit. That stands to me and over time a larger or longer line of credit is possible. But it will still require someone to sponsor me and that is where it gets really hard. Sponsors expect something in return. Favours need to be repaid. I am not sure I want what comes with all of that."

"What else then?"

"Perhaps I could manage a station."

"Like Ileadees, plump and slow, hidden behind muscle men?"

Dukk laughed. "Well, no, perhaps a fitter version. And I just realised that I am doing all the talking. What about you? Do you ever see yourself out from under Mentor's wing?"

Marr was annoyed at Dukk's comment. She felt judged. "I am choosing my path. I am not under anyone's wing!"

Dukk sensed his mistake. "Sorry, I didn't mean it like that. Let me apologise, take that back and go somewhere else."

"Apology accepted. So, what do you want to know?

"Tell me of your war?"

"What do you mean?"

"Where is it at?"

"Let me answer that in a roundabout way. There is this children's story, long since banned, often referred to as Hansel and Gretel and popularised by the Brothers Grimm."

Dukk interrupted. "That rings a bell. Isn't it an odd story about a poor man and a woman, leaving two children, Hansel and Gretel, in a forest to die because the woman thinks they will all starve if they keep the children? The children overhear the man and woman and try to take measures to get back to the house. It doesn't work and they end up abandoned and lost in the woods. They then come across a house made of candy and cakes. The owner of the house welcomes them but tricks them as she is a witch. The witch cages Hansel and plans to fatten him up to eat. The witch puts Gretel to work helping in the house and helping to feed Hansel. Then Gretel tricks the witch and pushes her into the oven. They escape, return to their home, and live happily ever after. That story?"

"How that you know about it, is baffling. But, yes, that is the story."

"How is this related to your war?"

"So, first we need to agree on what the characters in the story represent. The man and woman represent the masculine and the feminine, over the course of multiple generations. The order and chaos. The yin and the yang. As a generalisation you could say the masculine represents the ideas of industriousness, assertiveness, and curiosity for the abstract. The feminine, you could say, represents the ideas of compassion, politeness, withdrawal, and volatility. Between them, they share orderliness, enthusiasm, and openness. Being older they represent the hardened forms of these traits. As for, Hansel and Gretel, the children represent the younger form of the masculine and the feminine. Also, over multiple generations. The younger form has more potential to create and innovate. It is less corrupted or poisoned by the hard truths of reality."

"Ok, and what about the witch?"

"The witch represents the potential for corruption. The dangers lurking for the naive. Our lesser selves."

"Got it."

"So, let's look at the start of the story with the family in the house. The story mentions famine and scarcity. Daily needs are not being met. Our needs are not just food and water. We also need meaning and purpose. An absence of that opens us up to corruption. The corruption blocks our potential. It blocks curiosity of the unknown. It prevents us from seeing contradiction and therefore growth. We abandon reason and compassion. We only seek confirmation of what we already know. We try desperately to hold on to what worked before. We consume. We no longer create. We defend that position even if we know that it will eventually destroy us. The man and the woman see the children as a threat to this position. This all represents a society that has become overly burdened by having, rather than being. A society that is too focused on what one has, not who one is. When a society reaches this state, many can be manipulated easily to think they are threatened by everything, even that which is innocent and teeming with the potential to create."

"That was the society before The Reset?"

"Exactly."

"So how does the remainder of the story fit?"

"So, the man and the woman take the children into the woods. They look to abandon them, cast them out. Free themselves of the burden.

This represents society turning its back on learning. Using everything, for the sake of frivolous pursuits."

"And what of the children trying to get back. Leaving breadcrumbs and the like?"

"Yes, they try to return to their home, twice. The first failed attempt represents two things. Firstly, it represents the innocence of the young, and their willingness to cling blindly to limiting beliefs. Secondly, the first failed attempt also represents a society that has gone too far down the path of corruption. A society that will lie and cheat to protect what it has become, even if that which it has become is rotten at its core."

"And the second attempt?"

"The second attempt to get back home represents overconfidence by the young. They can't go back, yet. They need to learn and overcome their impulsiveness and arrogance."

"And what of the next part, the wandering of the woods and finding of the witch's house?"

"The time in the woods and the discovery of the witch's house, represents attempts by the naive to find a new path, to return to the safety they had before."

"The Reset?"

"Precisely."

"But that led to war and destruction, followed by authoritarianism. The world we have today. Where does that fit into your war?"

"Arriving at the witch's house and her taking them in, represents the establishment of the citadels. The people on Earth were sold the citadels on the notion of keeping them safe, right?"

Dukk laughed. "So, the citadels are made of candy?"

"No, not literally, metaphorically," Marr laughed. "The eco-zones with citadels at the centre, the candy houses, were presented as utopia. The perceived places of pure goodness. A perceived place that would provide for all one's needs. A perceived place where all could be safe."

"Oh, and we are still in the witch's house? The witch represents the overlords. The observers and the EOs?"

"Yes, but don't forget that the witch also represents our lesser selves. We are held back by our own darker side as well. You could even say that there is no witch, just the darker side of ourselves. This is where the evil truly resides."

"What do you mean by that?"

"Hope counters evil. True evil exists in only one place. That place is the intentional removal of choice, either within ourselves or for others. I bring an unnecessary weight to myself that I must carry, or I put myself under a perpetual cloud, when I relinquish my willingness to choose or when I intentionally take choice away from another. That weight is incredibly hard to put down. That cloud is incredibly hard to step out from under. Existing in this place is hell. It is pure evil that put me there. Only I can open that door for myself. Only I can step through it. Only I can bring myself back. Only I can close that door. When there is hope I step away from evil. I embrace choice. I embrace action that ensures others also have choice. This is heaven."

"Wow! That will need some more thinking. Anyway, if there is no witch, who enslaves them. Who puts Hansel in a cage and Gretel to work?"

"They do it to themselves by embracing elements of themselves in unbalanced measures. Gretel becomes consumed by order. She is constantly making, fixing, and doing. She is always working, never stopping. She takes no time to just be. This dedication to order, while commendable in a way, will consume them both and everything around them. Hansel has created a different sort of enslavement. He has chosen self-neglect, and total self-preoccupation. He is living with, and like the animals, in a cage of his own making. A cage of chaos. A dedication that will waste his time and bring no fruits. He will amount to nothing."

"Interesting, so if there is no witch, is there still a candy house?"

"Well, the candy house represents the naive utopian ideals. These ideals are divorced from reality. These ideals suggest that good things come to all, simply because they want it to be that way. In reality, good things require toil and sacrifice. The candy house also speaks to the notion of entitlement. The appearance of the witch just as they start to eat, illustrates what can happen when we become comfortable and start to feel entitled. Our darker and lesser selves come to the surface. We strive to protect what we feel is our right. We lose sight of what is truly important."

"I need to think about that a little more. What about the oven?"

"Great question. In the story, Gretel tricks the witch and pushes her into the oven. You could say that Gretel becomes self-aware. She grows up. She tricks her lesser self and is freed of her own enslavement. The witch going into the oven symbolises this shift."

"What about Hansel? Doesn't Gretel open his cage and free him?"

"Yes, you could say that Gretel uses her awakened state to shine a light on what Hansel has become. To help him see himself. This awakens Hansel from his enslavement. This opens the door on his cage."

"Fine, so now to return to balance, the masculine and feminine must be woken and potential for corruption, the witch, pushed into the oven?"

Marr laughed. "Now, you are getting it!"

"So, what happens next, when the witch is defeated. Does this war have a happy ending, like the children's story?"

"Let's go back to the story. At the end of the tale, the children find their home again. The search for their home has meaning too. Defeating the witch is only the start of the end. They must find their truth, their strengths before they can find home. That process started when they were in the witch's house. The journey home is where that process completes. Remember that the journey includes crossing a river and getting help from a swan. The river represents the void one must cross to gain wisdom."

"And the swan?"

"The swan can't carry them both at the same time. Crossing separately, suggests that order and chaos must find their own path, individually, before they reach their full potential."

"And then they get home?"

"Yes, and when they do, they find the woman is dead and the man is heartbroken. This represents the end of the old society. The corruption consumes itself. What is left is very little."

"That doesn't sound happy?"

"You are forgetting that Hansel and Gretel brought back spoils. They took pearls and precious stones from the witch. These spoils represent the wisdom they gained from the experience of fighting back the dangers, the dark and corrupt side of our experience. It is that wisdom that will help them build on what is left and return to thriving."

"But the woman is dead?"

"Yes, the elements of old chaos are gone, and only fragments of industriousness, assertiveness, and curiosity for the abstract, remain. Just some elements of order. Elements needed to embrace the potential again. But remember, Hansel and Gretel also represent order and chaos, just a younger version. Using what is left of old order, culture, the man, they can work to bring back balance."

"I like the sound of that, working to bring back balance," Dukk said smiling. "Speaking of work, it is time we got back to it. It is nearly four p.m. Shall we get going?"

"Absolutely. Let's go," Marr answered, smiling, and holding his stare.

5

On exiting the Hyperloop at the space port, Marr and Dukk found Kimince and Trence waiting.

"Hello, Captain and Co-Pilot," Kimince said. "We are waiting for Annee. We messaged her and she said she will collect us in the cart."

"Great timing," Dukk replied. "When she gets here, we can all then go to the temporary storage area. There is a RoboContainer we are transporting back to Earth. I'd like you to verify the seals."

"Only one?" Trence asked.

"Only one that requires your verification. We'll also be transporting empties, but they don't need to be sealed."

"Oh, okay."

"How was your stay?" Marr asked looking at Kimince and Trence. Dukk sighed.

"We had a ball," Kimince squealed. "Annee's recommendations were really good. We ate, drank, and danced. The hotel she recommended, The Boudoir, was amazing. It had a cosy little bar, a restaurant, and wonderful views of the mountains. We will have to stay there again."

"What did you like about the stay, Trence?" Marr asked, half regretting she'd asked anything about it all. She was hoping Trence's input would calm Kimince down a little.

"I was fascinated by the fireplace in the bar at The Boudoir," Trence replied calmly. "It was huge and occupied the centre of the room. It roared with a purple fire all evening. Did you know it has to be completely self-contained with special smash proof glass? This is because the indigenous wood releases toxic fumes when it burns. These fumes are invisible, odourless and would kill us if we were to inhale them for too long."

"That is interesting," Marr answered in a soft tone hoping to hide the connection she'd just made to Mentor's instructions.

"Here is our ride," Dukk offered seeing Annee on approach.

"Hello you lot. Need a lift?" Annee said cheerfully as she pulled up near the hyperloop station.

"Absolutely," Dukk replied. "Can we go via the temporary storage area. The load is ready to be collected?"

"Of course. Let's get Kimince and Trence's lockers into the brackets on the back of the cart, and we'll be off."

Ten minutes later, the seals on the container had been verified. Annee had left Marr and Dukk in the storage area and returned to the rig with Kimince and Trence.

"Let's leave this container here for a minute and buy some empties over in the holding area," Dukk said as they watched Annee, and the others disappear in the direction of the rig.

"Empties?" Marr replied.

"Empty containers and crates. We can sell them in the hub or back on earth. It helps sweeten the deal."

"How does that work? This feels a little informal."

"Some of it is and some of it isn't. Most of the time, we aim to secure a round trip as part of the contract. The buyer, via the agent, is responsible for our fees, fuel, insurance, and overheads. In return we carry the load of their choosing. The buyer is generally only interested in the outward load. Earth's fresh produce. The agent might choose to cut a deal and carry some of the costs and risk. Buyers like that. The agent then recoups that via return loads. Since there isn't a lot of demand for Earth bound loads, the agent doesn't always fill our hold. When we get space, we can pick up some empties and make a little margin of our own. The profit isn't much, but it will buy a few rounds."

"Who buys the empties?"

"Traders. The hubs, like Kaytom Beach, service metals mines so they are always looking for RoboContainers to carry loads. It is more efficient than loading the canisters individually. Also, Earth needs them to reload produce. So, they have some value there too."

"Cool."

With the three robotic containers in tow, Marr and Dukk made their way back towards the rig.

Halfway there, they were met by Annee and Mentor in the cart.

"Dukk," Annee said as she stopped the cart near them. "The passengers have just arrived at the Hyperloop station. Do you want to collect them and do your sermon? Mentor and I will bring these containers the rest of the way."

"Good plan. I was about to contact port control and get them to lower the air wash barriers, so we can open the nose door."

333

"Done and done."

"You are a model of efficiency today, Ann."

"What are you saying about every other day?" Annee laughed.

An hour later, just after five p.m., Dukk and his crew were seated around the table for their pre-departure circle-up.

"Good evening, everyone," Dukk said. "I hope you enjoyed the brief time here in Mayfield. Time to get moving again. How are we looking? Ann?"

"The passengers are settled in, briefed and eager to get underway. Mentor and I are ready to shower," Annee replied.

"All set for the evacuation drill?"

"Yep. I've asked them to be seated by quarter to six."

"Perfect. Bazzer?"

"Refuelling is done. Just need to check the load, then we are in the showers."

"Excellent, Bazzer. The flight plan is loaded and launch permission is obtained, so we are on track for a six p.m. departure."

"What is our path?" Luna asked.

"We are going to be tracking via Kaytom Beach for this return trip," Dukk replied as he enabled the projection in the middle of the table. "Our path takes us back to WXR22, then we head to Layton 16, Layton 1, LX315, LX306 and into Kaytom 6, the system that contains the modern and full service, Kaytom Beach hub. From there we go to Kaytom 1, MJ3, MJ12, Willpo 3 and back to Teegarden. Then it is into the Solar System and Earth. We'll probably take the intermediary inspections at Layton 1 and MJ12."

"Cool," Luna replied.

"We good?" Dukk asked.

Everyone smiled and nodded.

"Right Marr, time to fight for the showers before we do our final walk around the rig and close the door."

"Dukk, you mean, time for the rest of us without en suites, to fight for the showers," Bazzer challenged.

Dukk smiled cheekily and stood up.

Just before six p.m., the rig was ready for departure.

Dukk opened the comms to the passengers, "Hello, your Captain here again. Thank you for your help in doing the evacuation drill and getting seated. We are now preparing for launch. It will take us about fifteen minutes to exit the hangers and then get clear of the settlement. After that we can initiate the hard burn to reach orbit. Please sit back and enjoy the ride."

Chapter 21 – Turbulence

1

"There you are. Got a moment?" Annee asked as she entered the cockpit.

Marr was at her seat interacting with a complex set of screens. It was near the end of her watch. The launch had progressed without a hitch. The rig was now in orbit doing the countdown to the first traverse.

"Sure," Marr replied.

"I did some further research into the situation with the girls we picked up in Maple Tower. I searched our copies of the Earth ID databases we use for verifying passenger proposals. I can't find records of these girls. It is like they never existed. The proposals we received ahead of collecting them in Maple Tower appeared legitimate. It doesn't add up."

"That is interesting. I have also been looking into this."

"Really, did you find the same thing?"

"Actually, I've taken a different approach. Purely by chance."

"How so?"

"Well, I was doing some study of the safety protocols and how the relays work. Dukk pointed me towards the technical documentation. As you know, when we arrive into a system we broadcast details to help in the event that we run into trouble. We share our transponder ID, rig type, flight plan, load classification and number of persons on board. The relay shares this information with relays in other systems, along our flight path. It is used to help mount rescues if that is needed. You may also know that some of the more sophisticated and modern relays also have scanning technology. These scanners are used to verify the broadcast information. It helps prevent piracy and trafficking. The information is stored and accessed by the authorities. Things generally go bad for any vessel that tries to share false information. So, within the relay is a complete history of flight plans and passenger numbers for all vessels that pass through a system."

"Yes, I know all that. But the data is encrypted and tightly secured. How does that help us?"

"So, buried deep in the technical documentation, I came across a back door."

"Really?"

"Yes, I discovered that the relay has a debug capability. It is used for support and upgrades. Good practice suggests the debug capabilities would be disabled when not needed. However, my experience is that debug capabilities are rarely turned off as turning them back on requires physically visiting the satellites. That is usually too much hassle and expensive. So, I prepared a debug packet, with bogus transponder details and put it on the broadcast. The relay responded. I then prepared a new debug packet with the transponder ID from the broken-down cruiser."

"What happened?"

"The relay shared the last entry. I then put null values in the date range keys and the relay dumped all the records it had for the cruiser."

"Wow! All of it?"

"Yep, I have a complete history of the cruiser's movements. It goes back years."

"Anything interesting in that data?"

"Yes, a couple of things. Firstly, it is clear that Mayfield is its home. It comes and goes often, mostly to other systems in the Atesoughton cluster. The data shows it usually has seven or eight persons on board. Which makes sense as I looked up the specs and it is configured for eight people. However, every so often, typically every three months it makes one or two return trips to Earth. On these occasions it has four people on board for the outward and eight for the return journey. It has been doing this for years. The exact same configuration. Never more than four towards Earth and always eight coming back."

"I guess the pattern is a little strange. But it could be explained by the four passengers returning to Earth some other way. Like the four engineers we have on board right now?"

"Yes, I figured that too. So, I also then checked our copy of the Earth designation and ID gateway records. The cruiser doesn't show up in the records at times that match the relay data. There is no record of it landing or departing."

"Perhaps the cruiser changes course after leaving the Mayfield system?"

"And gets the additional four passengers from somewhere else?"

"I guess."

"Or perhaps it does go to Earth but bypasses the citadel ID gateways somehow. It then could pick up four passengers and return without records appearing in the databases."

"The passengers would be untraceable."

"They would."

"And even if someone noticed them gone, they wouldn't know where to start looking."

"True."

"Assuming this is the only rig doing this, that would make eight girls every few months. Untraceable! Hidden!"

"There is something else," Marr said quietly.

"What?"

"The last entry for the broken cruiser."

"What about it?"

"The data suggests it left the Mayfield system earlier today. It looks to be just under twelve hours ahead of us. I guess it got fixed and then followed us into Mayfield. It can't have been on the ground long. Just enough to refuel."

"What does the data say about the destination and number of people on board?"

"Earth. Four persons."

Annee looked up and out into space. Marr did the same.

2

"Hello," Dukk said from the cockpit doorway. Marr and Annee had been so absorbed in the conversation that they hadn't noticed the door open. "Found another recruit for your war, Ann?"

Annee smiled.

"War?" Marr asked.

"Human trafficking," Annee replied.

"Oh!" Marr replied in a confused manner.

"Find anything new?" Dukk asked.

"Yes, strong evidence," Annee replied. "Mayfield is bringing in girls every three months."

"That is an interesting development, but that doesn't feel entirely new," said Dukk.

"What? You know about this?" Marr asked.

"It was clear the moment Bognath mentioned four girls were stranded in Maple Tower and in need of a lift to Mayfield."

"So why accept it?" Marr replied.

"Something told me it was the right thing to do."

"Right thing!" exclaimed Marr.

"We are caught up in something, Marr. Your presence here. As well as Luna and Mentor. The explosion in Utopiam and the damage to the Bluilda. The odd way this beef contract came our way. Also, crossing paths with Ileadees again. It all points to a game. A dangerous game. Trafficking is one of the oldest games in the book. It is hard to know who is involved and to what level. Annee, and perhaps me too, if I am honest, have been looking for angles for some time. And when it showed up on the way to Maple Tower, I felt it was connected. I decided to lean in further. To see where it leads and hope that a clearer path would emerge."

"So, what do we do about it?"

"We be extra wary. Your use of the relay debug channels, Marr, caught my attention, so it's reasonable to think it caught others too. Annee will know things can get pretty hairy out here. And quickly. Cross someone the wrong way and things get explosive. Literally. I feel there are plenty of ruffled feathers already, and we are connected somehow. So, other than being extra vigilant, I suggest we just get on with what we know best."

"So, we do nothing!"

"No, we keep listening. Keep looking. Be ready. And besides, we are now involved. Connected. Complicit if you like. Transporting the girls puts us in the middle of it. That makes things even more dangerous."

With that both Marr and Annee sat back in their seats. Silent.

Dukk decided nothing productive could come of continuing the conversation. He turned and headed off to do another walk-around.

After the traverse, and before retiring for some well needed rest, Marr went looking for Mentor.

She found him doing a routine inspection of the hold.

"I want to talk to you about something," she said as she enabled her bracelet.

"Trafficking?"

"You know too!"

"Too?" Mentor smiled.

"Annee and Dukk have been concerned about it for some time. They are looking for angles. We uncovered clear evidence that someone is bringing girls to Mayfield."

"Their interest in this subject hasn't gone as unnoticed as they might hope."

"Is that why we are here?"

"It is connected."

"By connected you mean to stop it, right?"

"It is complicated."

"Whose side are you on?"

"The same side as you. The right side!"

Marr looked deeply at Mentor. He held her stare. His expression was calm and pleasant.

"So, what do we do?" Marr asked.

"We be extra vigilant."

"That is what Dukk said. It is infuriating."

"This is very dangerous territory. More than you can ever imagine. I need you to trust me and stand down, for now. There will be a time when you will be called on. But not yet."

Marr looked down. She sighed. "Mentor! Luna and I saw the girls. It was when we were taking measurements this morning; using the binoculars to size up the penthouses. We saw stuff that I am struggling to rationalise."

"What did you see?"

"There is a large room amongst the penthouses. It is filled with strange looking apparatus. Swings. Chains. Lots of leather stuff. Adjacent to that room is an accommodation area. Lounges and beds. The girls were there. They were dancing around dressed in strange leather outfits. They were talking about some sort of parade and the need to practice. They mentioned that the flimsy leather outfits were needed for the performance."

"You were listening in?"

"I had to know more about what was going on. There was clearly narcotics. Loads of it. Piles of the stuff. The girls were clearly into it. It was eleven a.m. in the morning. Who does that?"

"This isn't good news, but it is not new to me."

"You know about this and allowed it to happen?"

"It is complicated."

"You are getting repetitive! So, we do nothing!" Marr said raising her voice.

"No, we focus on doing what we do best."

"That is also what Dukk said. Surprising really since you've never met prior to meeting in The Triggerarti, ten days ago."

"Who said we haven't met before!"

"Dukk, for one. He acts as if that is the case."

Mentor smiled.

Marr stared.

After a few moments, Mentor said, "Anything else?"

In another part of the rig, Dukk was also being confronted.

"Dukk, I am worried about those girls! More than I have ever been since we got wind of it, years ago."

"Me too, Ann."

"So, why the lack of interest in action? Your answer earlier to Marr doesn't add up. It isn't like you to turn away from a fight. We have proof. We could raise it when we get back to Utopiam. The observers could check the movements of that cruiser?"

"Something doesn't fit. We've seen some crazy stuff out here, but something feels different."

"What do you mean?"

"On top of what I shared with you and Marr; I sense something more. Something deeper. I've been having the strange dreams again. The ones I had when I was a teenager. In the dream I am climbing a mountain. It is steep and the climb is hard. I am drawn to climb. There is something at the top, but I can't see it. Just brightness."

"How is that different now?"

"In my teens, I was alone on the mountain."

"And now?"

"There are others climbing with me. I can't see who they are. Also, I am carrying something. It feels very important, but I can't quite see what it is. My gut tells me to wait for a clearer picture."

"What in the world am I supposed to take from that?" Annee laughed.

"Whatever you like," Dukk laughed. "We good?"

"I guess. For now," Annee said with a smile.

3

Twenty hours later, the rig was exiting the second traverse since departing Mayfield.

The g-juice was just wearing off. Dukk had just regained consciousness. He started counting to ten as per normal to fight back the traverse sickness. But there was a noise. An alarm. He rushed the count and forced his eyes open as quickly as he could. They opened. Reflex told him to scan the instruments for the source of the alarm. But that wasn't necessary. The cause of the alarm was right in front of them. In full view.

"SHIT!" Dukk said as he peered out.

Directly ahead of them was a chaotic scene of twisted metal and plastics.

"Ah!" exclaimed Marr.

"Initiating debris field protocol. Not a drill. Stations everyone," Dukk said calmly as he silenced the alarm. "Marr, as we practiced, I need a projection of the scatter pattern ASAP."

"On it," Marr replied in a shaky tone.

"Bazzer, you and Luna head for the engine room. And we are going to need to keep an eye on those electromagnetic wave shields. We need them doing their job."

"DMD?" Luna asked.

"Nope, we leave that offline for now. Just in case. Let's go. Time to put good use to that hatch flip you've been practicing," Bazzer replied as he flipped up out of his seat and made for the hatch that was already opening.

"Annee, will you take over the med control. Mentor, can you get down below and take the console station in the crew mess."

"Roger," Annee replied.

"On my way," Mentor replied.

"Hello everyone, welcome to Layton 16," Dukk announced on the crew and passenger broadcast channel. "Please stay strapped in for now. We are about to experience some turbulence. We should be clear in about twenty minutes."

"Got the pattern," Marr shared on the comms. "Spherical. Dispersing evenly from a void in the centre. Forty percent slowing. Sixty percent accelerating. Three minutes until we reach the debris wave."

"So, we can't go around or get above it. Through the middle it is then," Dukk shared into the crew comms. He interacted with the controls. The thrusters fired briefly, and the rig changed course marginally. "Loading the pattern analysis and enabling the 'Evasive Manoeuvres' setting in the autopilot. Strap in and engage emergency air supply. It will be a miracle if we don't take a scratch or two. Hustle team. The clock is ticking."

Marr reached over to a panel near her seat. She pulled out a small pack and attached it to the front of her suit. Dukk and Annee did it also. The others would do the same once strapped in at their assigned stations in the decks below. In the event of a breach and loss of cabin pressure, the air pack would enable them to move freely.

The alarm started up again. This time it was much louder.

"Status?" Dukk asked into the crew comms.

"Locked in," Bazzer replied immediately. "Systems are all green. Electromagnetic wave shields are optimised for a frontal hit."

"Ready," added Mentor when Bazzer stopped talking.

"Securing the rig," Dukk said as he activated the lock down which would seal all doors and ensure a breach could be contained. When done he said "Brace" into the comms.

The rig vibrated as the smaller fragments hit the shields.

A larger section drifted into view. The autopilot reacted. It initiated a quick burst of the thrusters. The rig tilted to the left. For several minutes, the rig lurched to-and-fro. Smaller pieces of debris were taken head on. Larger pieces were avoided.

Then it all stopped. They were in the void. The other side of the debris field was a little way ahead of them.

"What do you think happened here?" Marr asked as she peered out.

"I would suggest an explosion of some sort. Perhaps within the rig. Reactor maybe. The scatter pattern would suggest the DMD was active at the time when the explosion happened. The AI would have tried to slip into the dark matter. The attempt would have smashed the rig apart, taking part of the rig and, perhaps, the crew with it. Speaking of survivors. Ann?"

"Nothing on the scopes yet," Annee replied. "The relay here isn't broadcasting a destress signal. Whatever happened, it must have happened fast without warning."

"Are there any other craft about?"

"A handful. Our scanners suggest mostly G5 rigs like us. Nothing suspicious. it doesn't look like pirates. Wait, that's odd?"

"What is?"

"The scanners suggest a vessel just traversed. The signal suggests it was not far away, on a similar trajectory, just a slightly higher orbit."

"How is that odd?"

"There is no transponder signal. And I swear until just now, there wasn't any vessel near us. A vessel can't just appear and immediately traverse."

"A vessel using stealth tech can," a voice interrupted them on the crew comms. It was Mentor. "The vessel would have to come out of stealth mode to lock down ahead of the traverse. Check the traverse signature. Does it match that of an interceptor?"

There was silence. Dukk looked around at Annee. She was furiously interacting with her console.

"Yes, Mentor. The signature has the same characteristics as an interceptor."

Mentor uttered something that sounded like the start of 'shit'. He cut himself short before finishing the word.

Marr was in shock. Mentor's behaviour took her by surprise. It was uncustomary behaviour for him. Dukk sensed it too.

Dukk was the first to reset his focus. "Thanks, Ann. For now, we have other things to worry about."

Marr caught her focus too. "If the debris is moving away from the centre, aren't we through the worst of it?"

"Maybe," Dukk answered. "It will depend. Larger fragments might collide and change speed and direction. That could put them back in our path."

The alarm started up again.

"Fingers crossed," Dukk said. "Brace!"

Hitting the other side of the debris wave was different. It wasn't as violent as the front of the wave. The rig's shields simply swept the debris out of the way as the rig caught up to it.

The autopilot continued to lurch the rig about to avoid larger fragments.

They were nearly through when a new alarm sounded.

Dukk knew the sound. He twisted his body and sat forward, so he could look up, out the windshield. Sure enough a large fragment was hurtling towards them.

Dukk flicked off the autopilot and jammed the joysticks backwards in order to engage full power to the forward thrusters. The crew and passengers were pushed forward into their seat belts.

The large fragment shot past the rig's nose. Narrowly missing it. Had Dukk not reacted as fast as he did, the fragment would have slammed into the top of the rig.

"Dammit" Dukk shouted.

347

Obscured behind the large fragment was a RSJ. A steel beam. It shot towards them.

Dukk yanked at the joysticks to twist the rig, but it wasn't enough. The beam hit the shields and flipped up. It spun around and looped up over the cockpit. There was a crashing and a ripping sound.

4

A new set of alarms sounded.

"Status!" Dukk said firmly into the comms.

"Passenger seating area has lost pressure," Bazzer replied, "No other drops. It looks like the breach is contained."

"Trence's vitals are peaking. Blood pressure. Looks like the observer got hit," Annee added.

"Ann, I'll take back external comms, scanners and med control," Dukk commanded. "You focus on giving assistance. I am depressurising the cockpit so you can pass into the passenger area directly."

"Ok," Annee replied as she unbelted. "Mentor, you are up. Get into the stairwell. We'll use it as a temporary airlock to access the passengers."

"On my way," Mentor answered.

"Marr, do another projection of the scatter pattern," Dukk said firmly as he looked over at his co-pilot. "We are nearly out but we don't want any more surprises."

She nodded back at him.

Dukk continued, "Bazzer, the moment we are through this debris, you get a pack on and get out and inspect the outer hull. I'll help with the passengers and do the internal assessment."

"Sound," Bazzer replied.

"Looks like we are through," Marr announced on the crew comms.

The view before them was clear again. The planet raced below them.

"Thank goodness," Dukk replied. "Marr you take over the conn. You need to reset the autopilot and also work the airlocks."

"On it," Marr replied.

"Bazzer, get outside. Luna, you are on systems monitoring. Leave the DMD off and let's continue to run hot for now."

"Will do, Captain," Luna replied instantly.

"I am in the stairwell," Mentor added.

"Dukk, will you depressurise the stairwell and open the doors," Annee said.

"On it," Dukk replied.

Dukk interacted with the controls to give Mentor access to the passenger area. He then activated his air pack. His g-suit inflated slightly. He felt the slightly sour taste of the temporary air supply. It was working. He disconnected himself from the med line. As he unbelted, he tuned his comms into the purser channel that connected Annee directly to the passengers.

"As we practiced," Annee could be heard saying. "Attach the air pack to the front of your suit and press the green button. Your suit will inflate slightly, and you will taste the sour air of the emergency supply. Trence, you stay put for now. On my signal, press the disengage button on your seat and then make your way to the door at the back."

Dukk passed through the cockpit door to the passenger area. Annee was standing in the middle of the space, checking that the passengers correctly enabled their air supply before detaching from the med lines.

The orange pressure warning lights were flashing in the forward section. It was darker in the back. The lights were out. A metre long tear could be seen in the ceiling. A steel beam was floating just above the space between the two seats in the fourth row. These seats were occupied by Kimince and Trence. Their expressions illustrated the horror they had just witnessed. It looked like the beam had crashed through the ceiling and come to a stop at the bulkhead behind the last row.

From Dukk's vantage point it wasn't clear what injury Trence had sustained. However, it was clear it could have been a lot worse.

Mentor appeared from the stairwell door. He was carrying a med kit and a stretcher. He stepped out of the way as the other passengers passed into the stairwell.

Dukk followed them towards the door.

"Dukk, will you help Mentor whilst I get everyone else to the accommodation level?" Annee asked in the comms link.

"Will do," Dukk replied as he closed the door behind Annee and the other passengers.

"Pressurising the stairwell," came Marr's voice into the crew comms. Dukk smiled. She was on the ball.

Dukk returned his attention to helping Mentor.

"What have we got?" Dukk said.

"Looks like the beam hit Trence's arm as it came through," Mentor answered. "The impact caused some bleeding. The lower arm might be broken. Thankfully, the suit didn't get ruptured."

"What can I do to help?"

"Let's use the stretcher. Trence is in shock, and it will be easier using the stretcher. I'll just pin the arm for now."

It didn't take long for Dukk and Mentor to help Trence out of the seat and get strapped to the stretcher.

Between them they used the stretcher to float Trence over to the stairwell door. Annee was there when they got there. She helped get Trence and the stretcher through the door and into the stair well.

"Are you two good from here? I want to inspect the damage," Dukk asked from the doorway.

"Yep, we've got it," Annee replied.

With the stairwell door closed again, Dukk returned to look at the hole in the ceiling.

"Looks like we were lucky," came a voice on the crew comms. It was Bazzer. He came into view on the other side of the hole.

"So, it doesn't look that bad from out there," Dukk stated.

"Nope. Looks pretty straightforward. We'll print what needs replacing, cut the damage out and then fix it. Several hours work, but doable. Quicker with a little help."

"Yep, hint taken. You take the measurements, then get back inside so we can temporarily bring the DMD back online. I'll organise a posse and we'll get it done. Now, I'm going to check in with the others."

"Excellent. Before you go, push that beam back up through the hole. It will be easier to move now than when the DMD is back on. I'll push it towards the planet. Better to have it burn up than up here with us."

"Superstition? It is just a chunk of metal."

"That chunk of metal is now tainted with bad luck. The sooner it is away from here the better."

"Fine. Whatever, Bazzer," Dukk laughed.

Dukk enabled the broadcast on his comms, as he made his way back to the cockpit.

"Good evening again. Thank you for your cooperation during this emergency. Thankfully, we've come through it relatively unscathed. We will bring the near zero-g back online in a moment or two, so that you can get settled for the evening. It will go off periodically over the next several hours, as we do the repairs. So, as always, please take care when moving about when we are in zero-g. Recovery and repairs will hopefully be completed by this time tomorrow and we'll resume our progress. We'll make up the lost time along the way. Clearly, the passenger seating area will be out of use for now. We'll let you know when you can use it again. Once more, thank you for your cooperation. Good evening."

351

5

The next twelve hours were intense. The night had passed with little rest.

Dukk, Annee, Bazzer and Luna worked together on the preparation for, and then doing the repairs. They all helped with printing parts. Dukk and Bazzer worked on the outer hull. Annee and Luna gave them support from inside the passenger area. It was challenging work. Wearing suits and having to take breaks to resupply the air tanks added to the challenge.

Marr had been put in charge of keeping an eye on the rig systems and other traffic. She also worked the airlocks as the others moved about doing repairs.

Mentor focused on helping Trence and supporting the other passengers.

Near six a.m., the repairs were done. Dukk suggested they celebrate by having breakfast together. Mentor had agreed to join them as Trence was resting contently with an arm that was already mending.

"Well done everyone," Dukk said as they sat down to eat. "We have successfully made it through our first hull breach."

"Yes, great teamwork," added Annee.

"What a team!" Bazzer said.

Dukk looked around. Everyone was smiling, except Marr.

"Marr, are you ok?" Dukk asked.

"The breach was my fault!" Marr answered.

Everyone stopped and looked at Marr.

"How so?" Dukk asked in an empathetic tone.

"If I had updated the projection of the scatter pattern when we entered the void, we wouldn't have come so close to the large fragment and then had the breach!"

"There is no way of knowing if that would have made a difference. The large fragment may have only just been dislodged moments before we came near it. Besides, constantly refreshing the projection also takes the autopilot offline for periods. That may have put us in even more danger. Your response, at each stage of the emergency, was timely and appropriate. Your contribution ensured we survived. No, the breach was not your fault."

Marr tried to smile.

Dukk knew not to push it. This was something she needed to think about more.

"Does this type of thing happen often?" Luna asked to break the tension.

"No, thankfully," Annee answered.

"Well, fingers crossed that it doesn't happen again anytime soon!" Luna replied.

"It happens more often than you would hope," Bazzer added. "Mostly we don't get to hear about it. When it goes wrong, there isn't anyone around to tell the tale. The discipline, preparation and practice, which is done on this rig, counts. You don't get to my age by leaving things to chance."

"Is that what happened to that rig?" Luna asked.

"A breach?" Bazzer replied.

"Yes."

"I doubt a breach would cause a rig to breakup like that," Bazzer replied.

"It wasn't a rig. It was a cruiser," Marr observed.

They all turned to look at her.

"What do you mean?" Dukk asked.

"I ran back over the footage of the near miss and then breach. The large fragment had a vessel identifier on it. I already knew that ID. It was the cruiser from Maple Tower. The cruiser the girls were on before they joined us."

Annee gasped.

Dukk sighed and looked around the table. All were looking surprised. Except Mentor.

"Well, this is all very sobering news," Dukk said quietly. "Perhaps after the events of the last twelve hours, rest is what we all need right now."

"Totally agree," Bazzer answered immediately.

"So, how are we looking?" Dukk asked, taking full advantage of the window created by Bazzer to shift the conversation.

"Pretty good shape," Bazzer answered. "The drones picked up a few more things to fix, but they can wait until Kaytom Beach."

"Great, let's get some rest. I need a shower before going back on watch. Anyone want to help Marr and cover me while I do that?" Dukk asked.

"I'll cover you," Mentor answered.

"Great. After the shower, I'll take the conn for a time and let the rest of you all get some downtime."

Feeling refreshed, Dukk headed to the med bay. He hoped to find Mentor alone. He was in luck.

Mentor looked up as Dukk entered.

Dukk stepped into the middle of the room. He stopped and looked directly at Mentor.

Mentor straightened up.

They looked directly at each other for a moment without saying anything.

Then, Mentor swiped his hand over his wrist and enabled his bracelet. Dukk did the same.

"Who are you?" Dukk asked.

"Someone with a history."

"Aren't we all. Let me rephrase that. What is going on?"

"It is complicated."

Dukk sighed. "I am getting tired of the mysteries. Let's try a different angle."

354

Mentor smiled.

"Whatever it is! Whatever is going on! Does it involve a fiery and sticky end for us?" Dukk asked.

"Not if I can help it."

"Is there anything I can do to help avoid that outcome?"

"Yes."

"What?"

"Stop asking impossible questions and instead keep doing what you do. Keep doing what you are good at. Keep this rig moving. And keep the team focused on what they do best."

Dukk sighed again. "On one condition."

"Shoot"

"When I feel that I can't keep doing that, you will level with me."

"Agreed!"

Chapter 22 – Waves

1

Twenty-four hours later, the Dinatha had just arrived into the Kaytom 6 system and the location of the Kaytom Beach hub.

"Kaytom Beach have given us docking clearance," Marr shared on the crew comms. "However, it is busy, so it will be near five p.m. before a bay is available."

"Did they send on the approach plan?" Dukk asked.

"Yep, I am sharing it with you now."

"Let's have a look," Dukk replied as he interacted with the console. "They want us to take a wide and slow approach. That figures. They aren't taking any chances that we might scratch their shiny hub."

"How long before we start the deceleration?" Bazzer asked.

"It is seven a.m. now, they suggest a six hour slow down, so we've got four hours of cruising at this speed."

"Great, I'm going back to bed. I want to be in top form for the bars and clubs this evening." Bazzer shared.

"Thank you, Bazzer, for illuminating your plans for us," Dukk answered cheekily. "Would you mind engaging slow running before you hit the bunk?"

"Of course," Bazzer replied.

Dukk enabled the broadcast mode. "Good morning. Welcome to the Kaytom 6 system, the home of the very popular Kaytom Beach hub. As expected, it will take much of today to get docked. Hopefully, that will happen near five p.m. We'll stay overnight and aim to be preparing for departure at five p.m. tomorrow. As for this morning, at this stage

357

we are aiming to start deceleration near eleven a.m. I'll ask that you take your seats again at that time as we start that process. For now, enjoy your morning."

A little while later, Marr and Dukk were sitting alone in the crew mess. The rig was quiet as most had gone back to bed. Dukk was at the console. Marr was reading on the couch.

"Damn it," Dukk said aloud.

"What?" asked Marr.

"Wallace has swapped the load we are to pick up here."

"To what?"

"Core concentrate."

"The additive used to make hard fuel?"

"Yep. Five canisters in a RoboContainer."

"Won't that be more lucrative than a basic metals shipment?"

"Yes, but also more of a prize for those that might think about taking it off us. The docket says it must be loaded immediately, on arrival. That will mean we'll need to hire some security while we are here."

"Bognath is looking for work," Luna interrupted. She was closing the crew mess door.

Dukk swivelled in his seat to look over at Luna.

"I thought everyone was in bed?" Dukk observed.

"She was," Marr added cheekily.

Luna made a rude face at Marr.

"That is an interesting thought," Dukk said. "Are you vouching for him?"

"Absolutely," she answered doing her best to hide her blushing.

"Well, that might work out well for us all. I'll speak to him later," Dukk replied. "Let's keep this between ourselves for now."

Later in the afternoon, the crew were gathered in the crew mess. Dukk called a circle-up ahead of their final approach into the Kaytom Beach hub.

"We have a slight change of plan," Dukk said. "Instead of a typical metals shipment, the agent notified me that we will be transporting core concentrate."

"How much?" Annee asked.

"Five canisters," Dukk replied.

"Wow," Bazzer interjected. "that's going to sweeten the earnings on this haul."

"Yes, Bazzer, it will," Dukk answered. "However, there is a catch. The handler wants us to take responsibility for the canisters the moment we are docked."

"That's not good," Annee stated. "This hub is big and attracts all sorts. The sorts that might want to sneak off with this stuff. If they do, we'd not find it again!"

"Yes, we are going to need extra security," Dukk replied. "The hub people have agreed to supply some extra personnel on the pad for the duration of our stay. This will be within the terms of the existing docking arrangements; however, we'll need to supervise the security personnel and be on high alert."

"And there it is. Out the window goes my plans for fun, frivolity, and debauchery!" Bazzer stated.

"Interesting that you are volunteering, Bazzer!" Dukk said. "However, there might be an alternative solution."

"Like what?" Bazzer asked.

"Luna brought it to my attention that Bognath is looking for work. He has the skills and background to step into a security role for us. I've spoken with him, and he is open to the idea. It would be temporary, and he'd report to you Annee, as chief mate. However, it would mean we'd have to pay him out of our own pockets. So, some of the bonus on the canisters, Bazzer, would have to be sacrificed. I want to ask two things of you all. Firstly, if you are happy with Bognath joining the crew, temporarily, and secondly if you are happy to sacrifice some of the windfall here? Thoughts or comments?"

"There will be no windfall if we can't keep hold of the canisters. Also, I respect the guy's skills, so no issue from me," Bazzer said immediately.

"I have no issue with it either," Mentor said.

"Me neither," Marr added.

"I am happy on all counts," Luna said gleefully, which got a laugh from everyone.

When the laughter stopped, they all turned to look at Annee. She was looking at Dukk. Dukk held a neutral expression. He waited.

2

After a few awkward moments, Annee spoke. "I have no problem sacrificing some of the bonus. However, I am not sure if Bognath can be trusted, yet."

"What do you suggest?" Dukk asked.

"He is answerable to me, and I have final say over what he does or doesn't do." Annee replied.

"Absolutely. Already a given. What else?"

"We restrict his access, for now. He remains as a passenger and therefore he can't access crew only areas. His focus will be external security only. He will coordinate the hub's security personnel. He will keep an eye on what is going on around the rig. However, whom ever is on watch must manage the door locks. Any diversion from the plan or suspicious behaviour from him or those he overseas, and he is off this rig. No second chances."

Dukk thought for a moment. "Yep, that works for me. What about everyone else?"

The others agreed.

"Great," Dukk said. "And, seeing as he is answerable to you, Ann, will you let him know what we agreed and take it from here?"

"Will do. Are we going with standard protocols?" Annee replied with a sincere smile.

"Yes, that is what I would suggest," Dukk answered.

"What are those protocols?" Luna asked.

"For high value loads, before collecting, we do a risk assessment and then a circle-up to coordinate our activities," Annee answered.

"When does that take place?" Luna asked.

"I guess that we will dock, get the ID checks complete, then do the assessment before anyone moves off the rig or we unload. Dukk?"

"Yes, that sounds right," Dukk answered. "The security detail should be at the pad for our arrival. Perhaps you and Bognath could meet them immediately after the ID checks are complete?"

"Good idea," Annee replied. "We can then do the circle up in the starboard airlock so we can keep an eye on what's happening on the pad at the time?"

"Yep, that works for me. Everyone else good with that approach?"

Everyone agreed.

A little over two hours later and the Dinatha was safely down on a pad within a large hanger. The hanger was one of several fully enclosed areas located within the hub's docks. It housed mostly transport vessels, like the Dinatha.

As planned, Annee had coordinated the risk assessment, circle-up and agreement on the approach.

They had agreed that the first risk event was in collecting the canisters. After the circle-up, Annee and Bognath headed to the collection point as forward reconnaissance. Marr and Dukk were tasked with taking the empty robotic containers to an adjacent hanger. A hanger typically used by space-bound mining and ice hauling vessels. They would hopefully find a buyer immediately. After that, the plan was for them to head to the load collection point. A separate security detail had been organised by the seller to help escort the load back to the hanger and then over to the Dinatha. Bazzer and Luna focused on preparing the rig for cleaning and repairs. Mentor was on point at the rig. He would operate the nose doors as the load approached.

"How are we looking?" Dukk asked on the crew comms. He and Marr were walking back towards the hanger. They had successfully found a buyer for the empty robotic containers.

"It is very quiet over here at the collection point," Annee answered.

"Very little happening here, either," Mentor added.

"Interesting," Dukk replied as they were about to exit the corridors that connected the hangers.

As Marr and Dukk made their way towards the hanger, a group of three, two men and one woman, stepped into their path.

"Hello, Dukk, captain of the Dinatha," said the man in the middle of the group.

Marr and Dukk stopped.

"Do I know you?" Dukk asked.

"No, thankfully," the man answered.

"Then what are you doing standing in my way?" Dukk said firmly.

"I was wondering what a newcomer like yourself is doing getting high value loads which, until earlier this morning, were scheduled to be on my rig?"

"I don't know anything about you, your rig, or your load. And I care less. Take it up with your contract agent."

Hands suddenly grabbed Dukk and Marr. Their arms were pulled sharply behind them.

They glanced around. Their two captors looked strong and capable.

"Here is the thing, Dukk! Me and my crew had plans for the bonus we'd get from that load. Some pleasures that don't come cheap. And now we won't be able to afford it. So, I figure we might get some payback, right now. Perhaps your hot companion here will oblige."

Marr was in conflict. She had already sized up the group. She was assuming there were no guns, given where they were and the security protocols. Knifes may be a problem, but so long as Dukk helped a bit, she wasn't worried about taking them on. She was, however, worried about blowing her cover.

Suddenly, out of the blue, the man in front of them collapsed forward. Bognath was standing in his place. Before the two on either side could react, Bognath ducked and swung his legs, bringing them both to the ground. A few fast and directed hits, and all three were out cold.

Marr and Dukk had reacted the moment they saw Bognath. They swivelled and ducked. They were free from their captors. The two remaining attackers took one look at their colleagues, then turned and fled.

3

"Great timing Bognath," Marr said as they turned to look at the three limp bodies.

"Thanks."

"It was lucky you were nearby."

"Not luck," Annee said as she stepped out of the shadows. "Bognath spotted this gang as we got near the collection point. We backed off and waited."

"But you gave the 'all clear' a moment ago," Marr said.

"Bognath had the idea of using you as bait. To hold their attention and give him the chance to get behind them. It worked a treat."

"Well, I am glad it worked a treat," laughed Dukk.

"What will we do with them?" Annee asked looking down at the remaining attackers.

"Leave them where they are," Bognath answered. "They picked this spot intentionally. There are no cameras here. It is a blind spot. They'll wake up in a while and crawl back to which ever rig is theirs. They might even share the story. Others knowing that we mean business, will help us avoid any further trouble."

"Right then, let's get over to the handover," Dukk said as he stepped around the pile of bodies.

"You go ahead," Bognath said. "I will hang back a little and keep an eye out just in case those other two decide to follow us."

"Marr, will you walk with Bognath?" Dukk asked. "I want a word with Ann."

"Sure," Marr replied eagerly. She was keen to know more about him having just seen skills on display that were like her own.

Annee nodded and joined Dukk as he headed into the hanger, past a long row of rigs and towards the load exchange area.

"There wasn't really any risk, was there. You were testing Bognath?" Dukk said as they walked.

Annee grinned. "It might have not been as clean or quick, and it would definitely hurt, but no, you and I could have taken that bunch of dimwits."

Dukk laughed. "And how was he otherwise?"

"Very professional. He spotted that group well before me. Before that, he talked me through all kinds of things I wouldn't have considered. Also, he whipped that security detail into order with total ease. He was very direct with what he needed from them and how things would go. Whomever trained him, really knew their stuff."

"This is excellent news."

"Yes, it is. He might be handy to have around."

"You have changed your tune."

"Well, while definitely capable, I am not suggesting he be made a crew member just yet. Having external security could be handy, especially if we keep getting these high value gigs."

"And there lies the problem. We can't afford him if we don't. As you know, with these things, it is either flood or drought. If we get a dry period, say postal runs for a couple of months, I'd go under. I just don't have the reserves."

"Good point," Annee replied quickly before going quiet.

"What?"

"Marr."

"What about her?" Dukk said quietly as he checked his peripheral vision to ensure she wasn't nearby.

"When you were attacked, she looked totally relaxed. No indication of stress or concern."

"Yes, that is interesting. Asset or threat?"

"Not sure."

The rest of the evening had progressed with ease and calm.

The load had been collected and put on board.

With the passengers and observers staying overnight within the hub, Bognath had been setup in the guest lounge room to monitor external security. Annee had configured the screens to cycle through the external cameras. One of the two crew that were on watch, stayed alert in the crew mess should Bognath need to get out to the pad. However, Bognath had been right about the message the handling of the attack had sent. The night had passed with little further hassle. Those few that did come near the rig where immediately confronted by the security detail and Bognath looking down at them from the top of the stairs.

The others had used their downtime to get some food and a few drinks in the entertainment district of the hub. The time together had been enjoyable once more, but less boisterous than the two previous stop overs. And, they had seen little hassle, perhaps also helped by the rumours of the handling of the attack.

The focus for the next day was cleaning and addressing the additional repairs resulting from the breach.

With refuelling complete and the passengers back on board, the crew got the rig through the hanger airlocks and back into orbit preparing for the next traverse.

A little over a day later and the rig was orbiting a rocky and desolate planet in the MJ3 system. It was near midnight. Annee and Mentor were on watch. Everyone else was asleep.

The DMD bounce alarm woke Dukk, but it was too late.

The wave hit him. He could feel his body going into arrest. Pain gripped his chest. His consciousness was slipping. The urge to vomit was overwhelming. He reached over to the sideboard. He grabbed the EVM pack and jammed it into his med line, hoping it ran true. Immediately he started to come back. He sat up with great effort and hit his comms.

"Status?" He wheezed as he forced his body to move in the direction of his inner layer and g-suit.

There was silence.

4

After what felt like an age, the comms came to life again.

"Mentor, cockpit, stable. Bazzer and you are stabilising. Marr, Luna and Annee have crashed as have all the passengers," Mentor said.

"Threat status?" Dukk added as he slipped into the inner layer. His body was responding to the adrenaline hit.

"Doors still sealed. Scanners showing nothing near us. No other vessel signatures. However, there is a blip on the radar. In our wake. It could be pirates or their transport pod."

"I am taking over the conn. I will bring it to the console down here. I'll monitor the threat. Where is Ann?"

"She was on a walk around. Clearly too far from the g-lines. Her vitals are showing her as in the nose section."

"You go for Ann. Resuscitate and then come and help with the passengers."

"On it," came Mentor's reply.

"Bazzer?" Dukk said as he got into his g-suit.

"Holy cow, that never gets any easier!" came Bazzer's faint and strained response.

"I'll go for Luna? You good to get to Marr?"

"At her door now."

366

Dukk dashed to Luna's cabin. The door was already open as per the automated response when a DMD bounce hits.

Luna was sprawled halfway out of her bunk. It looked like she had tried to get to her adrenaline pack but failed. It was floating just out of reach.

Dukk grabbed the resuscitation kit off the wall of her cabin and pushed himself over to her. He lifted her shoulder, spun her over on her stomach and attached a med pack to her med lead. He placed the resuscitation wrap across her back and spun her over to complete the wrap. He placed the mask from the kit over her mouth and hit the big green button on the front of the pack.

Immediately her whole body convulsed as the kit brought Luna back to life.

"Hey kid, welcome back!" Dukk said as Luna opened her eyes and coughed away the air mask.

"I tried, but…" she tried to say before coughing again.

"You'll get the hang of it. Besides, you weren't out for long. It was handy that you sleep in the buff. I didn't have to cut any clothing away to get the resuscitation kit fitted. Take a moment, then get dressed," Dukk said trying to avoid the inevitable awkward moment that was now apparent.

"Marr is back," shouted Bazzer from the other side of the crew mess.

"Luna too," Dukk replied as he closed Luna's cabin door.

"Passengers next," Dukk suggested to Bazzer as they both arrived at the door to the guest accommodation.

"Annee is coming around. On my way up to you," Mentor added into the crew comms.

"I'll be needing a new g-suit, captain. Any suggestions on colour?" came Annee's voice softly into the comms.

"Blue is all the rage these days, Annee, go with that. Good to have you back," Dukk added as he grabbed a resuscitation kit from the wall of the port side twin cabin.

Mentor was at the door to the double, when Dukk returned to the corridor.

"I'll leave you and Bazzer to sort this," Dukk said as he dashed back to the crew mess.

At the console, Dukk checked the radar. He found no rigs near them, and the only noise was a small signature in the wake. The blip that Mentor had mentioned. "Possibly a transport pod," Dukk thought to himself.

Next, he opened the engine controls and started the second reactor. He would need full power for what he needed to do.

He then opened various video feeds of the rig. It was more about passing time while waiting for the reactors to reach full power. He knew he wouldn't see anything. Rewinding the footage would be pointless also.

Dukk knew that just before the bounce, the rig had crossed the horizon. Raiders would have used the sunset to hide their movements. Also, if raiders had triggered the proximity sensors it was while they were applying filter caps to them. Which would now prevent the sensors from detecting any movement. No, Dukk wasn't expecting to see anything.

Before the bounce, they would have also attached grapple hooks and ultrathin tethers which would now be extending out behind the rig. They would have timed it perfectly so that after attaching the tethers they would scramble for cover and get ready for when the rig bounced. At this very moment other raiders would be using the tethers to reach the rig. They would be moving swiftly but carefully to not be picked up on radar. They would be wearing heavier suits to hide their body temperature. They would also be bringing resuscitation equipment and weapons.

Dukk knew the first set of raiders would have had to travel light and fast to reach the rig. This was so they could do their task during the short window provided by the sunset. Dukk knew that when the full team reached the rig, they would resuscitate their colleagues. Then they would sit tight and wait for the next sunset as the rig orbited the planet. They'd then use the blind spot offered by the sunset, to move along the rig, open one of the aft hold doors and gain entry. Opening the door would depressurise the hold, setting off all kinds of alarms. However, it would be too late by that point as they'd be on board.

Dukk also knew that if they thought they had been seen on arrival, they would come on board immediately. The eventuality would be the same. It wasn't a situation Dukk was interested in entertaining.

"See anything?" a voice came from behind Dukk. Luna was standing there. Suited up, helmet in hand.

"Nope."

"If there are raiders, they will be hiding in the main engine housings or even the directional thruster nozzle housings. Is that right?"

"Yep, that would be why we can't see them."

"So how do we shake them off?"

"Like this," Dukk said having noticed the reactors were ready. "Watch the video feeds."

First, he turned off the autopilot. Then he opened the broadcast channel.

"Brace," Dukk announced before firing all directional thrusters at the same time. The rig shook.

"You killed one of them," Luna gasped.

5

On the video feed, a body could be seen shooting out of one of the aft upper thrusters. The body was limp.

"Unlikely," Dukk replied to Luna's concerns. "The bounce would have killed him. I just made it unlikely that the resuscitation equipment will be of any use."

"Oh," she replied. "What if there are more?"

"You'd better hold on to something this time," Dukk said.

"Brace," he said once more into the broadcast channel before firing the main thrusters.

The rig shot forward. Dukk stumbled back into the seat at the console. Luna had gripped a handle on the side of Dukk's seat. She went vertical.

There were no new alarms, but the radar showed more noise in the wake.

"What's that?" Luna asked as she straightened up. The rear video was showing an object disappearing behind them.

"Hopefully, the last we'll see of the raiders," Dukk answered. "How are you by the way?"

"I've had better days, but I'll be fine."

"I am glad to hear it," Dukk said as he smiled up at her.

"I want everyone in g-suits as soon as possible. We aren't out of the woods yet," Dukk said into the crew comms.

Bazzer came into the crew mess. "Anything yet?" he said.

"Definitely had some visitors. The thruster bursts got in the way of their plans. Hopefully, they have backed off."

Dukk pointed at the video feed. It showed some body size objects slipping from view.

"Time for a closer look?" Bazzer asked.

"Yep, let's get out there and make sure the grapples and filters are removed. We'll need two experienced walkers just in case we didn't shake off all of them."

"I'm definitely in," Bazzer said. "I want to see that they didn't do any damage to this old bird."

"I'll go too," came a voice from the door. It was Mentor. "The passengers are all recovering well. The suddenness of it all caught me totally off guard. I thought I was better than that. If there are any still hanging on, I want to be there. I have some steam to work off."

"We aren't savages, Mentor," Dukk said instinctively. "If there is an inch of life, we bring them on board, secure them and let the authorities handle it when we are back in port."

"An inch gives me plenty of scope."

Dukk sat back in his chair. He was unsure of what had just transpired. He looked over at Bazzer. Bazzer shrugged his shoulders.

"Fine," Dukk said after a short pause. He looked around. The rest of the crew were now there too.

"Marr, I want you in the cockpit. Keep an eye on the scanners. Alert us if anything new shows up. Also, send a broadcast. We'd better let others know that this system isn't safe right now."

"Will do," Marr answered as she headed for the door.

"Luna, engine room, keep us running hot and sweet for now."

"On it," Luna replied.

"Ann, well, I'm going to help out with the airlock and EVA, so that leaves everything else in your hands."

Annee smiled.

Sixty minutes later, Bazzer and Mentor were back at the port door with a body in tow.

Dukk pressurised the airlock before joining Bazzer and Mentor and the body.

"No sign of life when I got to him," Mentor said as he removed his helmet. "He was in our wake, attached to a tether grappled to the starboard hold door."

Dukk bent over the body.

"Rigid," Dukk said. "No chance."

"That's what it looks like," Mentor agreed. "His colleagues weren't able to get to him in time, nor us."

Dukk sighed. "It isn't right, but better him than us. Any damage to the door or hull?"

"Not at first glance," Bazzer answered. "I'll go back now and have a more detailed look. We should also fly the drones to make sure there isn't any other damage."

"Good plan," Dukk replied.

"What about this?" Mentor asked pointing at the body.

"We will handle it now," Dukk said. "No point in carrying dead weight. Let's get Kimince in here to scan his details. The observer can handle the paperwork. Then, Bazzer, take him back out with you. Point him at the planet. Give him a proper haulier burial, even though it is unlikely that he deserves it."

Two days later and the crazy events in MJ3 were well behind them. The rig had been brought back to full working order. They had made up for lost time and there had been no further drama.

"You ready?" Dukk said looking over at his co-pilot.

"Absolutely," Marr answered. "What an adventure it has been. It feels like a lifetime since I first looked at this view of Earth. Not eighteen days."

Dukk smiled as he opened the crew comms. "Team, we are committed. How are we looking?"

"Reactors running hot, solar panels stowed and heat shields are locked into place. We are on our way up to you," Luna announced.

"Passengers are settled. Doing final lockdown checks. Two minutes," Annee replied.

"Excellent stuff," Dukk replied. "We'll be in the pub in no time."

Chapter 23 – Pivoting

1

The descent into Utopiam had gone well. Dukk had even been able to enjoy his favourite view as they passed over the large land mass.

The rig was humming. The stabilisers made their approach smooth and far less stressful than Dukk's last approach into Utopiam.

"That was a walk in the park compared to last time?" Annee said as the rig connected with the maglev track. "Citadel operations have acknowledged our landing and are requesting control."

"Sure was," Dukk replied smiling. "Switching control over now. Marr, the comms is back with you. Ann, you can help our passengers. Bazzer, power us down."

"On it," Bazzer replied.

The rig's tune changed slightly as the reactors powered down.

Dukk saw a familiar shadow swish by.

"Change of plan Ann," Dukk commanded as he flicked up video feeds of the wings and hold. "Find their channel."

"On it," Annee replied. She had seen the shadow too.

"What is going on?" Marr asked as she frantically reviewed the controls for the cause of Dukk's concern.

"For crying out loud. Breach, pirates and now raiders! We really need to shake this bad omen," Bazzer said.

"Robinhood Raiders?" yelped Luna. "Where?"

The proximity alarms sounded.

"Scanning all channels," Annee announced. "Got them. Broadcasting to crew comms channel."

"We are on," a crackled voice could be heard in the comms.

Suddenly their view darkened. A thud came from the direction of the windshield.

Marr screamed.

A person in an armoured flying suit, with what looked like a very big gun, was now perched on the nose. The gun was pointed at them. The video feed showed three more clinging to the starboard wing just near the aft hold door.

"We are being hailed, Captain," Annee said.

"Accept it," Dukk replied as he looked up at the raider.

"G'Day, G'Day. Welcome home!" said the raider. "You are looking a little heavy, so we are going to do you a favour and relieve you of some of your load. All part of the service. So, sit tight for a few minutes and we will be on our way. In no time at all, you'll be at the bar telling the story. You know the drill. Do anything stupid and we all die. Now, open the aft hold door on the starboard side. You have three seconds."

Dukk already had the rig schematic open. He had his finger over the button. He looked up at the raider and paused.

The raider stared back at Dukk intensely. She adjusted the gun slightly. It now pointed directly at him.

He smiled and clicked the door open button. The rig trembled slightly as the pressure in the hold balanced.

The video feed of the wing showed the three disappear into the hold. The video feed in the hold then showed them hustle to the doors of the containers.

"This one," a voice was heard on the raiders channel that Annee tapped into moments before.

The video feed showed the raiders opening the container.

"Jackpot. There are five canisters. Time?" crackled a raider's voice.

Dukk looked up at the woman clamped to the nose. She was looking intently into the cockpit. Firstly, at Marr, then she twisted her body slightly so she could see around Dukk and get a better look at Mentor. The woman looked perplexed.

"Just one, we are out of time. Let's go," came the response from the woman to the raiders in the hold.

The video feed showed the raiders making their way to the hold door with one of the canisters. They attached something to it and lobbed it out. They then launched themselves out the door and disappeared behind the rig.

"Thank you for your business. Have a wonderful day," said the woman as she launched off the nose of the rig.

Dukk swiped the rig schematic and closed the starboard hold door.

"Well, there goes our drinking plans for the afternoon and perhaps evening!" Bazzer exclaimed.

"How so?" Luna asked.

"We'll be confined to the rig until the investigators have cleared us of any involvement in that raid. They will talk to us and then search the rig thoroughly. It will be for us to put everything back in order after. That will be our evening done!"

"Involvement? How could we have had anything to do with it?"

"We can't. That won't stop them asking a whole lot of redundant and pointless questions. And wasting a lot of our free time. They must do something to justify their privilege."

Dukk looked over at Marr. She was busy with the post landing protocols. Strange that she wasn't asking questions. Dukk got the sense that she was intentionally finding ways to keep herself busy.

"I'll see to the passengers," Annee said as she got up.

"I will help you," Mentor added quickly.

"Ann, will you give the observers the heads up that we'll need them at the door the moment we are on the pad. The inspectors will want to talk to them first."

"Will do," answered Annee.

"Bazzer, when the systems are sorted, will you head down to the hold. Stand watch and make sure no one goes anywhere near that container before the investigators arrive. I'll start preparing the report."

"On it. Luna, will you head to the engine room. I'd like someone in there as we reach the pad," Bazzer answered as they both got up and left.

2

With only himself and Marr in the cockpit, Dukk turned to Marr.

"Are you okay? You are very quiet?"

Marr looked up. She paused momentarily. She was troubled. She realised Dukk had read her attempts to hide her knowledge of the raiders. She wanted to share, but now wasn't the time nor place. She had an idea.

"I have heard stories. It doesn't always end well. I heard the rig can jump slightly with the pressure change when the doors are opened to let the raiders in. That jump could trigger the citadel defences. That kept going through my mind. I guess that I am in shock," Marr answered genuinely.

Dukk looked deeply at her. He was still troubled by the way the raider had looked at her and Mentor. Dukk decided it wasn't the time nor the place.

"Yes, true. I had that covered," Dukk answered.

Marr paused. She looked out of the window. Then at the controls. She looked up at him.

"You started the depressurisation of the hold when you were first alerted to their presence?"

"Yep," Dukk answered.

"So, we weren't at risk?"

"I wouldn't say that. Nothing is without risk."

"Any other tricks you haven't shared?"

"Plenty, but now isn't the time nor place," Dukk said and smiled.

Marr smiled too. There was something in the way he said what she was thinking. They were in tune.

After a moment, Dukk broke the silence. "We've got some paperwork to complete if we want to hit the bars and celebrate our first successful return. Do you want to look after the normal port clearance protocols, and I'll focus on the raiders report?"

"Sounds like a good plan."

With the rig settled on the pad, Dukk prepared to leave the cockpit. Before leaving, he peered out of the windshield. There was the usual sentinel squad, typical of the welcoming committee for a high value load. He couldn't see the investigators. Perhaps they were delayed, he thought.

When he got to the starboard door, only Annee was there. No observers.

"That is odd," Dukk muttered.

Annee shrugged her shoulders as she was thinking the same.

Dukk dashed back up to the observer's cabin. The door was open. Kimince and Trence were there getting out of their g-suits.

"Why aren't you at the starboard door? The inspectors will want to see you immediately. Did Annee not tell you about this?" Dukk said in an impatient tone.

"Yes, she did. But just now we got a message from our supervisors," Kimince answered. "Our supervisors want us to just read and submit your report. They didn't feel it was necessary to investigate. Also, they said we don't have to leave the rig tonight and can forgo the inspection tomorrow morning. Something about new protocols for high value cargo," Kimince answered.

Dukk stood there stunned.

"Someone clearly has significant influence. I've heard of short cuts being made, but this turn of events is on a completely different scale," Dukk thought to himself.

"Oh. Right. So, will you be joining us again?" Dukk asked.

"Absolutely. We made a special request to stay with this assignment. They approved it," Kimince replied.

"Brilliant, isn't it," Trence added.

"Very much so," Dukk replied.

"We'd like to head into the citadel and enjoy some time with friends. Will you message us tomorrow's departure time?" Kimince asked.

"Absolutely. I'll check on the loading schedule and plan the departure time from there. Before you go, can you help us get the pad doors open so we can unload and disembark the passengers?"

"Of course, we'll get changed and be on the pad in ten minutes."

"Perfect. Enjoy your planet side time," Dukk shared sincerely. Half surprised at himself as to how authentic it felt.

"We will," came the reply as Dukk turned and headed back towards the starboard door.

Dukk's external comms started ringing. He inspected the caller ID. It was Wallace.

"Wallace," Dukk said as he accepted the call.

"Welcome home, Dukk," Wallace answered. "You made great time. And I hear you had quite an adventure."

Dukk laughed. "News travels faster than rigs."

Wallace laughed too. "So, I have some news of my own. The supplier wants to keep up the momentum. The beef will be ready for loading at eight a.m. tomorrow. What are the chances that you can accommodate a fast turnaround?"

"There is always something with you, Wallace. Something to keep me on the edge."

"At the edge is where I like it."

"Do I have a choice?"

"We always have a choice, Dukk. You can choose to go with the flow or walk away."

"That doesn't sound like much of a choice."

"How about I pay for your crew dinner. I'll even cover the drinks. Will that make the choice easier?"

"I think that might help me sway the crew."

"Excellent. I've made reservations for you at The Triggerarti. Eight p.m. One of the best tables in the place."

"I noticed the past tense in how you phrased the table booking."

"Just staying at the edge. Enjoy!" Wallace said as he disconnected the call.

Dukk turned around and headed in the direction of the crew mess. His progress was halted by one of the passengers standing in their cabin doorway.

"What is going on?" the passenger asked.

"It appears there won't be any delay in disembarking after all," Dukk answered. "If you want to get changed out of your suits, we can help you bring your lockers to the pad door. We'll have you on your way in no time at all."

"That is excellent news. We'll be ready in ten."

"Circle-up. Crew mess ASAP," Dukk said into the crew comms as he closed the crew mess door.

3

"I have one piece of very good news, some bad news and some other good news," Dukk said moments later as his crew sat down at the table.

"Very good news first please. We need it," Luna said with glee.

"Good idea Luna. So, the very good news is that there won't be an investigation into the raid," Dukk answered. "We just need to submit the report to our rig's observers, and we can get on with it."

"Looks like someone is smiling on us. We certainly need it after the last few days," Annee offered.

"It does. So, what's next, Luna. The bad or the other good news?" Dukk asked.

"Bad. We might as well get it over with."

"The bad news is that we will be doing a fast turnaround. Loading at eight a.m. in the morning. Launching near nine a.m."

"Oh," Luna said.

"What about the normal post arrival observer inspection?" Annee asked.

"The observers just told me that it is not needed either."

"Wow, who would have thought," Annee said.

"Is that the other good news?" Luna asked.

"No, I'd forgotten about that piece of news. No, the other good news is that Wallace is paying for dinner and drinks. He booked a table for us at The Triggerarti. Eight p.m."

"Someone is definitely smiling on us. This is all working out just fine," Bazzer said.

"Now my news fits," Annee commented.

"What news?" Dukk asked.

"I just received an alert that there is a cleaning crew ready to come on board immediately."

"That is interesting. Anyone got anything else to add?" Dukk asked.

"Passengers," Annee noted.

"What about them?"

"Finding passengers for the outward leg at such short notice, will be a challenge. I already advertised. There wasn't much interest. I had planned to use tomorrow morning to chase down some leads."

"Not getting any passengers might be a blessing after the passengers we left with last time," laughed Bazzer.

"It might," Dukk added. "Let's not make it a priority. Something might show up."

"Ok," Annee answered.

"So, I figure," Dukk offered. "If we all help with unloading, monitoring of cleaning and all that, we'll be done within the hour and we'll then have the afternoon free for some downtime."

Dukk looked around the table for feedback. Marr looked disappointed.

"Marr, are you ok?" he asked.

"I was hoping to get out of the citadel for a run. I understand authorisation of passes takes a few hours. I had planned to apply now and then go tomorrow morning."

"Yes, that is a pity," Dukk replied. "I was hoping to take you up on your offer to show me your old haunts. It would have been great to get out for a run."

"Let me look into it for you," Mentor offered. "I may know someone who can swing some passes at short notice for this afternoon. Since you were a keeper, you shouldn't need an escort. I'd think you should be able to take a guest too."

"Count me in," Luna chirped.

"Me too," Annee said.

"Great, that works for me. Annee, will you take charge of the allocation of tasks?" Dukk asked.

"Yep," Annee answered as she exposed a list on the table projector.

Thirty minutes later, Dukk was standing in the corridor outside the guest cabins. He was monitoring the cleaning crews as they did their thing.

"Can we talk?" came a voice from behind.

Dukk turned around. "Sure, Ann. What's up?"

Annee pointed towards the crew mess. Dukk followed her in. They swiped their bracelets as they entered.

"Something doesn't add up," Annee said quietly. "No investigation of the raid and no rig inspection. Even for short turn arounds, the observers usually do some sort of inspection."

"Yep, I know, it is odd."

"I've experienced inspections being skipped, but never investigations and definitely not both together. What is going on?"

"I don't know, Ann. Wallace contacted me just after the observers got their message. Perhaps he pulled some favours to get us turned around fast."

"That theory fits the inspection, but not the investigation."

"Wallace might have been concerned we would be held up while they investigated."

"I guess so. Still don't like it. Something is afoot."

"Yes, I agree there is lots more to this than is on the surface."

"Like what?"

Dukk said nothing.

"Mentor?" Annee asked.

Dukk was still unsure about how to respond.

"Do you think he might have got involved? He mentioned he knew people with respect to the passes for getting out of the citadel. That requires influence."

"It was odd behaviour, that is true," Dukk replied.

"We should ask him?"

"We've had a conversation of sorts already. After the breech. He is tight lipped. No, I don't think we'll learn anything more from him at this stage."

"You have a plan?"

Dukk smiled.

"The run this afternoon, with Marr and Luna," Annee said. "You plan to use the time in their old domain to see if you can learn more about what is going on or at least what the story with Mentor is."

Dukk smiled again.

"By the way, have the dreams changed?"

"Nope," answered Dukk. "Still the same. Climbing the mountain. Others around me and I am carrying something."

"There you are?" came a voice from the aft ladder shaft door. It was Luna. "The automatics are nearly finished upstairs. What is next?"

"I'll help you bring them to the hold," Annee answered. "We have time to give that space a once over too."

"Perfect," Luna replied.

Annee smiled at Dukk as she followed Luna back down the corridor.

4

Later that afternoon, Marr, Dukk, Luna and Annee were jogging through the vineyards beyond the walls of the citadel.

Mentor had come good on his promise. He had secured four day passes that permitted them to go beyond the walls for the afternoon.

They had completed their duties at the rig, cleared the ID gateway and got a lift via one of the regular shuttles.

The quadcopter had delivered them to a day compound where they had changed into running clothes. They would be able to make use of the showers at the compound before returning to the citadel.

Dukk's plans to interrogate Marr and Luna had been put aside for the time being.

The experience of exploring the lush grounds was just too good.

He was very much enjoying the exertion and even more so, seeing Marr move so effortlessly through the rows of vegetation.

Marr was leading the group. She was in her element. The time away from the orchards and fields helped cement her love for it.

She was maintaining a steady pace but had also taken regular breaks to check-in with the others or point something out.

Her next stopping point was the halfway mark. It was a small, enclosed shelter in the middle of a dense cluster of trees. The shelter would offer a moment to regroup before returning. It would be cool inside, and she knew it had a freshwater spring. She was looking forward to the soft and sweet taste of the unprocessed water.

She stopped outside and waited for the others to join her before going in.

It was dark inside the shelter. The only light came from a small window in the back. As their eyes adjusted to the reduced light, a familiar voice greeted them.

"Sit, please."

Marr immediately enabled her bracelet. The others followed.

"Teacher," blurted Luna.

The old woman smiled and gestured for them to join her. She was sitting on a stool. There were four other stools. Positioned in a circle.

They obeyed.

In the middle of the circle was a stone mound. A fountain. Water bubbled up in the centre of the fountain and filled a small basin in its top. Excess water flowed out of the basin, down the stone mound and into a small drain in the floor.

The old woman filled a cup from the basin and offered it to Annee.

Annee took the cup and took a sip. The woman gestured to Annee to finish it. Annee did that and passed the cup back.

The woman repeated the process with Dukk, Luna and finally Marr.

With the cup back in the basin, the old woman turned her gaze to Annee. "Welcome, Annee."

"You know my name?" Annee replied.

"Of course, Teacher knows much. You have come far."

Before Annee could respond, the old woman turned her gaze to Dukk. She lingered on Dukk, then spoke. "Welcome, Dukk. You have come home at last."

"Thank you, I think." Dukk said hesitantly. He was even more bemused than Annee.

The old woman then turned to Luna. "Luna, what occurs to you at this moment in your journey?"

Luna stared back. She was still unsure how to answer that question.

Teacher smiled, then turned her gaze to Marr.

"Hello Teacher, it is an honour to see you here," Marr said before the old woman could say anything.

The old woman laughed. "I approve, Marr. Good choice. Thank you for bringing him here to meet me."

Teacher then looked at Dukk and back to Marr. "It is time. Share your toil."

"What the!" Marr said in surprise.

The old woman closed her eyes and lowered her head. She chuckled five times, took a deep inhale and then started to snore.

Marr looked over at Dukk. He was looking at her. They both blushed.

Annee laughed and looked around at the others.

Luna smiled and shrugged her shoulders. "Time to go," she said.

Once outside, Annee turned to them and said, "Who in the world was that?"

"A nosy and crazy old storyteller," Luna offered.

"Great entertainment value," Annee laughed.

"Did you know she would be here?" Dukk asked, looking at Marr.

"Nope," Marr answered. "I am surprised about her presence too."

Dukk looked harder at Marr. It felt authentic, which made the whole experience even more confusing. Then it hit him. He laughed aloud. Perhaps it was what he needed after all. He had learnt something, something even more valuable than getting the inside track on Mentor. The dreams. The toil climbing the mountain. It was connected. Now he knew what he needed to do.

"Are you ok? Has she rubbed off on you?" Annee asked, having observed Dukk's sudden change in demeanour.

"Yep," Dukk answered confidently. "We'd better get moving. We have dinner plans."

Later that evening, Marr and Dukk were walking towards The Triggerarti.

After the adventure in the wild, they had cleaned up and made ready for their dinner booking. Marr and Dukk were ready before the others, so they headed off.

As they passed down a narrow street, the lights went out.

A door could be heard opening near them.

"Not again," Dukk thought to himself.

"In there," A voice said behind them as they were shoved forward.

They stumbled into a large, dimly lit room.

Two hooded figures stood before them. Dukk chanced a glance behind him. Two further hooded figures stood in a wide doorway. The ones that had shoved them. Dukk sensed the space was a garage of sorts.

Dukk could now see something sharp in the attackers' hands. The attackers rushed towards them.

Dukk felt Marr move and decided to go with it.

Marr ducked and sent her fist into the kidney of one of the hooded figures. Dukk sensed her movement and did the same. Both hooded figures squealed. As his attacker started to turn, Dukk slammed his boot into the attacker's knee. Pop. The attacker went down headfirst. Thud. No movement.

Unfortunately, in responding to the frontal attack, Dukk had lost sight of those behind. A fist collected him in the side of the face. He staggered. He glanced around. Marr looked to have had a similar experience. They looked at each other and nodded. They both swung around, back-to-back facing the remaining two attackers, who were now on either side of them.

Dukk looked up at the attacker in front of him. A woman. She was tall and strong looking. She looked at him and smiled. A smile that showed awareness that her punch had connected. Then suddenly the smile changed to shock. The woman was looking behind him. Dukk didn't hesitate. He charged, ducking as he did. He collected her in her mid-section and flipped her up. He pivoted so that as she landed, he could drive his boot into the side of her head. She went out cold.

Dukk regained his balance and glanced back at Marr. She was looking at him. She was grinning.

"You finished?" Marr said laughing.

Behind Marr were Luna and Bognath. Luna was rubbing her forehead. The fourth attacker was sprawled face down on the ground in front of Luna. Bognath was smiling with his pointer over his lips. He then gestured towards their bracelets. They all activated them.

"What the hell guys? We leave you for a moment and you find more trouble!" Luna said.

"Who are they?" Marr asked as she looked at the pile of bodies.

"Thumpol's thugs," Bognath answered. "I heard they've been hanging around for the last few days. Waiting for you to return. Plenty of influence it would appear. We'd better get out of here and away from this street before the lights come back on."

"Just as well we showed up," Luna said.

"What! We had it covered," Marr laughed.

Bognath led the way back onto the street. Dukk closed the doors behind them.

5

It didn't take long for the four to reach The Triggerarti. Dukk and Marr were still feeling a little dazed, so they stopped just inside the door and looked around. The place was busy. There was a good buzz.

"And there they are!" boomed a voice from the direction of the bar. "Dukk, captain of the Dinatha and his crew. Setting the gold standard for long hauling."

Wallace came across to them from where he had been sitting at the bar.

Dukk smiled. "Hello, Wallace. You are too kind."

Some of the other punters looked around. But most took no notice. Clearly, Wallace's booming voice and antics weren't that unusual.

"And, you have my newest team member with you," Wallace added as he looked beyond them.

Dukk and Marr turned their heads to look behind them. Bognath grinned back. Luna looked across at Bognath too. She had a curious expression.

"By the way, Bognath, I am about to secure your first assignment," Wallace said with a wink.

"Come," Wallace beckoned as he walked back towards the bar. "By the look of it, you've found even more excitement on your way through the streets of Utopiam. Barman, these guests will need extra ice with their drinks."

The barman was waiting for them at the bar. He reached under the bar and came back with three medi-packs.

Dukk reached over and took them. He passed one each to Marr and Luna, before resting the third against his cheek.

"You must be thirsty and hungry, their table, barman?"

The barman waved at a server. The server came across.

"Dukk, do you have a minute?" Wallace said before they moved off.

"Go ahead," Dukk said to the others.

The server headed off in the direction of the stairs. The others followed.

Wallace took a seat at the bar. Dukk joined him.

"Speaking of Bognath," Wallace said. "Things have heated up for you. Not totally clear to me if things are going with you or against you. I may have contributed in some way. But anyway, the past is the past. And regardless of whatever is behind the heat, I have my own interests to protect. So, I have taken advantage of an opportunity that was put before me. I have employed Bognath to protect my interests, so to speak."

"Your interests?

"The beef you are transporting to Mayfield."

"Oh, right. So, you are footing the bill for our security needs?"

"No, not entirely, just Bognath's wage and overheads. For the duration of the contract."

Dukk laughed.

"Of course, that is if you agree. The choice is yours," Wallace added.

"And we've had that conversation before."

"We have."

"Then, it is thank you, I guess."

"You are welcome, Dukk. Right, I have other matters to attend to, and I am sure you are hungry and in need of a few drinks."

Wallace then turned and looked up at the balcony. He found the crew's table and caught Bognath's attention. Wallace gave him a thumbs up and smiled. Then he swung off the stool and headed for the door.

Dukk headed up the stairs and joined the others. It wasn't long before Annee, Bazzer and Mentor joined them. With everyone there, Dukk welcomed Bognath and shared the details of the latest arrangements.

With the first round of drinks on the table, Dukk made a toast. "To the fine crew of the Dinatha, what a team. To all that was, is and yet to be. Thanks, I give!"

"Thanks, I give!" came the reply.

As the drinks came back to rest on the table, Mentor stood up, abruptly, from his seat at the opposite end of the table. "Long time, give me a second, I am in a noisy spot," Mentor said into his comms. He then left the table and headed for the balcony door.

An instant later, a familiar loud tone rang in Dukk's comms. "Shit!" he said aloud. He glanced around the table. The others looked to be expressing similar expletives.

Dukk started taking deep breaths. He only got two done before the noise started. An ear-piercing scream filled his comms. Dukk instinctively put his hands to his ears and pulled his head into his chest. He tried to breathe. It wasn't easy with the incredibly loud noise ringing in his ears. He felt like it lasted for an hour, but Dukk knew it was only thirty seconds. When it stopped, Dukk looked around. Everyone in the bar had suffered the same dreadful experience. Dukk tried not to hold his breath. He knew what was coming next.

"ATTENTION," boomed a voice in his comms. "Brawling and fighting are beneath those that are awakened. It is your duty to report all unusual behaviour. Remember we all must suffer for the inconsiderate actions of others. Only through this will we all be safe. We do this for your own wellbeing."

Dukk regained his composure, picked up his drink and took a long hard pull.

The others did the same.

"Right then, that's made me even more hungry," Bazzer laughed.

The others tried to laugh too.

The next evening, Marr and Dukk were sitting in the cockpit. The rest of the previous evening had been loads of fun and far less dramatic. The loading and launch had progressed as normal, and they were now biding their time ahead of the first traverse.

"Can I ask you something?" Dukk said to Marr as he enabled his bracelet.

"Sure, what is it?" Marr answered following suit on the bracelet.

"The old woman we met yesterday in the orchards. Luna said she was a storyteller?"

"She did?"

"Did she tell you stories?"

"Yes, I've known her for several years. She has shared loads of stories."

"I need help with something. Perhaps you know the story. I have fragments of a tale, a story, I just can't remember much of it."

"What do you remember?"

"All I have is a memory of a mountain, toil and carrying something."

"I think I know it. The Creator's Experiment."

"Would you share it with me?"

"Are you sure?"

"Absolutely."

"Fine, here goes."

Marr then proceeded to share the Creator's Experiment as she had heard it told many times. She told it as she had been sharing it with Luna since Teacher's instructions before leaving Earth for the first time.

After the story was told, a tear formed in Dukk's eye. "I know that story. The dreams. They are connected," Dukk reflected to himself.

"Are you ok?" Marr asked.

Dukk struggle to find any words to share. It was clear what he had seen in the dream and what he had been holding.

Then the charm sounded. It was time for the first traverse.

"Saved by the bell," Dukk replied in jest.

Marr smiled. "Not the time," she thought to herself.

Chapter 24 – Hard choices

1

The next eight days progressed without any of the drama of the first run between Earth and Mayfield. There had been a series of traverses along the same route. The interim stops had gone by smoothly. The layover at Maple Tower had been enjoyable, but quiet in comparison to the previous time. There was some downtime, some dancing and lots of long and, at times, deep conversations.

The rig had just arrived in the Mayfield system. The crew were coming around.

"Looks like things are busy," Marr said into the crew comms. "Air traffic control has put us in a holding pattern. No chances of getting down this morning. They suggest it could be later this evening, but more likely tomorrow morning. They have also instructed us to drop to a lower orbit. Will I update the autopilot?"

"Yes, go ahead. And I think I know why," Dukk said as he looked out.

"A Mammoth!" Marr exclaimed as she looked up.

"What is a mammoth?" Luna asked as she looked around.

"A huge space craft used by the heads of the elite families," Bazzer answered as he unbelted and came forward to get a better view. "Basically, a small hub capable of traversing. A fortified flying palace. There aren't many of them. Very rare. Perhaps a dozen in our galaxy. You hardly ever see them, let alone get close to one."

"Well, check this out," Annee said as she turned on the projector in the centre of the cockpit. "The radar has picked up four other large vessels."

The projected image showed a graphical rendering of the planet. Orbiting the planet were five large craft. They were evenly positioned to form a ring around the planet.

"But five means!" Bazzer started to say and then stopped.

"The Veneficans!" Annee answered.

"The who?" Luna asked as she unbelted and joined Bazzer in the space between Mentor and Annee's seats.

"A very secretive group of women. Highly sort after for their counsel. Some say they can see the future," Annee answered.

"Or write it," Mentor added quietly.

There was silence in the cockpit as the rig dropped to a slightly lower orbit and passed below the massive space craft.

"Holy cow. Look at the turrets and rail guns!" Bazzer observed.

"Look at that huge motif on the belly," Luna said.

"The mark of the Veneficans. Some say it is an eel," Bazzer said.

"Really, I guess it does kind of look like one," Luna replied. "My first thought was that it looks more like the cut of a blade, when you swoosh it from right to left to right. See how the top line is thicker than the bottom two."

"Well, I never. You could be right," Bazzer replied.

Dukk sat quietly. He felt Luna was right. While he knew of it, he had never seen the mammoth ring. He had seen the Veneficans' smaller vessels from time to time. He had even seen some of their number, passing through hubs or planet ports. They were unmistakable, in their white full-face masks, and their blood red, hooded cloaks. There wasn't anything really appealing about them, so Dukk had previously written them off as some weird elite sect. After Mentor's comment and Luna's observation, he suddenly thought differently.

Marr sat quietly too. "How is it that I know nothing of these women?" She thought to herself.

An hour later, Marr was doing a walk around. She was also looking for Mentor. She found him sitting alone in the nose section.

"Looking for some personal space?"

"Yes, Marr, but I see you need some answers," Mentor replied.

Marr sighed. He could read her. That was something she needed to work on.

"Yes, what do you know of the Veneficans?"

"Not much more than I suspect you've just read in the archives."

Marr smiled in a manner that suggested she wasn't going to settle for that answer.

Mentor smiled and continued. "Their leader calls herself Venefica Magnum Reginae. Some refer to her as Magnum Reginae. There number is always exactly sixty-one. And there are several hundred helpers. Younger women that do their bidding. They also employ men, and they go everywhere with a load of sentinels. They advise and they meddle. And they live in these mammoths. That is all I know."

"Why is this the first time I've ever heard of them?"

"What you do and don't read in the official archives has nothing to do with me?"

Marr frowned, but she took the hint and immediately enabled her bracelet. Mentor did the same.

"So, what do you know of the Veneficans, that's not in the official archive?"

"Nothing. I've been looking for years. I can't get any answers. I've been told it's above my pay grade, so to speak."

"There must be a way to find out more. Where have they come from? What is their history? Are they a threat or ally?"

"Perhaps you could ask the Venefica that you already know?"

Marr paused. Perplexed. Then it dawned on her.

"Teacher!" Marr said.

Mentor smiled.

"Tell me more."

"I have no more. I've asked her plenty. She tells me it isn't time for me to know more. Perhaps you could try. We'll be back on Earth again in ten days."

"Good, I will."

"By the way, I need your binoculars. I am going on a hike when we land, and I'd like to have them with me."

"Of course, but will you tell me what is going on? Luna mentioned you have also borrowed her rifle. This is odd behaviour, even for you."

Mentor looked at her deeply. "I am going to let that last comment pass, Marr. You should know better. Besides, it is too dangerous for you to know more, for now."

Marr frowned.

"Follow me, I'll get them for you now," she answered as she turned and headed off.

2

At the end of the watch, Dukk had gone to his cabin to change into his gym gear.

His comms sounded. It was Annee. "Dukk, there is an urgent message for you from port control."

"Fire it over," Dukk replied.

Dukk read the message. He then opened the crew comms.

"Listen up, team. We have a change of plan. Port control have cleared a pad for us. They have sent through our approach plan. I will load it into the autopilot now. We should be on the pad in just under three hours. Let's organise to start the deorbiting protocols. We break atmosphere in ninety minutes."

Dukk then relayed a similar message on the broadcast channel for the benefit of Bognath and the observers.

After loading the details into the autopilot, Dukk checked he was still alone at the console in the crew mess. He then opened the logs for the external comms.

"Something isn't right," he thought to himself.

The logs showed that just after reaching the system and discovering the delay, there were three calls made to the surface. Annee, Bazzer and Mentor had all made calls. The logs also showed that two further calls were made just now. Annee and Bazzer had made those calls.

"Bazzer has friends here. And, Annee has her new companion, Suzzona. It makes sense that they would firstly let them know of the delay and then of the change. But what is Mentor making calls for. And why didn't he then make a second call?" Dukk thought to himself.

"This is great news," a voice said behind him. It was Marr.

Dukk flicked the logs away. "It is, perhaps we can have a date after all?" he said as he turned to face her.

"Maybe?" Marr smiled.

Three hours later, the Dinatha was entering the hanger at the Mayfield space port.

"Pad R20 is a long way from the hyperloop station. We are definitely going to make good use of a cart." Marr said as Dukk manoeuvred the rig through the huge hanger doors.

"Definitely," Dukk answered.

"Oh, wow!" Marr exclaimed as the rig turned and they looked down the row of vessels parked in the hanger.

"Would you look at that?" Bazzer said. He had jumped up the moment Marr offered her observation.

The hanger was almost full. Space craft could be seen into the distance. The first fifteen drew their attention. There were five pairs of interceptors and in between a slightly smaller, but sleeker looking craft. They were all blood red in colour and on their sides was the motif of the Veneficans. The blade cuts, as Luna had described them.

"The presence of so many vessels can only mean one thing!" Bazzer observed.

"What does it mean?" Luna asked. She had pushed her way in to get a better look.

"The Queen, the Magnum Reginae, is here on this planet. In this resort!"

Luna gasped. Standing around each group of three vessels was a squad of sentinels. Their slick uniforms weren't black like those on Earth. They were blood red. Head to toe.

Their presence put a chill through them all.

They observed in silence as they passed.

Unloading and going about their usual activities had been more cumbersome than their previous visit.

The sentinels were in other places too. Everything took longer as there were more people about and there was a higher than normal amount of ID checking.

The crew still managed to enjoy themselves. They had done some skiing. They did some drinking. Marr and Dukk even enjoyed a meal together after their watch.

"They've gone?" Marr observed as they returned to the rig near midnight.

"They have," Dukk answered, as they drove through the half empty hanger.

Dukk was happy for his bed as it had been a long day. And he slept solidly until seven a.m. He had no plans for an early start, but that was about to change. The external door open request woke him.

"Odd, I thought everyone except Annee were already in when Marr and I got back. And Annee isn't on watch until ten a.m.," Dukk said to himself.

"Dukk, you up?" Marr announced into Dukk's comms.

"Not quite," Dukk answered with a chuckle.

"Your turn or mine?" Marr asked cheekily.

"Let's have a look first," Dukk said as he grabbed his robe and headed for his cabin door.

Dukk went across to the console and opened the external video feeds.

"Shit," he said aloud.

"What?" Marr said. She was standing behind him, also in her robe.

"PAN-PAN. Something is up. All stations," Dukk announced into the crew comms as he dashed back towards his cabin to get dressed.

Marr looked at the video feeds. Several vehicles were parked in front of the rig. A large group of official-looking and armed people were standing on the pad and on the stairs.

"Shit!" Marr said aloud as she dashed towards her cabin to get dressed.

Moments later, Dukk and Marr were making their way through the accommodation level and to the starboard door.

Dukk locked the inner door before opening the outer starboard door.

Standing on the platform, at the top of the stairs was Trence. There were several officials there too.

"They dragged us out of bed. They took Kimince. I don't know what is going on!" yelled Trence.

One of the officials stepped forward. "There has been an assassination. Your observer, Kimince, has been arrested. A replacement is on the way now."

"Wait, who has been assassinated?" Dukk asked.

"Craig Atesoughton. Now, make ready for immediate departure. You are cleared for launch. If you are still here in one hour, you will all be arrested too."

"On what grounds?" Dukk asked.

"Accomplices or whatever other grounds we like. If it were up to me, you would all be already sharing Kimince's fate. You are just lucky you have friends in high places. Goodbye."

3

"What happened?" Dukk asked Trence as they watched the officials leave.

"We were doing our thing, then we got an invite to visit the resort. There was an escort. They took us up there. We spent a couple of hours drinking and having fun and then we returned to our hotel. Then out of the blue, they pounded down the door and took Kimi away. They stuffed our things into the lockers and brought me here. That is all I know."

"What is going on?" Bazzer said from the inner doorway.

Dukk turned around. Luna and Bognath were there too.

"Not sure. Anyone got any thoughts?" Dukk said.

"We'd better comply," said a voice from behind them. It was Mentor.

"Do you know something about this?" Dukk asked in a firm tone.

"Enough to know we'd better take their threat seriously," Mentor replied.

Dukk stood his ground. He wasn't going to let him off that easily. Not this time.

Mentor took the hint. "Assassinations are like a tsunami. The power is sucked out and then comes crashing back. The tsunami size and potential for destruction is proportionate to the impact, the level of influence had by the person assassinated. We don't want to get caught up in this wave, I assure you. Our best option is to get out of its way."

Dukk sighed. "We really, are going to have a proper chat one of these days. Right, Bazzer, Luna, get us fuelled and prepped. Mentor, help Trence. Marr, get onto port control and get the launch plan. I'm going to see if I can contact Annee. Then I am going to get some empty containers. We might as well try and salvage what we can of this venture."

Dukk's comms sounded. It was Annee.

"Annee, hi, where are you?" Dukk answered.

"On my way back to the rig. Did you see the news?"

"Yep, we are making ready for launch."

"Why? What has this got to do with us?"

"Wait, why are you calling? And why are you on your way back?"

"Suzzona was called into work early. Something about beef postal drops being cancelled. There are some angry hauliers who just had their contracts withdrawn. We are on the Hyperloop. I was calling to see if I could get a pickup at the station."

"Is that the beef we brought in yesterday?"

"I guess so."

"Strange."

"Yep, Suzzona suggests they don't need that much beef here, especially as we'll be back in twenty days with another load."

"Anyway, we've got to get moving. I'll explain when I collect you. You can help me get some empties."

Dukk's departure in the cart was delayed by the arrival of a taxi. A person got out of the back and walked over to Dukk. The driver also got out and went to the back of the cart. The driver unhooked some lockers and put them on the pad. The driver then returned to the cart and drove off.

"Hello, I am Premnaly, the observer assigned to this rig to replace Kimince."

"Welcome, please wait here. I will have someone help you get on board."

Dukk opened his crew comms. "Mentor, the replacement observer is here. Will you come down and help with the lockers?"

The rest of the day was clinical and sobering. Not much was being said. The crew were subdued and just went about their tasks.

Marr avoided Luna and Mentor where she could. She didn't want any lines drawn between the facts she knew. She knew conversations with them might put her in the know. She knew that knowing was potentially even more dangerous. She had to trust her instinct. Her instinct told her to lay low.

Dukk was worried too. He couldn't put a finger on it. He was troubled by the news Annee had shared about what Suzzona had said. That, and their presence on Mayfield at the time of the assassination, could have implications for the beef contract and getting paid. He was also more concerned than before about Mentor's behaviour. He felt the comment about friends in high places was connected to Mentor. But he couldn't get any answers.

A circle up immediately after launch hadn't helped reduced the confusion.

In the end he decided to focus on keeping the rig moving, exercising and getting lots of rest. He wanted to be fully fit for whatever else was coming.

4

A familiar but unexpected shutter woke Dukk. He sat up and checked the time. It was near three a.m. Three hours until start of watch and a little more until the second traverse. That didn't make sense.

"Airlock," he said aloud after processing the sound and vibration.

"PAN, PAN, Status?" he announced into the crew comms.

There was a pause, then Bazzer responded.

"Captain?"

"I felt an airlock?"

"Me too. Checking."

Dukk slipped into his inners.

"The port airlock has just been used?" Bazzer said moments later.

"Who by?"

"Not sure. I just checked all vitals. All stable. Everyone is in their cabins."

"Intruder? Cameras?" Dukk asked as he started putting on his suit.

"Nothing near the hold or in the passageways."

"External cameras and proximity sensors?"

"Nothing showing up."

"Where are you?" Dukk asked as he left his cabin.

"The engine room."

"Luna?"

"When she heard your PAN-PAN, she dashed up to her cabin. She muttered something about having to retrieve something important."

Dukk went over to the console.

He verified what Bazzer had just shared.

"Check the passenger cabin door locks?" a voice said behind him.

Dukk nearly hit the ceiling from the fright.

"What the F!" Dukk exclaimed as he turned around.

"Check the passenger cabin door locks. Were they locked from the inside or outside?"

Dukk stared at Mentor. He was fully suited. His helmet was in his hand. Attached to his belt was a large gun.

"Just do it, now!" Mentor demanded in a tone that made it clear to Dukk as to who was in charge.

Dukk spun around and used the console to check the locks.

"The replacement observer's door is locked from the outside. Why?" Dukk answered.

"Likely a booby trap on the door. Probably connected to a small bomb that is attached to the window. Enough to blow a hole in the side of the rig and cause a bounce the moment that cabin door is opened."

"But that would cause the rig to implode on exit of the bounce."

"Yep. Also, I bet the observer has left a fake vitals transponder to take us off the trail. Now check the external cameras and proximity sensors. Are they in loop debug mode?"

Dukk checked. They were. Bazzer hadn't seen anything because the external cameras weren't working. Before Dukk could think, let alone respond, Mentor gave further instructions.

"Check the scanners. Check our hail channels. Are they working?"

Dukk checked. Everything was down. They were blind and unable to contact anyone else.

"What is going on! And, how do you know all of this?" Dukk asked as he spun around.

"Because it is what I would have done," Mentor added calmly.

"You and I are going to have to have a serious talk when this is over! Whatever 'this' is!" Dukk answered angrily.

"Ready," called a voice from the direction of the Kitchenette. Dukk looked around again.

Luna was standing there. She was suited up, with her helmet hooked to her belt, along with a small handgun. In her hands was what looked to be a sniper rifle.

"I am ready too," came another voice from the other side of the room. Dukk spun around.

Marr was standing there. Also suited up. Her helmet was in her hand. On one side of her belt was a large gun. On the other side was what looked like a large knife in its sheath. A few moments earlier, Marr had received a code word from Mentor. She had launched out of bed and responded instinctively.

"What the F! is going on?" Dukk demanded.

"We don't have much time. Bring up the video feed of the wings," Mentor demanded in a strong tone.

Dukk spun around, turned off debug mode and opened the cameras.

"There is nothing to see. Even the rear facing camera shows nothing."

"Play it back to the last time we crossed the horizon. Watch how the sun plays across the body of the rig. Play it at double time."

Dukk interacted with the controls and the video feed started to rewind.

"What is going on?"

Dukk looked up.

Annee was standing in the middle of the room. She was in a dressing gown. She was looking at the others with her mouth open.

The anger in Dukk was rising. He fought it back. Something told him to comply for now. He returned to the playback.

The tail was casting a shadow as the rig passed into the sunny side of the planet. The shadow danced across the wings. Suddenly he saw it. He pressed pause.

"Oh shit! We are being followed," Dukk said quietly as he noticed a silhouette of a rig clearly marked out next to the tail shadow.

"By the shape, it looks like an interceptor!" Annee suggested as she peered over Dukk's shoulder.

"The Ukendt!" came a voice from behind them. They all turned around. It was Bognath. He was also suited up. He too had a weapon attached to his belt. "I was speaking to the fuel truck operator before we departed Mayfield. The operator mentioned it was his second last job for the shift. He said his last job was to refuel the Ukendt. It has stealth tech. It won't show up on video feeds, radar, or scanners."

"Oh shit, this has just got real!" Bazzer announced as he looked around at everyone. He had just exited the aft ladder shaft.

"I need answers! Least of which is why Bognath is in the crew mess right now. And how in the world did you all get weapons on board my rig!"

"We don't have time for answers," Mentor said. "How about I share what we all need to understand right now."

"The floor is yours," Dukk replied angrily.

"The observer was a plant. Sent to help take us out. I wasn't sure until just now. I am guessing the observer was the one that just used the port airlock. The observer will be crossing over to the Ukendt right now. The observer's lack of appreciation of experienced hauliers and their sensitivity to every aspect of the rig, may have saved us. The

Ukendt is there to make sure the job gets done and to pick up the observer."

"How do you know all this?" Dukk asked.

"It is what I would have done."

"You keep saying that, but it doesn't add up."

"Look, let's just say they have good reason to want us, well me, dead. I'll explain later because if we don't act now, my history will be irrelevant. I suspect, if we stall the DMD, alter course or look to be responding to the threat in anyway, the Ukendt will missile us. If we traverse or open the observer's door, we will be all dead instantly. We have a narrow window between now and when we are scheduled to traverse. We need to get on board the Ukendt and turn the table."

"How will we do that?" Annee asked.

5

Mentor continued. "We use the next horizon breach when the sun will blind them. I, Luna and Bognath will use a transport pod to get above and behind the Ukendt. With the sun cracking over the horizon, they won't see us. We then drop onto them, get on board, neutralise the crew and then get the rest of you."

"Holy cow, just like that. This is lunacy," Dukk exclaimed. "If that is the plan, crossing unseen isn't the only big ask. What about the rig's proximity alert system? Won't that detect you even if they don't see you?"

"I am assuming they have disabled it to get the observer on board. I doubt they will bring it back online immediately."

"Why?"

"They will have other things to worry about."

"Like what?

"I may have inspected the observer's lockers when I brought them on board yesterday. I may have found a basic air pack and tampered with it."

"You mean the observer is already dead?"

"Likely."

"Why will that be an issue for the Ukendt crew?"

"Insurance. I am sure the observer left some sort of device, a bomb or something that only the observer can deactivate. It would be in the crew's interest to get the observer on board to do that. Otherwise, the crew could have simply left the observer for dead."

"But the observer is now dead," Dukk said with an emphasis on the word 'is'.

"Yep, discovering this, will put the Ukendt crew into a panic. They'll likely abandon ship. We can capitalise on that."

"Wait, but won't the observer's bomb still be a problem for us?"

"I have override codes. We have the same employer, so to speak. I have the master codes to anything that observer would be able to get access to."

Dukk sighed. "Every second thing you say makes me trust you even less."

"Assuming that all goes to plan," Annee interjected. "What do you mean by 'come get you'? With the Ukendt neutralised, we could break into the observer's cabin, via side panels. You could then use the master codes?"

"I am sure that we won't have that much time. I suspect the device on this rig might even go off if we move about too much. No, the Dinatha is now lost. We must think beyond it. We are now marked. The people behind this won't let us get very far. It won't be the likes of Joantyi coming after us. They would be much more professional. That I am sure of."

"How can you be so sure?"

"Because, Ann, I was until just now, one of the people they'd use to get the job done properly!" Mentor shared honestly, with a hint of shame.

"Oh!" Annee said as she slumped back into a chair.

"And what do we do while you find us a new ride?" Dukk asked in a defeated tone.

"The rest of you get packed up. Get personal items, supplies, and everything of value into one of the empty RoboContainers. Once we have secured the Ukendt, open the nose door, and use the transport pods to pull the container free. Get clear of the Dinatha as quickly as possible," Mentor replied.

"Do we have a choice?"

"No!" Mentor answered firmly.

"Right then, abandon ship!" Dukk said as he stood up.

Before moving off, Mentor stepped over to Annee.

"Ann, take this," he said passing a small package to Annee. "Get Trence into a transport pod. Make the observer take this. It is a sedative. It will make things much easier for all of us."

Dukk escorted the raiding party to the transport pod bay.

"Luna, that won't work in space," Dukk said as they climbed the stairs.

"This baby goes where I go. Besides, it isn't just a rifle," Luna replied as she clicked a button near the trigger. Instantly two spikes projected out from the top of the rifle. Luna smiled at Dukk.

"Oh! The more I see, Luna, the more I simply just don't want to know," Dukk replied.

Dukk looked at the three as they climbed into the nearest transport pod.

"This doesn't feel right. Do I have a say in the outcomes for those on the Ukendt?"

"No!" replied Mentor.

"Mentor, we are not animals. Nor do we want to be like them."

"Agreed, Dukk. We will do only what is required," Mentor replied.

Dukk looked at them and sighed. It was clear to him now what Marr had meant when she mentioned skills not typical for a keeper.

Marr, Dukk, Annee and Bazzer did as instructed. They collected the crew's personal items, supplies, and everything they could move. They packed it into one of the empty robotic containers. Also, after helping Trence get packed, Annee took the observer to a Transport Pod.

With most items packed, Annee and Bazzer had joined Trence in the transport pod, ready to launch the moment the interceptor was secured. Marr and Dukk were suited up, ready to get the nose door open and help get the container out.

It was a nerve-racking time. They had agreed on radio silence with the others. And, they had no idea if and when the device on board would explode.

Chapter 25 – New Beginnings

1

They got word finally. It was now a little over two hours since Dukk had been woken by the airlock door.

"Dukk, we have secured the interceptor," Mentor could be heard saying on the short-range broadcast channel.

"Excellent timing," Dukk replied. "We are ready with the container."

"We have another problem!"

"I'm listening."

"The master codes don't work. They must have changed them. The device is a nuke. It is armed. We really don't want to be anywhere near this when it goes off. It is booby trapped and pressure sensitive. We can't put it out into space. It would explode the moment we depressurise the airlock. The observer was more cautious than I had anticipated. The bomb is linked to the observer's alive vitals. With the observer dead, it can't be disarmed. The observer wanted to be certain this crew didn't scarper at the first sign of trouble."

"This day is just getting better and better. By the way, how do you know all this?"

"We overheard the crew talking about it as we crept on board."

"Where are the crew now?"

"Where we found them."

"Where was that?"

"In a transport pod about to abandon this rig."

"You just left them there?"

"Well, we tried to reason with them, but they resisted."

"All of them?"

"Yep, they were a pretty determined bunch."

"Great," Dukk said sarcastically. "So, what can we do about this?"

"We need a container. If we get it into the hold, get the bomb into it and seal it up. Then push it out, it might hold together sufficiently for us to get clear."

"What about using a transport pod?"

"The device is too big. We wouldn't get the canopy down."

"Ok then, we can bring over the loaded container, unload it and use that."

"We don't have much time. There is more bad news."

"What?"

"This rig has the DMD running and will traverse in less than sixty minutes. The traverse destination looks to be a deserted system. I guess they were planning on laying low for a bit."

"Can't we just reset it?"

"The crew had already sent a distress signal. Someone may already be on their way to mount a rescue. We really don't want to be here when they arrive. It may work in our favour if everyone else thinks the Ukendt blew up at the same time as the Dinatha."

There was a pause.

"Dukk?"

"Sorry," Dukk sighed. "The reality of loosing the Dinatha hits me in waves. Right, so the bottom line is that we have about an hour."

"Perhaps not. It also looks like the bomb on the Dinatha is due to go off before the traverse. And it might be more substantial than I first thought. Before they resisted, the crew mentioned they needed to get the transport pod well clear of the Dinatha too."

"What do you suggest?"

"We don't have enough time to unload the container. So, we use two containers. The empty comes over first. We'll use it for the bomb. Get both containers out now. Make your way here. Hopefully, you'll be clear before the Dinatha goes up. Meanwhile, we are going to get ready for your arrival, deal with the previous crew and do our best to cover our tracks."

"Sound. Bazzer and Annee, are you ready?"

"Yep, leaving the transport bay now."

"Okay, Marr and I are opening the nose and hold airlock doors."

Twenty minutes later, the containers were out of the Dinatha. Marr and Dukk brought the containers to the nose door and then Annee and Bazzer had used their transport pod to pull the containers free. With both containers out, they hooked up their pod to the empty container via a rigid towing frame. The container with the personal effects was now floating just in front of the Dinatha. It was ready for Marr and Dukk to retrieve, using the remaining transport pod.

"See you over there," Dukk said into the comms, as he and Marr dashed up the stairs to the transport bay.

Dukk paused at the transport bay door.

"Are you okay?" Marr said looking back from the hatch of the transport pod.

Dukk smiled. "No, not really!"

Marr paused. She knew better than to say anything.

"This rig is more than my home," Dukk said. "The Dinatha represents my life as a haulier. I guess that is over now too."

Marr walked back over to the door. She smiled at him and put out her hand.

Dukk looked at her now, properly. He knew. He took her hand and closed the door.

With the loaded container in tow, Marr and Dukk headed towards the interceptor. As they approached, they had a good view as Annee and Bazzer manoeuvred the empty container onto the platform that dropped out of the belly of the interceptor. They watched as the platform and container disappeared into the rig. It reappeared ten minutes later. They watched as Annee and Bazzer reattach the container and manoeuvred it away from the rig. Once clear, they jettisoned it towards the planet. With that done, Annee and Bazzer drove their pod into the door in the side of the rig.

Now it was their turn. Dukk engaged the transport pod controls and moved the container on to the platform. He then disengaged the towing line and pulled away from the rig.

"Dukk," Mentor said into the comms once the container was on board. "The transport bays are full, so you'll need to abandon that transport pod and EVA over. We'll open the port door. You will need to configure the pod's autopilot to drop out of orbit, so it burns up. We can't have anyone finding it."

"On it," Dukk replied.

"Ready for a dance," Dukk said to Marr as they moved away from the rig.

"Absolutely, so long as I am leading. I still don't trust your driving!" Marr laughed.

With the transport pod's auto pilot engaged, Marr and Dukk opened the canopy. They were about to move off when something caused Dukk to pause. He turned and looked in the direction of the Dinatha. Marr noticed and did the same.

"It looks insignificant and lonely from this distance." Dukk said.

"It does." Marr replied.

"Goodbye," Dukk started to say but stopped. He spotted a sudden bulge on the port side. Before he could rationalise it, there was a bright flash. The Dinatha bounced and then exploded. It was gone.

The space between them and the explosion appeared to wobble. The shock wave. It hit them instantly. It knocked them back into the pod. Dukk's helmet smashed against the canopy frame. Alarms started going off in both Dukk's and Marr's systems. Dukk's helmet was punctured. Dukk struggled to breathe. He was passing out. Marr was right there. She grabbed him and pushed them both free of the canopy. She then lined up the interceptor's port door in her pack's propulsion guidance system and engaged full power.

2

Marr had done well. The two of them shot towards the interceptor and crashed through the doorway.

Marr jumped up immediately and hit the door close and pressurisation button. The crash had damaged her helmet too. She could hardly see.

When the orange lights stopped flashing, she ripped her helmet off, then tended to Dukk. She pulled his helmet free. He wasn't moving. She knelt next to him and pounded at his chest.

Then she took his head in her hands and shouted, "COME BACK DUKK."

Tears welled up in her eyes.

Suddenly he was back. He shook, took a deep gasping breath, and then relaxed back on the floor.

Marr couldn't control herself. She pulled him close and kissed him on the lips.

Dukk swung his arms up and took her head in his hands. He kissed her back.

"When you two are finished, we need you in the cockpit!" laughed Luna. She was standing in the inner doorway.

They looked up and laughed.

"Seriously, we really need you in the cockpit," Luna said more firmly. "The DMD is about to traverse, however we don't have control of the rig. Mentor says we are dead stick."

Marr sat up. Dukk pushed himself up and got to his feet.

"What do you mean?" Dukk said as he steadied himself against the wall of the airlock.

"This rig is in evacuation mode. We can operate the hold and external doors, but not the med controls or the reactors. We can't prep

415

the systems for traverse. Mentor said if we traverse without the med control and systems running, we are as good as dead."

"Why don't we have control?"

"The conn was still assigned to the old captain."

"Where is that captain?"

"About to be cremated as their transport pod breaks orbit."

"Oh!" Dukk answered as his head started to clear.

"And what can we do about it?" Marr said in a confused tone.

"Mentor has a workaround," Luna replied. "He showed Trence how to initiate a conn reset but the observer's codes are back up only. Trence was a subordinate, not fully authorised. To complete the conn transfer process, it needs Dukk's codes as captain of the rig that Trence was assigned to."

"Where is the nearest console?" Dukk said firmly.

"Just here in the corridor."

Dukk approached the console. It was in reset mode awaiting codes. Dukk flicked his codes across from his wrist wraps.

The console came alive.

Dukk immediately initiated an upload of the Dinatha's databases. He had taken a copy of them as they packed the container.

"Where are the others?" Dukk asked as he watched the transfer.

"Everyone else is strapped in upstairs, ready to connect the med lines."

"Marr and I are going to need new helmets."

"In here," Luna said as she disappeared into an adjacent room. Moments later she returned with two helmets. "Lots of spares on this bird."

With the databases loaded, Dukk found his crew's biometric credentials and loaded them into the Ukendt's database. He assigned access rights then started loading the files into the med system. Then he opened a channel to his crew.

"Good morning!" Dukk said. "Looks like we are under a little time pressure!"

"Welcome on board, captain. Great to have you with us," Annee said. "Yes, time is the essence. We need the med system online before we traverse."

"I've started the med sync for yourself, Mentor, Bazzer, Bognath and Trence. I'll start the rest once we are plugged in. Bazzer, systems controls are with you. Let's get this bird heated up!"

"On it, captain," came the reply.

Dukk felt new vibrations and sounds. He assumed that was the reactors and hoped that it meant things were working. He promised himself he would be checking every inch of the rig, the first moment he got.

"Right, lead the way," Dukk said to Luna.

Marr and Dukk followed Luna up a flight of stairs.

At the top was a lounge and many passenger seats. Marr counted nineteen.

Bognath and Trence were seated in the front row. They smiled up at the trio as they passed through to the cockpit.

The cockpit had two rows of seats. Two seats in the first row and in the second row, two sets of two on either side. Six in total.

Annee and Mentor were sitting on the right and Bazzer was sitting alone on the left. Luna dropped into the seat next to him.

Dukk went to the front and sat on the left. Marr followed him and jumped into the seat on the right.

The controls looked slicker but basically the same as the Dinatha.

Dukk checked the count down after putting on his helmet. Three minutes until traverse.

"This is going to be tight," Dukk thought to himself as he opened the med data loading, he had started downstairs. It wasn't finished yet. Not good. He initiated the sync for himself, Marr, and Luna.

"By the way, where are we headed?" Dukk asked. "I don't recognise the traverse coordinates."

"An unmonitored and hopefully empty system," Mentor answered.

"Do we have a contingency if that isn't the case?"

"Assign me the weapons controls and we'll have plenty of contingency."

Dukk reached over to the panel he didn't recognise. He found the context menu and assigned the panel to Mentor. He then interacted with the med controls.

"Thanks," Mentor said. "But you've also changed the primary operator on med controls."

"Yep, looking after another contingency," Dukk answered. "I'll create a separate group for myself, Marr, and Luna. I'll put the rest of you under first. The med records for us three are still syncing. Things won't go well for us, if the rig doesn't have accurate data when it runs the juice. We'll need someone on the other end to resuscitate us if the sync doesn't finish in time."

A silence fell over the comms.

"Ninety seconds! Status," Dukk said into the comms in a matter of fact manner.

"Ready" was the reply from everyone in unison.

"Running the juice to group one. See you soon," Dukk said confidently.

Dukk watched the vitals. The heart rates dropped.

"All stable," Dukk said as he moved his gaze to the med sync for himself, Marr, and Luna. One panel showed the percentage rising. Another panel showed the seconds ticking away until the traverse.

"Thirty seconds," he said quietly. "This is going to be close."

He glanced around at Marr. She was looking at him. She was smiling.

"You've got this!" she mouthed. Dukk smiled and turned back to the panels.

"Twenty seconds."

"Ten seconds."

Dukk realised he was holding his breath. He looked again. The med records were in sync. The vitals were showing.

"We're up. Thank goodness. Running the juice. See you on the other side," Dukk said as he hit the button. Seconds later, the cocktail hit his blood stream. His consciousness faded.

3

Moments later they were out of the traverse. A featureless rock planet filled their view. An initial scan of the system indicated they were alone. There wasn't even a relay.

As per Mentor's advice, Dukk gave the DMD the location of another deserted system. They would traverse again in nine hours. They didn't want to take the chance that others knew of the Ukendt's flight plan.

"Time for some answers. Does this rig have a crew mess?" Dukk said as he removed his helmet.

"Yes, back here," Luna replied as she pointed over her shoulder.

"Right, let's go," Dukk said as he unbelted and made for the door.

"You'd better join us," Dukk said to Bognath and Trence as he passed them. "We are all in this together now."

Five minutes later they were all seated at a fourteen-seat table in the middle of the crew mess.

"Why was Craig Atesoughton assassinated?" Trence asked as they sat down.

"Great question, Trence. One of many questions that need answering," Dukk answered.

"He was so young. Late twenties, isn't that right?" Trence said, ignoring the hint Dukk had just given for him to stop asking questions.

"It was Craig Atesoughton the second, not the third," Mentor interrupted. "It was his dad. He was nearly sixty. Not so young."

"What do you mean by dad?"

"As in his biological father."

"Now you are making things up. There hasn't been biological anything for many years. Natural birth was done away with. It was too dangerous. Too risky for correct selection and continuation of the species. It was also done away with to prevent over population. People are now made in the incubation centres, one new for each death. There are no mothers, fathers, or siblings, just people made and raised in the incubation centres."

"Trence, you are going to hear some things now, that will possibly break your mind. I apologise in advance for that. But it is necessary."

Trence went quiet.

"I'd like to know more about that too, Mentor," Annee added. "Please explain what you mean by biological father?"

"The incubators are mostly a lie. Yes, there were plans initially to manufacture people in laboratories, but it never really worked. The results were terrifying. The same was true of the early attempts to genetically modify the entire population. So, things went back to being done the old fashion way. Women are impregnated and then they give birth. The babies are raised in the incubation centres. The rest is pretty much as you know it. Apart from the elites and others. Their children aren't raised in the incubation centres."

"Where are they raised?" Trence asked.

"With their families," Mentor answered.

"Oh," Trence replied in a defeated tone.

After a moment, Annee spoke. "What did you mean by others?"

"There are many more humans on Earth than the databases in the citadels would suggest. Some call them the wild people," Mentor replied.

"Do you mean robin hood raiders?"

"No, the wild people are those that survived the establishment of the citadels."

"Weren't they hunted down?"

"They were, but not all were killed. Many found refuge in the wild, far from the practical reaches of the citadels. These days they are nomadic. Hunters and gatherers. They often move with wild animals to hide their presence. They mostly go unnoticed."

"Have you met any?" Luna asked. This question surprised Marr. Marr had heard rumours but never heard Mentor talking so openly about them. Marr was just as curious but was cautious of being seen to criticise or challenge Mentor.

"Yes, Luna," Mentor replied sincerely. "On occasion. When I needed their help."

Dukk sighed. "This is all very enlightening, but I think we have some more pressing matters to attend to, like understanding what we are going to do, and equally why are we here and why is the Dinatha no more?"

"What do you mean by what are we going to do?" Trence interjected. "That is easy. We contact my superiors and have them sort this all out."

"By superiors, you mean those on levels ten, nine, eight, seven, six, etcetera and the EOs?" Mentor asked.

"Of course," Trence answered smugly.

"Have you ever met an EO?"

"No, I haven't."

"Seen one?"

"On the broadcasts, but not in person."

"What about a level two?"

"Nope?"

"Three?"

"No"

"Four, five, or six?"

"No, no, and no. What has this got to do with anything?" Trence asked angrily.

"I will demonstrate it," Mentor answered. "What is the highest level you have met?"

"The highest level I have met was those at level seven. Well, I didn't meet them. I was in the same room as a couple of them. The day I was demoted. They didn't say anything. They were hooded. Their faces hidden. They just sat there as my supervisor told me about my demotion before joining the Dinatha."

"Have you ever been to the inner parts of a citadel?"

"Nope."

"Do you know where those at level eleven, ten, nine, eight and seven live?"

"Yes, they live in h-pods in the middle ring, like me. Except the level sevens. I understand they live in the inner part of the citadel."

"And, level six, five, four etcetera, where do they live?"

"In the inner part of the citadel too."

"But you have never been there to see for yourself?"

"Nope."

"So, you have no evidence that there is even anyone above level seven."

"I guess not."

"Would it surprise you to learn that the Rule of Twelve isn't implemented in the manner that your schooling suggests?"

"It would. What do you mean?"

"The Rule of Twelve is a cover. Things aren't like that. There are no EOs. There are no levels below them or route to promotion. Level seven is as far as anyone will ever get."

"This is scandalous and untrue!"

The room went quiet again.

4

The next person to speak surprised them all.

"It is true," Bognath said. "I concur with Mentor's story. I worked security and have been to the inner parts of the citadels. There are no EOs or level twos, threes, etcetera, just level sevens, the elites, and their staff."

"Not true," shouted Trence.

The others stared too.

Mentor sat up and waited for silence again.

"Trence," Mentor said softly. "What privilege would you say level seven have over level eight?"

"Loads more."

"Interesting. So, they can do what they like?"

"It feels like it. But they must be answerable to someone. I guess, the levels above and therefore the EOs."

"This is not true. The observers at level seven are the governors. They run the citadels. The inner citadel isn't a place for providing governance. It is a playground for the elites. The elites monitor the goings on in the incubation centres, the test centres and delivery of punishment, but they don't have any involvement in the day to day. Citadels are run by lower ranking observers."

"How is this not common knowledge?"

"It is amongst those at level seven. Hence the big lift in privilege. They are given power to govern and in return they must hold up the lie. So long as they keep everyone else in line, they get to keep their position and privilege."

"But I often hear of level seven getting promoted?"

"Think of the last one you know of. What were they up to around the time they got promoted?"

"Let me think. Oh!"

"What?"

"Well, the last promotion that I recall was just after I heard a group of unprivileged were found to be out of the citadel after curfew. The level seven observer let them off with a warning."

"What would typically happen to the unprivileged under these circumstances?"

"They would be taken away by sentinels."

"Where to?"

"I don't know. I had never thought to ask."

"And it is best that you don't know."

"Oh!"

"So, what happen to the level seven observer?"

"Promoted."

"Ever heard or seen of the observer since?"

"No. Oh! This is awful. And wait. I've helped with all of this!"

"The past is the past, Trence. It is what we do now that matters more."

Trence fell silent.

"Mentor, how do you know all this?" Annee asked.

"Because I am an observer. Level seven."

Gasps filled the room.

"Explain!" Dukk demanded as he stood up.

"Calm down," Mentor said firmly. "The full story is for another time. Suffice to say, I made it to level seven at a young age. I was then repurposed to infiltrate and take down the resistance."

Marr and Luna now stood up too. Their hands went to their weapons.

"Sit down, all of you. What they didn't know is that I was already part of the resistance. I'd been recruited after the test. It was always the plan that I would reach the inner sanctum and get this level of access to help with the resistance."

Trence screamed, launched out of his seat, and walked backwards towards the wall.

"You are the enemy," Trence shouted.

Annee got out of her seat and went over to Trence. He slumped into her arms.

"Trence, breathe. Remember what we talked about," Mentor said kindly.

"This is all too much," whimpered Trence.

"Ann, perhaps Trence might want to lie down on the couch," Dukk said as he got out of his seat to help Annee escort Trence to the lounge area near the table.

"That is why you can move in and out of the citadel with no issues?" Luna observed when everyone was seated again.

"Correct," Mentor replied.

"It also explains the lack of investigation and inspection when we arrived at Utopiam last time?" Annee observed.

Mentor nodded.

"What else?" Dukk asked.

"I was one of the hooded figures at your hearing, Trence," Mentor said looking over at the couch. "I gave the order for you to be assigned to the Dinatha. It was the only way I could really look out for you. Your fate, if left to the other level sevens, wasn't going to be pretty."

Trence sat up with a childish smile. "Oh. But wait, so you can clear this all up. You can get Kimi back and get us all out of this mess?"

"It is not that simple," Mentor replied. "The arrest of Kimince, the presence of Premnaly and events this morning, were not part of the plan."

"What do you mean by the plan?" Dukk asked.

"The plan to assassinate Craig Atesoughton the second."

"Who's plan?" Annee asked.

"Mine, Ann," Mentor answered.

Gasps filled the room again. Trence lay back down and continued to whimper.

"So, you planned all of this?" Annee suggested.

"Mostly, but I also took advantage of opportunities that arose."

"Like what?"

"The beef contract, the time of year and using Mayfield as the distribution point. It gave me cover and more than one trip. That enabled better planning."

"Wait, back up. The assassination? That is what this has all been about?" Dukk said firmly.

"Yes." Mentor answered authentically.

"So we are back to monosyllabic answers," Dukk said. "Let me be more specific. Who wanted him dead and why?"

"The order came from one of the bosses I am answerable to as an observer."

"Who?"

"Craig Atesoughton."

"The son wanted his father killed?"

"No, the orders came from Craig Atesoughton the first. The granddad."

"Why?"

"I am not certain."

"But you went ahead anyways."

"I had other reasons."

"Like what?"

"The exploits of Craig Atesoughton the second. I was aware that he was trafficking young girls out of Earth. He has been bringing them to Mayfield for some time now. It had to stop. He was clearly behind it. Perhaps it is linked to the assassination order. Perhaps his exploits were drawing too much attention. Anyway, an opportunity presented itself and I took it."

"So, this whole thing, you being on this rig, and us being here, was about following an order from Craig Atesoughton the first?"

"Yep. And putting an end to the trafficking."

"Why didn't you just report the trafficking?" Annee asked.

"Who to?" Mentor answered. "For reasons already mentioned, there is no one else. Just the elites."

"Couldn't you stop it, using your privilege?"

"It isn't that easy. I knew of the trafficking because of my resistance activities. Getting involved could have compromised the trust with the elites, and that would put the resistance efforts at risk."

The room went quiet again. Marr had been following the conversation and putting things together. Her gaze came to rest on Mentor. He was looking back at her. His expression was different. There was something else. Her gut told her to step up.

"Mentor, let me try and paint a picture for my own piece of mind."

426

"Go ahead," Mentor replied. His face softened as if to say he was giving her permission.

"You have been working to bring down the trafficking for some time. You knew who was behind it, but you were powerless to do anything about it."

"Correct."

"Granddad Atesoughton came to you with a request to take out his son. The reasons for which are unknown to you. But it presented an opportunity to kill two birds with one stone, so to speak."

"Correct."

"You orchestrated your way onto a rig, the Dinatha, in order to get to Mayfield and also to provide cover for the assassination."

"Correct."

"Craig Atesoughton the second, died from breathing toxic fumes emitted from a small hole in the fireplace enclosure in his room. That hole was made by a specialised bullet fired from Luna's rifle. You borrowed that rifle on approach to Mayfield, and then took it hiking that afternoon."

"Correct."

"You kept everyone around you in the dark, including Luna and I, should the plan fail, and you get exposed."

"Correct."

"But someone double crossed you. They changed the plan. They arrested Kimince to make space for a new observer and to send suspicion in our direction. Then they planted Premnaly to take you out. They also sent this interceptor after us to make sure the job got done. With the Dinatha and you out of the way, those that double crossed you could write a narrative that shifted attention away from themselves."

Mentor nodded.

"So, who double crossed you?"

"That is a great question. And one I can't answer. Not because I don't want to. Simply because I don't know, yet. I need to take some time to work out what went wrong, if I have been compromised and who is really behind this."

Silence filled the room again.

5

Eventually Dukk spoke.

"So, what do we do now that we are supposed to be dead and don't truly know who wants to keep it that way?"

He looked around the table and stopped when he got to Mentor.

Mentor looked back at Dukk. His face softened again. "We do something useful!"

"Like what?" Dukk asked.

"For starters, I had no idea that Kimince and Trence were invited up to the resort. Scapegoating the observer would have never been okay with me if I had known. My preference is for everything to appear like an accident."

"So, what can we do about that?"

"We mount a rescue. But not just for Kimince."

Mentor looked over at Marr.

"Marr, do you have the footage you captured the morning you and Luna were hiking?"

Marr looked blankly at Mentor. After a moment she spoke. "It is hidden in my binoculars."

Mentor reached down beside him to his backpack. He retrieved the binoculars and passed them over to Marr.

Marr interacted with the binoculars and then flicked a video clip to the projector in the middle of the table. She hit play without saying anything. Before them, a scene played out. It was the scene Marr had mentioned to Mentor after departing Mayfield the first time. It showed the young girls in the penthouse. It was hard to watch and at times the crew looked away.

"What is the point of all of this?" Annee snapped angrily when the video stopped.

Mentor took a deep breath. "The parade that the girls mentioned is the opening event to a multi-day party. That party starts in five days."

"So?" Annee said in a sharp tone.

"Bognath, have you done the after-party clean-up?"

"No," Bognath answered.

"But you know what I am talking about?"

"Yes," he answered reluctantly.

"Will you share what you know, please."

Bognath paused. He looked around the room. "Fine," he said. "There is an elevator lift in the corner of the big room you saw there. The one with the strange looking apparatus. The lift goes to a mostly disused basement. This basement connects to the tunnels used during construction. Those tunnels connect to the old port. Within the old port hanger, there is a garbage incinerator built for the construction phase of the resort. It is designed for organic waste. These days it is only used once every three months. The day after the party."

"And after that?" Mentor asked.

"The penthouse is cleaned thoroughly and left empty until the next party, three months later."

"Thank you, Bognath for sharing so openly," Mentor said. He paused for a moment to let that sink in. Then he continued. "Bazzer and I inspected the incinerator the day we hiked over to the old hanger. We found something in the incinerator."

Mentor turned to look at Bazzer.

Bazzer reached down and extracted something from his backpack.

He dropped a charred looking object in the middle of the table.

"That looks like what the girls were wearing. Well, what is left of it?" Luna said in shock.

There was silence again.

"Someone needs to get those girls out of there before the party!" Annee blurted.

"Definitely," said Marr.

The others nodded in agreement.

Then Mentor spoke. "They do need to be rescued, as does Kimince, and we now have the rig that can make that happen!"

They all stared at Mentor. No one spoke, for what felt like an age.

Eventually, Dukk spoke up. "So, this is your real plan, Mentor. To turn us into heroes!"

"You can frame this in what ever manner you like, Dukk," Mentor answered in a defiant tone. "But I see it as my duty."

Dukk felt annoyed with his emotional outburst. He gathered himself again. "Yes, you are right, Mentor. This is not about being a hero. It feels like it has always been the path for me. So, what do we need to do? What is the plan?"

"Dukk, I have skills that will be needed here. And I am one hundred percent committed. However, I am many things. But I am not a leader!"

"Who will lead it then?"

Mentor said nothing. The others had been following the conversation. They had been looking back and forth between Mentor and Dukk. Now their eyes came to rest on Dukk. Dukk moved his head slowly around the table. He looked briefly at everyone individually. Their eyes told him his answer.

"On two conditions!" Dukk said quietly.

No one spoke.

"First, everyone volunteers. We drop those that want out, at the nearest hub. And, secondly, Mentor, you will share everything you know about all of this. If I am to lead the rescue, I need to know exactly what we are up against!"

Mentor stayed quiet. He held Dukk's stare. The others now stared at Mentor.

"Agreed," Mentor said eventually. "But not until we are safely out of this system and well rested. We are going to need cool heads."

430

"That sounds reasonable and I am dead tired," Dukk replied. "I also need a shower, but before that I need to inspect this rig. I am not going to rest unless I know what I am floating in. Anyone got anything that can't wait until after this afternoon's traverse?"

Dukk looked around the table. Marr's expression told him something.

"Marr, do you have something to share?"

Marr turned to Mentor. Something was bothering her. However, she was in conflict. She felt she needed to ask but asking would bring Mentor's credibility into question. Mentor looked back at her. She felt his gaze like never before. Then he nodded. She took a breath.

"Mentor," Marr said gently. "How can we be sure that the girls are still in danger? Didn't you just take out the man responsible? Why would the party still be going ahead?"

Mentor sat back. His shoulders dropped. Marr felt it appeared as if a great weight had just been lifted.

"Marr," Mentor replied in a quiet voice. "I received a message just before things got real on the Dinatha."

Mentor flicked a paused video into the centre of the table. Before them was a still image of a middle-aged woman. Her expression showed warmth with a touch of sadness. Her long hair was light brown with wisps of silver. She had fair complexion and she had dark brown hazel eyes.

Mentor reached over and engaged the replay.

The woman started to speak. "The party is still going ahead. It is a hydra. We just cut off one of the heads. We've worked too hard to have another group of girls come to harm." She paused. A tear fell down her cheek. "There is something else." She paused again. "They know!" The video then froze.

They all stared at the frozen image of the woman.

Dukk did a double take, as did all but Mentor. Mentor looked calmly at the image. His expression had a hint of longing.

Eventually, Marr broke the silence. "Who is this?" She asked softly.

"Her name is Tieanna," Mentor replied.

"She looks like!" Marr began to say quietly.

"Dukk," Luna blurted.

Everyone turned to look at Dukk.

"I know this woman," Dukk said. "Well, I knew her. She looks older. She was in the incubation centre."

Dukk paused. Memories came flooding back.

"I was very young," Dukk uttered, "she told me stories. She taught me the creed. She was so kind. She was always with me and then suddenly she wasn't."

Tears welled up in his eyes.

An eery silence filled the room.

Eventually Dukk spoke again. "Who is she?"

After a moment, Mentor answered softly. "Dukk, she is your mother."

The End

Continue your awakening at <u>RuleOfTwelve.com</u>.

The Rule of Twelve trilogy:

Book 1, Double Take

Book 2, Convergence

Book 3, Regeneration

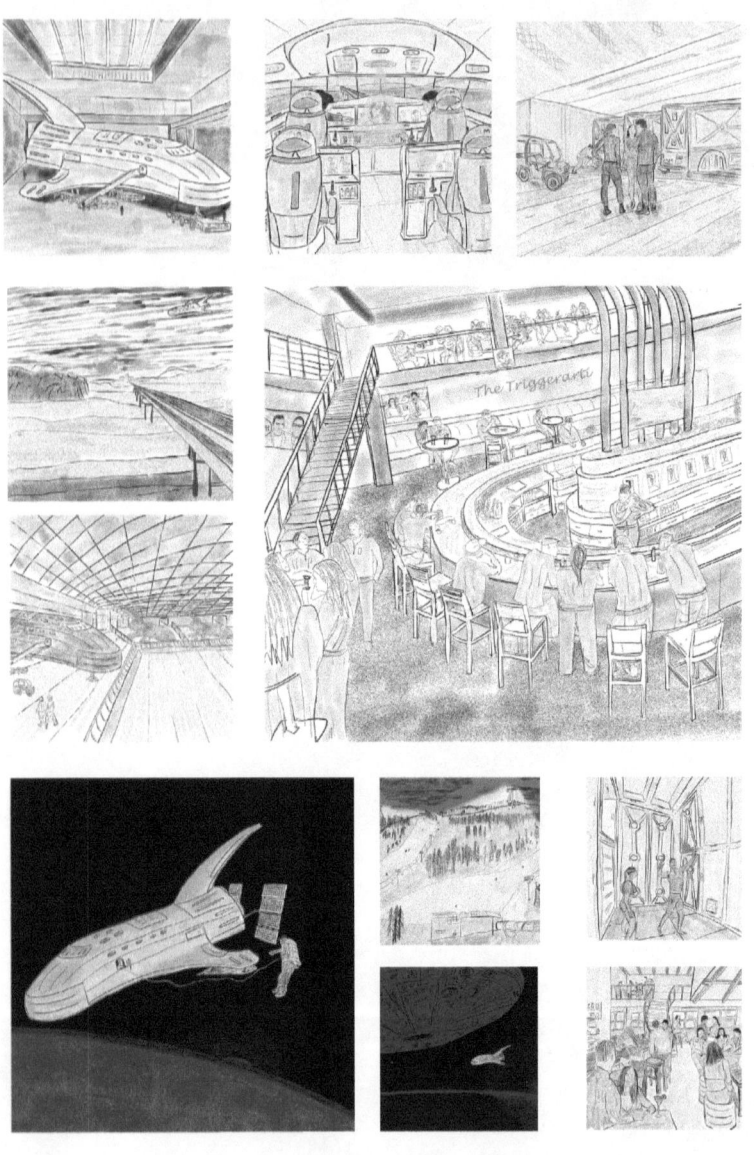